LOST THRONE

LOST THRONE

ARIN L. BLACKWOOD

Atlantis Rising Book One

LOST THRONE

Published by Under the Blackwood Tree
Buffalo, NY 14075
Undertheblackwoodtree.com

Book Design: Arin Blackwood
Map illustration: Arin Blackwood
Cover: Arin Blackwood
Art: Heather Menz
Chapter Art: Heather Menz

ISBN: 979-8-9944056-1-1
Printed in the United States of America
1st Printing

Books by Arin Blackwood:

<u>Fyrala Chronicles</u>
Between Light and Shadows
Woven of Ash and Gold *Coming Soon*
<u>Atlantis Rising</u>
Lost Throne
Echoes of a Queen *Coming Soon*

<u>McKlean Mysteries</u>
Published under A.L. Blackwood

Blood of the Rose
Darkness of Youth Coming Soon

Your mental health is important. This story is a fictional fantasy, but any good story has real-life elements. This book includes the death of characters, intense violence, sexual assault, and an abusive relationship, as well as themes of grief and loss. It also includes depictions of emotional, physical, and/or sexual abuse and may be disturbing to some readers. The romantic elements in this story include why choose where the FMC has multiple love interests but never at the same time.

Note About AI. It's alarming that authors need to write this but...
Myself and most other fiction authors were using em dashes and various creative and stylized punctuation long before AI was being used to write or enhance books. Since AI programs were trained using thousands of authors' works, most often illegally, make sure to understand that AI resembles the authors' works not the other way around. Please refrain from accusing authors of using AI because we use similar punctuation...

Fyrala
Fallen Ember
Shadow Court
Greenwood
Iron Mountain
Greenwood Outpost
Blood Plains
Rafe's Camp
Atlantis
Sea Court Lands
Sanguine Court
Legend
Fallen Borders
Court Borders
Stolen Borders

Shadow Court
Iron Mountain
Greenwood Outpost
Blood Plains
The Wilds
Raef's Camp
Atlantis
Sea Court Lands
Legend
Court Borders
Stolen Borders
Rory's Path

PROLOGUE

MY STORY DOESN'T START WITH a sordid tale of death, abandonment, and suffering. Despite having a very Disney princess name, I never had a Disney princess life. It's not some damn fairy tale. I mean, it is by the strictest of definitions, but I wasn't some lost girl who needed to be rescued and belong somewhere. I *was* happy, genuinely happy. If anything, I had too much curiosity and not enough fear. But that's hindsight for you. Hindsight is always 20/20.

I grew up an orphan. Now, don't start thinking that I was some lost little puppy who needed a family, my found family. I was adopted as a baby by a wonderful set of parents, and yes, they told me I was adopted as soon as I was old enough to understand. My parents are amazing, loving, and supportive—the best parents a girl could ask for.

They built me a sandbox and called it a 'dig site.' I spent hours unearthing bottle caps and fossils from the local rock store while they cheered like I'd discovered a lost tomb. I never once felt unwanted. I only ever felt...home, wanted, and loved.

History has always fascinated me. I love the mystery behind it, taking the little clues left to us and turning it into a story and a lesson. My dreams started at an early age. At first, I attributed them to a fanciful imagination after watching the animated classic movie with adventure and love. As time passed, though, the dreams became more vivid, and there were parts that felt so real that they hadn't been in any movie. And sometimes I woke up with sand under my fingernails. Once, seawater in my bed. I told myself it was sleepwalking, stress, or anything else. But deep down, I wasn't sure.

Atlantis became an obsession for me, one that only my nearest and dearest knew about. I'd chosen my career path and didn't want my obsession with the lost city to negate my capabilities as an archaeologist. I didn't want academia to think I'm completely nuts. When I could manage it, I wrote papers on the topic, making sure I was discreet and professional, laying out the details and the evidence, and either debunking a current theory or analyzing old ones. I was careful not to reveal my interest—at least I thought I was.

But obsession is a hard thing to mask. And secrets have a way of slipping through the cracks, especially when they want to be found.

If I'd known what was coming—what those dreams truly meant—I might've run instead of chasing them.

I thought I was chasing stories in stone. Turns out, they were waiting for me.

1

How to Make the
Wrong Choice

"W HERE YOU OFF TO THIS summer, Mattie?" I sit sideways in my favorite chair reading the latest fae fantasy smut, as he calls it, twisting the smooth lock of hair that lies behind my ear. Mattie had walked into the kitchen; the smooth pop of the fridge door and the clink of glass are my perfect signs that he had moved on to the celebratory beer, having finished his latest article.

"Nowhere, yet," he answered, twisting the metal cap off with that telltale *pfft* and tossing it in the sink with a clink.

I sit up, shoving the bookmark between the pages. "What do you mean nowhere yet? It's a little late in the year to not already be attached to a dig."

"I got sidetracked by this article. It's a big one, could open some significant doors for me. I missed the deadline for that underwater dig in the Mediterranean; it completely passed me by." He plopped his considerable form back onto the couch, taking a long draw from his bottle. By considerable form, I mean my bestie is whatever the blond version of tall, dark, and handsome is, sporting two hundred pounds of lean working muscle. There wasn't one dig we've been on together where I didn't have to play-act his girlfriend to keep the ladies at bay. Not that he wasn't interested; they simply weren't his type.

Mind you, at this point, I'm not sure what his type is. There was this one grad student who practically threw herself at him during the Belize excavation. She brought him iced coffees every morning and hung around the trench pretending to need help cataloging bone fragments. Mattie was polite, as he always is, but the minute she slipped him her number, he passed it to me with a grin. "She's more your type, Ror," he whispered before heading back to his notes like the whole thing hadn't happened. Another time, in Peru, a local guide invited him to a village festival and made it very clear she had plans that involved more than dancing. He thanked her, turned her down, then spent the night teaching kids how to play soccer with a ball made of knotted rags. I keep waiting for him to actually say yes to someone, but he never does.

Also? He once carried me three miles uphill in a sandstorm because I sprained my ankle after ignoring his advice. Never lets me live it down. But that's Mattie. He shows up. Always.

"What about you?" he asks, and I start chewing on the nail of my pinky finger. It's my worst tell. Screams, I've got a secret. I don't answer, and if anyone knows my tells, it's Mattie. "Roorrry?" he says, elongating my name in obvious accusation. "You're keeping a secret. Spill, now."

I get up and rustle through the drawer of my desk. You know the one everyone has, that all their important stuff goes into for safekeeping only to be lost in the chaos. Fortunately, or unfortunately for me (jury's still out on that one), the large manila envelope with the expensive lettering is still sitting right on top.

I'd checked at least a dozen times in the last twenty-four hours to make sure it hadn't vanished. Some parts of me expected it to melt away, dreamlike, like so many other things that came in the night and left with the dawn. But no—there it sits, solid and real, though entirely odd. Something about the logo feels off, like I'd seen it before, but I hadn't. Had I?

I shove the envelope toward him, not daring to open it myself and risk more exposure to some curse (because my luck is never this good). Sitting back on my heels, I bite my lip hard enough to taste copper and watch as he breaks the seal.

My stomach twists as I watch his eyes skim the page. What if it is happening? What if this is the moment everything changes?

"This is a joke, right?" he asks, eyes darting back and forth across the page. His brow creases deeper with every line, beer bottle forgotten at his side. I lean in, heart thudding, catching words like "fully *funded*," "*exclusive rights*," *and* "*lead researcher.*" They're not dangling an impressive grant; they're throwing a fortune at me to chase Atlantis, as if I were some treasure hunter in a movie instead of a postgrad with overdue rent.

"I don't know, honestly." And that's the truth. Because I can't decide if this is the start of my big break or the beginning of a horror documentary where people shout at the screen, 'Don't take the money!' right before everything goes to hell.

"You said no, right?"

I don't answer. Deciding to chew on the nail of my pointer finger this time, hoping to hide my true answer. My hands won't stay still. My brain won't either. It's like the words in that letter struck a chord I didn't even know was there, and it's still humming in my bones.

"You said no, Rory, right?" he asks again, more emphatically, like adding in my name is going to make me answer faster. I thought invoking names was only supposed to make someone appear.

"I haven't answered yet," I spit out as fast as my lips will let me, throwing my legs back out to rest my feet on the floor.

Mattie grabs at his forehead, tapping the stack of papers in his other hand on his knee. "Rory, you can't be serious. This can't be real."

"But what if it is?" The words are out before I can stop them. Unexpectedly, I want to cry, because it's not just a letter; it's the city. The one I've seen since I was a child, the one that's haunted my dreams like it's waiting. Like it remembers me.

He wipes his hand down his face, pulling at his mouth as he passes. "If it is, if you are fool enough to agree to this, I'm coming with you."

"Mattie, come on. This isn't even your area of expertise. You have other ambitions, and I can take care of any sleazeballs all on my lonesome. Don't get caught up in my crazy and potentially ruin your career."

I aim for flippant and casual, but what comes out sounds more like a balloon losing air. The idea of doing this without him hits like cold water down the spine. I've gone on digs alone before. But this...this feels different. This feels like stepping into the unknown, and the only hand I'd trust to grab if I slip is his.

"Ruin my career? What about yours? If word gets out that you took part in this and found nothing, no one will take you seriously. You'll be the crackpot of the field."

"My life, my choice."

"Ditto. I'm going with you. You need to have someone sane by your side." He tips his beer toward me like it's a toast, an easy grin softening the weight of his words.

"I haven't decided yet." But God, I want to. I want to tear into maps and archives and put my name on something that matters. Deciding means admitting I might actually believe this isn't a scam. And believing means I'm setting myself up to be the idiot on a cautionary podcast titled 'How Not to Fund a Dig.'

"If you do—"

The doorbell rings through our apartment, cutting him off. His long legs take him to the door much faster than mine. I always look like a chihuahua trying to jog to keep up with a Great Dane with this guy.

I follow, slower, nerves twisting like kelp in deep water. Something about the timing of that knock feels too perfect. Too rehearsed. Like a line hitting precisely on cue.

"Is Ms. Aurora Darling at home?" A very snooty-sounding British accent asks from somewhere on Mattie's other side. Yes, my parents were Disney fanatics, and yes, they thought it was a good idea to pair Aurora with Darling. A good chunk of my childhood was full of shoot-me-now moments of embarrassment. I've never liked hearing my full name spoken aloud. Every syllable sounds like it should belong to a debutante or a queen, not the girl who still forgets to water her plants.

"Who's asking?" My overprotective best friend growls politely, using his entire body to not only block my view of our guest but also his view inside our apartment and therefore of me.

"Lloyd Blakely, Esquire. I'm here to inquire about a recent proposal that was sent to Ms. Darling. She has yet to respond, and time is of the essence. Ms. Darling," he calls to me over Mattie's shoulder like he knows I'm right behind him, not hidden by a two-inch steel core door.

The way he says my name again, every syllable clipped neat. It scrapes along my nerves, the way chalk does on slate, and I can't pin down why it feels so wickedly familiar.

"Do you have an answer? My employer is eager to hear your response and get the project in motion."

Mattie flicks a finger up for silence, pushes the door closed with his shoulder, and lowers his voice. "This sets off so many red flags, I can't—say no. I don't like this at all, Rory." He says in a hushed voice behind the door.

"I know. I know. But Mattie, what if he's just excited? This is a huge opportunity for me. I could end this once and for all, and maybe the dreams will finally stop, my subconscious satisfied. They want an answer now, not to leave now, I think." Even as I say it, something inside me itches. A wrongness I can't name. Like I've been here before and said these words before, and the ending didn't go well.

"No. The expedition is set to leave in a month from tomorrow. The ship will sail out of Barcelona." Mr. Blakely doesn't raise his voice, but every word slides past the door anyway, neat as bullet points.

Mattie raises his brow in complete shock while I whisper-scream, "He can hear us."

"I assure you, Ms. Darling, I can hear you loud and clear. Your metal door does not block much sound at all," he says. "My employer is excited and eager to get this moving, as he believes you are correct in your research. It shows great promise."

I open the door again; there's no sense talking through it when he can hear us anyway. "Who is your employer?"

"He wishes to remain anonymous at this time," he says, twisting an actual bowler hat brim in his hands like he's auditioning for Nervous Businessman of the Year. He's all clean lines and polished vowels, the sort of man who probably irons his socks. Except for the hands. The hands give him away—nails bitten to the quick, knuckles raw like he's been knocking too long on doors that don't open.

"How convenient for him," Mattie says, attempting to mutter under his breath.

"Most assuredly," Mr. Bowler Hat remarks. "I do understand how challenging that can be, that he remains anonymous and you take all the risks of failure. However, he is confident you will not fail."

"If I say yes, will you leave? I can always change my mind."

"Indeed, it's a pleasure to finally meet you, Ms. Darling. We will be in touch with the rest of the paperwork and your airline tickets. We will need a list of equipment you will require within the next week. Good day," he says, pats his hat back onto his head with a bow, and starts back down the hallway toward the stairs, not the elevator.

"Wait," I call after him. "I didn't actually say yes." But he keeps walking like he didn't hear a word, like his leaving cements my yes. It feels like some invisible gate slammed shut behind me.

"Well, fine! But Mattie's coming too!"

"I will add Mr. Matthew Beauregard to the manifest," he says and disappears into the stairwell.

"What the fuck just happened? How did he know your name?" I ask of Mattie. I'm not sure he hears me by the look of complete shock on his face.

2

ALWAYS BE PREPARED...BUT FOR WHAT

MY DUFFEL BAG SITS OPEN like a yawning mouth, half-stuffed with cargo pants, field notes, books, and the same weather-worn boots that have seen a dozen digs and as many airport security pat downs. The heel on the left is coming loose again—I make a mental note to re-glue it, fully knowing I'll forget until I'm ankle-deep in seawater.

It's a ritual at this point, packing. Socks, gear, and lists in my head. But this time the rhythm feels... off. Each motion snags, like muscle memory hitting against a wall that wasn't there before. Like I'm not just packing for a trip—I'm packing to become someone else. Someone new and complete.

I crouch beside it, rolling socks with mechanical precision, pretending I'm prepping for any ordinary summer expedition. Pretending I'm not about to hop a plane toward the world's most famous maybe-real-maybe-not sunken city on the dime of a stranger with too much money and too many secrets.

I'm also pretending I didn't wake up last night with salt in my mouth again.

My parents linger in the doorway like ghosts of reason past. Mom clutches her ever-present mug of peppermint tea—ceramic chipped at the rim, steam ribboning in the cold. She's in her weekend uniform: leggings, one of Dad's oversized flannels, and that skeptical look that could shrivel steel. Dad stands beside her, pretending to inspect my camera bag but mostly rubbing the strap like it might offer him insight or comfort. He's tall enough to loom, but his hairline gave up years ago, so the effect is more nervous professor than protective patriarch.

"You packed sunscreen?" Mom asks.

I pause mid-roll and look up. "It's in the side pocket. With bug spray, Dramamine, and the tiny sewing kit I'll never use but always bring."

She gives a half-smile but doesn't move. "And your backup inhaler?"

"Middle zipper pouch."

She nods, silent for a moment. Her eyes are glassier than I like, her fingers white around the mug. "You sure this is safe?"

"Nope," I say, honestly. And I hate that I don't even sugarcoat it. Because I think she already knows the truth, and so do I. This isn't a detour. It's a door, and once I step through, it stays shut behind me.

Her lips press into a thin line. I can almost hear the words she isn't saying—don't go, stay, this isn't worth it—but she'll never be the kind of mother to clip wings. She's the one who will hover while you take flight, heart in her throat the whole time. She raised me better than to lie, even by omission. I stand and pull her into a hug. She's warm, soft, and smells like cinnamon and garden soil. Her hands clutch my back tighter than usual.

For a second, I'm ten years old again, muddy from digging holes in her flower beds with a plastic trowel, insisting I'd found Atlantean ruins beneath the daisies. She didn't even yell, before bringing me juice and a towel. Called me her little explorer. God, I hate how much I want to hear that now.

"I'll be fine," I murmur. "Mattie's coming, remember?"

She pulls away enough to look at me. "He's the only reason I'm not chaining you to the water heater."

Dad clears his throat, finally abandoning the camera bag and folding his arms. "You know, this funding offer sounds like the kind of thing you see in thriller movies. The 'too good to be true' kind. The kind where someone always ends up running through a jungle with a cursed dagger and a leg wound."

"Sounds like a Tuesday," I mutter, slinging the duffle strap over my shoulder.

"It's serious, Rory," he says, voice low but even. "They contacted *you*. Not a university, not a foundation. *You*. That's personal."

"That's why I'm going," I say. "If it's a scam, I come back with a suntan and a great story. If it's not…"

I trail off.

Mom's gaze catches me off guard, cool as a fingertip pressed to the back of my neck. "You'll chase it until it kills you."

"Maybe." My voice cracks, but I cover it with a quick smile. "But at least I'll know."

I step toward the front door, brushing my fingers over the bookshelf as I pass—pausing at the spine of a worn hardcover I'd practically memorized by age ten: *Legends of the Deep: Atlantis and the Lost Civilizations*. A birthday gift from them, back when they still thought my obsession was cute.

The moment my fingers leave the book, it tips forward slightly on the shelf. Not enough to fall, enough to make me stop and stare. I push it back, but the hair on my arms rises anyway. Coincidence, I tell myself. Stupid nerves. But it lingers, a weightless touch at my nape. Funny. They used to call me their little explorer. Now they look at me like I'm a soldier going off to war.

I don't look back.

3

If Something Seems too Good to be True, it Usually is.

THE SECURITY LINE AT JFK is unusually short for once, which should be a win. Instead, it makes the back of my neck itch. The whole thing runs too smooth, like someone greased the wheels ahead of us. And if there's one thing I've learned, it's that my life doesn't do smooth without a catch.

"Not to sound like a conspiracy nut," Mattie says as we step into the terminal, "but I'm starting to think your mystery benefactor paid off airport karma too."

Scanning the room for any signs we're wrong doesn't help. The boarding gate is sleek and unmarked, cordoned off from the rest of the traffic like it has something to hide. "Or cursed it."

We reach the private terminal, where a single dark-suited attendant waits without a smile. She checks our names—no passport scans, no boarding passes—and ushers us down a corridor that smells like fresh paint and too-new money. The type of hallway where your footsteps feel too loud and the silence listens back and judges.

Mattie bumps my shoulder with his. "We're totally being trafficked. You know that, right?"

"If we are, I better be getting assigned to a penthouse."

He snorts. "You would haunt the shit out of them." Implying I'd get myself murdered. But his voice isn't quite as light as usual. He's joking, yeah, but I can see him checking the corners, watching the walls like he's expecting something to peel away, a secret door giving way to whoever's going to nab us.

The plane itself is—of course—ridiculous. Gilt trim. Crystal decanters. Plush seats the color of old money. Someone has laid out a box of macarons with a note that reads, "*Welcome, Ms. Darling. You're right where you belong.*

Mattie picks one up, sniffs it, then puts it back. "Okay, that's serial killer behavior."

"That's bait," I say. "Pretty, pastel-colored bait."

I work on keeping my voice even, but my stomach twists at the note and my ears start to ring. Not because it's threatening. Because it isn't. It's warm. Familiar. Like someone knew I needed reassurance—and that makes it creepy warm.

We buckle in, because why tempt fate even more than we already are? Thumbing through research notes I've already read a hundred times, I use my tablet to try and distract myself from the growing uncertainty that we're stepping into something much, much older than either of us. Like the ending's already been written and no one bothered to hand us the script.

"I did some digging before we left," Mattie says quietly, pulling out a worn leather notebook from his bag. He flips to a page sketched with stars and rough coordinates. "These are the exact coordinates listed in the proposal. Problem is, the spot's there—but nothing should be. No island, no wrecks, no documented sea floor anomalies. It's been explored before."

"But nothing?" I ask.

He nods. "Weirdly so. I mean no shipping traffic. No sonar readings. It's like no one ever goes near it anymore. Like the ocean itself forgot it existed."

That same chill hits the base of my spine. "You think it's a mistake?"

"Trust me, Ror, nothing this big gets forgotten. Somebody made sure of it."

I lean my head against the window. Cloud cover stretches out beneath us like white velvet. For a second, I can almost see something dark swirling below it. But I blink, and it's gone. Just nerves. Or maybe the pressure is finally getting to me.

I think I've made a huge mistake.

4

IF ITS NOT AS IT SEEMS, ASK QUESTIONS, DUMMY

BARCELONA WELCOMES US LIKE A ghost wearing a mask, only solidifying my mistake.

The air smells of salt and sun-warmed stone, but something in it feels...filtered. Off. I can't quite name it, like a word stuck on the tip of your tongue. It's like someone scrubbed the edges of the world before we arrived, or we were on a sound stage for a movie before the actors started the show.

A black SUV idles on the tarmac as we step off the jet—no airport staff, no customs. A lone driver in a navy suit sits in the front seat, gloved hands gripping the wheel, sunglasses hiding his eyes. He says nothing as he steps out to open the back door, only dips his head in the barest nod.

Mattie gives me a sidelong glance. "That's not ominous at all."

"No, no. Totally normal. Just how all funded research expeditions begin." The laugh I tack on dies quickly, swallowed by the cabin. My throat tightens, skin prickling hot, the way it does when every eye in a lecture hall swivels toward me at once.

The SUV is silent inside—soundless tires, dark windows, and the air too cold for how bright the sun looks outside. I keep waiting for the driver to say something. Anything.

He doesn't.

The city unfolds around us, but not the Barcelona I remember. No mopeds whining in the lanes. No street vendors hollering. No clatter of tourists dragging suitcases over cobblestone. It's clean. Controlled. As if someone has bleached the life out of it and polished what's left. Like a postcard of a city instead of the city itself.

Mattie leans forward slightly, scanning the sidewalk. "Where are we?"

I press my forehead to the cool glass and peer out the window. Narrow streets wind below, lined with crooked stone balconies and faded banners strung between them. The air should be alive with music and chatter, but—

"Gothic Quarter, maybe? But it's…quiet."

"Too quiet."

The SUV turns down a narrow street flanked by buildings that lean like they're whispering to each other. Vines twist up ancient stone facades, blooming with flowers I don't recognize—too pale, too perfect, like they've been painted on. At the end of the road, behind wrought iron gates, stands our accommodation.

Calling it a hotel would be like calling the Parthenon a fixer-upper. It looks like a small palace—white stone veined with gold, sharp black roofs, and a single mosaic trident embedded above the entry arch. Same logo as the envelope. Same logo as the jet with some swirl design with entwined circles on the handle.

It's starting to feel less like branding and more like a signature.

The doors open as we approach. No bellhop. No reception desk. A woman in a slate-gray suit stands waiting with two keycards in hand.

"Miss Darling. Mr. Beauregard. Welcome."

Her voice is flat and perfectly enunciated. It's like someone took it out and ironed out both the accent and the humanity.

"We didn't give you our names," Mattie says. I elbow him even though I thought the same thing. I can feel the tension in his arm before he finishes the sentence. He's still joking, but his shoulders are tight, and his fingers keep tapping the side seam of his pants. A quiet, nervous tell I've only ever seen during university exams.

She stares straight through me, like pausing to take a breath never occurred to her, and says, "Your suite is ready. You'll find all necessary materials and briefings inside."

I don't remember walking inside, but suddenly we are in a marble-floored atrium with ceilings two stories high and chandeliers that look like spun glass. No music plays. No other guests in sight. There's the quiet echo of our footsteps and the lingering perfume of something sweet and spicy and nothing else.

The woman hands me a slim envelope before disappearing down a hall that swallows her whole. I turn it over. No logo or return address. My name is the only thing handwritten in a deep green ink that shimmers faintly when it catches the light. The letters tilt slightly left, stylish in that old-fashioned, boarding-school sort of way. Something oddly familiar, like the love letters tucked into the back of my nightstand I can't seem to throw away. I shake the thoughts loose. Coincidence. Another coincidence.

Mattie takes the other key and opens the suite.

If the lobby was eerie, the suite is worse. It looks as staged as the city outside. Two bedrooms and a sitting room with antique furniture that hasn't seen a speck of dust. A decanter of amber liquor beside two crystal tumblers. Maps pinned to a cork board, dotted with coordinates we never sent to anyone.

"What the actual hell?" Mattie mutters, making a slow circle. "This looks like an Airbnb designed by someone who's never met a human."

I drop my bag and approach the maps. One was circled in red. The coordinates were exact. I haven't even memorized them yet. Never published them. My stomach clenches.

"This is too curated," I say. "They have information I haven't given anyone."

Mattie runs his hand along the bookshelf. "Like they've been watching you?"

A faint hum fills the silence—something low, almost electrical, like a freezer in the garage or a bee hive in the middle of summer. It vanishes as quickly as it comes. Neither of us moves. I think we're both waiting to hear it again. We don't. But the silence it leaves behind feels worse.

In an attempt to ignore my growing nerves, I wander over to the window to look out over the strange city. Even from here, Barcelona doesn't look like Barcelona. It looks staged. Like a memory someone built from scratch. I don't know if I've been brought here to find something... or to be found.

Or, my dad's thriller comments were getting to my head.

WE BARELY HAVE time to unpack our thoughts or things and put our feet up before the knock comes—three brisk raps on the suite door.

Mattie opens it to a tall, sun-browned man in cargo pants and a faded blue tee that says *S.S. Calypso*. A second figure huddled behind him—a woman with auburn curls pulled into a high ponytail, her arms full of folders and gear. The man smells faintly of sunscreen and metal tools, with a faint side of engine grease and salt wafting from the hall.

"Evening," the man says with a crooked grin. "You must be our fearless archaeologist and her sidekick."

"Excuse me, co-lead researcher," Mattie says, offering a hand with mock indignation.

"Good man. I'm Beck, the ship's second-in-command. That's Kya— logistics and mechanical genius, unless she's modest today."

Kya doesn't smile, but she does nod—efficient, like she's already cataloging our luggage and our pulse rates. Her voice is dry when she finally speaks. "You'll like the ship. Bit of an older girl, but she's sturdy. Captain's prepping her now. Wanted you two to meet the crew before we sail."

She shifts the folders in her arms with practiced ease, like someone who's used to multitasking mid-squall. There's a grease smudge on the hem of her shirt. Her boots are steel-toed and scuffed. I relax a little. You can't fake wear like that.

Mattie shoots me a look, then shrugs. "Finally. Something normal."

I exhale through my nose, quiet, almost embarrassed at how much I needed something like this. The comfort of strangers existing around me, instead of the cold hush of suits and silent halls.

They lead us down to the lobby, then into a van that looks suspiciously civilian. Beck cracks jokes the entire ride, most of them terrible. Something about waterproof socks and squid attacks. It feels...good. His laugh is too loud for the quiet car, but I can't help smiling anyway. It's chaotic, completely unpolished, and exactly what I needed.

Kya rolls her eyes at him, muttering something about rehearsed material. I catch the smell of engine grease on her clothes and the scuffed knees on her jeans, yet another reminder of the kind of ordinary chaos I've been missing since this started.

The port is bathed in gold light when we arrive. The ship isn't sleek or ominous—it's a mid-sized retrofitted research vessel, complete with visible rust, patched paint, and a scuffed blue hull. It looks like it's worked hard. The ropes are frayed at the ends. Someone's shirt hangs from the railing like a forgotten flag. My heart unclenches more.

A few more crew members greet us on the deck—divers, medics, and a linguist named Ben with bright blue hair and too many bracelets. Someone hands me a mug of coffee. Beck introduces them one by one, and I stop holding my breath. The place is all tired, sun-worn faces and people stepping over tangled hoses to argue about bunks. They laugh. One is trying to fix a broken winch with a butter knife. Someone has a playlist of '80s hits playing softly over the intercom. It's the first time since stepping on the plane that I feel like maybe I haven't made a huge life-changing mistake.

Mattie leans against the railing beside me. "There. Not so bad."

The hint of a grin sneaks out. "They feel real."

"Which means the horror movie's probably just been delayed a scene or two."

I elbow him lightly. He grins and sips his coffee. The setting sun catches his eyes, and suddenly it's like we're back on a dig, dirt under our nails and dust in our lungs. Another adventure. A brief flicker of the familiar. My world, not theirs. Mine. But later, when I'm alone in my room, I open one of the folders Kya handed me. Inside is a passenger manifest. My name sits there in black ink, right next to Mattie's and the rest of the crew. The last line is smudged out, black ink thick and ugly, like whoever did it wanted me to know they'd erased someone.

I stare at it for a long time, wondering if it has always been like that or if this was for me alone. I press my thumb to the page. The paper is still warm, like it was printed not long before I opened it. But, then again, this is the Mediterranean. It's hot.

The lights flicker once. Enough to stop me cold.

I close the folder and go to bed before my imagination starts to run on overdrive.

5

SOMETIMES DREAMS REFLECT TRUTH

NIGHT SWALLOWS THE SHIP, BUT the cabin is too bright. A phosphorescent glow filters through the curtains—unnatural and drifting. The light crawls along the walls, soft and uncanny, moving on its own.

I lay in bed, boots at the foot. Water creeps higher in my cabin, inching up their soles. The sound is gentle, almost soothing, until I realize it shouldn't be there.

Beneath the surface, I see a city of red and silver—towers shimmering, spires cracking. Waves of red light pulse through the streets. A scream echoes from the stone, far off. The buildings tilt inward, the city drawing in on itself.

My bare hand brushes the wet floorboards, and when I look, my skin glows faintly like sea foam. Fingertips trace unfamiliar runes tattooed on my wrist—runes I didn't ink in reality, but they pulse like living veins in the bluish light. The markings shimmer and shift, never quite staying still. I force my brain to memorize them, what they look like, so I can look them up, but I can't.

A voice calls my name.

Aurora.

It's a whisper and a command. I rise in the water, searching for the source. My body floats without effort, like the rules of gravity have loosened.

Below the waves, I see him—Mattie. His face is half-submerged, eyes blazing gold. He reaches out. My heart feels like it's going to stop. He opens his mouth, but no bubbles rise.

"Help me."

Then the towers shatter in slow motion. Water turns to fire. Glass explodes. The city's reflection cracks, looping into horrifying swirls of sea and flame. The scream breaks free at last, deafening, everywhere, and then the water is gone, the fire gone, only the silence curling in the wreckage like smoke.

MY EYES FLY open.

A harsh light floods my room. The ship's internal alarm beeps—low and insistent.

The voice over the PA crackles to life, tinny and cold, like it's coming from underwater. "Casting off in five minutes," the voice calls, clipped and unfeeling. "All personnel prepare to disembark."

My heart thuds in my ears. I bolt upright, chest tight. The blankets are damp. My shirt clings to my skin. My breath tastes like salt. The air in my chest has suddenly decided it wants to be bricks instead of oxygen. I reach automatically for the nightstand, fingers twitching toward the bag with my inhaler, but stop myself. It's fine. I'm fine.

Mattie is already awake, silhouetted in the doorframe. His light hair is mussed, his t-shirt is inside out, and he's watching me like he already knows what I saw. His eyes find me instantly. We had decided after only one night in the suite that the boat was much preferred.

"Dream?" he asks softly, voice rough with concern.

I can only nod, skin cold and damp. I feel hollow, like something followed me back and is still clinging to my spine, pulling.

The cabin lights brighten further, readying us for sea. I stare at the ruined towers behind my eyelids.

They don't fade. Not yet.

Atlantis has called—and somehow, I knew I had answered.

6

When It All Goes to Hell, Try Not to Panic. Good Luck With That.

THE SEA IS TOO CALM. It's as flat as glass in a way that makes my skin crawl.

Waves we create lap gently against the hull, but the sea itself refuses to move, stretched flat around us. It's wrong. Oceans aren't supposed to hold still. They breathe, they roll, they argue with the wind. This one waits. Above it, the sky sours into a shade of grey I've only ever seen in old frescoes, storm gods daubed in ash and pearl, the kind of color that makes you brace for thunder even when the air is silent.

Mattie leans on the railing beside me, squinting into the fog bank rolling in from the west. "That doesn't look natural," he mutters. "It's moving against the wind, right?"

I glance up. The flags hang still. A held hush; metal answers in soft creaks while the water churns below. "No wind."

And worse—no birds. No buzz of insects. It's silence that feels like being stalked. Something waiting for its moment to pounce.

Behind us, Beck stands at the helm with one hand on the wheel, the other raised in salute as Kya comes stomping from the main cabin, a clipboard clutched like a weapon. Her curls are frizzing at the temples. It's better than a weather app for telling me when a storm's about to roll in.

"GPS is down," she snaps. "SAT-NAV too. Instruments are spinning like a drunk octopus."

Beck shrugs. "Bermuda Triangle, baby."

Kya doesn't so much as crack a smile. Her fingers tighten on the clipboard as she says, "We're leaving the Mediterranean."

"Triangles are everywhere if you squint hard enough."

Mattie chuckles, but the sound falls flat. He runs a hand along the railings, fingers tapping in that restless rhythm he uses when he's calculating risk. Moist heat packs in around us, like something large settling closer.

I pull my jacket tighter around my shoulders and look back to the sea. The calm isn't calming. It's sterile. Like the ocean forgot how to move or is too scared to.

That's when I feel it.

A faint pulse against my chest—soft at first, like a second heartbeat. I slip a hand beneath my shirt and touch the necklace. Cold metal, but not still. It buzzes under my fingers, as if sensing something beyond the edge of the horizon. The chain shivers against my skin. It isn't painful, but it sure as hell isn't comfortable either. It feels like it's warning me, buzzing too close to my bones. It's the only thing I have from my birth parents. Found with me when I was a baby. It's never done this before.

No one else moves. No one else notices.

I press my palm over it to steady it. It doesn't stop.

Mattie's eyes flick to mine. "You feel that?"

I nod slowly. My mouth is too dry. I want to say yes, but the word lodges in my throat. I don't know what I feel. All I know is that it's weird, and it has that cold, déjà vu edge, like an old bruise pressed again.

There's a prickle on the back of my neck, like eyes I can't see. A moment later, the breeze stirs.

On it is not the usual tang of sea salt or engine oil. It smells like wet stone and crushed violets, and it whispers over the deck like a caress. It's sweet at first, turning sour, like blossoms wilting against hot granite, flowers on a gravestone.

Kya pauses mid-sentence. Beck tilts his head. Even the ship seems to still. The creaks quiet. The air presses down with silence again. The fog rolls in, swallowing the horizon whole.

I grip the railing tighter and breathe through the weight building behind my ribs.

The sea is too calm.

THE FOG EVENTUALLY blurs the sun until it's nothing more than a smudge of light.

The muscles across my chest cinch up on their own, my body ducking before the swing clears its arc.

It thickens so fast the light dims in real time. One moment, we have shadows on the deck. The next, they're gone—consumed by a colorless shroud that blurs the line between sea and sky until the ship floats in pure, featureless nowhere. The horizon disappears. The world flattens. I don't know where I am. I don't know if I'm still moving.

Mattie moves closer to me without a word. Beck has slowed the ship, but it doesn't matter. We can't tell if we're still moving. Can't tell which way we're going. Even sound seems dulled, like someone has thrown a blanket over us. All I can hear is my own breath, harsh and papery, like dust grinding down my throat.

The change creeps in, subtle at first, then undeniable. A hum—not loud, but deep. Resonant. Like the low purr of a cello played underwater. I feel it first in my ribs, then in my teeth. It layers on itself, over and over, until it's not a hum anymore.

It's singing.

Dozens of voices. No, hundreds. All female. Soft and distant, like lullabies sung in a language I don't know but almost remember. They sing from below, from under the ship, lifting out of the depths on a late swell. It brushes the back of my mind like a forgotten name.

I step toward the railing, drawn. My feet move before I think. I feel heat blooming in my chest—like the necklace is waking up from a long sleep.

The mist glows faintly, pulsing with the sound. I lean out over the water. It's beautiful. I know it shouldn't be. But it is. It's timeless and hollow, a voice pulled out of the dark, finally remembering how to sing.

"Rory." Mattie's voice breaks the spell. His hand closes around my arm and jerks me back from the edge. I gasp. My knees lock. I didn't realize how far I'd leaned.

"You're hearing it too, right?" he asks, words pressed out between his teeth, his jaw working like he's chewing on the question.

I nod, throat dry. "What is that?"

Before he can answer, someone behind us groans.

It's Quinn, one of the riggers—a quick-witted, efficient woman who'd handled the ropes like extensions of her own limbs. She's slumped on the stairs now, muttering to herself, eyes wide and unfocused.

One of the younger deckhands staggers to the rail, freckles standing out stark against skin gone gray-green, and heaves, the splash hitting the waves hard enough to make my stomach lurch in sympathy.

Kya is already shouting orders from the bow, trying to get everyone to regroup. "Get below deck! Stay together! Beck, sound the—"

The intercom crackles—then bursts into a shriek.

It's not feedback. It's alive. The sound isn't sound—it's *teeth*. It's pressure and rage and wet heat. A guttural, inhuman scream pours from the speakers, louder than anything that should've come from a human throat. It hits like a wave, flooring half the crew. I drop to one knee, hands over my ears, heart hammering.

My vision blurs. My necklace burns cold against my skin. My whole body wants to run, but there's nowhere left to run to.

The ship's lights blow out all at once.

Darkness falls, absolute and smothering. The mist around us glows faintly still, but now with a sickly green edge.

From somewhere below deck, we hear it—metal tearing. Screeching. Like something is crawling up from the deep. The deck vibrates beneath me. My bones feel out of tune. Something has woken.

THE WORLD HAS gone still, like a class full of anxious students holding their breath right before the test results drop.

Fog presses in and erases the edges of the ship. There's only shadows— faint outlines of crew moving like ghosts through smoke. The sea has gone silent again, too silent, the kind that makes you check if your ears are still working. My breath fogs in front of me. It's the only thing that moves.

Mattie grips my wrist. Hard. "Something's wrong," he says. His knuckles are white. His voice cracks under the weight of fear. I've only heard it once before, during a dig site collapse. He doesn't rattle easily.

I open my mouth to answer, but the hum returns. Low, vibrating through the planks under my boots. My necklace buzzes hot against my sternum. I yank it out from under my shirt. The metal glows faintly—for a second. Then it goes still, like whatever it was gave me a nod and kept moving.

Almost immediately, something massive rakes against the hull.

The sound is wet, hard, and criminal. A deep shudder runs through the ship's bones, and heads swing to the railing in unison. Kya shouts something—cut short by a second blow, this one louder. The groan of the ship answering back. It sounds like the sea is trying to peel us open.

Beck curses and runs for the wheel, but it's already too late. They come over the side in near silence.

The water stays unbroken, while something moves, fluid, exact, not possible for human bones.

Dark shapes vault the railing, quick and liquid, like gravity doesn't exist for them. For half a second, I think they're human. Men in dark wetsuits or black diving gear like I've never seen before, lean and tall and quick. But then the mist catches their faces.

Their eyes catch the dark, glowing amber-gold like a cat's caught in headlights, only there's nothing cute about it, just that predatory gleam that makes my stomach clench. Their ears taper to sharp points, not cheap plastic or costume props, but real, grown that way, unnervingly beautiful in a way that feels wrong. And the way they move—too fluid, too practiced—it's somewhere between a dancer and a predator, every step balanced like they're born for the hunt.

I can't move. I'm frozen in place, my body rejecting the evidence of my eyes. One of them looks at me as he passes—a face both ageless and cruel, features sharp enough to cut. He doesn't pause. Doesn't speak.

It starts with one scream, sharp enough to slice through the fog, and then the rest of the crew joins in like they've all been waiting for permission. The sound claws up my spine, and I clamp my jaw shut, because the last thing I'm doing is adding my voice to the chorus.

Blades flash. Real ones—gleaming curved weapons like obsidian fused with steel. One cuts through Beck before he can get his hands on the flare gun. Blood sprays against the mast. Another crewman tries to swing a wrench—his attacker slits his throat before the wrench hits the deck.

In the space between defiance and death, chaos breaks loose. They don't waste time with threats or speeches. They carve through the crew like they've done it a hundred times before, every strike efficient enough to make my stomach jump in protest.

Mattie hauls me backward. I stumble over a coil of rope and go down hard on my hip. Pain flares white. I bite down on a scream.

The fog has turned red in places—soaked with blood, swirling like mist caught on a battlefield. It's eating it, making it a sick part of itself.

My hands land on something soft.

Kya.

She's lying flat, mouth slack, eyes wide open and still reflecting light. There's a single red line across her throat, clean and deep. Her fingers cling stubbornly to a flare she never fired. Her uniform shirt is half untucked, streaked with grease, and one braid has come loose across her face, clinging to the blood at her collar. She had freckles across her nose, I notice that now, the kind of thing you'd expect to catch in sunlight instead of under this gray fog. Her lips are parted as if the next breath should have been a scream, a curse, or one last attempt to keep living. Her knuckles are raw, nails broken, like she fought for every second she could get.

My knees shake uncontrollably. The boards are slick beneath me, her blood already soaking into my jeans, sticky and warm against my knees. My stomach lurches, bile burning the back of my throat, but I can't move, can't look away. She's right there, alive one second, gone the next, and all I can think is how easily it could have been me. How easily it still could be.

"Rory—get up!" Mattie's voice cracks. He's dragging me to my feet. His hand under my elbow is slick with blood. I don't know whose.

Someone behind us screams—gurgles—and then goes quiet.

We run.

I don't remember making the decision. My body moves, obeying Mattie's grip and the shove of his shoulder as he pushes me toward the stern. Blood slicks the deck, tacky under my boots, and I almost slip. Damp fog clings to my skin, clammy, not even close to normal, and every part of me screams to look up when a shadow passes overhead—a rope? A body? I don't; I can't. Looking would make it real.

We reach the stairs. One of them stands at the bottom, blood dripping from his blade, all casual as if slaughter were all a part of his routine. My chest locks up. Mattie doesn't stop. He slams into the fictional fae thing full force and takes us both down. I hit the deck, dazed, the crack of the impact ringing through me. My shoulder jars. My temple bounces off metal. Stars burst behind my eyes, and for a fractured second I wonder if this is it, if this is how I end, sprawled faceless in someone else's nightmare.

Mattie lands on his feet and grabs me—again, always Mattie—and shouts something I can't hear over the ringing in my ears. Then the water surges.

A roar tears across the deck, drowning out thought, rattling the boards under my hands. A wall of red water surges over the starboard side, crashing down like a beast's open maw. The weight of it pins me where I am, salt burning my tongue, the tang of metal sharp in the back of my throat.

It rushes in at once, warm and heavy, alive in a way that makes my skin crawl, clutching at me like a hand with too many fingers. I stumble, coughing, slick with it. Blood on my hands, in my eyes, and in my mouth. It coats my tongue with the taste of copper. It stings my throat. It smells like rust and something older.

Mattie shoves me—hard. I stagger toward the railing.

"No—Mattie!"

I whip around. Something dark and sinuous—not a rope, not a vine—slithers from the water and wraps around his ankle like it always belonged there.

The thing convulses around him, each pulse squeezing harder, forcing the air from his chest in short, jagged bursts. Veins of red light ripple through it, spreading faster with every beat, drinking him in. His jaw locks tight, muscles straining, but he doesn't scream.

I grab for him. He grabs for me. I catch his wrist. Our fingers clench—white-knuckled, frantic, a lifetime of inside jokes and shared ramen and dig-site dances hanging between us in that impossible grip. My nails dig into his skin. His grip bruises mine. Neither of us lets go. Not yet. He tries to smile. That Mattie smile. But his eyes are wide. Terrified.

"Don't—" I choke. "Don't you fucking dare—"

It pulls. His body jerks. My shoulder wrenches. Skin burns. I hold tighter—until the wet, sucking strength of the sea wins.

Our hands tear apart. He falls backward. Legs first, then hips, then arms—his eyes never leaving mine.

His lips shape my name—*Rory*—and then he's gone, the sea swallowing him in a crash of red and black. The water seals shut as if it was never broken, but the sound of it lands inside me like a slammed door, like something final and unforgiving. The silence that follows is anything but empty, it presses hard enough to splinter me from the inside out.

I scream. A raw, jagged thing that scrapes blood from my throat and still doesn't feel like enough. The world tilts. My knees buckle.

I scream again, because what else is left? He's gone. Gone from reach, leaving only absence. All I hear is nothing. I don't care a lick that I'm exposed. I don't think about it. I don't care that the ship is splitting. I don't care that someone could be stalking me right now. I see only the gap where he was—the world missing his shape. It feels like the end of everything.

I pick him out across the deck. A man—tall, regal, the epitome of darkness, untouched by the chaos around him. He stands alone in the fog, long coat billowing, dark hair streaming behind him like ink in water. His eyes are glowing—not like the others. Gold, not amber. Sunlight instead of wildfire.

He clocks me. And stops.

The chaos keeps raging, but he's still as stone, trying to decide if I'm real as I do the same. Our eyes lock. He doesn't move. Doesn't attack. There's no clear emotion there, only a bare hitch in his gaze, a flash that looks too much like surprise.

Something behind him moves—another attacker, blade drawn—and the moment snaps. The tall man disappears into the mist like he'd never been here.

The ship groans again, louder this time, the sound deep enough to rattle through the boards and into my ribs. The air is heavy in my chest, my skin prickling tight as if I don't fit in it anymore. The deck shifts under me, pitching enough to send me stumbling toward the rail. Ahead, beyond the fog, a glow pulses in the water, steady and insistent, like a heartbeat I can almost feel. Like a promise I'm not sure I want kept. My throat goes dry. The light should mean safety, discovery, something worth chasing, but bodies cover the deck and blood sticks to the boards, and I know better. Whatever's down there isn't a gift. It's the reason the sea demanded payment.

My legs don't hesitate. My chest does. My heart does. But my legs move anyway.

I jump.

The sea catches me and drags me under.

7

When An Island Is Not Nearly As Lost As Advertised

THE OCEAN SPITS ME OUT like something it doesn't want to keep.

I hit the sand hard, face-first, grit scraping my cheek and grinding between my teeth. Pain fractures through my ribs, sharp and white-hot, while my knees drag across crystal grains that cut like glass. Salt rushes in fast, searing every scrape, every tear in my skin, branding me with proof that I survived when maybe I shouldn't have. Or maybe I didn't. For all I know, this is what death feels like, salt in my cuts and sand in my mouth. Figures.

I roll onto my side, choking, and vomit seawater and blood. It splatters across the sand, red streaks catching under an alien sky, and all I can think is that it looks like someone else's life is leaking out of me.

So much blood. On my hands. In my mouth. Somewhere, I register it might not all be mine, and that thought guts me worse than the pain. Mattie's laugh, Beck's terrible jokes, Kya's pointed grin, and Quinn's quiet patience. They flicker through my head, ghosts tied to every drop of red on my skin. I don't know whose blood I'm wearing. I only know it means they're gone.

The sky above me is alien. Not cloudy, nor stormy, but a purple-black so deep it looks endless, dusted with stars I don't recognize. There are more of them than there should be, brighter than they have any right to be, and the way they flicker makes it look like the whole sky is breathing. Two moons hang over the water, pale and watchful, and I can't shake the feeling they're staring straight at me, weighing whether I deserve their pity or their judgment.

No sound but the sea behind me, hissing against the shore like whispering teeth. I lift my head, and something cracks in my neck. My skull pounds. My chest locks, then jerks. I push up, but my arms shake. The weight of my body feels unfamiliar. Everything is too heavy. My bones don't fit right anymore.

Sand bites into my palms—jagged, crystalline, sharper than any beach I'd ever seen. I crawl forward an inch at a time, each movement a battle. Every breath feels like betrayal. Like my lungs resent me for surviving.

"Mattie." His name catches in my throat. Too big to swallow. Too sacred to spit out.

I didn't scream it under the water looking for him. I didn't fight. I'd let go.

I let go.

"God." My voice cracks, barely a whisper. "Oh God, I didn't—" It hurts to say it. It hurts more not to. My fingers curl in the sand. I choke on another sob. I want to scream. I want to bite the world in half. But all I can do is cry.

He's gone.

They're all gone. Beck, Kya, and Quinn.

Quinn, who showed me how to braid fishing knots. Beck, who pretended to be the captain when we hit calm water. Kya, who handed me a flare and told me I'd need it more than she would. Faces I'd laughed with over instant coffee and a few long days under the sun. All of them torn apart—ripped into nothing while I ran, while I survived.

Survived for what?

The wind shifts, tugging strands of my dark hair toward the land. It reeks of wet stone and something floral that doesn't belong here, too sweet against the salt still burning my skin.

I raise my head—slow, aching. It feels like lifting a mountain. My body doesn't want to obey anymore. My elbows shake under me, muscles fluttering like birdsongs ready to snap.

Something flickers in the distance. A faint, golden glow, pulsing like a neon sign on its last legs. It doesn't look real. It looks placed, the type of lights that lures ships straight onto the rocks.

One by one, lights spark to life along the ridge of a massive stone plateau, revealing the edges of a city that should not exist. Not here. Not after everything. Not now. Each light calls to me, like a bait hanging on a hook, or a signal that promises rescue but only brings the sharks.

I push up to my elbows. My arms shake. My legs barely move. But I move. Not because I want to. Because I have to. Because some stubborn, feral instinct deep in my bones refuses to die here.

I crawl, dragging myself up a slope of biting sand and scattered black stones. Each grain cuts like glass. I leave a trail behind me—blood, salt, the ghost of someone who didn't deserve to live. Each step is a curse. Each inch a scream. But I don't stop. What if they're still looking for me? What if one of them made it? What if Mattie—I slam the thought down before it can finish. If I let it take shape, I'll collapse.

The wind picks up as I climb—cool and strange, thick with that same scent of wet stone and something oddly floral, like violets soaked in iron. The smell is different. Beautiful and wrong. Still like funeral flowers. Like blood and perfume mixed together.

The whispering waves hiss below.

Finally, I reach the ridge and freeze.

It's circular. A great series of concentric rings, land and water weaving together like a labyrinth. The sight knocks something loose in me. A primal awe. A wordless recognition. Like I've been here before. Or dreamed. Or was born remembering it.

Canals glint faintly between them, bridged by arched spans of glowing crystal or dark, metallic stone. Each tier rises higher than the last, until at the very center stands a towering palace complex, illuminated from within by a cold, silver flame.

The outer walls shimmer—metallic, burnished with something that looks to me like orichalcum, the lost alloy Plato had claimed once glowed like fire. But this isn't fire. This light shifts color with the movement of the sea wind, sliding from amber to blue to violet, alive in a way that feels reactive, almost aware of me watching.

Something well beyond human hands.

The buildings aren't ruins as I expected. They're almost sleeping. No, not almost.

Columns climb the air like trees, twisted with vine-like carvings that glow faintly under the moons. Domes gleam like seashells. Some of the structures curve in impossible directions, geometry bent by something otherworldly. Light spills from the narrow windows in slow pulses—waking circuits finding their rhythm. The entire city breathes. Not metaphorically. I feel it in my spine. In my teeth. A deep rhythm that syncs too easily with my own.

It's not completely silent. Beyond the waves, a faint harmonic hum rides the wind. A frequency that doesn't belong to this century. Or this planet. Or maybe even this reality. Atlantis is alive around me in ways I don't understand, waiting with a patience that feels too deliberate, and watching as if it already knows me.

The legends hadn't lied. Not exactly. Plato couldn't have described this. Not like this. His words had been guesses. Stories built from secondhand tales and whispers. What I see now isn't ruins. It's not sunken. It's not lost. This isn't a city pulled from the sea. It doesn't belong to time. Or erosion. Or the world I know.

I stare as rings of stone and water wind inward, impossibly perfect. Structures carved from black stone gleam with metal too smooth, too polished for weathered history. It doesn't look forged. It looks grown. Like the city birthed itself from the ocean floor. Light ripples along the ridges. Bridges stretch between concentric canals in arcs too fine for ancient hands, every span intact, every surface untouched by time, with no erosion or collapse to mark the centuries.

None of this is decayed.

It's preserved, whole and untouched, impossible in its perfection. It mocks what I know. It mocks everything I believed. Every dig site. Every failed expedition. Every sleepless night spent with books and maps and doubt, and I don't know how. I don't know why. It shouldn't be here in a part of the ocean that's been explored and photographed from space. But it is here, waiting, as if it expected me, as if it had been calling all along.

The lights flicker again—growing brighter, casting long shadows across the high stone ridge where I kneel, shaking and soaked in blood and salt.

I should feel awe. Should weep with wonder. But all I feel is guilt. All I feel is the hole Mattie left.

Mattie.

His laugh would echo in a place like this. He would've hated it. Called it too pristine. Too stage-set. He would've said something stupid to make me smile. I blink, blood in my lashes, throat tight with rage and grief and something I don't have a name for yet.

I'd lived. Somehow, I'd lived. And nothing—nothing—would ever be the same again.

My limbs tremble beneath me. My chest heaves, each breath jagged and shallow. There's not enough air here. Or maybe I've forgotten how to use it. I push myself up, to stand, to keep moving forward. But my arms fold beneath me like broken branches. The sand cuts new lines across my skin. I don't even flinch anymore.

Darkness pools behind my eyelids. I think I hear his voice—Mattie's— just for a moment. Maybe memory. Maybe madness. The cold seeps through my skin. The last thing I hear before the world slips away is the whisper of stone walls stirring to life.

8

MANY POISONOUS THINGS LOOK VERY PRETTY

SOMETHING SCRAPES AGAINST MY CHEEK. Sand. Sharp, sunless. Each grain shifts like splinters against my skin. I cough, salt burning my throat, and roll onto my side. Everything hurts. My ribs grind. My shoulder screams. My stomach clenches with the memory of blood and seawater and Mattie—

Where am I?

The last thing I remember is Mattie's hand slipping from mine. Blood in the water. The ship cracking apart.

Mattie.

My stomach twists. I retch. Nothing comes up but air and grief. I barely have the strength to cry. My body's a ruin, my lungs feel bruised, and I'm shaking from the inside out. Something glimmers at the edge of my vision. I cant my head—slow, painful. The movement grates like rusted gears. Every muscle a betrayal.

Atlantis.

I blink hard. Once. Twice. Still there. Rings of light. Columns that glow like moonstone. A palace that shouldn't be. It can't be. This can't be possible. I'm dreaming. I'm dead. Something other than lying on a sandy ridge looking on the not decaying, ruined city of Atlantis.

I hit my palm against the sand. The sting tells me I'm not. The pain feels too specific to be death. I drag myself upright, swaying on my knees. It takes everything I have. The sky pulses behind my eyes. My vision tunnels. Each movement lights another path, another rune, as if the city is happy to see me. Like it recognizes me. Like it missed me. Welcomes me.

My necklace vibrates softly against my skin, the hum steady and warm. Like a heartbeat pressed to mine. Like it's answering. Or calling. I touch it with numb fingers. The heat bites back, searing in a way that makes me snatch my hand away before I realize I can't.

What are you doing?

I stand on shaking legs and stagger forward. The ground sways beneath me. My knees threaten to buckle. My skin crawls. But still, I move. Because I don't know what happens if I stop. Because part of me, some part I hate, wants to figure out what happens next.

More light bursts into bloom. A high wall etched with glyphs lights up like sunrise. The carvings shift when I blink, changing slightly. It's enough to make me question if they ever stopped moving at all. I stumble, but I can't stop. I don't know what would happen if I did. I don't know if I'd survive the silence that might follow.

Somewhere above, a sound breaks the natural quiet. A whisper. No— whispers. Dozens. Skimming under the wind like a secret passed from mouth to mouth. Too high to understand. Too low to ignore.

The woods beyond the ridge rustle, and glowing eyes watch from the trees. Not two. Not ten. Dozens. Pale and lidless, blinking slowly in unison. Animal and not. Curious. Calculating. My chest knots tight, every instinct screaming to run, though I'm not sure my legs would obey if I tried. They watch me like I'm something new on the menu, or maybe their nightly entertainment. Neither feels better than the other. One creature breaks from the shadows and vanishes into the brush. The others don't follow, but their eyes stay fixed on me, and I can't shake the sense that they're also waiting to see what I'll do next.

The city still responds with each movement.

"You need to stop." The voice cuts through the fog in my brain, smooth and deep, close enough to make the hairs on my arms lift. The sound wraps tight around me, strange in its calm, the way a predator quiets the world before it strikes. Not like the whispers carried on the air, this voice has weight, aimed straight at me.

I spin, nearly falling, blood rushing in my ears. A wave of dizziness hits so hard I taste metal. My foot slips on a loose stone. I catch myself on the ridge with one scraped palm.

He stands at the edge of the stones, half shrouded in mist. The mist doesn't touch him the same way it touches me. It curls around his boots but never clings. Like it respects him. Or fears him. The man from the ship. I can feel all the remaining color drain from my face.

A bolt of memory fires through me. Amber eyes flashing in the storm. Blood blooming against canvas. Mattie's hand disappearing beneath the waves. And this man standing in the middle of it all without a scratch, the chaos sliding off him like the sea itself refused to touch him.

He found me. Or maybe he never lost me.

I remember those eyes—glowing gold, not like fire but like a predator in the dark. I remember how he stood untouched by the chaos, how everything around him died while he didn't lift a blade—he watched, still as stone while bodies fell around him. While Mattie—

I gag, bile catching at the back of my throat. I double over slightly, my vision flashing red for a heartbeat. "You," I manage, the word splintering out of me, thin and ragged, barely more than a gasp. It scrapes my throat raw, and even as it leaves my mouth. I hate how breakable it sounds.

He steps closer. The light from the glyphs caught on the curve of his armor, under the coat—dark, rippling, almost wet looking, like it's been forged from ocean shadows and starless sky. It doesn't reflect light. It absorbs it. And something about it—about him—makes my skin tighten like a bad burn.

"I said, stop," he says. "Stop moving. You're lighting up half the realm. Every fae lord within a hundred liorin will see the city alive. If you want to survive. Stop now."

Fae.

The word rings sharp in my mind. I don't know what it means, but it rings like a bell struck inside my skull, a fictional word used in books and fairy tales. "You were on the ship," I whisper.

He doesn't deny it.

"You didn't help anyone. You just watched."

A flicker of something crosses his face—anger, maybe. Or regret. I can't tell. I don't think his expressions are built for human understanding.

"I didn't kill you," he says, like it's a great favor. Like I should be grateful. The words crawl under my skin, twisting hot and cold at the same time. Gratitude is the last thing I feel. Rage, maybe. Shame, definitely. Because he's right, I'm still breathing, and Mattie isn't. Beck isn't. Kya isn't. The fact that he spared me makes me feel less alive, not more.

"That's your defense? That's the bar now?" I laugh, but it cracks in the middle—more of a sob. "Everyone else died."

Mattie died.

A gust rolls off the water behind me, sharp with metal and blood. My dark hair whips across my face, and the distant towers flare brighter—like they're listening. Like they're reacting. Like they know his voice, too.

His teeth press together, a muscle twitching in his cheek. "You were already waking it. I didn't see any sense in killing you at that point."

I don't understand what he means, but I can feel it: the city pulsing with every beat of my own heart, responding to me. And behind his words— behind his stare—I feel something else. Recognition. Not me knowing him. A familiar face in all the chaos, even if he is the enemy. But him knowing me. Like I've crossed his path before. Or someone else's path wearing my face.

He extends a hand—not kindly, not with comfort, but with purpose. There's nothing soft in it, no pretense of choice, it's a command dressed up as an offer.

"Come with me. You don't want to face what comes next without protection. You won't last a minute in this world alone. I'm the only one who has a reason not to let you die now."

"I'm not going anywhere with you."

"You don't have a choice."

"Watch me." I wheel and take two steps back toward the trees, toward the wild edges of the island—where the whispers keep moving. Where the eyes are still watching. Where the brush rustles like breath caught in teeth. Something moves there. Dozens of eyes blink in the dark. Too many. Too high up. Some flash silver, others violet. A ripple of movement—not one creature, but many, shifting as a single, hive-like thing.

He doesn't stop me, saying, softly, "The city called to you. Now they'll come for what answered."

I go rigid as the air shudders beneath my skin. The stone burns brighter under my feet. Lines of golden light race outward, speeding across glyphs and bridges I hadn't noticed until now. The city is stirring faster, answering me, reaching for me, and I can't stop it. My arms fold tight across my chest, a useless shield, as if I can make myself small enough to escape its notice.

"I didn't mean to."

"I know." His voice is quieter now, like trying to calm a scared animal. It almost works. Almost. But even gentleness from him feels dangerous. Like the kind of quiet that precedes the kill. "But they won't care."

"Care about what?" I whisper.

His gaze shifts to the tree line. "That you didn't mean to wake it. That you didn't know what you were doing." Any warmth drains from his tone, leaving it clipped and hard. "And they don't take chances with threats they don't understand."

My mouth goes dry. "What does that mean?"

He tilts his head, gaze steady. "Some will want to dissect you. Others will want to bind you—to a throne, or a stone, or a grave. You woke something none of them can afford to let live unclaimed." His bright blue gaze lingers on me, unblinking, before he goes on. "They will come wearing smiles. Or teeth. Sometimes both. You won't know the difference until it's too late."

I swallow hard, heart hammering. It feels too loud. Like it might draw more things to me. Like it might draw him closer.

Somewhere, something howls—a sound pulled from nightmares, echoing across the waves. High and wet and nothing I've ever experienced before. It sounds like bone grinding over stone. My whole body flinches.

He extends a hand—without cruelty. But also without apology.

I stare at that hand. Then at the city glowing with life behind him. I'm not standing at the edge of salvation. I'm standing at the edge of consequence, and I realize this is another kind of drowning.

9

If It Blinks Sideways, You're Screwed

THE FOREST WATCHES US.

And I mean that literally. Not the way haunted places feel watched, or how paranoia gnaws at the back of your mind after too many sleepless nights. Every branch creaks like an old spine turning. Every head tilts to track our passing. I swear the trees breathe. Not fast or loud, but slow and deep, like sleepers dreaming with their mouths closed.

The trees aren't trees, not really. Their bark shimmers in places like beetle shells, and their limbs curl upward like fingers waiting to close around something. Some of those fingers twitch. I don't think it's the wind. I can't tell where the roots end and the bones begin.

Behind us, the city still pulses.

I look over my shoulder once and nearly stop walking. The glyphs across the high stone walls flicker like the world's slowest warning light, steady and impossible to ignore. They glow in time with something under my skin. The necklace. My pulse. I can't tell which. As if Atlantis isn't just awake now, but...aware. Watching me go. Like I've left in the middle of a conversation I didn't realize I was having.

"Don't look back," he says.

I don't ask how he knew I had. His voice is too close, almost brushing my ear, and his hand stays firm between my shoulders. The pressure isn't soft, but it isn't forceful either, it keeps me moving, steady and unavoidable. His palm lingers like an anchor I can't shake, the heat of it sinking through my shirt. It feels less like he's guiding me and more like he's staking a claim, holding me in place as though the moment he lets go, the forest will reach in and take me for itself.

His name still hasn't been offered, and I'm not sure I'd take it if it was. If I know it, I might start thinking of him as real. As someone I can understand.

I wrap my arms tighter around myself and keep walking. My shoulders ache. My calves scream. Every step tears at the skin along my heels and the edges of my toes. My feet bleed, shredded from coral and stone, but the shock makes it distant—like I'd left my body behind somewhere in the surf with Mattie.

That thought cuts deeper, sharper than the physical pain. I almost face back again. Not for the city. For the sea. For the part of me still floating in it.

We move through winding paths where the light refuses to follow. It should be day. Somewhere, above the trees and beyond this alien sky, the sun should exist. But here, it's like the light has forgotten how to land.

The moss underfoot pulses in faint ridges—not green, but bruised indigo and violet, like spilled nebulae trying to crawl back to the stars. I don't walk on it so much as sink into it. Every step leaves behind a faint imprint that slowly swells and fades, the forest is swallowing the memory of my presence.

Above us, twisted trees arch so tightly they scrape one another, shedding leaves shaped like knives and thorns that gleam blue when they hit the dirt. A thorn tears skin, and blood spreads across fabric, but my body stays locked in place. The shock doesn't even register anymore.

The air feels wetter than fog—thick, cloying, smelling of crushed violets and burnt copper. Too thick and heavy for my asthmatic lungs still raw from seawater, and now each inhale tastes of perfume and pennies. I cough once, and it comes out red. He cuts me a look. Says nothing and keeps walking.

Shapes move beyond the trees. They don't walk. They shift—gliding on too many limbs, bones jointed and backward, spines protruding at odd angles like they'd grown wrong on purpose. One has arms but no fingers. Another has ribs outside its skin. None of them blink, except one. It pauses, half-emerged from the bark of a tree it isn't part of, its eyes vertical and rimmed in bone, glowing like molten gold through milk glass. It blinks—sideways.

It doesn't move. Neither do I. My heartbeat stutters. For a second, I think it recognizes me. Not as a person. As prey. My lungs scream for oxygen. But I don't make a sound. I don't run.

He doesn't slow down. But his voice drops, low and tight. The calm is gone, pulled taut and strained in a way that makes my stomach drop. "Too late."

I look at him, heart hammering. Not from the exertion. From the fact that he's not alarmed by the creature I saw.

"Someone else saw the city wake," he says. "They're already here."

He doesn't say who. Doesn't need to. My stomach twists hard enough to make me stumble. Whoever 'they' are, he isn't surprised by them. That's worse than the creatures in the trees, worse than the forest watching us, because it means he expected this. And if he expected it, then maybe I should've too. But I didn't. I was too busy drowning. Too busy losing everyone. Now I'm the one left standing in a place I never should've reached, and apparently I'm not even alone in that.

I spin toward the dark—no shadows move, no wind stirs the leaves—but the air presses harder now, like the whole island has drawn a blade against a new foe. There's no sound, only a vibration under my skin, the warning tremor that comes a heartbeat before a trap slams shut.

Behind us, I can feel the light of the city dimming—not dying or going back to sleep; banked to an ember. Like it's watching the same things. Like it's waiting to see who survives. I wonder if it's rooting for me or the others?

A soft screech echoes from the cliffs hiding above—not a bird or human, but something caught in the middle. The sound rakes through me, sharp as teeth sinking into bone, and my body reacts before I can think. I jolt, knees locking, vision narrowing to a tunnel of dark and gold.

Mattie.

He's not here. He would've cursed and made some stupid joke and shoved me behind him. I almost call his name. Almost.

He grabs my wrist, his fingers tight, not rough or cruel, but with no room for negotiation. "You will not run. You will not speak."

I nod without thinking. My mouth is dry. My thoughts are loud and scattered.

"Who is it?" I whisper.

His eyes glow in the shadows. "Pray you never learn their name."

He takes a step toward me, positioning himself between the sound and my body, and says nothing. Not a threat or even comfort. It's a fact. He will shield me from what comes. But not because he cares. Because I am still useful. Maybe.

The hunter keeps to the dark. But I can feel it. And it feels old and hungry and like it already knows my name. And names are a powerful thing, right? That's what all the fairy tales say, never tell them your name.

WE KEEP MOVING. Each step feels heavier now, drawn out by the weight of what I've seen. The forest doesn't thin; it closes in tighter, branches knitting overhead until the path feels swallowed whole. Bark creaks as trunks bend inward, their limbs dipping down like nosy neighbors pressing in too close, waiting for me to screw up loud enough to notice.

Moss gives way to stone—black and veined with silver, slick beneath me. The stone bites at the torn soles of my feet. Each step leaves a smear. I nearly slip, but he catches my arm without looking. His grip is too strong. Too fast. Like this isn't the first time he's walked someone through this place.

And then something…chirps. I go statue-still, because apparently my body's survival plan is to impersonate bad garden decor.

It emerges from a tangle of roots up ahead—small, round, and catlike, with oversized ears and iridescent fur that shimmers silver-blue in the gloom, except for the membranous wings along its spine like a bat. Its eyes are impossibly large, deep violet, and glow faintly. It tilts its head at us and chirps again, softer. The sound makes it look more curious than dangerous, almost harmless, though I'm not stupid enough to trust appearances here.

The little chirp punches through the fog in my brain like light through water. For a second, I almost cry from the sheer relief of seeing something that isn't sharp or screaming or dead.

It's adorable. Not nearly as scary as everything else I've seen so far. I was convinced this world was only deadly. My body starts to relax before my brain catches up. My fingers even twitch forward, like I might crouch and coax it closer.

My heart does something stupid. "Is that—?"

"Don't move." The words bite out of him so fast and precise they leave no room for argument.

The creature pads closer, fluffy tail twitching. It blinks slowly at me, then bares a tiny mouthful of needle-like teeth. A low purring whine vibrates from its chest. The sound is warm. It curls into my skull like lullabies from a childhood. I sway enough to hate myself for it. For showing weakness. This isn't the place to show weakness.

"That thing is not adorable," he says like he's correcting a dangerous mistake, not making conversation.

I didn't realize I had said that part out loud. My cheeks flush from shame. I almost let myself believe something was safe.

"It's a liorwyn. It kills by mimicry. Getting into your mind to find a way to set you at ease. The purr is to lull prey. The glow to hypnotize. It'll climb your spine and hollow you out from the back of your skull."

The explanation hits, not cold but corrosive, eating through whatever excuses I might have reached for.

The liorwyn sits. Its tail wraps neatly around its paws, like a house cat waiting to be fed. I take one step backward. Every hair on my body rises. "Got it. No touching the creepy cat-bat."

"Not unless you want to die smiling."

The way he says it makes me shudder, like he's seen someone do exactly that. The forest swallows the liorwyn whole. One blink and it's gone—like it was never here. I walk on in silence, each step harder to count than the last, my lungs locked tight until the ache in my chest forces me to draw air again.

It's only then I notice my hands, trembling so badly I curl them into fists to hide it.

He walks ahead like none of this fazes him. He doesn't even glance back. Not a flicker of surprise that I'm still here, or that I almost wasn't.

I scowl at the back of his head. "You know," I say, louder than necessary, "for someone dragging a traumatized stranger through the murder forest, you're real stingy with the introductions."

He doesn't slow or so much as shift when I speak. His stride stays even, the same measured pace as if I hadn't said a word. The quiet stretches, thick and grating, and I push faster to close the gap, slipping once on the slick moss before catching myself. Close enough now to glare at the line of his broad shoulder, daring him to turn.

"What do I call you? 'Hey you with the glowing murder eyes'?"

He leaves me hanging in the quiet until my jaw tightens, and only then does he give me a name without so much as a glance, "Raef."

"Raef." I test the name in my mouth. "That a first name? Last name? Serial killer codename?"

"Just Raef." The way he says it makes it clear there's more, but he's not about to hand it over. It feels like a scrap tossed my way; a single word is supposed to keep me satisfied, and I despise myself for almost letting it.

We move deeper into the forest, though it doesn't feel like any forest I've ever known. The trunks shoot up higher than they should, straight and rigid, too perfect to be natural. The leaves snag the last scraps of light and flash metallic green and copper, as if plated instead of natural. And the eyes— because there's no mistaking them for knots or tricks of shadow. Wet and unblinking, set deep in the bark. Some shut the instant we pass, only to peel open again behind us. I keep walking, but every step tightens the knot in my spine.

"Where are we going?" I ask, mostly to break the silence crawling between my thoughts.

"Off the island," Raef says. "Before whoever's watching decides to follow."

I glance over my shoulder. Nothing but trees. But the air behind them carries weight, as if thought itself has grown teeth. It presses at the edges of my mind, not a whisper, not a voice, but the shape of one trying to take root.

"How far?" I ask.

He keeps walking, steps a steady pad, and for a moment I wonder if he's ignoring me until finally, "Two liorin. Maybe three."

I frown. "And that translates to...?"

He gives me a look that's either pity or exhaustion, his brilliant, light blue eyes shadowed beneath dark lashes too long for someone this ruthless, his mouth set in a line that never quite softens. "You'll learn."

He's not unkind, but not kind either. I mean, he is a cold-blooded murderer, so what am I expecting? But I get the sense that whatever patience he has left is reserved for something worse than me.

THE PATH EVENTUALLY narrows, forcing us single file through a cleft in the trees. On one side, thorned vines coil around a crumbling statue. Their barbs hooked deep into stone as if feeding from it. Moss clings thick across its chest and jaw, but patches of pale granite show through—fingers reaching skyward in a gesture caught between prayer and demand. The face is worn flat, features eroded until it looks more mask than human, hollow where the eyes should be. The other side drops into shadow—a sheer pit that looks shallow at first glance, until you look twice and realize you can't see the bottom at all. A trick of the light, darkness swallowing itself. I edge closer to the middle, silent except for the squelch of my bare feet in the damp earth, skin raw, toes numb, and ankles rimmed in blood where coral or stone cut deep.

Raef hasn't spoken since his name. But I can feel him watching. Judging. Maybe calculating. Maybe all of the above.

When we reach a flat ledge carved with half-buried symbols, he stops and faces me. "How did you find the island?" His voice drops, smooth enough to unsettle, stripped of anything kind.

My eyes snap to his, narrowing before I even realize I stopped walking. "What?" The word comes out rough, half-broken from my throat, more challenge than question. My gut twists, not only from fear but also from the way he's staring, like I've tilted his axis, like he's seeing something in me he didn't plan for.

"You come from the mortal realm. That's not a guess—it's all over you. The clothes. The smell. The disorientation."

"Gee, thanks." I cross my arms, then stop when I feel dried blood flake from my sleeve. It's not mine. I don't think. I don't know whose it is. I try not to think about that.

"How?"

How? Like it was something I planned? Like I chose to be dragged underwater and spit out in a world that's actively trying to kill me? I hesitate, arms crossing over my chest, hugging myself tightly. "I—I was on a research expedition," I say finally, though the words feel hollow now. "A ship. Funded by someone I never met. We followed coordinates, but there was a storm. I think. Fog."

Mattie. The image of him being pulled under flashes behind my eyes like a knife in the dark. My voice catches, and I skip the part where I let go. "I didn't find the island. I washed up on it."

Raef closes the space between us, his boots whispering against the moss until he's near enough that the air shifts with him. "You're saying the portal simply opened for you?" His presence prickles under my skin, too close, and my pulse stutters. I want to lean back, to put distance between us, but I make myself stand still, because giving ground feels like giving in.

"I don't know what I'm saying." I look up at him, pulse quickening. "We were in the Atlantic. One second it was water, the next—nothing made sense. Fog that didn't move. Lights in the deep. Then...well, you're well aware of what happened next."

I attempt at keeping my voice level, but it's unraveling. Every word makes this place feel more real. The city, the deaths, the fact that I might be the one who broke something sacred by existing. The air hangs heavy between us, with no sound but the faint stir of leaves, each second dragging longer than I think it should. He studies me, eyes narrowed, mouth a hard line. "That's impossible," he says.

"I'm living proof that it's not," I snap, but the defiance dies in my throat. Because he's not annoyed. He's afraid. Not of me—of what I represent. "You think I want this?" I gesture to myself—torn, filthy, barefoot, and blood-spattered. A walking disaster. "You think I *meant* to be here?"

"No one can." The words land stripped of inflection, heavy enough to feel like stone dropping between us. "That portal was sealed before your kind could write their name in ink." He strides past me, each step slipped and controlled, shoulders tight beneath his dark coat. His fists flex open and shut at his sides, knuckles pale against skin that looks carved too smoothly to be human. "The last known mortal crossing was before this city fell many thousands of years ago. The gates were bound by oath and blood. Nothing slips through."

My mouth goes dry. Many thousands of years. The kind of number you only read in footnotes. The kind of weight that buries civilizations.

"Well," I force out, "maybe your magical gate has a leak."

He rounds on me, fast. "That leak is going to cost my court ten centuries of war."

I jerk back, his words hitting harder than any physical blow. He isn't shouting—but because I finally understand what he's saying. I didn't stumble into another world. I cracked it open.

"Mattie died," I whisper, like it's a defense. Like it excuses any of this. "I lost everything. Do you think I wanted to tear holes in your magic and wake up in a place where trees bleed and cats try to eat your brain?" I wheeze on the last word. My chest tightens suddenly, not from grief this time, but from air that won't come. Not now. Not here. I double over, hand to my sternum, gasping. The world spins for a second, but it's long enough to remind me that my inhaler is gone.

Raef is at my side before I hit the ground, dropping to one knee without a word. His palm presses flat to my chest, steady and unyielding, the weight of it sinking through skin and bone. His touch is cool, not icy, carrying a faint thrum that makes me wonder if it's his pulse I feel. Magic. Nothing like the spectacles at home, but something steady that pushes against me until my chest finally drags in air again. It isn't gentle necessarily. It feels imposed, like my body's been forced to remember how to work.

"Breathe," he says, voice quiet but firm. "Soft, light, just breathe."

I do. Slowly. Each inhale is jagged but growing easier. The worst of the pressure eases, though my hands still tremble. When I glance up, I find him watching me. Not with pity, but calculation, measuring how broken I already am and deciding if I'm worth the effort of fixing.

He looks past me, jaw flexing. "It shouldn't be open. And if it is...if you can open it..."

"Then what?"

Raef cuts himself off, leaving the rest unsaid, but the look on his face is enough. He's still gripping the idea of me like I'm a loaded weapon he didn't know existed. And maybe I am. Maybe the city picked me. Maybe their gods did. Maybe I'm the idiot who wandered too close to the edge of something that's been waiting to open. Whatever power he thinks I possess that's strong enough to tear open a sealed gate isn't one he wants walking free. And now I'm standing here, covered in salt and blood, the city of Atlantis still glowing in my wake.

"I didn't do it on purpose," I say, quietly. The words taste like sand and failure.

He gives a bitter breath of laughter. "Intention means little here."

I get up and look away, teeth gritted, eyes burning. I want to scream. At him. At the city. At the sky. But there's nothing left in me but the ache. The silence isn't comfortable—it's thick with too many unspoken things. The grief of what I lost. The terror of what I've caused. The truth that neither of us is free anymore.

"How far is your camp?" I ask because it's easier than saying sorry. Or asking what happens next.

"Close," he says. He says this quieter, with a certain clip at the edge, his gaze flicking toward the trees with that feline flash of gold as if he's listening to something I can't hear. The change knots in my stomach before I can even process it, a warning threaded into the air between us.

The shadows slip across the ground in ways that don't match the light, sliding over roots and stone independently. The air grows heavy and damp, metallic on my tongue, and the trees groan, their trunks bending slightly, like they're making room for someone or something else.

Raef tenses. His hand drifts toward the blade strapped at his thigh. "We need to move."

"What is it?"

No reply. He keeps scanning the dark, fingers brushing the hilt of his weapon because he's already chosen violence over explanation.

10

TRAVEL TIP DONT LOOK DOWN, DONT LOOK BACK

THE PATH DOWN IS BARELY a path at all—a broken line of stone scraped into the cliffside, slick with moss and crusty with salt. One wrong step and the ocean would take me. Again. My fingers curl against the rock, already trembling. My body remembers drowning even if my mind hasn't caught up. Salt still stings my throat. My lungs ache from memory alone. Part of me still thinks maybe it should. Maybe I should've let it.

Raef goes first, his movements fast and sure-footed, like he's done this climb a hundred times. He doesn't test his steps or check his grip; he moves, balanced as if falling isn't a problem for him. The wind snaps his coat against the rock, the fabric dragging shadows with it that shift in ways I don't comprehend. For a second I swear they ripple under the surface, more liquid than cloth, smoke one moment, dark water the next. I blink hard and look back to my own footing before I can decide if it's a trick of the wind or just him.

"Step where I step," he calls over his shoulder. "If you fall, I'm not climbing down after you."

I don't reply. I can't waste air on being witty. My throat is still raw from the screaming—screaming Mattie's name, screaming as the ship cracked apart, screaming as the sea dragged me under. I swallowed blood, salt, and grief so thick it lodged in my lungs like sand.

My feet bleed with every step, cut from stone and broken shells. I keep moving anyway, because stopping means thinking—and if I think, I'll watch his hand slip from mine again. I'll feel it. I'll fall. Not from the cliff, but into myself.

The wind claws at us now, sharp with sea brine and something stranger beneath it. Something sweet and coppery—like blood and crushed flowers. I taste it at the back of my throat.

Beneath us, the water churns black, blue, and gold. Light shimmering beneath the waves like lightning trapped under molded glass. My stomach lurches. I never want to see that color again. The color of Mattie's eyes when they vanished. The color of something ancient waking up.

"How much further?" I ask the question, squeezing it out before I can swallow it back. My legs feel like they've been traded for lead, every muscle trembling, and I hate the weakness in my voice almost as much as the fact that he's still moving like the climb costs him nothing. It's a fine time to realize I'm out of shape.

He keeps climbing like I never asked a question, his silence doing all the talking. Typical. Mattie would've had three bad jokes ready by now, plus a lecture about conserving water or not slipping on moss. Anything to make me forget how much my legs hurt. I grit my teeth and push on, hating Raef for being steady, chastising myself for wishing Mattie was here instead, for thinking of him constantly.

I catch myself on a jagged outcropping, palm scraping open. I hiss but don't stop. Pain's a distant thing now, another buzz in the static. My hands are shaking. Could be fear, could be the cold, could be my body finally staging a revolt. Take your pick.

The jungle presses in around us, the usual hum of insects gone, the leaves holding still. I think everything is bracing for the next bad thing. I sure am. High above, something screams. It isn't human. It isn't a bird, either. The sound spirals down in waves—a whistle, then a warble, then a shriek that bends the air.

Raef's head snaps up. "Glint. Move faster."

"What the hell is that?"

"Hunters," he says grimly. "Their sight is sound. And they like the taste of new things."

I shrink back, shoulders hunched, folding in on myself. Of course they do. Of course this world wants more blood. It hasn't had its fill.

I don't ask for more. Why waste my breath when I know he won't answer. One foot. Then the other. Don't stop. Don't scream. Don't let the wind rip the last of Mattie from your throat.

Halfway down, my foot slips on slick rocks. My body tilts, weight lurching out from under me—and then his hand shoots out and catches my wrist.

Everything halts in an instant. The wind claws at us, but neither of us moves, caught in the pull between his grip and my balance. His grip is iron, fingers burning hot against my clammy skin, holding me so tight it feels like the cliff itself has me. For a second, I swear the air between us sparks, a charge crawling up my arm until it settles in my chest. I drag my gaze up to his face.

And I hate him.

I hate the way he didn't move when Mattie was torn from me, like the sea taking him wasn't worth Raef lifting a finger. Hate that he's steady now while I'm falling apart. Hate that I need his hand not to die, to keep from tumbling into the dark, that I need him in this moment to survive when all I want is to tear free.

His face is too close. His eye flashing gold, even in the light.

"Let go of me," I whisper.

"If I do, you die."

That's fair, *asshole*.

He pulls me up with one hard yank, and I stumble after him, not letting go this time. Not because I trust him. Because the air screams. The rocks bleed. The sky tilts. And my hands still remember the last time they let go. I'm not making that mistake again.

We descend the last stretch in silence, if silence can include the howl of wind and the rush of blood in my ears. The path ends in a narrow shelf of stone and a cave mouth that opens to the sea. There, half-shrouded in mist, is a boat. I stop. Hard. My body locks up before my mind understands why.

It's nothing like the last one. Slender and black, riding low to the water, with sails that shimmer like beetle wings in the dim light. The hull is carved with shapes that make my eyes ache if I stare too long, as if the boat refuses to stay fixed in one place. The air around it smells faintly of salt and metal, like blood lives in the seawater. My stomach flips. The last boat I set foot on gave me nothing but screams and loss, and this one looks eager to finish the job. I don't want to touch it. I don't want to go anywhere near the water. The sea already took everything.

Raef steps lightly onto the deck and looks my way. "Get in."

I can't. My brain refuses. My feet root to the stone. The last boat I boarded ended in blood, screams, and the sickening sound of a throat opening underwater.

Something stirs beside the boat.

The water swells. Tall, pale, faceless. Like someone draped silk over a shadow.

I lurch backward, shoulders hitting rough rock, my throat locking tight before a sound can escape. Not again. Not the water. Not this.

Raef murmurs a word I can't understand. Low and rhythmic. The thing tilts its head, then slips beneath the surface without a ripple.

"What was that?" I ask, voice shaking.

"Not your enemy," he says. "Yet."

Not comforting. Not even a little.

"Get in," he tells me again.

"I can't." I shake my head, tears pressing sharp behind my eyes. My lungs feel too tight. My chest is too small. The cave is too dark. The boat too still. Mattie went into the water and didn't come back. Why should I?

Raef steps forward, his hand hovering in the space between us, close enough to feel but never touching. When he speaks again, the edge has slipped from his voice, leaving it quieter and more grounded. "Nothing will happen to you in this vessel. I swear it." Up close, tension cords his shoulders, his jaw ticks, and a weariness hangs on him that doesn't match the predator from the ship.

The way he says it—swear, not promise—sounds like an oath. Like something weightier than trust.

I force myself forward. Legs leaden. Knees trembling. It feels like walking into a grave.

We cut away from the island without sound. No creak of wood, no snap of canvas, the boat gliding forward while the water parts cleanly around the hull. As we drift into deeper water, I force myself to look back. The cliffs glitter faintly, and the glyphs along the edge of Atlantis fade, dimming one by one, leaving the stone cold and dark.

I wonder if it's mourning me.

Or everything I brought with me.

WE LEAVE THE lamenting sea behind right before sunrise. The twin moons have vanished, swallowed by the dawn. In their place, light breaks across the sky in warm golds and pale rose, casting long shadows through the trees. I should feel familiar and safe. But nothing about this place is home, and even the sunlight feels like it's watching me.

I keep my eyes on the path.

Each step sends pain shooting up through the soles of my feet—split skin and bruised bones grinding on moss-softened stone. I don't cry out; I no longer have the strength for it. Raef walks ahead of me, always far enough to remind me that I'm following, not traveling beside.

He didn't speak much on the boat. He doesn't speak now, either. One hand rests on the hilt of a knife at his hip, dark metal that shimmers in the rising light and drinks it in. The runes etched into it gleam soft and pale, echoing the ones in the city. I don't ask him about it. I don't ask him anything.

My body moves out of habit now. Everything else—mind, soul, whatever's left of me—drags behind like driftwood.

We made landfall at the edge of a cliff-lined inlet, then hiked through another forest—this one thicker and less luminous than the one on the island. Here, the trees rise like pillars. Their bark is dark and threaded with veins of light. The moss beneath our feet still glows faintly violet, softening the sounds of our steps. The air buzzes with hidden life.

And right when I think I might collapse, the trees part.

We step out onto a ridge that overlooks a narrow gorge—almost invisible from above. A series of stone outcroppings have been shaped into structures—half cave, half tent, each one draped in fine cloth and ringed in glowing blue stones. Moss coats the walls, like the whole place has grown into itself, nature creating the camouflage needed to hide it from the rest of the world.

It's beautiful, and nothing about it feels safe. Not when every shadow might be something watching back. Not when I'm still bleeding between my toes. Not when the man beside me hasn't decided yet if I'm a threat or a burden.

As we descend, movement catches at the edges of my vision. Figures peel out of the shadows, tall, lithe, and silent. Fae, I'm guessing. Like him. Tall. Broad-shouldered. Not human, but close enough that the difference strikes like static. Uncanny in the worst ways. One has curved horns braided into his long black hair. Another's skin shimmers like wet ash with every pull of their lungs. All carry weapons. All stare.

The moment they notice me, my muscles betray me again, freezing like stillness will somehow save me.

A few of them edge backward, boots scraping over stone, eyes cutting toward one another before snapping away again. The shift runs through the camp like a ripple, small but easy enough to notice. No one speaks at first.

A female warrior steps forward. Her armor shines hazily in the pre-dawn light, and her eyes are rimmed in silver like polished metal. She drops her gaze, barely, and speaks in a voice scarcely more than a breath.

"Nightmare Queen."

My heart stutters.

What?

A broad-shouldered male near the fire spits, the glob landing in the dirt at my feet. His skin is pale as ash, his hair matted with grease and leaves, and his eyes slit sideways like a serpent's. He doesn't look away when he does it, jaw working slow, daring me to react.

I lock up so hard my jaw aches, a cold sweat breaking out all over. Doesn't it figure that I survive drowning only to choke on nothing.

My hands twitch at my sides like I should defend myself, like I even could. I don't understand what I've done—what they see when they look at me. All I know is that I wish Mattie were here. I wish someone were here. I wish I didn't feel so completely and utterly alone.

Raef steps in front of me—not protective, but a silent warning to the others. He's drawing a line in the dirt. His presence crackles like a blade pulled halfway from its sheath. The other fae fall quiet. The one with the horns looks away.

I feel like I've been skinned open. Like they're seeing parts of me I don't even know yet.

Raef's voice cuts through the air, clipped and curt. "Where is a tent?"

A younger guard with blond curls down to his shoulders, barely older than me, maybe, nods sharply and leads off. "This way."

The camp winds inward, spiraling toward a central fire pit ringed by jagged black stones. The cliff hides a smithy tucked away, its coals banked low. A pot hanging over the fire smells faintly of herbs and meat I can't name. There are weapons, books, a birdcage strung with bones.

They live here. These aren't simple soldiers. This is a place of waiting. A war camp without a war, or one they're preparing for.

And me? I'm the ghost they didn't expect. The thing they feared might one day arrive.

They whisper when I pass. I catch pieces. Words that crackle like static. None of them kind. But none of them stop me either. The path bends, and there it is, the place they've been driving me toward.

A low stone nook set back against the cliff wall. It's not ugly, but it's not welcoming either. The mouth is draped with heavy fabric the color of bruised stone, faintly iridescent. Two guards stand at either side, weapons crossed. I stop outside, my whole body vibrating with exhaustion.

"This is it?" I ask.

"It's not a prison," Raef answers, obviously reading my face.

But it is. A gilded one. A clean one. But still a cage. I duck beneath the curtain.

The fabric walls deaden sound until the world feels hollowed out. No footsteps follow me, no rustle of wind through leaves, not even the scratch of birds outside. I hear only my breath, uneven in my chest, reminding me I'm still here.

The space is cool and dry, lit only by the soft pulse of glyphs etched into the stone walls. They definitely aren't random lines. They spiral and intersect in ways that remind me of early cuneiform or Linear B, but twisted. They're a language, I know that. The pale blue light spreads across the walls, cold as moonlight on ice.

A cot made of leather and what looks like polished bone sits near the back, beside a low table. A folded blanket rests on top. The table squats beside it, made of twisted dark wood, warped and gnarled like something pulled from a nightmare.

There's a silver basin shimmering in the corner, full of clean water. A small bundle of folded fabric lay beside it—clothing, dark and stitched with faintly shifting threads. Something practical, built for use rather than show.

None of this is normal. None of this was made for me.

I move to the basin and drop to my knees, bracing my hands on either side. The water inside doesn't ripple. It glows faintly, viscous and still, like mercury caught in a dream. My hands shake as I brace myself on the edge. The stone floor is cold, almost numbing against my knees. Raef steps forward, fast, but stops short when I hold up a hand.

"I'm fine," I croak. I'm not. But I need space. I need silence.

He lingers. I can feel it. The weight of him behind me like another storm waiting to break, the energy radiating off of him is suffocating. But he backs off.

I splash water onto my face. It smells like wild herbs and metal. The first pass stings—the cut across my brow, the salt in my mouth, the blood dried in my hair. The second pass washes it clean. And the third? It breaks me. I don't sob. I don't scream. I sit there with tears running into the basin, silent and stunned, while the image of Mattie's hand slipping from mine plays over and over and over.

The water doesn't change. It doesn't reflect me. It doesn't forgive me either. Hair tangled. Neck bruised where Mattie's hand had slipped while guiding me.

I wipe my face with the hem of the offered tunic, then reach up and feel the necklace against my chest. Still warm. Still pulsing. Still the only thing that's mine. I tuck it further beneath my shirt, fingers shaking, not wanting anyone to see.

Behind me, close, Raef's voice cuts through the silence. "They don't know what you are. Most of them, anyway."

"Do you?" I ask, not looking back.

He hesitates, the quiet stretching long enough to make my skin prickle, before he finally says, "I know you shouldn't exist."

I laugh. It sounds broken. "Yeah," I whisper, "join the club."

He takes a single step closer, the leather of his boots whispering against stone. I keep my eyes fixed on the floor, refusing to give him the satisfaction of meeting his stare, but I feel his presence tighten like a cord between us. I don't trust him. But he hasn't left. And that's more than I can say for anyone else.

"We'll talk later," he says. "Clean up. Rest. Don't leave this tent."

"And if I do?"

His mouth twitches. A shadow of a smile flickering at the edge of my vision, more warning than warmth. "Then I'll have to carry you back." He leaves without waiting for a reply.

I stare at the curtain swaying in his wake. The silence swells again, but this time it's not empty. It's filled with the ache in my chest, the heaviness dragging at my limbs. I sit down on the edge of the cot. It's firm. Cold. I press my face into my hands and finally, finally, let myself break.

11

ON THE PROPER CARE AND FEEDING OF MORTAL WOUNDS

T HE TENT IS QUIET, THE kind of quiet that presses on the inside of my skull.

Not the absence of noise other than my own breaths and my own beating heart, but silence that settles like frost on bare skin. Heavy. I sit stiffly on the cot, legs tucked under me, the strange tunic brushing my ankles every time I shift. Its threads shimmer softly, blues, greens, and shadowed violets, like an oil slick trying to pass for silk. Beautiful and strange. I hate how soft it feels. Like something meant to soothe.

The basin of now-cold water rests beside me, stained pink from when I'd scrubbed my hands until the skin burned. I hadn't noticed the dirt under my nails until I saw the blood. Not my own. Maybe Kya's. Maybe Beck's. My stomach flips again. Across from me, a shallow table holds a plate of food I haven't touched: flatbread, soft cheese, and slices of pale fruit I don't recognize. The smell alone turns my stomach. It looks like bait. A trap dressed in civility. I sit pressed against the back wall of the tent, knees drawn up under the strange tunic, spine taut against the stone. Every inch of me aches. Every sound from outside that manages to seep through the canvas makes me flinch.

The silence deepens until it has weight, until it presses into my ears and chest like a second heartbeat. My thoughts feel too sharp. I count the rising and falling glyphs along the tent walls, not because they comfort me, but because if I stop, I'll remember what the sea took. What I left behind.

When the tent flap stirs, my shoulders snap tight and my hands clench against the cot.

A sharp gust of salt air pushes through the seam, curling under my skin. My whole body coils. I reach for the necklace beneath the tunic and press it flat against my chest, half-wishing it would stop pulsing. Half-hoping it won't.

Raef enters without ceremony, armored and clean, like the chaos of the island had rolled right off him. His wet-look coat is gone, replaced by something darker, fitted to a frame built on long muscle and harder scars, every line carved with discipline and danger. The kind of body that looks shaped more by battles and hard work than by time. His expression reveals nothing.

"Don't you knock?" I ask, twisting my face into a glare sharper than I feel. It's armor. A cracked, rattling thing I wear so I don't fall apart in front of him.

"It's a tent," he says. "You're awake."

"You left," I snap.

He lets the quiet stretch long enough that my pulse won't settle.

"I had things to tend to."

I almost laugh, but it comes out rough, closer to a cough than humor. Definitely not joy, but rather a sound that doesn't belong in this moment, my body realizing that too late.

"Like hiding the war crimes you committed on that boat?" The words spill out before I can stop them. Too loud in this hush-heavy space. The echo of blood in the water still clings to the back of my tongue.

He doesn't so much as blink. The planes of his stunning face stay rigid, jaw locked, cheekbones cut sharp under the low light. His plush mouth holds in a flat line, neither cruel nor kind, and his eyes don't waver, the blue fixed steady on me.

"You lit the city. Came through the closed portal."

My eyes snap wide. "What?" The bottom drops out of me, locking my chest tight and sending a chill racing down my spine. "That makes it my fault. You're saying I'm the sole reason all those innocent people are dead?"

He steps closer, shadows folding behind him like a trailing cloak. "That hasn't happened in ten thousand years," he says. "You touched the stone and the shore, and it woke. Don't even try and claim to me that those people were innocent."

I shoot to my feet. The blood rushes from my head so fast I have to plant one hand on the wall to steady myself. The glyphs behind me flare softly in response, pale blue shifting to violet under my palm.

"Mattie was," I breathe out. My voice cracks. So does everything I've been holding back.

"Mattie was—" I can't finish. The tears are welling in my eyes against my will. I swallow, hard. My throat aches. My hands shake. I didn't mean to say his name out loud. Not like that. Not to someone who let him drown.

"I didn't even know it was real," I whisper. "I just wanted to find something. Something from my dreams. I knew it wasn't just a story."

Raef's eyes darken, not with anger but with something calmer, stripped of heat. His gaze fixes on me like I've confirmed a suspicion, recognition flickering there, unwelcome but certain.

"It's not a story," he says. "And now it's too late to stay out of it. I am sorry your friend fell. Truly."

His voice holds a gentleness now, and I hate him for that.

I open my mouth to ask him something, anything, because I need an anchor. I need someone to blame. I need someone to tell me I didn't break the world by waking up on the wrong shore. But then the tent flap tears open like a wound.

A gust of sea wind sweeps in with the intruder—cold and sharp, scattering the ends of my damp hair like ash across my cheeks. I twist toward the flap, heart slamming against my ribs. He steps inside like he owns the place. Exceptionally tall, lean in the torso, but wide in the shoulders with muscles layered upon muscle. His armor catches the pale light in greenish sheens like old copper. The layers resemble fish scales and bone, ancient and ceremonial, something worn more for ritual than protection. His hair is a pale gold, nearly white at the ends, and is slicked back like sea foam frozen in motion, and his eyes—silver, sharp as broken shell—glint with polished cruelty.

"Vaeryn," Raef mutters, the name bitten off like it tastes bitter in his mouth.

The new fae ignores him. His gaze pins me head to toe and lingers in ways that feel like a strip search of the soul. "So this is her," he says, low and interested. His voice curls like smoke around something venomous.

Raef stiffens. "She's not yours to inspect."

"Please," Vaeryn replies, stepping forward with the smooth, predatory ease of something that's never heard 'no.' "You took the ship. I call that an invitation."

He steps closer—predator smooth—and circles me like I'm something he's considering devouring whole.

I stand stiff, not shrinking back, even when his fingers ghost an inch from my shoulder like he wants to touch me to see what I would do.

"She looks soft," he says, not to me. "Doesn't smell like a god."

My spine straightens. Rage flares, fast and fragile. I bare my teeth. "Glad I disappoint."

Vaeryn laughs, easy and confident, like he's the only one who knows how this ends. Like he knows the punchline to the joke I have yet to hear. His silver eyes stay fixed on mine even as he angles a fraction, predator posture, like he's testing my edges.

"You're mouthy," he says. "That won't last."

Raef moves then. Not fast, but with a finality that thuds through the ground like a thunderclap. His hand hovers near the curved blade at his hips, the one I now realize hums faintly in my bones.

"Vaeryn. Enough."

They face each other, two storms, but different kinds. Raef is tension coiled in silence. Vaeryn is the wave that already broke and wants to break again.

He smiles like a shark. "Careful, cousin. You can't shield her forever." And then he's gone—out the flap, trailing salt and steel. No goodbye. I'm left the sharp taste of danger lingering like metal on the tongue.

The tent flap still sways. A thread of wind lingers, brushing the back of my neck like fingers that haven't quite finished reaching. I stare after him, lungs aching, only realizing now I'd locked myself rigid the whole time.

Raef holds himself perfectly still, shoulders drawn tight beneath that fitted coat, the kind of tension that looks carved there rather than worn. The faint gold in his eyes fades back to something guarded, all watchfulness and restraint.

"Who was—"

"He would've bled you on the altar to see if your bones glow," Raef says.

His words stop me cold. I suck in a hard breath, staggered. "That was your *cousin*?"

Raef still doesn't look at me. He keeps staring at the place Vaeryn stood, like his shadow hasn't faded yet. Like he expects it to crawl back in.

"You think me cruel," he says. "He is of the Sea Court, who swore an oath when the island closed the portal. No outsider was to ever reach it again. Not a toe on the shore. They've killed more for that vow than your mortal wars ever tallied."

He holds the words back long enough to make me wonder if he'll say them at all. When they come, they're quieter, worn thin. "They'll kill again."

My knees tremble. I sit down, too fast, on the edge of the cot, fingers digging into the strange fabric for grounding. "And the city?" I ask.

He finally faces me, blue eyes burning with knowing. Like he's weighing the answer for what it might cost us both. "You woke it," he says. "That means something."

My stomach twists. The words press behind my ribs. I didn't mean to. I didn't ask for any of this. I want Mattie back. I want air that smells like exhaust and rain, not blood and crushed violets. Instead, I say nothing.

"And now every court in Liorin'ae will want to know why. Will want to know what you are and how they can use you." Raef says nothing more. What more is there to say? Basically, my life is over. Everyone here either wants to kill me or enslave me, and I have absolutely no idea why.

He slips through the flap, disappearing again without a sound—no creak of stiff armor, no parting words. He's gone, like the tension he leaves behind is enough to speak for him.

I sit there, staring at the empty space he left, heart pounding too hard against the weight of everything I don't understand. The strength bleeds out of me and I crumble on the cot, legs folding under me, ribs catching on a sob I can't swallow. My arms wrap around my stomach like that will hold the grief in, but it doesn't. I tug the strange tunic tighter, curling into myself like I can vanish inside it. Like cloth could hide the fact that everyone here either wants to kill me, use me, or dissect me for parts.

Nightmare Queen. What the hell does that even mean?

I press my palm against my chest. The necklace—still warm. Still pulsing, soft as if it's mocking the rhythm my body can't keep.

I lay back slowly. Staring at the shadow-draped ceiling of a tent/cave in a world that shouldn't exist.

For the first time since the ship split in half, I let the real grief come slow and steady.

The tears break loose and run, streaking salt over already burned skin. My jaw aches from holding everything else back.

THE AIR HANGS thick and warm. Spiced with something dry and bitter, like cedar bark cracked over coals. My cell is dim, the light low and blue, shifting with the pulse of the glyphs etched into the walls. It's not enough to see clearly.

I don't know how long I've been lying here—only that I haven't moved since I collapsed onto the cot. The woven surface bites into the bruises on my back. My legs still throb in low, persistent waves. My arms ache from the climb and the swim. My lungs still remember the water. My heart...well, that is another matter.

The silence settles like moss now, gentle and soothing. There's no more footsteps, leaving the sound of the shift of weight on my cot, the rustle of cloth, and then his voice, low and emotionless.

"Give me your feet."

I flinch, pushing shallow breaths. He's crouched beside me now, all shadows and sharp angles in this strange, shifting light, sleeves rolled, armor stripped to a dark tunic that clings to his broad shoulders. His hair is damp, curling at the ends and tickling his waistline, like he's washed away whatever blood or seawater had clung to him. I thought he cleaned up before. I was wrong. This Raef looks...unfinished. Like something he hasn't decided to be yet.

"What?"

"Your feet," he says again, quieter. "The cuts will rot if you don't salve them."

It's a quiet insistence. I wouldn't call it kind exactly, but it's not cruel either. It's almost like he doesn't know how to speak gently, only quietly. That might unsettle me more. I almost laugh—a bitter, breathless sound. "You destroy a ship full of people with me on it, and now you want to play medic?"

That gets a flicker of something across his face, but it isn't guilt, and it sure as hell isn't humor. "*I* didn't destroy it. And I'm not playing anything." He could say more. Could once again say I woke the city. That I started all of this. That I'm the variable. But he doesn't.

I hesitate. Not because I don't trust him, but because my soles feel like they've been flayed open, and if I don't let someone help, I'll never walk again, and it kills me that he's the one offering.

I shift slowly, muscles stiff as rusted gears, and extend one leg, flinching as the movement stretches the broken skin. Without a word, he uncorks a small clay jar and dips two fingers into a greenish salve. The smell hits first—biting and cold, like mint and crushed nettle. Then the sting.

I suck in a breath. "What is it?"

"Cleansing balm. It'll sting—"

"No shit, Sherlock."

He raises a single black eyebrow. Just one, and it's almost smug. More like he's saying, 'You're still alive enough to be annoying.'

"Then it'll numb." His voice is calm, clinical. And it does. Slowly. The fire recedes, leaving only a faint buzz under my skin. But it's his hands that surprise me most. Gentle. Calloused in the right places, precise in pressure, but never harsh. The way you might touch something fragile even if you didn't know how to fix it.

Not what I expected from someone who watched people die without blinking.

Not what I expected from someone who left me to drown.

He works quickly and efficiently but with a strange sort of reverence, like tending a relic, not a girl. The bandages are unnervingly smooth under my fingers, stitched from the same shimmering not-fabric as the tunic I wear. Slicker than silk, tougher than anything I've ever seen.

He doesn't speak again until both feet are wrapped in the strange cloth, cool and faintly waxed to the touch, like pressed petals hardened with preservation. His hands are steady, practiced, and surprisingly not rough. Each motion is precise and controlled. A soldier tending a wound, not a friend, nor a lover. But something caught in the middle, a distance that's confusing to say the least.

When he finishes, I don't thank him. I sit staring at my own hand, the one that let go. The skin is raw from coral and rope burn, every line of it a reminder. Mattie's grip had been solid until it wasn't, until the sea decided it wanted him more than me.

Raef follows my gaze. His expression is still professional, but his voice changes. Less stone and more heart. "It wasn't your fault. No one holds against a Veylun Maw. Its pull would have torn you under too."

The name coils in my gut, ugly and final. A thing I can't fight. A thing I'll never forgive. "Maybe that would've been better," I mutter.

"Never," he says, his tone biting enough to cut through the thought before it can take root. His eyes catch mine then, steady and unflinching. "Not you."

He reaches toward the inner wall of the tent, fingers closing around a long shape wrapped in cloth. A weapon, of course, now carefully placed across his lap.

Longer than a dagger, thinner than any sword I'm used to. Curved slightly, almost like a crescent moon. Black at first glance, but beneath the surface...light stirs. Not shines. It brews and flickers. It gleams with pulse lines trapped beneath glass. Etched lines run the length of the blade—more glyphs, maybe. Or something like them.

He holds it in both hands. Carefully.

He doesn't offer an explanation right away, staring at it like it still speaks to him, like it remembers something he would rather forget.

"When I was young, I found this buried on the island, amongst the trees," he says softly. "It burned when I touched it. Not with heat, but it left a white mark." His gaze stays on the blade, not me. "I was never supposed to go there, no one is. I told you that. But I couldn't stop myself. I felt...called."

His voice shifts, and he's no longer guarded or speaking in that clipped tone I'm used to. It's quieter than I've ever heard it. Rawer. Like he's telling me the truth without knowing why he's doing it.

I watch him, not sure what to say.

He offers it now, across both palms, not handing it to me, but presenting it, like an offering.

"This is Atlantean steel."

I don't move to take it.

"You felt it, didn't you?" he continues, eyes flicking to the necklace hiding under my tunic. "In the city. The way it responded to you. The light."

I nod slowly.

He inhales once. "Atlantean steel doesn't kill like mortal weapons. It wounds, yes, but it also unbinds. Cuts through what keeps us fae tethered to this world. No healing. No resurrection. Not even the most ancient magic can undo it. Life ends."

"Why would it...react to me?"

His gaze meets mine at last. There's a strange softness in it now. Or maybe not softness, but truth.

"Because it's made for you. For what you are."

The words drop between us, edged, daring me to touch them. I'm not sure if I want to pick them up.

I swallow hard. "And what is that, exactly?"

His eerie eyes hold mine for a long moment, unreadable, before he sets the blade down beside me on the cot—its edge gleaming in the low light— and says, "When you're ready." He rises and leaves the tent without another word. The moment lingers long after he's gone. I stare at the blade and wonder if it's a gift...or a warning.

I STARE AT the blade for a long time after he leaves, its black edge catching the low blue light. Sitting next to me on the cot, it doesn't hum like the city had. Doesn't pulse like the necklace with the ring still warm against my skin. It...waits. Quiet. Patient. Like it already knows I will reach for it eventually.

The cot beneath me creaks with every shift of my weight. My back rests against the cool stone wall, knees drawn up, blanket wrapped tight around my shoulders despite the warmth. The basin in the corner still smells faintly of nettle and mint. Somewhere outside, a voice calls out in a language I don't know—low, then gone. The silence returns too fast, too complete.

I lift a hand; one finger—tentative—touches the blade. Cool. Smooth. Not what I expected. The metal doesn't fight me. Doesn't bite. No burning. No death screaming in my ears.

I let out a shaky breath, then lift the thing from the cot with both hands. It's lighter than I expected, almost impossibly so. It feels like it would remember how to move for me. Perfectly balanced. The metal whispers as it moves—too quiet to be actual sound, but I feel it in my bones. Like it speaks to me specifically. Like it already knows the shape of my grief.

I turn it over. The writing shines faintly. I was mistaken. They're not etched. They live inside the blade, lines of silver-gold that pulse like veins beneath translucent skin.

He says it unbinds. That it kills what can't be killed. A light touch burns. But if that were true, why hadn't it hurt me? Unless I am—no. I shake my head. This isn't proof. He could be lying. He's probably lying. He didn't show me the scar he claims it gave him. Didn't give me the real story behind the oath his people swore or what happens to someone who breaks it. Hasn't told me anything that matters.

But still... I run a finger down the length of the blade. Nothing. No mark. No cold. No pain. It's steel that almost feels like it's waiting to be remembered. If it truly ends things, if it's a cold-blooded killer, why does it feel like it fits in my hand? Like it belongs there?

A knot twists in my chest. Mattie would have known what to say. He would've rolled his eyes. Called it my 'emo archaeology heroine era.' Said it looked like something out of a fantasy exhibit. He'd have made me laugh. Dragged me back from the edge.

But Mattie is gone. Now the edge is all that's left. And I'm here, alone, in a tent that isn't a prison but feels like one. Holding a weapon made for a war I don't understand.

I set the blade across my knees and stare down at it. I don't blink. Don't flinch. My hands are shaking again, but the blade doesn't. It gleams in the half-light, steady as a calm breath. Steady as the necklace still humming faintly beneath my shirt.

Maybe I'm not what Raef thinks I am. Or maybe...he's not wrong. I clench my jaw. "You still should've shown me the scar, bastard."

The blade doesn't argue.

12

Signs Your Destiny is About to Ruin Your Nights Sleep

T HIS TIME, MY DREAM DOESN'T feel like a dream or like fantasy. It feels like walking home.

Not in the way you recognize a familiar door or remember the way your mother folded blankets. No. This is deeper. Cellular. My body answers the pull of this place like it's coded into my very makeup. Like my bones knew the shape of this place before my skin ever saw it.

I move through the city as if it were written into me—every turn instinctive, every rising spire an echo of something I once knew in a forgotten life. The streets are paved in pale stone, shot through with veins of silvery mineral that gleam faintly in the low light. Each step is soundless beneath my bare feet, the ground warm and pulsing like the skin of some great sleeping beast.

Alive.

The walls curve like the inside of seashells, their surfaces etched with glyphs and whorled reliefs that glint gently when I pass, catching the light in shifting patterns. Blue and gold light spills from their lines—subtle, like candlelight filtered through honey and sea glass. It's not static. It quickens my steps, answering in waves I feel deep in my ribs, as if the city is aware of me. As if it's listening.

My hand lifts of its own accord. Fingers trail across the stone, brushing symbols I cannot name, and the wall sings.

Not a melody. More like a low thrum, a language made of feeling and light. The sound hums through my skin, resonates in my spine, and fills my chest with a weightless ache that has a familiarity I can't explain. Each pillar carries its own note, each arch a different cadence, and somehow I understand them. I know which stones mark mourning and which ones are for birth. I know where lovers once met. Where vows were broken. I shouldn't—but I do.

Tears sting the backs of my eyes, from some buried part of me that remembers what the rest of me doesn't.

The air carries a strange scent—ozone, like the moment before lightning strikes, layered with salty wind and crushed violets.

Above me, the sky is vast and still alien. Three moons hang suspended in a deep cobalt sky, casting shifting silver shadows across the city's central hall. Their light filters through the high open space like slow-moving water, illuminating rings carved into the floor—concentric circles of stone inlaid with copper and quartz that catch the light and refract it into soft halos.

I pass beneath an arch and find myself in a wide circular hall. The chamber is massive and open to the sky—yet it feels enclosed and protected. Trees with ghost-pale bark rise from within the inner ring, their leaves a translucent green that catches the moonlight and but also glow faintly from within. Between the branches and their roots, white blossoms drift lazily, falling even though there's no breeze.

And there she is.

Her hair is white, not with age, but luminous, like snow under starlight. It drapes down her back in loose, gleaming waves, adorned with threads of silver and blue. Skin pale as pearl and shifting under the glow, like moonlight given form. The robe around her clings and shifts like liquid opal, impossible to pin to a single color. She stands at the far end of the hall, beneath a tree growing from stone. Blossoms drift around her like snow. She doesn't speak, but I hear her voice anyway.

You found the door.

I move toward her. My legs move on their own, pulled by a gravity I can't fight. My hand lifts—drawn to her or the ring glowing bright on my finger.

I grip the front of my shirt in a fist. It's the ring I thought was still around my neck. But there it is, solid and real on the ring finger of my right hand, warm with light. Familiar in a way that makes my chest hurt. My ring.

Her lips curve in the saddest smile I've ever seen. She lifts her hand too, palm out like a mirror. Our fingers meet. Not quite touching, a sliver of space separating them. A spark crackles between us, sharp and alive, biting against my skin like the universe rewired me without asking.

Light swallows everything—and I jolt awake. Breathless. Sweating. My cot creaks beneath me. My skin is clammy, the blanket tangled around my legs like vines. My heart a trapped thing.

The tent is dark and quiet. The ring around my neck glows, steady and unyielding, each pulse echoing against my ribs like it wants to sync with me. I stare down at it, the light washing over my chest as if it's mine. My fingers tremble as I reach up and touch it, feeling metal warmer than my own skin under my fingertips.

Outside the tent, through the thin slit in the fabric, a glow ripples across the moss. Tiny threads of light pulse through it in time with the ring—like the ground itself is inhaling my light.

I close my eyes and press a hand over the ring. "I don't know who you are," I whisper to the woman in the dream. "I don't know what you want from me." But something inside me answers anyway.

You've always known.

Once, when Atlantis still sang above the waves,

there was a court older than crowns and deeper than any trench.

They named it the Court of Souls,

and its queen wore starlight on her brow and seawater on her hands.

Where she walked, wounds closed.

Where she spoke, ghosts listened.

She held the balance between realms like a lantern in a storm.

—Book of the Atma, The First Age

13

CARD TRICKS FOR THE DAMNED AND THE DESPERATE

THE FLAP RUSTLES, AND SUNLIGHT cuts across the tent, real morning light, soft and silver-gold. Dust swirls in it like motes caught in honey. The smell changes too, with less salt and ash. Warmer, like damp moss and crushed grass left in the sun.

Raef ducks inside without fanfare, carrying a wide ceramic bowl balanced in one hand and a slim lacquered box in the other. "You're awake."

"Hard to sleep after a murder cruise and an apocalypse welcome party." *And ghosts are now talking in your sleep*, but I keep this last thought to myself.

"Fair." He sets the bowl down on the small table with a subtle finesse I didn't expect from him. "Eat. Carefully. That purple fruit numbs your tongue if you don't peel it first."

The food smells strange, sweet and sharp at once, like overripe nectarines soaked in something floral and spiced. My stomach growls before I can stop it. I ignore it. I eye the slices with suspicion. "Some of this info would've been good to know before I passed out in your not-a-prison tent."

His mouth moves, the barest twitch, like he's fighting a smile and winning.

He kneels and sets the box down between us, then opens it. Inside are circular cards that shine faintly, their edges beating with opal hues. We're closer than we've been since the cliff. The box sits between us, but his presence takes up more than half the space. Not in size per se, but in gravity.

"I thought you might want something that isn't prophecy or blood. Just a game."

"You people do games?"

"Sometimes. When we're not waging civil war."

I lean forward, curious despite myself. The ground beneath us is cool stone, covered in a fur-soft mat of violet moss. The contrast against the hard tension in my shoulders is defined enough to sting. "What is it?"

"Thirel. It's a card game, yes. But also a kind of teaching tool. For children and diplomats. And sometimes spies."

"Comforting."

"The rules are simple enough. Match a House, Mask, or Fate across three cards in sequence. But the power is in the pattern you create and what that pattern means." He fans the deck into a spiral on the floor between us. Each card glimmers faintly—some gold-touched, some deep red, some seagrass green. "You won't recognize the Houses yet. Or the Masks. But you'll learn. The cards...help."

"They help?"

"They're attuned to intent. Your thoughts, even ones you haven't fully formed yet, affect what they reveal. Most cards have three faces—but you'll only see the one you're ready to see, or need to."

"That sounds rigged."

"Everything worth knowing is." He smiles, a thin curve that looks like it cost him something, but at least it isn't one of his rehearsed ones. It throws me for a second. It's not the kind of smirk he's very good at or the mask he wears when he wants to look untouchable. This one feels unguarded, like he slipped and forgot who he was talking to. And I hate that I notice. Hate that for half a heartbeat, it makes him look almost human. Almost someone I can believe.

"Play with me. I'll teach you the Houses. You'll teach me how someone like you ended up in a place that should've stayed buried."

"You're not going to give up on that are you?"

"Can't."

Raef spreads the deck in a spiral with practiced ease, fingertips brushing the backs in a soft circle. The cards shimmer in rhythm, faint throbs of light tracking across their surfaces like a searching spotlight.

"Pick one," he says, nodding toward the spiral. "Left hand only."

"Why?"

"The right hand is for lies."

"And which hand do you use?"

"I don't play fair."

I snort but extend my left hand. The card I brush lights faintly under my skin, tingling as I slide it free from the others. It's like the sensation you get right before a limb falls asleep. I pretend not to notice. The face reveals itself with a ripple—first blank, then ink swirls into form. A figure emerges, crowned in stars, a chain around her wrist, blood trailing from one hand into a chalice at her feet.

"That's...cheerful."

"The Bound Queen," Raef says, tone neutral. "One of the Fate cards."

I arch a brow at him, card pinched between two fingers. "What's her deal?"

"Creation and destruction. She governs choices made under duress. If she appears first, it means your game will be governed by sacrifice. Or power. Sometimes both."

"You said this was a children's game?"

"Fae children. Far more vicious than your poor mortal sensibilities, obviously." The corner of his plush mouth pulls up, self-satisfied, like he thinks he's clever.

I don't smile back. He didn't scare me, not in the slightest. It's that the first card cuts too close—chains, blood, choices made with no good way out. I know all three intimately now. I shake my head and draw another. This one glares blue green, the image slowly resolving into a spire wrapped in ivy, an anatomically correct heart etched into its stone base.

Something about the shape pulls at me—like I've seen it before, in a book, or the edge of a dream. The stonework nags at me, like a half-finished sketch I left buried in a notebook.

"Sea Court," Raef murmurs. "The Spire of Oaths. That's a House card."

"So what does it mean when I pull it after the bleeding queen?"

"Depends what your third card is. Could mean loyalty under pressure. Or a lie. Or that you're about to betray someone important."

I raise a brow. "This is a therapy session, isn't it?"

"Involves less blood than a war trial. Usually."

I pull the third card. This one flashes gold. A mask. No face beneath it—dark hollows where eyes should be.

Raef goes still.

Something tightens in my spine. I don't know what the card means yet, but I feel the way he looks at it, the way he stops breathing for half a second, and it tells me enough. "And this?"

"The Empty Veil," he says after a moment. "One of the Masks. It means unknown truths. Things hidden even from yourself."

"So, if I understand the game correctly..." I gesture at my lucky spread. "I'm a chained queen from the sea who doesn't know what the hell she's doing."

"Not wrong, necessarily," Raef murmurs, gaze still locked on the mask. "Or you can interpret it as your loyalties are still bound by someone else's choice, and your power—if it is power—has yet to know its shape."

He doesn't look up. The silence congeals; his eyes fixed on the card like he's willing it to say something else.

The cards seem to hum faintly between us, or everything in this cursed place hums. I feel them, like pressure at the edge of a wound. Like they're waiting to be played.

"So, part of this game is drawing the cards, and the other is playing them in a way that outmatches your interpretation of your cards?"

"In the simplest way, yes."

"Fine, your turn."

He reaches out and plucks three cards. Laying them out one by one. The first lights a deep red, with ink bleeding across the surface into the shape of a crowned figure kneeling in chains. Wings bound tight. A broken blade before them.

I frown. "Why does that look familiar?"

It echoes mine too closely. But where mine held blood and power, his bleeds grief.

"The Fallen King," Raef says. "Not a warning, but a mark of what's already been lost."

The second card shimmers silver, then resolves into a tower rising from ice, its spire cracked, leaning slightly. Crows circle it as smoke drifts from the windows.

"House of Ash?" I ask. I know the House cards are the backbone of the deck. Each one ties to a court or bloodline, a way to stake a claim. Raef explained that much. Houses set the field, control alliances, and decide what patterns even count. Ash was one of the ruined ones, though, a House that doesn't grant stability so much as collapse. In play, it can double the value of a chain...or burn it to cinders if you risk too much.

"What's left of it." His voice barely moves. But the weight in it lands heavy. Like the ruin still burns behind his eyes. The third card takes longer—black at first, then flaring white-gold, until the ink settles into a half-circle. A mirror. Its surface is blank.

A muscle jumps in Raef's jaw, tight enough that it looks like he's grinding down a word he won't say.

"What is that one?" I ask, my voice catching low in my throat, barely louder than the cards shifting between us.

"The Mirror Unnamed," he says. "It shows what you can't hide."

"So, what does it say about you?"

"That I know what I am," he says, "but not what I'll become."

The words land cold. Not because they're untrue. Because they sound like a sentence he's already served. Raef gathers his own three and sets them aside, careful. Not hidden—but out of play. Then he nods toward the spiral again. "You win that round. Your turn."

"You lost?" I ask. "How?"

His mouth flicks into the ghost of a smile—mocking, maybe, but it doesn't reach his eyes. "Let's say I'm conceding."

"Conceding," I repeat. "To someone who doesn't know the rules?"

"You're learning."

"And you're hiding." I edge closer across the cards, close enough to crowd his space. "You pulled something you don't want me to see."

His jaw shifts as he grinds his teeth, a tiny tic that cracks the smooth mask he wears.

"That's not how the game works," I say quietly. "You said every card tells a story. Even yours."

Raef keeps his eyes on the cards, hands resting too still in his lap, like stone carved to wait me out.

So, I tap the ground between us. "Show me."

Stillness stretches. Long enough for me to count the rise and fall of my own shoulders.

Raef's fingers ghost toward the discarded cards and pause. Then he withdraws his hand, folding it into a loose fist in his lap.

"No."

"Why?"

His voice, when it comes, is flat. "Because some stories end with everyone dead. Ends the game before it even starts."

I sit back, fixing my gaze on him until my eyes sting. "So do shipwrecks." I regret the words the second they leave my mouth. But I don't take them back. He's not the only one with things he won't say aloud.

His eyes flick up, gold catching the low light. "You're not afraid of me."

I don't answer. Because I'm not sure if it's bravery or being too broken to care. Sometimes you have to make up for a lack of physical strength with wit, intelligence, and a sassy mouth.

"Fine. Your turn then."

RAEF SETS HIS hand down, calm and precise, as if he's simply closing a book mid-sentence.

I tilt my head, suspicious. "That's it? You're done?"

He nods once, calm, as if folding a hand after crushing me for an hour is the most natural thing in the world. No hesitation, no flicker of doubt, the cool confidence of someone who thinks conceding is strategy, not surrender. It grates, because part of me wants to call him out, and part of me wonders if that's the lesson—he never loses; he just decides when he's done playing.

I narrow my eyes. "You're forfeiting?"

"Strategic withdrawal," he says, smooth as glass.

"Oh, come on." I lean forward, cards fanned loosely between my fingers, their strange ink still glistening under the lantern light. "You've been wiping the floor with me for an hour. You've got at least two towers and a worm left in your field. Why fold now?"

He shrugs, lazy on the surface, but there's a tightness in the way he leans—like a predator stepping out of reach. "Because you laid a Rogue Mirror Thorn three turns ago. Which means your next move puts me in check—unless I waste a draw chasing shadows. It was a good play."

I narrow my eyes at him, lashes sticking from the damp. "That's it? No cryptic lesson? No eerie warning or blood prophecy?" My lips quirk. "So, you're saying I beat you?"

"I'm saying," Raef says, sinking back against the tent pole, "if I kept playing, I'd have to show more of my hand than I'm willing to. And I don't play to bleed."

Something cold and bright coils low in my chest. It isn't victory, not really, but close enough to taste. He didn't fold because I beat him. He folded because showing me more would have cost him. That says more than any card could. That makes more sense. What I've been able to suss out is that here, losing isn't a weakness. It's a...refusal. Protection. Every card holds meaning—symbolic or personal, depending on how one plays. Raef clearly prefers strategy to exposure.

I shuffle my own deck, the familiar weight of the cards less foreign now. Or maybe I'm starting to recognize myself. "So, what now?" I ask.

His eyes meet mine—steady, unreadable, twin shards of sapphire flashing molten gold. "Now you build your deck again," he says. "And I teach you how to win without a lucky draw.

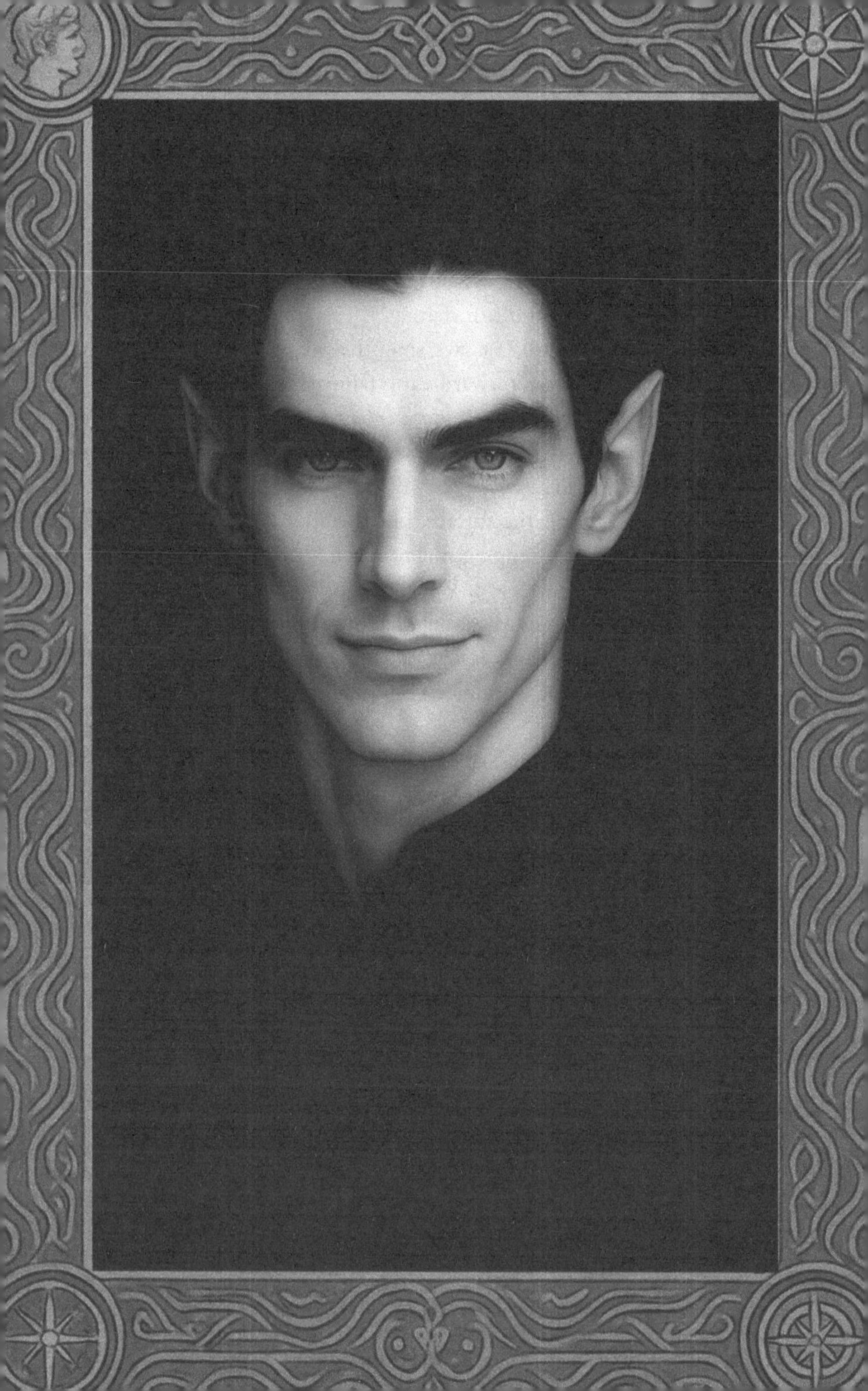

14

ON THE MERITS OF SAYING HELL NO

RAEF LAYS HIS FINAL CARD, and the glow across the table dims. The spiraling light fades like a fuse burning low. Then he looks at me.

"You were on that ship."

"Obviously." I flick my fingers at him like, 'Congratulations, you solved the mystery.' He won't let go of this topic, and it's starting to grate.

"But how?"

I arch a brow. "What do you mean, 'how'?"

"You shouldn't be here," he says, and this time the edge in his voice isn't tempered or hidden. It glares. "No one should be here. That portal was sealed before your kind built your great pyramids."

His words cut, and my shoulders jolt before I can stop them. He catches it, of course, because Raef notices everything, and the edge in his tone slices clean through the fragile calm we'd managed.

I lean away, putting more space between us, the humor draining from my expression. "I didn't exactly RSVP. I went looking for an ancient human civilization. I found...this."

The space between his spoken thoughts drags, my pulse thudding too close to my ears.

Raef stands slowly, legs wide apart, his hands clasped loosely behind his back. "That gate should have remained closed. It opened for you," he says. "Something broke."

"I didn't break it."

"Didn't you?"

The air in the tent pulls tight. The glint in the cards dulls. Ink bleeds from vibrant to gray. The mask's face—one of the trickster cards—melts into blank parchment like it's hiding too. I look down at my hands sitting limp in my lap. Not as much as before. But enough for me to feel it.

"I didn't ask for any of this," I say.

Raef doesn't speak right away. When he does, it's soft again, but heavy in the way a sealed tomb is heavy. "Neither did the last female who lit the city. They buried her in salt and steel."

This new revelation hangs between us, stretching thin. His gaze doesn't shift, and the silence presses harder until my blood turns cold. It feels like standing too close to lightning and knowing it's about to strike. "That's not comforting," I mutter.

"It wasn't meant to be."

He sits again. Slowly, so controlled, a predator resettling its weight, deciding it's not quite time yet. Then taps the edge of the spiral. Light ripples outward. The shimmer returns in pale threads, hesitant at first, then brighter. The blank card reforms, the mask smirking once more in fresh ink.

Raef's face gives nothing away. But his fingers don't leave the edge of the table. Like he's bracing himself for what comes next.

"Your turn again."

I stare at the mask, and for a heartbeat, it feels like it stares back. The smirk carved in ink looks too knowing. Too cruel. My fingers hover above the deck, but I don't draw.

"I still don't know what this game is about," I say finally.

Raef leans back. His silhouette cuts hard lines against the tent wall behind him.

"It's not about knowing. It's about playing."

"Cryptic. Very fae of you."

He doesn't argue. The silence between us tightens like a drawn string.

Then he says, almost casually, "The moss outside your tent glowed last night."

I jerk my head back. "You saw it?"

"So did everyone else. A half-mile radius lit up like starfire. Threads ran from your cot to the roots. Some reached the ward stones."

My mouth goes dry. I press my palm flat to the stone floor to steady myself. "What does that mean?"

"It means they'll know what you are. Or think they do." He stands again, not slowly this time, not like before. His movements are clean and sharp, like something in him snapped back into place. "Which means they'll come. Not just the Sea Court assassins. The Gray Host. The Mountain Watch. Half the northern houses would kill you to keep that island asleep. It represents everything we've been taught to fear."

"But I'm not—"

"No one cares." The words land like a hammer on already fractured stone.

My eyes sting, but I don't look away. He doesn't raise his voice, but the air in the tent drops a degree. His posture stays rigid, every movement trimmed down to precision, and that restraint coils tighter in my gut than shouting ever could.

The hard line of his mouth eases a fraction, his shoulder loosening like he caught himself too late. "I'm not here to coddle you, Rory. I'm here because the rules are already breaking. You lit the dead city. You left a trail through the wards like a bloody footprint. They'll come, and they won't be subtle."

The cold creeps into my gut now, tight and metallic. "And you think I should what—hide in this tent forever?"

"No." His gaze holds inextricably for a moment, steady and unblinking, before the next words drop like a guillotine, "I think you should marry me."

The silence slams back into the tent, thick enough to choke on. My stomach drops, my pulse skitters, and for a second, I'm convinced I misheard him. Marriage? Here? Now? My brain scrambles for logic, for a joke, for anything that makes this make sense, makes it less insane, and comes up empty. I stare at him like I misheard, like maybe the tent warped his voice. "Excuse me?"

Raef stays utterly still, not a flicker in his expression. "A fae marriage bond is old law. Foundation. Even the Sea Court would have to respect it. If you're under my protection, you can move safely. Access my resources to train, to survive."

"Oh," I say. "Survive. How romantic."

"It's not about romance. I don't want a mate." His jaw locks, the lines around his mouth sharpening like he's biting down on the words. "But I don't want to watch you get dragged through a court of blades, either."

I push to my feet, every muscle protesting, the chair leg scraping against the tent floor with a grating drag that makes the moment feel sealed, irreversible. "So let me make sure I understand. You want to chain me to you in magical marriage because *other* people might hurt me?"

"I'm offering you safety."

"No. You're offering me a gilded leash." My voice spikes sharper than I mean, my chest pulling tight as my hands knot into fists. "You're offering me a sad and lonely lifetime chained to the person who signed my best friend's death certificate."

His jaw tightens. A flicker of something dark flashes in his eyes, but he doesn't snap. Doesn't apologize. He doesn't bother to defend himself either. "It's the only option that gives you power and some sense of freedom."

I shake my head. "You don't even know me."

He doesn't argue. Doesn't explain himself. The silence that follows is worse than any denial, settling heavy in my chest until my heart beat drums too loud in my ears. I let the words hang between us, then exhale. "Yeah. Hell no."

Raef looks away, but not like someone backing down. The light cuts across his profile, turning his features stark, indecipherable, but still carved into something I can't mistake for comfort. His gaze stays fixed on the dark outside, as if he's already weighing a future I don't want. "You'll change your mind," he says, almost gently.

I meet his gaze. Let him see the grief. The fury. The sharp, unwilling burn of who I've become. I bare my teeth in something that isn't quite a smile.

"Watch me."

To her side came a king of another court—

the Sanguine, crowned in iron and fire, keeper of endings.

Life took Death by the hand, and the old laws trembled.

They bound their wrists with bloodroot and gold,

not as conqueror and conquered,

but as two stars defying the dark that tried to name them apart.

-Book of the Atma, The First Age

15

WHEN 'HELL NO' MEANS 'HE'LL ASK AGAIN TOMORROW'

I AM DONE PLAYING THIREL.

Not with the cards, but with the unspoken rules. The careful silences. The way he looks at me, like I'm a puzzle box that's only halfway solved. Three days in the tent. Three mornings of Raef gliding in like he owns the place, setting down that deck of shifting cards with the same smug expression. Three games that started in snark and silence and always ended the same way:

"You should accept my protection," he'd say, dealing the last hand like he was flipping fate itself.

And I say, "Absolutely not," and then, win or lose, he'd nod like he has all the time in the world to wear me down. But I'm not wearing down. I'm cracking, piece by piece, and he knows it.

Today, I don't wait for him. "You can't seriously live here," I snap, slamming my cards face down. "What is this place? A war camp? A graveyard? It's like someone carved tents into a canyon and called it civilization."

Raef doesn't look up. "It's temporary."

"So is a sneeze. When do we leave?"

He places a single card on the table—The Mirror-Faced Queen. "When it's safe."

"For whom?" I demand. "Because I don't feel particularly protected, locked up in a tent with guards who flinch when I blink."

His azure eyes flash to mine. Calm. Icy. "You're not protected yet. That requires a bond."

"There it is," I mutter. "The daily proposal."

"I'm nothing if not consistent."

My throat tightens, but I cover it with a scoff. He says it like a joke, but he means it. Every day, a little more certainty. Like he's already decided I'll say yes. Like it's a matter of timing. I stand, pacing. The woven floor mat near the cot prickles under my bare feet, warm from sunlight that can't decide if it wants to shine or hide behind clouds.

"You keep saying it's for my safety, but let's not pretend this is selfless. You want leverage. You want to control the woman who lit the city."

"And you want to survive long enough to see your world again."

That stops me cold. Because he's right. And because I hate that part of me screaming *no* has started whispering *but what if he can help?*

I angle slowly toward him. My eyes catching light shining off the necklace beneath my tunic. I press my fingers against it as if that might slow the thud of my pulse. "If I agree to this ridiculous betrothal...you'll help me get back."

He studies me. Too long. Like he sees more than he should. "There's no guarantee the portal can be opened again."

"You'll try?"

"Yes."

"And this bond? It's not a marriage until we make it a marriage?"

"No," he says. "It's an oath. Breakable only if I betray you...or you betray me."

I don't like the sound of that. "And if I change my mind? If I fall in love with someone else?"

"You won't change your mind, and that won't matter. Most of us aren't averse to multiple partners. We live a long time and get bored."

My jaw tightens, teeth grinding against the urge to laugh in his face. The confidence in his voice is pure arrogance—fatalistic, like he's already decided love isn't part of the deal. Which it isn't. How could I ever love someone that was, at least a part of what took Mattie from me?

I roll my eyes, but my heartbeat skids as he reaches into his coat and draws something out. A band of silver-black metal that shimmers like moonlight on deep water. A pale gem at its center—moonstone, but alive somehow. The air stiffens again, sharp with ozone and something old. Like lightning is about to strike me down for my stupidity alone.

"This is meant for the heir of my court," he says. "The true one. The city responded to you, that should be enough for the old laws to accept your magic."

"I don't have magic," I scoff, "and I don't need a magic ring."

"Too bad," Raef murmurs. "It doesn't need *you* to work." He looks at it longingly between his fingers. "It belonged to my mother."

He raises a single brow in question.

I hesitate. Of course I do. Every instinct in me screams to run, but there's nowhere left to go. No other card to play. My throat tightens as I give the smallest nod. I don't trust him, not in the slightest, but I don't have another move.

He steps closer. When he slips it onto my finger, the ground lurches under me, like I've stepped off solid rock into open air.

A jolt hits—cold first, like stepping barefoot into deep water, then hot, like static crawling up my spine. Not pain. But invasive and too much. The band doesn't sit on my skin—it sinks. Threads of light spider under the surface, thin veins of silver weaving down from the gem like roots into soil.

I choke on a sound and stumble, catching the table's edge.. My knees threaten to fold. The feeling passes too fast to scream, too slow to forget. My hand shakes. The ring is gone—no, not gone. Still there, but different. The metal has thinned, fused to my skin like filigree, the gem pulsing once, faint as a heartbeat.

"What the hell was that?"

Raef's expression doesn't change. His voice is too calm. Like this is all expected. Like he's done this before. "The seal," Raef says, his voice unreadable now. "It won't come off unless one of us breaks the vow."

Seal. Vow. Bond. The words make my stomach twist.

"That's horrifying," I breathe. "It's *in* me."

He doesn't deny it. He can't. It's right there.

"Welcome to the fae," he says. "We don't do anything halfway."

I stare at my hand. It doesn't even feel like mine anymore. It feels claimed. Tagged. Like something wild, caught and marked.

"A warning would have been nice." I stare at my hand, heart thundering.

Raef breaks from me and leaves. As if the moment is over. As if I'm supposed to carry this now. Then he adds, all too casually, halfway through the flap of my tent, "We leave at dawn. Hopefully you'll be the lucky one to survive me."

"Say what?"

But he's gone. Leaving me alone with a ring that hums too softly and a future I didn't choose. I mean, I did, but what the hell did I choose?

16

On Accepting Boots from the Enemy and Other Bad Life Choices

THE FIRST THING I NOTICE is the light.

Not the sun, but the way the world drinks it in. Someone has taken dawn and stretched it into silk, draping it over trees that bend gracefully, too gracefully to be natural, over moss that shimmers like velvet dust. The air even looks softened by it, as if color and shadow forgot how to fight. Even the shadows aren't gray—they're violet, gold at the edges, as if night here doesn't know how to end cleanly.

The air feels different too. Thicker, but not humid. Alive, buzzing under my skin. I can't tell if it's the place or me finally losing it. I mean, I might be dying...

I step out of the gorge barefoot. The stone is smooth beneath my feet, worn by time or magic, or both. Still tender from days healing in the tent, the soles of my feet flinch at the coolness, but I don't slow. I can't. The ring embedded in my finger pulses once, steady and invasive, like it's reminding me who I belong to now. It doesn't hurt, but it sure as hell doesn't feel like comfort either.

Raef walks a few paces ahead, dark against the morning light. His coat catches faint glints of indigo where the fabric curls. He doesn't look back to see if I follow. He never does. But somehow, he always knows.

Two guards flank him, one to either side, their expressions impenetrable. Their armor catches the light like molten metal, but they don't glance my way, don't speak, and don't even bother with the courtesy of a nod. Two sets of eyes sweeping the tree line, hands hovering near hilts, as if I'm cargo instead of company. I wonder if they've been told what I am. What they think I am. If they have, they're a step ahead of me. I don't even know what I am.

I don't ask where we're going. I don't even ask what we're walking through. I try to meditate. Deeply. Slowly. Like if I can master the rhythm of this place, maybe it won't eat me alive.

Behind us, the gorge fades into mist. Raef's hidden camp vanishes like it never existed in the first place. Ahead, the world unfolds into strangeness. Like a dream half-remembered—real only in fragments. Too vivid to be false, but too impossible to be true.

Twisting trees with bark like obsidian glass. Ferns with tiny golden buds that curl in on themselves as we pass. A river—thin as a ribbon—that weaves through the valley, drifting above ground at some points like it changed its mind about gravity. My brain keeps trying to assign logic to it all, like plugging data into a formula that won't compute. But there are no equations for floating water. No science for how the forest hums when I'm near.

I'm not meant to hear them. Their voices are low, meant to blur into birdsong and wind. But I'm tired, and the quiet has a strange sharpness here. The one on Raef's left, Draven I believe, taller, with a jagged scar vanishing into the collar of his armor, tilts his head enough for the words to slip to my ears. "...the waypoint at Vaeloris is dead," he murmurs, voice rough like gravel rubbed between fingers.

"Fast travel risks too much here," the other, Taren, says. He's younger than the scarred one, though the lines at the corners of his mouth make him look older when he frowns. His helm hangs loose at his hip, revealing dark hair cut close on the sides and long on top, already curling in the damp air. His eyes flick toward me once, quick and assessing, the gray-green of storm glass. Then he looks away again, jaw tightening like he wishes he hadn't spoken at all. "Even for her."

Her. Me. My spine prickles.

"That's not an option anyway," Raef says in a hushed but forced tone.

"But...it's the safest option, considering what happened to the others," counters Draven. His scar catches the light when he turns, running from the corner of his jaw into the collar of his armor like a mark carved there on purpose. His build is heavier than Taren's, shoulders squared beneath burnished plates, but there's no looseness to him; every movement is clipped and economical. His eyes, when they cut my way, are the color of tarnished bronze, unreadable but sharp, like he's measuring what I cost them by standing here.

What others? The words dig in like splinters, catching places I don't want touched. My stomach knots, but I can't even panic properly; I don't know enough to. That makes it worse, somehow, like waiting for a blow I can't see. What happened to them? Who were they? People like me? Mortals dragged through by accident? Or fae who didn't make it back? The possibilities stack too fast. My feet stutter, for a few steps, and I stop, long enough to feel the weight of it settle, long enough for the question to sink its claws in.

Fast travel, waypoints. Whatever they're talking about, it isn't metaphor or some clever trick. It's magic, and they speak about it like ordering supplies or checking the weather. I'm the one left scrambling to catch up, like a student who walked into the wrong class and can't admit it. Maybe that's the point. Keep me quiet. Keep me following.

I catch up again, breathing heavily with the effort, which is beyond embarrassing. My voice comes out before I can stop it. "Wait," I say. "Fast travel sounds good. Considering the danger and all."

The guards look at Raef in shock, like I'm not supposed to know I'm in danger. Like the doll they're escorting has suddenly spoken out of turn.

"Can't you just use magic, and poof, we teleport where you want to go?"

Raef doesn't stop walking. "We don't call it that."

I tip my head, narrowing my eyes enough to make my point. "Oh? What do you call it, then?"

"Gatework."

"Great. Cool. Can we do that?"

The muscle in his cheek jumps, a twitch he probably doesn't mean for me to notice. "Not here."

"That's not an answer."

"It's not an option. Gatework is unstable this close to the wild threshold. And even if it weren't, my father controls every working circle between us and his court."

"Your father is the one you're dragging me to, yes?"

The look he gives me over his shoulder is flat. "I wouldn't be in any rush to go before him."

That doesn't bode well. But it confirms what I've suspected. He doesn't trust his own blood. So why would he ever trust me?

I slow, staring at the ring on my hand. A thread of warmth pulses from it down into my wrist. It's not threatening. It's more like subtly telling me to pay attention. Like I've been marked, and it wants me to remember that.

"You're not very good at the reassuring thing."

"I'm not trying to be."

My feet throb. I glance down at the cuts from the island that haven't fully closed, and the soft ground here offers little relief. I stumble over a root, curse under my breath—the pain flares quick and bright. It jerks me out of the dreamlike haze and slams me straight back into my body. I bite down on the sound rising in my throat, but it slips out anyway, a low, ragged growl of frustration that makes me feel smaller than I want to admit. That's what finally gets him to stop.

Without a word, he unbuckles a bag in the leading wagon and pulls something from inside. Boots. Soft and strange in a dark weave that catches the light like everything else—like oil on pavement. They lace up the sides, and the insides are lined with something that looks warmer and softer than any fur I've touched.

I didn't realize how tight my shoulders are until he holds out the boots. There's no pity in his eyes, or mockery; it's a plain and simple offer, like I'm not dead weight dragging behind him. His eyes say this should have happened hours ago. Like I'm still someone worth helping. That thought stings more than the cuts on my feet. Because I should've asked. Should've admitted I needed it. But I kept limping along, too stubborn, too afraid of being the human liability in a fae war zone. And now he's the one handing me mercy, while I'm the idiot who made it harder than it had to be.

I take them, careful not to brush his fingers. "Thanks."

The word scrapes on the way out. Too small for everything I want it to mean.

No answer. He starts walking again. Like it didn't cost him anything. Like my pride isn't frayed around the edges. Like maybe, just maybe, I'm not alone.

I crouch by the trail to pull the boots on. My hands still shake, a barely there twitch that I'm hopefully the only one who can see. Whether it's pain or exhaustion or the slow crash after days of panic, I can't say. The lining is warm. The fit is exact. It's such a small mercy, but my throat goes tight anyway. I'm a burden. Maybe I'm a burden someone here decided was worth carrying. I don't know what that means yet. Not really. But I walk steadier after. But that's the boots...

THE BOOTS KEEP me going until dusk paints the trees in flame-colored streaks. The light drips gold and crimson down their bark, turning every leaf into a burning coin. It doesn't feel like sunset. It feels like the forest is catching fire from the inside, glowing with some hidden meaning. The light isn't dying; it's coming closer to watch. Sifting me apart in layers.

They don't camp so much as pause. Raef and the guards have no tents, no fire, and no food. They don't even sleep, as if sleep is a formality. There's not even the usual creak of armor or shifting weight. Only the quiet of predators who know they're safe in the dark.

I curl up near a half-circle of stone that judders indistinctly under my palm—low and continual, the way a cat might purr if it decided you were tolerable. Heat seeps into my skin, not searing or artificial, but the deep kind that feels like it's coming from marrow instead of surface. The moss beneath it glows with crushed-violet color, soft as velvet and strange as bottled twilight. For a second, I almost believe it's inviting me to rest, promising comfort if I give in. But comfort here always feels conditional.

Raef is the only one who lingers close—ten feet away, maybe less. His coat is off, folded with military precision beside him. He sits cross-legged, silent, spine straight. Like he's been carved out of obsidian and stitched back together with willpower and war. And maybe he has. I don't know anything about him.

A long blade rests across his lap—dark, etched, alive with the same unsettling pulse that clings to this place. He draws the whetstone down its edge in slow, practiced strokes, each one sending a thin spark of blue-white light skittering along the steel. The glow doesn't look like moonlight so much as something stolen from it, fractured and bent to another purpose. The sound of stone on metal rasps through the quiet, crawling along my spine until my skin prickles. Beautiful, yes, but wicked. It's a song that starts sweet and ends with a knife twist.

The guards linger farther off, eyes ever outward. Their posture never changes. Like they don't sleep so much as recharge, or maybe they're waiting for something to kill, stealing someone's soul to use as an eternal battery. One of them has eyes that catch the last light like a cat, like Raef. The other hasn't blinked since we stopped.

I tuck my knees into my chest. The stone behind me thrums faintly against my back. I should ask what it is. Why the moss is warm. Why the air tastes faintly of ozone and something sweet. It smells like rain before it falls. Like thunder about to break. And something sweet beneath it, faint, like honey left too long in the sun. But I'm too tired. The tired that feels like it lives in your marrow, like something has scooped out your center and left a hollow echo.

I shift onto my side, half-dreaming already. Just before sleep claims me, I think I see him look at me. Not like a predator or protector. Not like a soldier calculating odds. Not like a savior, or a captor, or anything else I've labeled him as so far.

Like a man.

And that might be the most dangerous thing of all.

17

KISSES, LIES, AND OTHER SURVIVAL TACTICS

WE LEAVE THE FOREST BEHIND. The air changes first—thinner, lighter, but charged, like the hush before a thunderclap. It smells faintly of rain and rosemary, a scent that doesn't exist outside of a fancy candle shop. Mist curls low across the hills, shrouding everything in pale gold. This place is too perfect to be real. Like a painting trying too hard to convince you it's a live video. Like Barcelona...

The sky above is too vast, streaked in copper and green, and the grass underfoot isn't green at all. It's lavender. Feather-soft and buzzing. Everything fucking hums.

It's music. Low and resonant, it thrums through the soles of my boots and up my spine like it's tuning me to something older than real language. Each step sets off a gentle vibration beneath my boots—like walking across an endless harp string. Draven's jaw works, tight as if the sound is a headache he refuses to acknowledge. Taren's eyes flick once to the ground, then away again, his stride never faltering. Raef doesn't break pace at all, like the whole forest could rearrange itself beneath him and he'd still walk through it untouched. Meanwhile, I'm busy pretending the shifting tones don't make me want to trip over my own feet. I play around with the steps anyway, nudging the notes higher or lower, seeing if I can change the song. Pretending I belong here has become a reflex. Maybe my only coping mechanism.

"This is normal," I murmur, more to myself than anyone else. I don't even know what normal is anymore. Normal has a completely different definition because this isn't my world. My worldview will never fit here, which also means my values and norms are obsolete and foreign. I have no idea what I'm doing, but what I can do is learn and stop wallowing in the novelty of it all.

Raef hears me anyway. "This is the Fractured Wilds. It stopped being normal before your species stood upright."

He says it like it's a simple fact. He's not being judgmental for once, despite his word choice; he's educating me on very, very old history. As if my confusion is nothing personal, it's another wrinkle in a long line of entropy.

We pass a river that runs like glass—clear and slow in a way that shouldn't be possible, but here, it is. Silver-scaled fish drift mid-current, fins trailing behind them like silk ribbons. A few even hover above the surface entirely, suspended by nothing but magic.

Farther on, we pass ruins. White stone, split down the middle, carved with glyphs I can almost read, different from the others I've seen but with some similarities. Almost. They tug at something in me. Like the curve of the letters matches something I once carried. They whisper when we pass. The words slide sideways through my thoughts, not quite translation, not quite sound.

The ring throbs under my skin again. Like it knows something I don't and isn't sure I'm ready to hear it. I don't remember exactly when it started, only that now, whenever something ancient stirs, it answers. A throb against my bones. A weight behind my ribs.

Raef hasn't said a word about it. Neither have I. If I do, it stops being a strange coincidence and becomes something real. Something binding. He watches me like he already knows, but I keep my mouth shut, because the second I admit what the ring is doing, I lose whatever scraps of control I still have.

We stop at a waypost before dusk—three sharp towers made from obsidian and bone, set into the cliffs. The structures rise like broken teeth from the land, half-swallowed in mist, glowing at the seams. The guards aren't like Raef's. Their armor gleams like beetle shells. Their eyes are polished opals—no pupils, no whites. Their faces are impossible to read, but I still somehow feel the weight of their judgment. Everyone here is a judgey prick.

Raef speaks with one at the gate, words too fast and guttural for me to follow. This language sounds like large stones rolling on a frozen lake, like thick nails bouncing across a chalkboard. The gatekeeper shakes his head. Points to me.

"What is it?" I ask, suddenly cold. My arms wrap around my ribs like they could block the answer.

Raef's eyes flick to mine, then away. His jaw shifts, like he's grinding down words he'd rather not say. For a moment, the silence stretches so tight I think he won't answer at all. When he finally does, his voice drops low. Only for us. "They think you're an illusion, or bait."

"Great." My voice comes out thinner than I want, but I force my chin up anyway. "And bait for what?"

"They want proof." He looks at me head on. The dying light sharpens the lines of his face, casting shadows through the loose strands of his dark hair. He looks every inch a prince and a blade disguised as a man.

"Since I said you are my bride, a kiss."

My eyebrows shoot up, and I can feel my mouth fall open before I manage to snap it shut again. "You're kidding. That's ridiculous."

He doesn't smile. "No, I am not, and yes, it is."

"And if we don't?"

"They'll gut me. Then you. And not necessarily in that order."

I swallow, hard. My heart gives a single, traitorous flutter from panic. I might be desperate for a soft touch instead of all this mayhem and death, but I'm not this desperate. Before I can tell him to go to hell, he steps forward. One hand at my waist. The other brushes along my jaw. His fingers are calloused and warm. His eyes locked on mine like I'm the storm he's bracing for. Like I'm a danger. Ha.

"It doesn't have to mean anything," he says, his voice soft, barely more than a whisper.

"Of course not," I lie.

His soft lips meet mine. The world doesn't spin. It tightens. I startle, muscles coil, and I can't tell if it's fight or flight. His mouth is warm and dry. Gentle—infuriatingly so. It's not a conqueror's kiss. It's not passion. It's restrained, thank God. It's perfectly measured like everything else he does. I don't close my eyes. The atmosphere flares around us like someone struck a match in a room full of stars.

The moss beneath our feet blooms. Blue and gold spirals burst outward, curling like ink dropped in water. It's like it recognizes the bond before I do.

Draven and Taren inhale as one. One of those at the gate drops to a knee.

Another hisses through clenched teeth, "Nightmare."

Raef pulls back like nothing happened. His eyes flick to the moss, then back to the gatekeeper. "Let us through."

The gates creak open, unfurling like petals if they were made of raw, ragged metal.

I can still feel the kiss. Burned into my lips. This means nothing. It can't mean anything. But my hand brushes my mouth without thinking. Like my body hasn't gotten the memo. Like it already knows the lie.

18

When the Rulebook Wants You Dead, Don't Read Aloud

THE INN SITS WHERE THE wilds begin to bleed into something colder. The shift is subtle at first. The light grows brittle, almost metallic, as if the sky itself has been scraped thin. Clouds gather pale and bone-colored overhead, stretched tight like parchment. No more lavender grass singing or flying rivers. What's left are frostbitten shrubs and bare branches knocking together in the wind, clicking like teeth. Raef explained that the wilds and places like this were once courts and kingdoms but fell during the great war, left to manage themselves, hence their wild nature.

It's not what I imagined when Raef said 'inn.' No warm fire or bustling hall. The structure hunches low into the earth, grown rather than built—knotted roots shaped into arches, bark peeled into walls. Moss gives off a wan

113

green glow around the doorway, and the windows blink faintly like sleepy eyes. A part of me wonders if they're actually blinking. If this place is alive in some strange fae way, watching us approach.

A fae woman greets Raef without warmth, her horns adorned in silver thread and tarnished bone. I'm given one glance, one sniff, and nothing else. Thankfully. She doesn't speak to me. That one glance already decided everything—what I am and what I'm not. The way her nostrils flare like she smells something broken makes me want to shrink or spit.

Inside, there's no bar, or other guests. There's one room with thick rugs on the floor, shelves of withered herbs, and two low beds against opposite walls. There would be no privacy here. Not even the illusion of it. Not with open space and tension thick enough to choke on.

"Luxury," I mutter.

Like always, he doesn't answer. He drops his pack and sits on the bed closest to the door like a soldier claiming high ground. I guess it makes sense. He's always closest to the exits. Closest to the blades, or the ones that might come anyway.

Dinner comes in the form of thin root stew and bread that looks like bark but tastes like honey and a touch of ash from the ovens. We eat in silence. I chew slower to avoid filling it with words. The bowl warms my hands but not my insides. Nothing about this place feels nourishing. Not the food, not the company, not the hollow quiet that swells between us like a bruise.

"You were quiet today," I finally say, breaking first. The silence had been clawing at me. The stew had long since gone tepid, and I'd already memorized every crack in the floorboards. I wasn't sure what I expected him to say, but the not saying anything is rather unpleasant.

He doesn't look up. "You had questions." It's not a question. His tone is clipped, clinical. Like my questions are a splinter in his left ass cheek.

"You ignored them."

"I didn't like the answers."

I set my spoon down hard. "That's not how this works. You want me to play your fiancée in front of whoever you're trying to impress—or terrify? Fine. But I'm not just your puppet."

"No," he says, voice cool. "You're the one who lit the city. And there are rules to what that makes you."

"Would you drop that already? I get it. I lit the city. Big bad." The words spill out faster than I mean them to, brittle with exhaustion. I don't want to talk about the city. I don't want to remember the way the runes bloomed under my feet like they knew me.

I'm halfway through planning my next jab when Raef finally looks at me. It's not the look I was expecting—no cold dismissal, no easy arrogance. There's something else in his eyes, something I can't pin down. Warning, maybe. Or pity, which is somehow worse. His gaze doesn't waver when he says, "Magic doesn't respond well to lies, Rory. Not bold ones spoken aloud. Intentions are fine, as long as they are not spoken."

My eyes sting, a dryness forcing me to squint at him. "Wait. What does that mean?" My stomach sinks. There's something about the way he says it, like he's quoting scripture. Or repeating a rule that got someone killed.

"It means if someone asks if you love me, you say, 'That's none of your business.' Not 'of course I do.' It means if they ask you when the wedding is, you say, 'we haven't decided.' You don't make up a date. You don't lie to a realm that listens."

A knot catches hard in my throat, forcing me to press my tongue to the roof of my mouth before I can get words out. "Because if I do?"

"Lies bend magic. Enough of them, and it breaks you instead."

The firelight flutters across his face, casting shadows in the hollows of his cheeks. I want to ask what it means to break like that—but I'm not sure I actually want to know the answer. A long silence follows. The stew cools in my bowl.

"That's a hell of a rulebook," I mutter.

Raef stands and walks to the narrow window slit, staring out into the gloom. "You asked earlier why the long road," he says. "This is why. You're not ready."

"Not ready for what?" I stand, heat rising to my chest. "For your father? For your court?"

He doesn't answer me, and it's infuriating. He stands there and watches the fog crawl down the hills like fingers. The wind outside howls low against the bark walls, like it's trying to get in.

I cross the room. "You've barely said anything about him. About where we're going. If I'm in danger, I deserve to know what I'm walking into. Especially since this," I wave the embedded ring in his face, "was supposed to protect me."

Still nothing.

"Raef," I snap. "Talk to me."

He faces me at last, the motion tight and controlled, until his jaw ticks and a flicker runs through his eyes, like a fault line opening where I didn't expect one.

"You think I wanted this?" he says, low and harsh. For a moment I think he means this, us, but then he continues. "You think I asked to be birthed into a kingdom of knives and trickery?"

The words slice the air between us, and my chest locks up tight. Air claws at my throat, but it won't go down. His voice carries a weight I haven't heard before, measured but strained at the edges. It isn't anger, well, not only anger. It isn't even pain. It's something deeper, forged from too many years of surviving a place that demanded more from him than anyone should have to give.

He doesn't stop. "The Shadow Court rewards pain. It breeds monsters because that's the only form ruler who survives. My father is the worst of them. And I—" he catches himself, jaw clenched tight. "I killed my brother to keep my place at his side. That's what you're walking into."

I don't know what to say. There were too many answers, and none of them felt safe. The silence between us isn't hollow anymore; it's heavy like a sponge full of water. Dense with all the things I never thought he'd admit. None of it makes sense, and yet all of it does.

For a moment, Raef looks like he might say more. Might let the silence stretch towards softness.

I sigh. Not in relief, but to steady myself. The air in the inn feels tighter now. The apprehension so strong, the room itself waits to see what I'll think of next. *You and me both, tree, you and me both.*

"I haven't known you very long, but you don't seem like the type to murder anyone in cold blood, not unless your hand was forced, Raef," I say, laying a hand on his shoulder. His body goes still under my touch, not tense, just still, like he's not used to it. Like he doesn't know what to do with softness when it comes.

I don't offer the words to provoke. I offer them because I mean them. Because whatever he's been taught to believe about himself, it doesn't match what I see—not in this moment. Not when the mask slips.

He keeps his back to me, but I can sense him relax a bit. Not all the way. Enough that his lungs release a loud exhale. Enough to prove he heard me. "You were tasked with killing me, and yet here I am. You had the opportunity more than once, and instead I'm to be your bride."

"Moments of weakness, I assure you," he smirks. The humor is brittle, like glass that'll snap if you press too hard. But it's there. A flicker of who he might've been if he hadn't grown up in the shadows.

My mouth pulls into something that almost passes for a smile. "Of course."

He looks away, not shutting me out, but giving me the space I would need to backtrack if I wanted to. I don't.

He seems so lost right now, and I can't let it be, even though I should. Some part of me still wants to draw a line in the dust and hold it. But another part, a quieter part, knows what it's like to carry a story no one asked for.

"No parent should force their child into darkness. It's not your fault and not a punishment. Who you're born to isn't a choice you get to make. Sometimes the people who choose to be in our lives—who we *let* in—are much better."

"You sound as if you speak with experience," he says softly, barely turning his head from the window slit. His voice is low but warmer. Like the edge has been dulled by something.

"I don't know my real parents. The only thing I have of them is this ring on a chain," I tell him, pressing my hand to my chest, where the familiar weight of it rests beneath my tunic, solid, warm, strangely present.

"I was adopted by a lovely couple who couldn't have children of their own. I was one of the lucky ones, and I was happy and loved."

Raef is quiet, saying nothing as he stares outside. The tension that plagues him has left. Like my story knocked something loose, and he doesn't know where it landed.

Outside, the strange wind stirs the leaves with a sound like whispering paper. Somewhere deeper in the woods, something croons low and melodic, nothing human. But for once, it doesn't feel ominous but a natural part of the rhythm of this place. Another voice in the wilderness. This land has a pulse, a voice, and a thousand watching eyes. For once, they all feel distant.

"I didn't know that," he says at last. "About your parents."

"Of course you didn't. I haven't talked much about home," I admit. "There's not a lot to say. They're kind and good. My mom taught kindergarten. My dad collects really ugly mugs. I mean hideous. He calls it a 'conversation piece.'"

Raef looks over, one brow raised. "Hideous mugs?"

"I said what I said."

He lets out a quiet breath—almost a laugh, if Raef is capable of such things. He glances toward the small shelf of curved wooden cups the innkeeper left behind. "I'm afraid we don't have any such treasures in the Shadow Court."

"Pity," I say, settling cross-legged on the woven rug. "I could've brought a legacy of tragic kitchenware."

He exhales through his nose, one corner of his mouth twitching. Like he wants to smile, but hasn't remembered how in years.

He eases down opposite me, studying my face. His expression is still shadowed but softer at the edges now. "Thank you," he says.

"For what?"

"For reminding me there are things in this world that don't begin in blood."

I think about joking that we fit that description did but change my mind. The statement settles heavy and real between us, and then he straightens, shifting the mood with a practiced flick of tone. "Tell me something else."

"Like what?"

"Something not tragic," he says. "Something ridiculous. Something yours."

My eyes snap to his, searching for the joke. "Now?"

"I insist."

I think for a moment, then grin. "Alright. When I was seven, Mattie and I thought we were part dragon. I used to climb up on the roof and try to roar at the neighbor's dog."

Both dark brows climb up his forehead as I tell my story. "You tried to intimidate a dog."

"It was a very judgmental dachshund."

"I don't even know what that is."

"It's small. Suspicious. Basically a low-slung menace."

That gets a sound, an actual laugh that's real and unguarded, low in his throat. It's short, but it was there, and I want to hear it again.

"Your turn," I say.

Raef leans back on his hands, eyes on the crooked wood ceiling. "When I was ten, I was caught sneaking off palace grounds with a shadow beetle stuffed in my pocket. It bit a hole through my coat and released a stench so vile it sent three guards into convulsions."

I give him a slow, flat stare. "You smuggled an actual monster?"

"In my defense, I thought it would make a very loyal pet."

"You have a truly concerning definition of pet."

For once the silence doesn't scrape. It sits there, rough around the edges but holding.

Raef looks at me again. "The road will only get harder from here."

"I figured."

"But tonight—" he pauses. "Tonight, I don't mind pretending."

For the first time since the ship, since Mattie, since the blood and the liorwyn, and the kiss at the gates—neither do I.

19

How to Lose a Guard in Three Easy Stabs

THE SPACE BETWEEN US HAS changed. I can't explain how—not in any way that makes logical sense. Raef is still Raef. Still sharp-edged and armored in silence, still treating the world like a trap waiting to spring. But something shifted after that night at the inn. It doesn't crackle the way it used to. Something about the way he looked at me that morning and every day since was different. Not soft, exactly, but not hostile either. Like he's starting to see me as a person again, not a liability or a political headache.

And worse—I'm starting to notice how often I look at him too. The way his eyes scan for threats before his hand moves to the hilt of his blade. The way his voice dips, softer, when speaking to me, even when the words are curses. The way I'm starting to listen. And all of this is more dangerous than anything else in the world.

We walk in near silence as the landscape shifts around us. The trees thin. The ground hardens. By midmorning, the forest breaks open into a vast plain of red with a new forest in the distance.

It looks like a prairie someone has bled into. Long, reed-like grass sways in slow waves, the color of old wine and rust. My boots make a dry hiss as I step through them, but the stalks don't bend or snap—they resist, like they don't want us here. It pushes back, like it's testing me or being difficult.

"Okay," I say under my breath. "Where the hell are we now?"

"We don't linger on the Blood Plain," Raef says in answer. His attention is somewhere far ahead. The guards fan out again, Taren closer to me, subtle but unmistakable—like they've done this before, like they don't trust open spaces.

I tug at the too-stiff collar of the tunic I'd been given. "So...does the murder grass have a name?"

Raef's gaze skates over me without a word, sweeping the horizon like the question never mattered. "Stay close."

I move closer without arguing. I am definitely scared of what makes someone like him nervous.

The longer we walk, the more I realize how off the silence feels. No birds being the first clue, but no bugs either. There's only the soft crunch of boots and the swish of reeds brushing our sides. Not even wind. The stillness is one that usually comes before bad things happen.

"We're too exposed," Taren mutters. Not to me—to the group. But I catch it.

Raef nods once. "Half a liorin. Stay alert."

I press closer, eyes scanning the horizon. The reeds whisper against my legs with every step. My shoulders knot tighter with every ticking second. I don't like the way the ground feels. Like it's waiting for an excuse to bite.

The reeds sway, and for a split second his shape cuts through the red.

A man—standing perfectly still in the reeds maybe thirty feet away. Too far for detail, but something about him tugs at my brain like a memory caught sideways. He's on the taller side with strong, broad shoulders and brown hair too neat for this place. Eyes I can't see, but somehow still feel.

Familiar.

"Remy...?" I whisper. Not sure if I mean it as a question or a curse. A trick of the light, maybe. Or a ghost from the past. I blink—and he's gone. Nothing but reeds. My heart gives one hard kick. Then another. But I don't say his name again.

I barely have time to process it before everything changes. The air tightens. The reeds are still as the trap snaps shut. A sound cracks across the plain like a whip against the sky. Then another. Shouts. Metal drawn.

Raef's voice bellows, sharp and commanding: "Form up!"

The field slams into motion. A thrum hits my chest like a hammer, and everything in me screams *move*. My limbs are too slow. My thoughts sluggish. My instincts? Gone. There's only panic. Raw, physical panic.

From the tall grass, figures emerge—dozens. Armored, fast, and fae. Weapons gleam with blue and silver edge-light. Their faces are hidden behind carved masks—some like beasts, others like death itself. I can't see their eyes, but I feel their intent like a wall slamming into my chest. They're not here to have a chit-chat.

Raef pulls off, already drawing his blade. "Get her out—" he snaps to Taren, but another masked warrior drives a pike through the fae's shoulder before he can move.

"*RUN!*" Raef roars, his voice cutting through everything else.

I run. Not gracefully. Not with purpose. I bolt, feet tearing through grass that slices open my skin with every step. My boots snap on the reeds. My lungs seize. My thoughts are a blur of noise. This is the ship again. The storm. The screaming. Mattie being pulled away—

The plains blur around me, a riot of reeds slashing at my arms and face. They aren't soft like grass but sharp-edged, slicing thin lines across my cheeks as I push through. The air itself feels charged, pressing against my lungs like it doesn't want me to leave.

The woods are still distant—they're too far away. I look back once, and I shouldn't have.

The field is chaos, with fire sparking, blades flashing, and lightning cracking through the air. Raef stands at the center of it all, his blade carving arcs of silver blue through the air like it's alive. A fae warrior lunges at his back, and Raef wheels without looking—driving his elbow into the figure's throat hard enough to collapse it. Another comes, and another. He cuts through three in seconds, fluid, brutal, and terrifying.

His guards are breaking ranks, trying to shield the opening I made—buying me seconds, heartbeats.

That's the moment they break from the main line. Three warriors, masks shaped like wolves, breaking from the main line. Running—not toward Raef. Toward me.

A chill rips through my spine. They're not chasing me. They're hunting me. Panic catches in my throat. I surge forward, nearly stumbling. The reeds snag at my ankles. My boots aren't made for this. My breathing comes in hot gasps, vision tunneling. I don't look back again.

One of the guards shouts something behind me. There's a scream.

I hit a rise in the field and vault down the other side, tumbling into a shallow ravine where the red reeds grow sparse and jagged stone juts from the ground. My shoulder slams into rock. I keep going. Blood smears my arm. My knee burns.

Still no trees.

They're gaining on me.

I can hear them—footfalls too light for anything human, fast, deadly. The crack of reed stalks, the whisper of blades drawn from sheaths. One of them lets out a low warble, like a horn and a laugh at once.

Mocking.

A shadow flickers ahead, and I duck without thinking. A knife hisses past my ear, embedding in the trunk of a black-barked tree twenty feet ahead.

Almost there. Almost.

I break into the edge of the woods as another blade slashes across my back—not deep, but enough to stagger me. I scream, spin wildly, and throw a handful of dirt in the direction of my pursuer.

They laugh. I can feel the hunger behind their masks. Not for blood. For me. For whatever I am, or whatever my death will reward them with.

I dive into the trees, branches whipping across my face. My necklace flares against my skin, bright and hot, like it's warning me—like it's reacting.

I don't stop. I can't. My body's running on raw panic now, muscle and instinct and that horrible truth thrumming through me. They're not chasing to scare me. They're chasing to catch me, and I don't want to think about what they'll do to me when they do.

Because behind me, I hear one of them call out, "She's the one." The words slam into me harder than any blade. What does that mean? The girl from the ship? The one who lit the city? Something else? I don't want the answer. Not now. I'm not ready for the answer.

"Take her down."

Branches claw at my arms. Roots threaten to catch my boots. I'm bleeding, limping, and too loud, but I keep going, because stopping means I find out exactly why they want me. I don't even know how long I run—I know I have to keep going.

Eventually, the sounds behind me fade to nothing. I don't know why, but I'm not about to question it. The sounds surrounding me, footfalls and shouts, fade to wind through the trees, sharp and fast; it hasn't caught its breath either.

I duck under a low-hanging limb, heart punching against my ribs, and finally stop in a shallow hollow choked with moss. My whole body shakes. My lungs burn. Blood worms down the back of my leg as it drips from where the blade grazed me, and my hands tremble too badly to clean it.

Everything aches. My shoulder, my side, my jaw. There's dirt in my mouth and blood drying on my hands, and I can't even tell which cuts came from blades and which came from the goddamn reeds.

I press my back to a tree and melt into it. The bark is damp and oddly smooth. The moss beneath my boots shifts—blue-green, almost radiant— and I realize I, once again, stepped into something not entirely ordinary.

But nothing moves.

I lean forward, hands on my knees, heaving chest making my back pulse in pain. Safe, I tell myself. Just for a minute. Just breathe.

Leaves rustle above—soft, gentle.

I glance up, and everything in me seizes like I stepped on a live wire.

A face hangs upside down from the branch above me, inches from mine. Rancid breath steaming my skin.

Pale skin stretches too tight over sharp cheekbones. Eyes milk-white, rimmed in red. Hair stringy as wet rope, dripping in strands that almost touch my face. Blood cakes its chin, lips parted in something that is not a smile but shows *all* its teeth.

I open my mouth, but no sound comes.

It tilts its head and whispers, the words leaking out thin and wet, like a sound forced through waterlogged lungs, "You glow."

20

HOW TO GET EATEN ALIVE AND MAKE IT WEIRDLY PERSONAL

THE CREATURE LUNGES.

I scream, but it's already on me, its weight slamming me to the mossy ground. My head cracks against the dirt, vision spinning, a blinding jolt of white behind my eyes. It smells like rot and sap. It's broken. All of it is so unbelievably strange and new.

This is how it happens, whispers a useless corner of my brain. Not on a ship. Not in the sea. Here, beneath a forest sky I don't recognize, with no one left to scream my name.

Panic scrambles up my spine. I'm on the ship again. Mattie's screaming. The water's glowing. I'd screamed for him then, useless and human. I scream again now; only this time, no one comes.

More of *them* come.

I catch flickers of them in the trees—four, maybe five. One crawls like a spider on too few limbs. Another twists midair before landing way too close.

I don't even see them—I feel them. Bodies, too fast, too strong, blurring through the trees like wind turned solid. Cold hands, burning breath, mouths smeared in old blood. Their eyes glow with frenzy like sharks with blood in the water—bloodshot, rimmed with red. Teeth snap at my neck.

Everything is noise. White-hot. My thoughts shatter into reflex. I scream again, twisting, ramming an elbow into something hard. It gives a grunt and staggers back, enough for me to scramble up, but another is already there.

I grab a branch. Swing it wild. It cracks across a cheekbone, splitting skin, but the creature only smiles. Red drips down its face. Its pupils are blown wide, lips slicked with old blood.

"You'll sing when we open you," it whispers. Its breath stinks, like old copper and dry bones. It burns when it hits my face, but the coldness of its skin seeps through my clothes, numbing. The moss under me is damp and strangely warm.

I hurl a rock at its head. Miss. Another tackles me from the side. I land hard on my hip, a shockwave spiraling through all my bones. My hands scramble in the moss and find something sharp. I don't hesitate. I stab it upward. The creature shrieks and jerks back, dark purple ichor pouring from its collarbone. The blood smells like burnt salt.

My hand is slick and shaking, but I push to my knees.

A fourth leaps from the trees. I spin to meet it—and punch with the sharp stone still in my grip. It catches my wrist mid-swing. Cold fingers with too many joints.

"No more hiding," it says, voice like nails on a chalkboard. "No more veil."

I pull away. Kick. Bite. Scream. My heart is fire in my chest. The ring on my finger burns. But the creature pulls me down. I hit the earth again, head ringing, shoulder screaming.

The weight shifts. Teeth tear into my throat. Skin splits too deep and certain. They've found the exact place to unmake me. It's an invasion. Like its mouth is searching for something beneath my skin. Pain lances down my spine.

The others gather, whispering. "She bleeds starlight," the one at my neck whines.

No. No, I don't. That's not real. That's not—

I gasp as the others descend, choking on the weight of them. My fists flail weakly, slipping against slick skin. I feel the blood, warm and spilling. One pins my shoulder with its teeth, another my thigh.

Another mouth latches onto my neck on the other side.

Fire rips through me, searing and raw. The bites aren't clean; they tear. Skin splits, muscle gives, and the heat of their teeth drives in deeper. It isn't a wound like a blade would make, but a pull, a siphon, as if they're unpicking me thread by thread from the inside out.

My scream is animal. Raw. I don't even know if I make it out loud. My world shrinks to white pain and pressure.

I kick wildly, hit something hard, but the mouth only latches deeper. The suction turns greedy, a slow, brutal siphon. My heartbeat stutters, and I feel it. My limbs go dull at the edges. Everything inside me shrieks *no*.

This can't be how it ends. Not here. Not for something I don't understand. Not again.

Fingers scrape at my ribs. Another set holds my jaw. "Soft," one of them hisses. "So soft."

The pain twists—sick and hot and dizzy. I sob, barely able to move now, breath catching in jerks. My legs stop kicking. My vision blurs around the edges, tunneled.

Still they feed.

I think I hear Mattie's voice. A blip in the chaos. A trick of blood loss or madness. Doesn't matter. I hang onto it anyway.

A crack splits the air, close enough to rattle through my ribs. The weight crushing my chest jerks once, shudders, and then it's gone, ripped off me in a blur I can't follow.

A shriek rends the air, high and choking, then abruptly cuts off with a wet, splitting sound. Something heavy thuds beside me.

I blink through sweat and blood. The forest swims—dark shapes, limbs in motion too fast to follow. I roll, but the moss grabs at me. Or maybe that's my body failing.

Boots slam into the ground near my head, scattering dirt and blood. A sword arcs through the air. Another creature drops, neck half detached, body twitching.

A male stands over me. He's real, solid, no tricks of fog or magic. There's blood on his blade, and the brutal certainty of someone who knows how to kill is written across his face. Tall, built like a dancer carved from marble—clothes torn, knuckles split, silver hair tangled and darkened with gore. His grin is crooked and wicked. He's enjoying this.

"Couldn't let you have all the fun," he says to someone I can't see.

A second figure slides in behind him—quieter, careful. A fae man with honey-brown eyes shot through with gold, sun-warmed skin, and dark hair swept to one side, a thin beaded braid skimming in front of his ear. No weapon out, but his hands spark faintly with green-white energy. He kneels at my side. "Stay with me," he says, voice like a prayer. "Don't close your eyes."

My vision trembles. I blink blearily at a face that's calm in a way that feels illegal against all this blood. He doesn't look like someone who should be here, not in this nightmare. He's so steady and composed. His touch at my throat is gentle, but even that makes me cry out. I want to shrink away, but I don't have the strength. My limbs feel like they've been packed with wet sand.

"Bite's deep, jagged," he says. "We need to stop the bleeding."

I tilt my head slightly. He has freckles. A calm face made for trust. He touches the wound again, and I flinch, but he doesn't pull away.

"You'll live," he says. "If we're quick."

Live. That word doesn't feel real anymore.

"Do you smell that?" the silver-haired one asks, wiping his blade on a fallen cloak.

The one beside me goes still. His gaze flicks to my face. He doesn't answer right away.

The silver-haired male lowers himself until his face fills my vision, his knees sinking into the moss beside me. Too close—his shadow cuts across my chest, hot air brushing my cheek, the copper tang of blood still clings to him. I can hear as he inhales slowly through his nose. The sound is small but there, the way an animal tests the air before deciding if you're prey or kin.

I jerk back. I don't care if it's weak; I want space.

"You smell like home," he says, voice suddenly far too quiet. Then his eyes dilate. "And war."

I sit up. My muscles don't obey.

The calm one presses a hand to my shoulder.

"Don't," he says. "You lost too much."

He looks at the blood still slick on his fingers. My blood. Then up at the silver-haired man, whose smile has thinned into something unreadable.

I want to ask who they are. What they are. If they're going to finish what the others started. But I can't. My throat is closed. My mind is spinning. I can't hold on to the questions spiraling down the drain in my head.

I hear them say something—names, maybe, or places. But the words blur. My body pulses with heat. My veins buzz, too fast and too loud. And underneath it all, a hum that doesn't belong to me.

"Hey," the calm one says gently, hand still on my shoulder. "Stay with me."

I want to. I want to tell him I'm trying. I want to say I'm not done, that I can't be done. I try to. But my eyelids sink, too heavy now. The edges of the trees slide out of place, and the last thing that registers is the stranger's blade flashing once.

Not at me. Past me. Defending me.

The darkness claims me.

21

BEDSIDE MANNERS A FIELD GUIDE TO SANGUINE JERKS

THE FIRST THING I NOTICE is warmth. Not a desperate warmth that comes from clawing your way back from almost dying, but steady heat, low and constant. Something soft is tucked around me, and a nearby fire snaps and pops, small bursts that sound like they're keeping time for themselves.

Then, pain. Everywhere. A deep, dragging ache across my chest, side, back, and legs. Like someone took me apart and stitched me back together with barbed wire. My neck takes first prize, pounding in time like it wants to make sure I never ignore it again.

My eyes drag open, heavy and reluctant. It's night again. Shadows press close beyond the flickering firelight, but the camp itself is small and calm. The flames sit hemmed in by a ring of carefully placed stones, and moss-lined bedrolls are tucked beneath a crooked canopy of roots and bone-white trees.

It smells like smoke and crushed herbs. Not the wild rot of the Blood Plain, not the scent of salt or blood. Something cleaner.

I sit up and hiss at the throbbing. Pain tears up my spine, bright and immediate. My hands instinctively curl in the blankets. Not mine. I don't like not knowing where I am.

"Oh good. You're alive." The voice is velvet-wrapped in thorns—amused, low, and too pleased with itself.

I swing my gaze around, finding the voice the best I can.

He lounges against a tree root like it has been made for him, every line saying he could be kind—or wicked—depending on who asks. His hair is true silver, pulled back clean with a couple of free strands brushing his cheekbones. The ears are gently pointed, the face all fine planes and light—arched brows, clear skin, and eyes the shade of blue-violet glass that catch and hold. When he smiles, it's never centered; one corner tilts up as if he's in on a joke you haven't heard yet. He dresses for mischief rather than war: a fitted moss-green tunic edged in quiet knotwork and a burgundy scarf that softens the severity, except for the blood. None of it looks like his own. It's not fresh; it's dark, dried, and crusted where it clings to his sleeves.

His eyes are violet, and the way they pin me down feels less like looking and more like cataloging. Great. Another fae who thinks I'm a specimen.

"You owe me," he says simply, and smiles.

Something in that smile makes my skin crawl.

A laugh almost breaks loose, fragile, and I choke it into words instead. "Do you charge interest?" My voice comes out hoarse and rough, but I'm not letting him have the upper hand. Not after everything.

He stretches, blood powdering down his arms like a decoration. Of course he's not bleeding. Of course he looks relaxed; like dragging someone out of a feeding frenzy is just another Tuesday.

"Seriously," I mutter, easing back against the bedding, "next time just let me die with some dignity then."

"Tris," the other voice chides. The sound slips through the campfire crackle, not tough, someone who doesn't raise it often. He looks like the trouble you smile about later: eyes the color of honey with flecks of gold bright as firelight, set under strong brows that lift when he's amused. His skin holds a warm bronze cast, the sort that says he lives outdoors. Dark hair is cut short along the sides but left longer on top to tumble across his forehead; a single, beaded braid slides down in front of a lightly pointed ear—a quiet tell of what he is. The rest is practical and handsome: a fitted moss-green tunic trimmed in subtle knotwork, a worn leather strap over one shoulder, forearms roped with lean muscle. When he faces into the light, the gold in his eyes flashes; when he smiles, the whole clearing tips toward him. A gentle steadiness in the way he moves, like someone who heals more often than he fights, but his forearms are scarred, and the daggers at his side are well used. He offers me a crooked smile. "You gave us a bit of a scare. Lost a lot of blood. We weren't sure you'd wake up tonight."

I blink at him, sluggish and slow, my brain still playing catch-up. The fire flickers too green, shadows curling instead of moving the way they should. A bedroll cradles me in softness that isn't mine, and the voices, one sharp and one steady, still feel like they're coming from underwater. None of it is familiar. My fingers twitch against the blanket at my sides, half-expecting dirt under my nails, moss clawing at my skin, and teeth at my throat. My body hasn't caught up to the fact that I'm alive. Instead there's this male, calm, grounded, and real, and it takes effort not to lean toward him like a drowning person grabbing for a floating log.

"Who…" I try, then swallow hard. My throat feels like it's been scraped with broken glass. "Who are you?"

"I'm Javi," he says. "That's Tris. We were nearby when we heard the fight. You made quite a bit of noise."

"You're lucky *we* were the ones who found you," Tris adds, stretching like a cat. "Most wouldn't bother. Or, they'd finish what the Frenzied started."

Frenzied. The word clicks in my ears. I don't know what it means, but I remember their eyes, their teeth, and the way one of them whispered at my neck. My hand drifts up, fingertips grazing the rough edge of the bandage at my neck. Heat spikes beneath it, mean, like pressing on a bruise that isn't ready to be touched.

I flinch slightly, hand rising to the sore, sticky place on the other side. "What were those things?"

The silver-haired one, Tris, I think he said, glances over from where he leans against a low branch, keeping his distance. He arches a brow, his smile all teeth, canines slightly longer than normal. "Frenzied," he says simply. "Starved, mindless. Used to be fae. Now they're just hunger."

"That wasn't...normal?" I ask. "They looked like people, sort of—except their eyes, their teeth—"

"They are what's left of people," he says, tone sharp enough to cut. "Sanguine curse. When one of us goes too long without blood, we lose the thread of who we are. The hunger eats everything else."

My eyes lock on him, searching, the words scraping out of my lungs. "One of us? What does that mean?"

Tris pushes away from the tree, movements lazy and liquid, like a jaguar stretching before the pounce. "We're called Sanguine. Fae born with a curse or a gift, depending on who you ask. We don't drink blood because it's fun. Most of the time we live on food like you. We drink it because without it, we shatter."

"You're..." I trail off, my mind scrambling through half-baked folklore. Vampire is the first one that pops up, but it doesn't fit. Doesn't cover the blood and the teeth combined with the way he's still alive in front of me. It's too neat a label for something this disturbing.

He smirks like he can hear the word forming in my brain. "Not undead. Not some coffin-sleeping myth your kind tells around firelight. We were born this way. We bleed, we breathe. And if I don't feed every few days, I become what tried to rip your throat out."

The way he says it makes my stomach twist. He's so matter-of-fact, like he's not trying to scare me; it's how it is. A chill creeps under my skin. I don't think he wants to hurt me. But I believe he knows exactly how to. I've seen that edge before. In Raef. On the battlefield. Now it's staring me in the face again with fangs and a grin.

Javi lets out a soft cough, then steps forward, kneeling to offer me a waterskin. "Don't mind him," he says gently. "He's bad at introductions." He flashes a kind smile that somehow makes my racing pulse slow a bit. "You're safe now. I promise."

"Thanks," I fumble the word out, my voice far rougher than I want it to be. My eyes flick between his calm face and the fire, trying to catch up, maybe if I keep my eyes moving, I won't feel so far behind. "I think I'm a little behind."

"That's all right," Javi says. "You'll catch up."

"Unless you die first," Tris adds helpfully, flashing another smile.

Javi lets out a long sigh through his nose, shoulders dipping as if he's used to cleaning up after Tris's sharp edges. "We're also working on his bedside manner."

THE FIRE CRACKLES low, now a greenish-blue hue and scentless. Not wood, not flame—not any fuel I recognize. It gives off enough warmth to make the air bearable, casting shadows that curl instead of flicker.

Javi hands me a blanket woven from something too soft to be cotton. It shimmers faintly in the firelight. "Here," he says, crouching beside me again. "You're still shaking."

The blanket nearly slips from my grip before I manage to clutch it, my fingers clumsy and stiff. "Thanks," I mutter, tugging it around my shoulders. "Not exactly in the habit of being almost eaten alive. Second time in less than a month."

"That wasn't your first frenzy encounter?"

"My first what?"

He drags a hand over the back of his neck, eyes skimming the fire instead of me. "Right. You're...new."

"Very," I say. My voice is dry, but the blanket does help. Or maybe it's the closeness, the normalcy of someone handing me something warm and speaking in full sentences that don't sound like prophecy or threat.

Across the way, Tris sits with a dagger and a whetstone, his movements smooth and slow as fingers through silk. He hasn't stopped watching me. Not with malice, but curiosity, like I'm a puzzle piece he hasn't quite fit into place.

I keep my hands in my lap, trying to hide the way they still tremble, trying to act like the blanket is enough to ground me. But the memory of those mouths, the feel of teeth in my skin—

My eyes squeeze shut, trying to trap the image before it claws free again. Teeth and cold hands. The way my own voice cracked into something I didn't recognize. My stomach knots, and for a second, I swear I can still feel them at my throat. I shove it down, hard, burying it under the scrape of the blanket in my fists and the steady rasp of Tris's whetstone.

"So," he says, voice too casual. "You glow."

"I don't."

"You did. When they fed on you. Light under the skin."

"I didn't mean to." Even as I say the words, I hear how useless they sound. How many times now have I been told that my intentions don't matter? That I lit the city, woke the wrong things, and tore through a gate I wasn't supposed to touch. That accident, or ignorance, doesn't erase the wreckage left behind. It's like I keep handing out excuses to a world that doesn't care.

He tips his head like it's nothing, like I asked if the sky was blue. "That doesn't usually matter."

The whetstone rasps once more. He's still smiling, but it's smaller and less smug. It's more like someone watching smoke curl in the air, interested, but waiting to see if it's going to choke you.

I pull the blanket tighter around my shoulders and glare at him. "Do you always start conversations by bringing up traumatic moments?"

"I find it cuts through the small talk," he says. His grin hooks sideways, the kind that says he enjoys watching me squirm. "Besides, I'm saying—it was beautiful. In a terrifying, what-are-you sort of way."

"Tris," Javi warns gently.

"What? I'm being complimentary."

I cut my eyes to Javi. "Is he always like this?"

"Unfortunately," he says, smiling. "But I promise he means well. Mostly."

"Mostly," Tris echoes, flashing teeth.

They volley words back and forth like they've done this a thousand times, and it grates. Part of me wants to snap at them and tell them it's not funny and that I'm still bleeding and still shaking, but the other part aches for normalcy. I'm trying to piece myself back together, and they're already slipping into banter like this is another regular evening. It shouldn't help me, but it does. At least a little.

I shift the blankets higher, trying to stop the chill that's creeping into my bones. Not from the cold. The feel of their hands, their teeth. The sound of my own voice breaking. That desperate, raw moment before the world tilted sideways and everything went red.

I should say something. Ask about the Frenzied again, or what the hell is happening to me. But my voice sticks. I'm a chicken and far too scared the answer will only make everything worse.

They both watch me for a beat, then Javi asks softly, "Do you have people waiting for you? On the other side?"

I hesitate. "I don't know. I didn't mean to end up here."

"You mean you didn't travel through a portal from the mortal realm on purpose?"

"I more like...fell through it."

Tris lets out a low whistle. "That's rough."

"Tell me about it."

Javi's eyes soften, careful in a way that tells me he's patched up people before, like he knows how easy it is to break someone by accident. "We'll help you however we can. If you need to get back."

He digs under my skin, stirring the same hollow ache I've been trying to ignore since the ship. I look down at my hands, scraped and dirty, the ring still faintly glowing beneath my skin. "Thanks," I say, "but I think getting home's going to be harder than I thought."

I catch myself glancing between them, two strangers who killed for me, bled for me, and now sit like we've always known each other. Like this is totally normal. Like I'm not still trying to piece together the edges of who I was before this place cracked me open.

Finally, Tris taps the hilt of his dagger against a log. "Well, at least you've got good company now. Me, the sunshine boy—" he jerks his chin at Javi, "—and a body count."

"I *was* promised a fae prince," I say, dryly. "Instead I got the blood-soaked comedy duo."

Javi laughs. "Sorry, he comes as part of the package."

"Lucky me," I mutter, the sarcasm thin, brittle at the edges. My mouth tugs, almost a smile, but I'm too tired to get there. But my next question catches despite the smile. "Do either of you...know Raef?"

Javi glances at Tris before answering. "We've crossed paths. Why?"

His name lodges in my throat like a stone I can't cough up. "He said I'd be safe," I murmur. "That the bond would protect me. But they still came. They knew."

Tris's eyes narrow slightly. "The Frenzied don't care about bonds. Neither do half the courts."

My hands ball tight in the blanket. "Then what's the point of any of it?" The heat in my throat scrapes with every word. "The ring, the oath, the rules that shift every time I start to understand them—"

I'm still half-shouting when Javi's voice cuts in, low but loud enough to slice through my anger without pushing against it. "Raef may have believed it would hold. But the wilds don't follow court law. If you are what they think…"

"I'm not anything," I snap. "I'm not special. I'm not chosen. I didn't mean for any of this to happen."

Tris leans back, eyes narrowing slightly, and lets out a slow, loud breath through his nose. "Doesn't matter what you meant. You're in it now."

I stare at the fire, trying to let the strange blue-green flames anchor me. They twist clean and strange at the edges, with shadows that stretch across the clearing like claws instead of comfort. My chest tightens. Back home, fire meant warmth, laughter, and Mattie's terrible marshmallow technique. Here, it only reminds me I'm in a place where even fire feels foreign, like it's watching me instead of keeping me safe.

"Yeah," I say. "I keep hearing that." It doesn't make it any easier to swallow. Doesn't make it feel any less unfair. The blanket shifts in my lap as I adjust, trying to keep the ache in my side from flaring again. They both go quiet. Patient. They're giving me the space to unravel without pushing. And maybe that's what does it. Not the words or the pity, but the way they simply stay.

I smile in spite of myself. A tired, cracked sort of smile. I can't go back, but maybe I can go forward—even if the path is crooked and full of monsters.

For a moment, I don't feel entirely alone on the crooked path.

22

WHEN THE WIND GOES QUIET, PAY ATTENTION

I WAKE TO BIRDSONG. Blessed birdsong. Normalcy. It doesn't even matter that I don't recognize the birds—sweet and spiraling, like flutes in the wind. The trees overhead are thin-limbed and silver, their leaves the color of wine and rust. The moss beneath me pulses faintly with heat. Someone had tucked another blanket around me during the night.

Javi sits cross-legged nearby, humming softly as he stirs something in a strange little bowl—no fire, but it steams anyway. When he sees me sit up, his whole face lights up like I've given him a present.

"Morning," he says. "Or...close enough."

"Where are we exactly?" My voice comes out raspy and small.

"Just east of the Blood Plains," he says. "A clearing we use when we need to...not die."

"Charming."

141

"We decided you'd earned a full night of not dying too."

I smile, "That's thoughtful," but my brain is already spinning in the space he left empty. Where is Raef? If I nearly died, wouldn't he come looking? Wouldn't he be here, grim and brooding, tossing insults like skipping stones?

What if he can't? The thought catches me off guard. That he might be dead. That he might've fallen on that plain, buried beneath a wave of masked blades. That I might never see him again. I swallow hard, unsure what I'm reacting to more—the flicker of fear in my chest or the fact that it's there at all.

"You're welcome."

Tris is already awake, of course—leaning against a tree with his boots off and his shirt open, silver hair a tangled halo around a face that shouldn't look this smug after a night like ours. He's all long limbs and lean muscle, a body that looks lazy in repose but wired for violence underneath. His forearms are roped with veins and faint scars, and the knife flipping easily between his fingers looks like it belongs right where it is. Firelight catches on his eyes, that deep unearthly blue, and his grin cuts the rest of his face into something reckless. "Don't worry, little star. We kept the monsters away. Unless you count Javi's cooking."

"I heard that," Javi mutters, a blush creeping up his cheeks.

"You were meant to."

The banter rolls off them like it's second nature. Tris throws barbs, Javi swats them away, and the rhythm between them doesn't hitch once. It should feel harmless, maybe even comforting. I think that's their intent. But it's annoying how easily they fall into a rhythm. It's like someone bursting into laughter at a funeral. Like none of this touched them. Like the world isn't burning somewhere behind my ribs. Then it hits me why it's clawing under my skin. They sound like Mattie and me. That easy back-and-forth, the shorthand you don't even have to think about. Only I don't have it anymore. It was torn out of me on a deck slick with blood and salt. Every time they laugh, it feels like someone's prying that wound back open.

Javi hands me a small wooden cup. "Drink this. It'll help. Don't ask what's in it."

I sniff it anyway. "This smells like licorice and armpit."

"Then I got it right."

I stall, sniff it again, then force it down. The taste is worse than the smell, sweet and bitter and earthy all at once, but within seconds, the fog in my head begins to lift. The shivering dulls. My fingers stop twitching with phantom panic.

Javi watches me over the rim of his own cup, eyes steady and kind. I think he's trying not to hover. Trying not to look worried. Which only makes me more aware of how wrecked I must look.

It *did* help—whatever it is. My ribs still ache, and there's a dull throbbing where the Sanguine had bitten me, but I don't feel like I'm going to pass out again.

Across from me, Tris shifts where he lies sprawled on the moss near that tree. His eyes flick to my bandaged leg, then away again. I can't tell if it's worry, revulsion, or hunger. But he doesn't move closer.

We pass the day in this strange peace. Almost safe.

They ask questions—not hard ones. What I like to eat. Whether I've ever ridden a horse. What movies are. (That one took a while.) In return, I ask how long they've been out here. How many people live in their court? Tris's answers are slippery. Javi's are laced with cautious hope.

"You're mortal? Human?" Tris asks at one point, confusion creasing his brow, spinning a stone between his fingers.

"Last I checked."

"Huh." He tilts his head. "You're more interesting than the last one."

I frown. "Last one what?"

"Last mortal I met. She cried a lot and tried to stab me with a comb. That was a very long time ago."

"She sounds like she had good instincts."

Javi snorts. "You're not wrong."

Tris throws his head back and laughs. A loud, reckless sound that rolls out of him like thunder cracking through a clear sky. It's too loud for the quiet woods, too bright even for someone who looks carved from moonlight and shadow. It startles a flock of crystal-winged birds from a nearby tree, and they spiral upward in a flurry of color.

It does something to me, something I'm not ready for. My chest flutters in a way that has nothing to do with fear. I don't trust it, and I don't trust him, but for a fleeting second, I forget what he is. A boy's laugh rings out, wild and full, like the world never broke him. For a second, I forget the claw marks on my back, the bite at my throat, and the blood on my hands. I want to laugh with him. Which is probably the most dangerous part. Then my gaze drifts to the edge of the clearing. And I wonder again where Raef is. Why hasn't he come? I know he was fighting. I know he told me to run. But he should have found me by now.

What if he didn't make it? The thought curls in my chest. I drag my eyes back to Tris, to the way his grin still lingers like this is all some joke. *Last mortal I met*, he'd said. My stomach plummets.

"How old are you?" The question slips out because I apparently have no brain-to-mouth filter anymore. "Because Raef said the gate's been shut for thousands of years. So unless you've been hanging around since the dinosaurs, explain how you met a mortal."

Tris twirls the knife once, lazily. "I'm not that old, little star."

My pulse stumbles. "Then how? Is there another gate?"

"No." His gaze tracks my face, the intensity of his eyes unsettling. "Some humans were already here when the gates closed. They'd been taken. Slaves. Buried so deep most courts pretend they don't exist."

The fire pops. Javi looks down into his cup, shoulders climbing.

"Buried where?" I press, throat suddenly dry.

Tris's grin thins. "In the north. In the mines. Shackled where the sun doesn't reach."

The words sink heavy. My skin prickles. Slaves. Hidden in some court's shadows, close enough for the fae to keep their claws in.

And I hate myself for asking the next part. "Are they still there?"

Tris doesn't answer right away. That silence says enough.

By evening, Javi is teaching me a card game called Wildling—something fast-paced and clever that involves tricking your opponents and capturing sigil sets before the spiral turns. It reminds me of rummy, if the cards sometimes hiss at you and try to bite your fingers off.

"You're not bad," Javi says as I lay down another card.

"I'm motivated by spite."

"Ah. You'll fit in just fine."

Tris lies nearby, watching with lazy amusement. Always keeping his distance. "I give it an hour before she beats you blind."

"I'm letting her win. You know, on account of that she almost died," Javi says.

I arch a brow. "Uh huh."

I'm about to play another card when it happens. The wind shifts. The air squeezes enough to make the hair on my arms stand on end. Even the biting cards twitch like they want to crawl out of reach. The trees go still, and I know for a fact that this quiet means something ugly's about to step out of the dark.

Tris freezes. Knife already in hand.

Javi's smile fades. "Stay behind me," he says softly.

He shifts in front of me, his hand brushing my arm—barely a touch, but I feel it everywhere. Warm and grounding. I flinch, ridiculous and shaky, and I hate how grateful I am for that contact. For him. I shouldn't be. I don't know him. But I want to. I shouldn't want that, either, not here, not like this, not while my body still aches. But his presence doesn't ask anything of me. It just *is*.

He's different from Raef's sharp edges and shadowed silences. Javi is light, solid, and sincere. And when he looks at me, it's not like he's weighing my value or potential. It's like he sees me as a person. A girl afraid and trying not to be.

I shift to follow him, adrenaline still buzzing too hot, and pain tears through my thigh like someone struck a match under the skin. I hiss, stumble, and the ground lurches sideways. My gut knots hard enough I nearly fold. Warmth blooms and drips. I look down. One of the deeper bites in my leg has split open again. Blood seeps through the bandages, soaking the fabric of my borrowed trousers.

Javi pivots immediately, eyes going wide—not in fear, but worry. He reaches for me, catching my elbow as I sway.

"I'm fine," I lie, biting it off too fast. It's a stupid thing to say. I'm clearly not. But I hate the way weakness feels in my mouth.

From ahead of us, Tris makes a sound low in his throat—a growl that ends in a hiss between his teeth. He stalks away into the trees. Toward the noise. His movements aren't frantic, but that doesn't mean anything. I don't think Tris could be frantic if he tried.

Javi doesn't watch him go. He's already lowering me back to the bedroll, his touch gentle and encouraging.

"Where's he going?" I grunt out.

Javi hesitates, the look in his eyes torn, debating if he should tell me the truth. "Your blood...it smells good to him. Enticing. That's why he keeps his distance while you're healing. He's going to go take care of the problem while we stay here."

"Oh." It sinks straight through me, leaving the rest of me empty. I needed to know this, but I don't want to think about it. Smelling appetizing. Knowing I smell like food makes my skin crawl. Makes me want to scrub every inch of myself raw.

"You're not fine," he says under his breath. "But you will be. Just...stay still."

I nod, dizzy from more than blood loss. The clearing tilts again, the spin slow. Javi's voice is the only thing that holds. Maybe the look in his eyes, too.

NIGHT FALLS HARD and still, the sort of stillness that makes your skin itch before your brain catches up. It's like the woods are bracing for something ugly.

Javi hasn't left my side. Tris hasn't returned. The shadows press in thick around us; the strange-colored fire burns low to embers. The cards lay scattered, forgotten. It's not the cold that walks up the back of my neck. A hush crawls down my spine like a thousand sand fleas.

I should've known something was wrong when the wind shifted, carrying with it a metallic tang I've come to dread. That deep means something out there hungers and has me in its sights.

Javi locks up like a trap waiting to spring. "Stay low."

He reaches for his blade and pulls it free with a soft hiss. The edge gleams faintly in the moonlight that filters through the canopy, blue runes flickering to life along the hilt. I don't know what they mean, but they don't look purely decorative.

"Javi—"

"Don't move," he whispers. "Not again."

The first shape launches from the trees like a shade ripped from the earth. Javi meets it mid-air with a grunt and a flash of steel. Another comes behind it. Then two more.

They move flawed—too fast, limbs jerking in ways that defy balance. Their eyes glow a faint red in the dark, and their skin is slick with sweat and something darker that I don't want to think about again. One lets out a wet, gurgling laugh as it charges.

I scramble back, boots sliding in the pine needles, heart lodged somewhere in my throat.

Javi fights like he's done this before—quick, clean, and terrifying. But there are too many. And they're not after him.

They want *me*. One slips past his guard. Fangs bared and charges.

Javi roars—yes, *roars*—and crashes into it mid-air. The impact rattles the ground, followed by a crack that jerks straight to my throat. It's a bad sound. My gut knows that sound. Bone, not wood. I wish I hadn't recognized it so fast.

He gets up slower this time. Blood's already soaking through his shirt. It's spilling from his side like something important gave way.

My vision pulses at the edges. "No," I let the word shiver out.

Another frenzied springs, and Javi throws himself in the way. Claws rake down his back. Then a sharp stone is rammed straight into his side. He staggers. Drops.

"Javi!" I scream his name as he falls, the stone blade buried deep in his side.

A different frenzied leaps over his crumpling body, barreling toward me. I don't think. I move.

Javi's sword lies half-buried in the grass, slick with blood. Faintly glowing. Like it knows what it needs to do. I grab it with shaking fingers, nearly dropping it. It's heavier than it looks, thrumming against my skin, burning cold, alive.

The frenzied snarl, arms outstretched, teeth gleaming.

I swing. The blade connects with a sickening crunch. The creature screams as its head rolls off its shoulder. I don't have time to be shocked. The head drops. So does the body.

No time to think on that.

Another comes from the left. I pivot. My form is trash, but the blade moves anyway. My hands are unsteady, but the sword—the sword moves with me.

I swing again, harder this time. The blow cleaves through another neck.

Nothing about it satisfies. It's chaos and impact and the ugly rush of blood on my hands.

My heart pounds like a war drum, like it wants out. My hands sting. My body should hurt more, but adrenaline's smothering everything.

I hear him. Not a scream or a cry. An agonizing suck of air that rattles like a window about to shatter.

"Javi—"

I drop the sword, falling to my knees in the dirt.

He's so still, blood seeping beneath him, soaking into the earth. Too much. His shirt is drenched and torn where the blade had gone in. His eyes flutter, half-lidded and dazed, and his lips part, but no sound comes out.

I crawl to him, palms scraping the ground. My knees hit the earth hard with each move forward. I barely feel it. "No, no, no, please—" I press my hands to his side. Warmth meets me, wet and slipping between my fingers. "Stay with me. Stay here. Don't leave me."

His fingers twitch. A flicker. Barely anything.

A single breath leaves his lungs, then nothing.

"No—" My throat catches halfway through, the sound snagging on a sob before it's even free. It scrapes out of me raw, like I've been shouting for hours instead of seconds.

My hands press harder against the wound, but it's useless. Too much blood coming too fast. My palms are slick and shaky. His body, so strong minutes ago, now sags like the fight has left him completely.

"Please," I whisper. My chest knots, and the next comes faster, rougher, tearing through me before I can stop it. "Javi, please, you don't get to do this. Not for me. You don't get to—"

Tears spill down my cheeks, hot and relentless. I close my eyes tightly, trying to blink them clear, and lean closer, my forehead nearly touching his. I can still smell him beneath the blood—sun-warmed cedar and spice. Still feel the warmth of his skin. But it's fading.

"Don't leave me," I choke out. "You can't... I'm not ready. I can't do this again. I'm not—"

A phosphorescence appears above him, a blur in my teary vision. It shimmers up from his chest, slow and spiraling—golden.

A sharp ache builds behind my ribs. It's not real. I don't know what it is, but I know what it means. He's leaving.

"No," The word cracks out of me. The light floats higher.

"No, no, no—" I reach for it, my hands shivering and bloody. "Don't go. Don't you dare go." I don't think. Don't weigh the logic or wonder what I'm touching. I grab it, and pain roars through me. White-hot, blinding pain. It tears through my arm and buries in my chest like fire has taken root in my bones. I scream, my back arching, every muscle locking as that golden thread pulses in my hand—alive, fighting, slipping. It's like grabbing a live wire and holding on while it tries to gut me from the inside out.

I hold on tighter. "You don't get to leave me." My voice hisses through clenched teeth. "You don't get to die for me, Javi."

The light writhes. Something surges inside me, uncoiling, answering a command. It pours from me—through my hands, through that thread, burning and electric, threading its way back into his body.

I shove the light back into his chest with both hands. The impact detonates between us, blinding, deafening, a shockwave that tears the air apart. White fire bursts outward, searing through the clearing. The ground shudders under me, trees rattling as if their roots want to rip free. The frenzied on the ground disintegrate to ash. The trees tremble.

I collapse across Javi's chest, sobbing now, throat raw and open, his name falling from my lips like a prayer. I can't stop shaking. My skin feels peeled back. My heart won't stop pounding.

I feel his heart stutter. Then beat.

Once.

Twice.

My chest seizes, air catching like it forgot how to work. The sound that scrapes out of me is jagged, broken, and nothing even close to steady. His chest shifts, once, so slight I almost miss it. The smallest rise, the barest proof he's still here. I lock in place, muscles trembling, afraid if I move, I'll lose that flicker.

My body quakes, wrung out and cracked open. The energy from inside hasn't stopped pouring out. It surges beneath my skin, alive and aimless. My hand rests haphazardly over his wound that's started bleeding again. It glows with a faint green light. A deep, radiant green. The color of spring flowers punching through the snow. Light pulses from my palms in slow waves, sinking into Javi's body. The torn flesh beneath my touch begins to knit. Bit by bit, like time rewinding. Muscle reforms. The blood clots, then clears. The gash seals.

I gasp, blinking hard. Every nerve in my body is screaming.

Then I hear them again, and my heart aches. More are coming. I can't see them yet, but I know they're coming. Their scent hits first—rust and rot and ruin.

I don't have the energy to grab the sword. I try but fall woefully short.

Figures dart between the trees. Eyes like open wounds. Teeth bared.

I work at standing. At fighting. But I can't. Everything in me wants to run, or scream, or drag Javi away. But my legs are lead, and my body's giving out. The strength I had is gone. Burned out. I reach for anything—rage, fear, adrenaline—but nothing answers. My body's empty.

I reach for Javi again, heart clawing its way up my throat. My hand finds his shirt, still damp with blood. Still warm. I cling to that as a scream rings out that isn't mine.

A blur of silver and black crashes into the clearing.

Tris.

He hits like a blade through smoke—clean, fast, and merciless. His boots slam into the chest of the first frenzied one and sends it flying. His blade arcs in one fluid, brutal motion. The next one falls in pieces. Blood already drips down the fine edge, his silver-white hair a storm behind him. He moves like a hurricane. Graceful, lethal. One, two, and three fall in quick succession. When the last frenzied hits the dirt, ash billowing from its ruined chest, Tris drops to his knees beside me.

His hands frame my face, so gentle, thumbs smoothing across my cheeks, swiping at blood, sweat, and tears. I don't know which.

"Rory," he says, breath ragged. "Gods, you're—" His eyes search mine—burning, wild. There's something behind the violet now.

"Apparently," he whispers, voice low and in awe, "not human after all."

I try to answer. Try to hold on. But the fire in me has burned to cinders. The green light starts to fade, and the cold comes fast. The last thing I feel is Javi's chest rising beneath my hand.

The dark rushes in and swallows me whole.

23

How to Survive the Moment You Realize Shes More Dangerous Than You

Tris

I'VE SEEN BLOOD BEFORE. Rivers of it. Waded through it waist-deep on battlefields that reeked for weeks. I've weighed it, cataloged its colors by the way it dries. Drowned in it until even my lungs tasted of old coins. But this isn't blood.

It behaves wrong. It thrums in the air, clinging to my skin—bright where blood should be dark, endless where it should clot. Not mortal, nor fae. Something older. Something that remembers fire and crowns and oceans parting.

This is power.

I stand over the ashes of the frenzied, the stink of their final scream still thick in the air. And she—this mortal woman—lies curled around Javi like a broken promise. Hair dark as wet soil fans across his chest. Her dark eyes closed, lashes black as soot, and her hands still glowing faintly green and gold. She's soft where the world isn't meant to be, curved, scarred, and strong. She's built for warmth and laughter, not war, and yet the ruin around her says otherwise.

My blade drips, still hungry, though the fight is already over.

She glows, they had said. The Frenzied. The dead. "She's the crack in the world."

They aren't wrong. Even her scent tilts the glade, she's intoxicating.

Javi should be dead. I saw the wound. It was deep, precise, and meant to kill. I smelled his soul leaking from his body. That copper-salt pull that means someone's past saving. And she—gods, she reached out and stole him back.

I've only heard of magic like that once. What remains in this realm is a bastard craft. Some of us still have some innate skills, but most have to memorize spells, potions, and runes to do the most basic of things. This, this is the magic of the old stories whispered by seers too scared to say her name aloud. A queen with light in her veins and fire in her voice. The last heart of Atlantis before the sea swallowed her whole.

That queen burned kingdoms to protect her own, and she died for it.

I crouch beside Rory, smoothing a blood-tacked strand from her brow. Her face is soft in sleep—but her magic still simmers under her skin. It coils there, restless, waiting for an excuse to burn.

She looks nothing like a queen. She reads as prey—small, bruised from head to heel, ribs barely lifting. But even prey can tear a god in half if you corner it.

Javi stirs, a ragged sound tearing out of him. His chest catches on something uneven, and the wound at his side seals clean. Relief slams into me so hard my jaw locks. He's still here. Barely stitched together, but here. I swallow the surge and set my shoulders. He shouldn't be alive. Not after a wound like that. He's alive because of her. And if she hadn't—

"Rot me hollow," I whisper, dragging a blood-slicked hand through my hair. She has no idea who she is.

I study the Shadow ring embedded in her finger. And if the wrong people find out before she does—if anyone saw what happened, if word spreads—there won't be a realm left to save.

I need to move her. Hide her. Question her. Protect her. Kill her, if the ledger demands it. If I can do it—

The world would burn again.

And she might be the match.

24

HOW TO HATE A GIFT YOU DIDNT ASK FOR

Rory

I WAKE TO PAIN FIRST. A deep, burning pull in my ribs that makes it hard to breathe. Then the scent of lavender and smoke, with something biting underneath. Sweet at first, but tainted, like fruit left too long in the sun, sugared over rot, with a bite of scorched iron in the back of my throat.

It's not the sky above me, filtering through silver and red trees. It's thatch, uneven and old, draped in cords that hold dozens of tiny, glowing bones. They sway gently, casting pale blue reflections across the walls like fireflies caught in jars. The light shifts when I blink. The bones twitch when I look too long. I can't tell if they're real or carved. And right now, I don't care.

I sit up, but pain laces through my side, white-hot and blinding. My arms give out, and I drop back against the pallet, teeth clenched hard enough to ache.

"Don't be stupid," says a voice, dry and cracked. "You've already torn the stitches twice."

A figure shuffles into view. An old woman—or something close enough to pass. Her hair is a mess of white braids and coarse twine, with bones and beads tangled in the ends. Her skin is tanned and wrinkled like tree bark, her eyes clouded with white... but I get the feeling she can see straight through me. She looks like she belongs in a museum display labeled 'Don't Touch. Still Bites.'

She moves slowly, but there's no uncertainty in it. Like she has nothing to prove and no reason to hurry. That, more than anything, unsettles me. I don't like not knowing what I'm dealing with.

My eyes struggle to focus on her shadowed outline, vision swimming. "Who...are you?"

She grins. Her teeth stark against that tanned skin. "Child, you say that like it matters."

My gaze drags back to the ceiling, the cords and twitching bones swaying like they might drop down on me if I move an inch. My pulse hammers in my ribs, uneven, angry at me for moving. "Is this...your house?" *Who lives under a roof of bones and thinks that's normal?*

"No, it's the Queen's palace." She cackles and flicks a glowing twig into a bowl of burning herbs. "Of course it's mine. I'm the one keeping your ribs and blood inside your body where they belong."

I shift slightly, testing her words. Pain blooms down my side like someone's taken a hammer to my ribs. Okay. Probably not a bluff.

"I don't mean to sound impolite, but what are you?" I ask.

She huffs out a laugh. "No bother. You're meeting all sorts of new people. A healer. A hedge witch. A mistake, depending on who you ask."

"You're a witch?" My tone fractures between disbelief and exhaustion.

Her grin tilts sideways, lips pulling far enough to catch on a crooked tooth capped in tarnished silver. It's not a warm or welcoming grin, but one that says she's already decided where I fit in her world, and I'm not sure it's safe. "You say that like it's an insult."

It kind of is, but I don't bother correcting her. I've dealt with grave robbers, looters, and one guy who thought he was a reincarnated druid, but never someone who felt like the bones in their house might get up and walk.

"Where are we? I mean beyond your house," I ask, breathing shallowly because anything else still hurts.

"A place between places," she says, clearly unhelpful on purpose. "It appears where you need it, when you need it." Her voice creaks like old floorboards, comfortable in how little sense she makes.

"The boy brought you here. The golden one. The silver right behind him."

"Javi—" I push myself up, too fast, too desperate. Pain flares like fire under my ribs, stealing the rest of the words from my lips. My mouth twists around the unfinished question, the end trembling in the air. "Is he—?"

"Alive," the witch says, already turning away. "Mostly."

I slump back, vision swimming. Tears well up without warning, hot and unwelcome. I don't let them fall.

"Thank God."

"No gods helped you, girl."

Some part of me had hoped that was a dream, that something did help. But no. It was me. Whatever that was, it was all me. Her fingers brush over my arm, rough and papery against my skin. My muscles snap tight on instinct, a jolt I can't hide, but she doesn't even pause. My eyes drop, searching for what she touched, for proof. My wounds are covered in new bandages, thin as paper but translucent, glimmering faintly like silk soaked in moonlight. They catch the flicker from the bowl of burning herbs in the corner, throwing faint patterns across my skin. None of it smells familiar.

"I don't understand what happened," I whisper.

"You cracked the veil," the witch says simply, her blind gaze finding me. "Now the world will bleed to find you."

I don't know what to say to that. My chest hurts. My hands ache. My body feels like it's been emptied and filled with something that doesn't belong to me. Something hot and strange and awake. It's still there, sitting under my skin like a second heartbeat. Waiting.

I work at the lump rising in my throat, voice dragging out so embarrassingly small. "And Javi?"

She tips her head again—toward the door, maybe. "Changed."

My lashes drag closed, shutting out the bone-lit ceiling. Darkness presses closer, heavy, like I can hold back the answer if I stop looking. He's not dead, but not exactly fine either. And whatever I did to save him... I didn't know I could. I didn't know I had anything to give.

Something inside me has changed too, and I don't know how to change it back.

"I don't want this," I whine softly, and for once, it feels like the truth is dangerous too. The words scrape out low, almost swallowed by the crackle of the herbed fire. My throat feels raw, but it isn't from a wound; it's from the weight of everything I am saying and everything I'm not. My fingers curl tighter in the blanket draped across my lap, nails digging into the fabric like I can anchor myself there, like I can hold onto some version of me that existed before light poured out of my hands. I never asked for this. I don't even know what *this* is. And still, it sits under my skin like a fuse already burning.

The witch doesn't respond. She moves with quiet efficiency, grinding something in a stone bowl, the scent bitter and harsh—copper, nettles, and a deeper sweetness that reminds me of burnt sugar. My stomach turns. I don't want to be here. I don't want to smell this or breathe this or watch her stir whatever she's making like it's no big deal that I brought someone back from the dead.

She hums quietly. No real tune, but it sticks in my head anyway.

I shift against the pallet and instantly regret it. Fire streaks down my ribs, sharp enough to steal sound from my throat. Every nerve screams that my body is still broken, still fragile, no matter how neatly the witch stitched me back together. At least the pain is real. Something I can trust when nothing else makes sense.

My fingers twitch against the blanket, restless, like they're still searching for something to grip, for stability. I clench them hard, knuckles aching, but the memory slips through anyway, light burning my palms. My body remembers before my mind does what it felt like to hold that light. Javi's blood spilling hot between my fingers, the terror of not knowing if I was dragging him back or shoving him further away.

I didn't want this. Any of it. I didn't want him to die.

"What do you mean...changed?" It sounds steadier than I feel, which is a joke, because steady left me hours ago.

She pours the mixture into a cup carved from bone. It's not human bone, it couldn't possibly be, but at the same time, I don't want to know about a creature large enough to hollow out to produce this cup. "Drink."

"That's not an answer."

"Neither was your question."

I glare at her—but the look slides right off. Her milk-pale eyes still seem to watch me too closely.

Finally, she sighs, crouching low by the pallet.

"The boy you saved is not as he was," she says. "No one is, who experiences death. He carries something now—your thread, your light, your mark. He walks differently. Breathes different."

It lands too easily, too offhand, like she's brushing lint from her sleeve. It's how casually she says it. Like he's a coat I threw over a puddle, and now it's stained for good. Like he's another side effect.

"That's not possible."

"Not for most," she agrees. "But you cracked the veil."

She keeps saying that like it explains everything. It doesn't. The phrase that means everything and nothing. She keeps saying it like I should already know. Like, *of course* you cracked the veil, dear; didn't anyone tell you?

"I don't even know what that *means*."

"It means this world sees you now." She says it like a secret, soft enough that I almost have to lean in. "It means the dead might stir when you speak. That old blood might wake when you cry. And it means those who crave power will chase the scent of it on your skin."

My fingers freeze halfway to the blanket. "Is Javi okay?"

She straightens, slow and creaky as dry wood in winter. "Alive, because of you. Changed, because of you."

That part, I already know. The part I'm scared to ask is the one she answers last.

"Whether he is okay..." Her head tilts. "That depends on what comes next."

I look down at my hands—bandaged in silk, faint green light still ghosting along my palms. I clench them, hard, until the glow vanishes. It takes a second longer than I want it to. Like it doesn't want to go. Like part of it is waiting for me to acknowledge it. Whatever's inside me now…it's real. Even if I didn't ask for it. Even if I hate what it means. Something inside me has most definitely changed. But I know this much, I'm done with anyone getting hurt because of me. Not Javi. Not Tris. Not even Raef.

I might not understand what happened, or how to control it, but I'll damn well figure out how to keep it from killing someone or hurting someone.

A knock rattles the door.

The witch only blinks, slow as stone. "Your prince waits."

The name slips out before I'm sure I believe it. "Raef?"

Her mouth curls into a grin, all teeth. "No, girl. The other one."

The door creaks open, and Javi stands there silhouetted by the sunset, eyes bright as morning. There's something in the way he holds himself now, still and careful, like he's listening to the space around him. But when his gaze lands on me, it softens.

Different. But still him. Still smiling.

25

WHEN GOAT JOKES COUNT AS TRAUMA THERAPY

IT'S LATE AFTERNOON, LIGHT SLANTING low enough to paint everything gold whether it deserves it or not. The air hangs heavy with crushed herbs and woodsmoke, heat pressing close until it feels like the whole hut is steeped in someone else's tea. A fly buzzes near the doorway. Smoke curls slowly, clinging, like it doesn't know where to go. *Ditto, smoke, ditto.*

Javi sits with his back against a sun-warmed stone outside the witch's hut. I'm tucked between his legs, leaning back into his chest. The warm body feels steady behind mine, strong, real, a wall I didn't know I needed. His arms are around me—one resting across my stomach, the other lazily curled around my waist like it's the most natural thing in the world. It should feel strange and foreign, but it doesn't. It feels so natural after what we survived, after what I did.

His heartbeat is steady against my back. I know the rhythm, but something in it feels different, changed. Maybe it's too strong. Or just...off. Or I'm reading into something that isn't there simply because the seed of doubt was planted in my mind. My bandages are dulling everything. But I can't bring myself to ask him about that yet.

We're watching Tris feed a fire. Every move is proficient, like he's done it a thousand times, but there's flourish in it too, because, well, it's Tris. He tosses something into the flames—dried petals, maybe—and the fire flares blue in a spark then settles. His eyes find mine through the smoke, steady but searching, searching for the girl he thought I was and realizing the edges don't match anymore, the puzzle piece doesn't quite fit. He hasn't said anything about what I did. None of them have. But that silence is starting to weigh more than words. Since I did something not even the fae can name.

"You should eat," Tris says, looking away and flicking another piece of whatever into the fire. "You're still pale."

Javi chuckles softly, his warm breath stirring the hair at my temple. "You always say that like it's not true for *you*."

Tris rolls his deep blue eyes, but his mouth twitches.

"Don't start," I mumble. "I've had enough of almost dying."

"Only *almost*," Javi teases. "That's the part that counts."

I huff out something that's almost a laugh. But it's a hard breath through my nose, and I hope it passes for normal. It's easier than flinching. I lean back against him a little more, letting myself rest, for a second. Everything still hurts, but for now, it's quiet, and I'll take it.

I smile despite myself, the effort pulling at something deep inside. Everything around me still feels fragile, like spun glass—but for this one moment, I'm warm and safe and surrounded by people who don't look at me like a weapon, or a tool, but a person.

The fire crackles. It's therapeutic, the calming sounds of nature. Even though the sounds can be different, it still has the same effect as a campfire and woods back home. A place I'm starting to realize I will never see again. It aches, that thought, but not as much as I thought it would, or should. I miss my parents and my life, but I seem to have found something here, too, and that softens the blow.

Tris finally sits, closer than he has before. His legs stretch toward the flames, and his fingers toy absently with a charm at his wrist—bone, braided thread, something old.

"You could have let him die," he says quietly.

It's like he yanked the plug, and everything in me cuts out at once. He's not angry; there's no edge to his voice, or even his body. I think he's stating a fact no one wants to say out loud.

"But you didn't." His eyes meet mine, sapphires catching in the firelight. "You bled to stop death. That's not something I forget."

My throat tightens. I look down at our hands; Javi curls his around mine, warm and sure, confident. I don't think he's stopped to feel what happened yet either.

I'm not sure I want to.

He squeezes gently, like he can hear my thoughts. I hold onto that. Not the warmth of his hand, even though it helps, but because he's here breathing behind me. I haven't let myself think too hard about what I would've done if I hadn't reached him in time. About how close I came.

Tris edges closer to the flames, his shadow stretching long across the ground, dragging my attention back to him. "That form of magic," he says, "hasn't been seen in a very long time."

Those words are intriguing enough to force me to lift my incredibly heavy head, the muscles of my neck and shoulders protesting a great deal.

He keeps staring into the fire like he has the answers and won't give them up. The flames lick higher, blue at the edges, and for a second I wonder if he's seeing them or me in them. "You didn't just heal him. You pulled him back."

Every muscle forgets what it's supposed to do. My body's waiting for the verdict before it dares to move again. Part of me wants to argue, deny it outright, but the rest can't stop replaying the moment—Javi's skin cooling under my hands, the panic in his eyes before they closed. If I hadn't—if I hadn't—

"I didn't know what I was doing," I say. "It happened."

He dips his chin, barely a motion. "That's the part that matters."

\#

JAVI'S VOICE IS warm beside my ear. I want to lean into it and let it mean I'm safe. The rest of me bristles, though, because safe is a lie, and I'm not ready to believe in lies again.

"...and the look on Tris's face when the goat kicked him was better than any punchline I've ever heard."

I laugh, a hearty sound straight from my belly, though it scrapes my throat raw. "You're lying."

"I swear on every last one of Tris's expensive boots."

Across the small hut, Tris snorts without looking up from sharpening his blade. "They were imported from the Iron Market."

"So was the goat," Javi adds.

The laugh that catches in my chest is easier this time. Something about this, about them, makes it easier.

I lean back against his chest, my head tucked beneath his chin. His arm is curled lightly around my waist, familiar now, like it's always been there. His thumb traces small circles ever closer to the underside of my breast, sending little shivers up my spine. A part of me registers it. The rest clings to the comfort. I need steady, and Javi is everything right now.

The witch stirs something in a bowl by the fire, humming to herself. Lavender smoke curls in the air, softening the walls.

A long creak cuts through the hut, enough to pull all of us toward the sound.

Raef fills the doorway, wind still tangled in his hair, dust streaking the shoulder and tails of his coat like he ran through the world to get here. His face is carved into that careful mask he wears so well, with the hard, unreadable lines. His eyes find mine instantly—I'm pale, bruised, battered, but alive—and something cracks beneath the practiced stillness of his face. A muscle ticks in his jaw, the only break in his composure. He lingers on the threshold, held there by something elusive to me.

Javi's hand tenses where it rests. His thumb stills, and I feel it ripple through his chest against my back, the whole of him drawn tight.

Raef's gaze snags on Javi's arm around me, long enough to tighten his hand into a fist.

"You're...alive," he says. The way he says it, you'd think it was the last thing he expected. Which is fair considering. I almost didn't survive and wouldn't have without these two.

"I tried not to die," I rasp.

That tugs the faintest smile from him. It's gone almost as soon as it starts.

He looks at Tris next. "You found her."

Tris nods once. "You were looking in the wrong direction."

He chews on the silence for a moment. "Apparently." He looks tired. Physically, yes, but more like he's dragging baggage he doesn't know how to drop.

I push myself upright, gently slipping out of Javi's hold. My legs tremble under me, but I stand.

Javi doesn't stop me. He watches, though. Just like Raef does. Like they're both waiting to see if I'll fall.

Raef's eyes track the movement, but he doesn't reach for me. He looks at the smudges of dried blood on my clothes, the dull green glow clinging faintly to my skin when I'm not concentrating.

"You came all this way," I say, my voice rough but steady. "Did you think I wouldn't survive?"

His Adam's apple jerks as he forces down something he doesn't say. "I thought if anyone could...it would be you."

That sounds a little like faith.

"But?"

"But it nearly killed me not knowing."

His words send out a shockwave, knocking the air sideways. My body forgets what to do with itself, eyes burning, mind blanking, like I should say something, but nothing makes it past my teeth.

Whatever cracked a second ago vanishes as he leaves, voice clipped, barely lifting his mouth back over his shoulder. "And next time, maybe try not to bleed out in the middle of nowhere."

I'D MANAGED TO steady my legs when Tris appears behind me, eyes bright and unreadable. He places a casual hand on my shoulder before glancing at Raef.

"Well." Tris stretches the word, a smile tugging at his mouth, though his eyes stay sharp and focused. "This reunion is lovely, but you look like you want to snarl at each other."

I open my mouth, but Tris is already nudging me gently toward the blankets.

"Back down, little star," he murmurs, using the nickname with that practiced ease that makes it hard to push back. "Snuggle up with Goldenboy. The prince and I need a...chat."

I give him a look, but Javi is already shifting to make space for me, his hand warm on the curve of my back. Exhaustion drags heavy through my limbs, and I sink beside him, too spent to argue, giving Tris a look. The fire crackles, my chest aches, but I feel some healing, some normalcy.

Tris faces Raef, smile disappearing as his face edges into shadows.

"Walk with me, Shadow Prince," he says softly. "There are things we need to speak of. About her. About what she did."

Raef hesitates—his eyes lingering on me longer than they should—and something shifts in his expression. But then he follows.

The door creaks shut, leaving behind a silence that makes you wonder what you missed.

26

HOW TO KEEP YOUR TEMPER WHILE EXPLAINING SEX TO AN IDIOT

Tris

1 LEAD RAEF INTO THE trees, far enough that the hedge witch's wards stop tingling along my spine and the ears of his guards won't hear. The night air is still damp with the stink of blood and old fire, though dulled now, like a battlefield scrubbed but never cleaned. They apparently didn't take any time to wash.

Raef doesn't speak. He never does unless it matters. Not until I stop again beneath a leaning birch, its branches pale as bone in the starlight. I refuse to face off with him, knowing he'll crack before I do.

When he finally speaks, it's barely above the hush of the trees.

"I saw the city light to life under her feet."

Now, I look over my shoulder.

"She stepped into the boundaries, and everything answered. Walls sang. Glyphs woke. She didn't even realize she was doing it."

"She wouldn't," I mutter. "She thinks she's human. Which she's not with the magic I saw."

Raef takes a single step closer. "What kind?"

I pivot toward him, meeting his stare, folding my arms tightly across my chest, a barrier and a dare all at once. "The kind that belongs to the Atma. Older than any fae or human magic."

"They were soul-binders," I add. "Magic that answers to blood and memory. The kind that hasn't existed in full strength for millennia. Even the distant descendants have but a whisper of what she can do."

He shuts up, finally thinking. About strutting time. Maybe he's finally listening instead of brooding in a corner like he does best.

I say, "I recognized the magic that saved Javi. I've spent a lifetime being taught what that power looked like in a body. What it does to the world when it wakes. They said it was a myth. The blood of Atlantis. The spark that mends flesh, the hands that snatch souls from the fates."

His brow creases, doubt written plain as ink, that princely mask slipping. "You're sure?"

"I know when death has dug in its claws. That boy was *gone*."

I let that hang between us before finally saying, "I watched her hold Javi's soul in her hand like it was fragile glass. I didn't think it was possible." The space after my words turns pointed. "But she did it." I give him my back. Let the silence grind.

Raef, of course, fills it like a knife fills a sheath. "She's dangerous."

"No," I snap, spinning to face him again. "*You're* dangerous. She's still figuring out which way is up."

"She nearly tore the fabric of the Blood Plain apart with a scream."

"She was dying. *Javi* was dying."

His jaw ticks, but he doesn't argue. He knew what she'd done. What it means.

I jab a finger toward his chest. "You were sent to kill her. And instead—what? You stitched a ring to her finger like a lovesick mutt?"

He locks up, spine straight as if I'd driven a pin through it. The soft flicker of guilt crosses his face before he can bury it again.

"I couldn't do it," he says quietly. "I tried."

I blink back the fury that's now boiling inside me. "You *tried*?"

"On the ship. I had my blade out. I had the time, the opportunity. I—" he breaks off, exhaling. "I felt it. Something pulling tight. Like a thread wound between us. A bond. I didn't choose this."

He looks up at me and, for once, doesn't wear the tired mask of princely restraint. "I didn't know what she was in that moment," he says. "But I knew I couldn't put a blade in her. The moment our eyes met...it was already too late."

Pressure builds in my jaw, tight enough to ache. "So you *bound* her instead? Does she know?"

"No. She wouldn't understand. She was unprotected. The courts will tear her apart. This way she's safe."

"You think you're different?" I take a step closer my fists balled tightly in an effort to keep my hands on my own person, but the desire to strangle him is winning. "You think binding her to you is better than bleeding her out in an alley? You still *took* her choice."

"She agreed."

"She compromised. Did you explain to her the rules? What happens if you rut her because of this thread?"

He doesn't answer, and that's answer enough.

I'm nowhere near done putting his ego in its place. "You know what happens if you sleep with her. That's it. The bond seals. Souls fuse, and whatever choice she thought she had, it's gone. She was raised human; she doesn't know how to stop feeling what she feels to keep that at bay."

I feel the burn in my chest, and it's not my anger. Fire she rouses in all of us.

"You're not the only one who feels it," I say, voice dropping. "Whatever's humming in her blood—it calls. To me. To Javi. And you think binding her is going to keep that from breaking you?"

His eyes darken. "You're one to talk. You saw her magic and practically offered your throat."

I let that accusation hang a moment before saying evenly, "I'd rather bleed with her than collar her like an animal."

Raef jerks back a fraction, too small to pass for anything but guilt.

Then—soft, like something he hates admitting—he says, "I don't want her *caged*."

"Then start acting like it."

The silence that follows is tense but cooler now. Like a storm has broken and left the air cleaner in its wake.

He nods once.

I let out a slow breath. "We need to tell her. The truth. About Atlantis. About the ring. About what she did to Javi."

He lets the quiet drag, buying himself a moment. But when he does speak, it's something I haven't heard from him in a long time. Resolve. "Then we tell her together."

I nod. "And we train her. Her magic. The blade. She needs sword skill so she can protect herself, and you can release her from that damn binding."

He dips his chin, controlled, like he's signing a contract, like this is some diplomatic negotiation rather than the life of a woman I know he's starting to care for.

"And we're coming with you. You're going to need as much backup as possible if you're going to drag her into that cesspit you call home."

He bristles, but I'm not wrong, and he knows it.

"It's still better than your home," he counters.

"Taking her there never even crossed my mind. The frenzied grow in number every day, and they salivate and hone in on her blood. Even in your court, she cannot walk alone."

"Fine, let's go break the news."

"In the morning, let her rest."

27

HOW TO HANDLE BEING THE DAUGHTER OF A DISASTER

Rory

I WAKE TO THE SCENT of cedar smoke and that now familiar sweetness—like overripe plums soaked in brandy. It makes my mouth water. For half a second, I think I'm back at the dig in southern Italy. The scent of firewood and fruit wine and too much sun. Then the ache sets in—chest, limbs, skin—and I remember.

I lay there for what feels like forever. My head feels less foggy, but still like I slept too deep for too long. My chest still aches. My arms, my legs, and even my skin feel sore. But I'm not alone.

Muted voices drift through walls. Low, murmuring, too careful to be genuine arguing. Almost like play. Whoever it is, they're trying not to wake me. I open one eye.

The hedge witch's hut is dim and cluttered, thick with dried herbs and knotted bundles of new roots bundled and waiting to dry. The morning sun slants through the thatch in places, catching the silver threads woven into the walls. I blink blearily and feel the warmth of Javi at my side.

He's already awake. Propped on one elbow, tracing something into the dirt beside us with his fingertip. A rune, maybe. Or a doodle for all I know. I don't know enough yet to tell the difference.

"You never sleep?" I ask softly.

He looks over, and his smile is pure sunlight. "I did. You snored."

"I did *not*."

His shoulders tip in that easy way that says he's not arguing. "A little."

It makes me laugh, even as my ribs twinge. I shift, his arm brushing mine, heat rolling off him in a way that feels deeper than skin. Like something lives underneath it all now, woven through the seams of him and into me.

I watch him for a long moment, memory flickering behind my eyes. His blood on my hands. His soul in my grip.

"I thought I lost you," I say quietly.

His smile fades, the brightness slipping from his face. "You didn't."

"No," I agree. "But I don't think I understand what I did."

Javi takes my hand, lacing his fingers through mine like it's easy. Like it's always been this way. "Whatever it was... I think it made me *more*." He tilts his head, studying me. "And I think it's changing you too."

I look down at our hands. I don't feel more. I feel like a girl who didn't hesitate, who acted and didn't think, and now everyone keeps calling it magic. Imagining the green pulse that will still flicker there on and off. "I don't know how to be someone who does this," I say.

"You already are."

"You didn't just heal him, you brought him back from the brink," Tris says. "You also vaporized three of the frenzied."

I startle—half from the suddenness of his voice, half from the realization that I didn't hear them come in.

Tris stands near the doorframe, arms crossed loosely over his muscled chest, one light brow cocked over his keen violet eyes, like he's still trying to solve me, but it doesn't bother him as much that he can't. Raef leans beside him, cloaked in shadow and silence. Back to normal with his unreadable expression. No armor this time, only dark clothes and that ever-present edge that makes it impossible to relax around him.

Javi squeezes my hand once before releasing it. I sit up straighter, aware of both how small I feel and how they're all watching.

"I didn't mean to," I say carefully. "I know I say that a lot, but none of any of this makes a lick of sense to me. They were hurting him. I just...I didn't want him to die for me."

"Just a side effect of the strength of your magic, I would presume," Tris says. "I don't think purpose or intent had anything to do with it. It appears, little star, that unlike most here in the outer realms, you still possess innate magic that's quite powerful. The three of us here are some of the handful of fae that still possess innate magic and ours doesn't even come close to what you possess combined."

"Is that supposed to scare me?" I snap before I can help myself. "Because I've been scared this whole time. You're just late to the party."

He chuckles low, eyes glinting like he's caught me out. "Not scared, little star. Impressed."

Raef moves closer, the space between us narrowing with his stare locked tight. "You kept a soul from leaving a dying male and completely healed his body in seconds. Then, you burned the frenzied to ash with nothing but will. That's not accidental power. It proves your heritage once and for all."

The bitter taste in my mouth turns thick, hard to push back down where it belongs. "What are you saying?"

"I'm saying," he says, voice cool but no longer cruel, "that you're not what I thought you were. You're worse."

The words are harsh, and it's not fear they press on me; it's anger. I didn't ask for this. I didn't offer. The burn flares hot under my skin, but I look away, shoving the sting down where they can't reach it.

But then, softer than I've ever heard from him, he adds, "And I think I'm starting to like that."

That earns him a sideways look from Tris, who mutters, "Gods help us all."

I push for a better angle, pulling the blankets tighter around me. My skin still aches at the bites. My veins feel...stretched, like something inside me is still trying to remember its shape and fit the rest of me around it. The sensation makes me want to crawl out of my own body, but I hold still, pretending the cocoon of fabric is enough to keep me together. If I think too hard about it, I'll start believing I'm already coming apart.

"I want answers," I say, my jaw aching with how hard I force the words through it. "Not vague warnings. Not cryptic bullshit. Tell me what the hell is happening to me."

Raef looks at Tris, who nods once. Javi stays close, his hand brushing mine, like he can already sense how hard the next words will be for me to swallow, whole or in pieces.

"You were never simply a girl who opened a closed gate," Raef says finally. "You're a ripple from a story the courts have tried to erase."

I freeze, lungs tight, air sticking in my throat as the world narrows to his words.

"Your magic—it's old," Tris continues. "Too old for someone so young, and yet here you are. It doesn't align with any court we know ourselves. You vaporized an enemy and healed a soul in the same breath. Life and death. Creation and destruction."

The words scrape at something in me, but I can't latch onto them. It sounds like poetry. It feels like a threat. I look between them, grabbing for Javi's hand, for anything to make the room stop spinning. "So...what? I'm some weapon?"

A faint shake, like denial tastes bitter on his tongue. "You're the daughter of a tragedy. One that was only whispered about, and most thought a myth."

My mouth opens, then shuts again, the silence winning outright before I can scrape together a comeback. My mouth goes dry, my tongue heavy; I've got nothing. Part of me wants to argue, call. It's another fae story meant to box me in—but another part can't, because some thread deep inside me twists in recognition of what he said.

He steps forward, and whatever he's thinking, it's locked down behind that careful mask. Like he's afraid and wants to choose his next words very carefully.

"There was a queen, a high queen," he says. "White-haired. Powerful. A healer without equal. She ruled in peace over a now extinct court, the highest court—the Court of Souls, though that name means little to most fae now. This was the court of the Atma, seated at Atlantis, a court of deep magic, magic that's been lost to us for millennia. Soul magic."

Something cold coils at the base of my spine. Soul magic. My hands still remember the weight of Javi's almost-death. My chest still echoes with the moment I pulled him back.

"This queen fell in love. She had thought she had found all her mates, her council, but never undying love. Something so distant for so many. It was a forbidden love, but the fates don't care about our laws and rules."

Tris takes over, his voice lighter but still reverent. "The Sanguine King. Fitting, isn't it? Death against her life, blood against her water. Everyone expected war. Instead they got a secret love affair."

"They kept it secret," Raef says. "And the myths say she bore a child, but no one ever knew or saw or spoke about it."

"This queen was hunted down," Javi says softly, resting his cheek on my head, "by the other courts. She had betrayed them—chose love over allegiance. Chose mortals over fae."

"What?" The sound leaves me low, more like surrender than relief.

"Worse," Raef says. "She closed the gate. The one between your realm and ours."

Their words punch the air from my lungs. "She—what? Why?"

"Atlantis was once the meeting ground between the fae and the mortals. Councils met there for trade and such, the usual pomp," Tris explains. "They started dragging mortals through—servants, toys, fuel for whatever scraps of power they could wring out of them. She saw what they were doing, both of them did, and she shut it down. Started a war. Locked the path. It's been sealed ever since."

"Until me," I whisper, the words sour on my tongue.

His head tips in the smallest concession, nothing more. "And now the world will bleed to find you."

"If she was punished, killed for this, what about the King?" I ask.

"Where do you think the Sanguine curse came from?" Tris asks, smirking, but it wasn't a pleasant one.

I tip my chin, a small surrender. "And you think I'm some very distant relative of this love child who somehow has her powers after thousands of years of genetic mingling?"

Tris crouches in front of me, less predator now. "You're their daughter. A myth. Healer and reaper. The spark that burned Atlantis down."

I laugh, well, I try and fail.

"I'm not—I'm no one. I'm a mediocre archaeologist. I grew up over the last thirty years. I had a childhood, a recent one. I'm not ten thousand years old."

Raef answers with a look of pity, maybe. "We haven't figured out all the answers, all the mechanics of it yet. Much of your story is shrouded in myth."

Javi reaches for my hand again. "You're not no one," he says gently. "You're the reason I'm breathing."

Raef's voice drops low. "And you're the reason the courts will go to war again."

I whip my face away from him, removing my burning eyes from his keen observation. Not from the fire behind them or the heat in my cheeks—but from something deeper. A pressure rising inside me that has nowhere to go. I'm not crying, not yet. But if I let myself blink too long, I might. They talk like I've already been chosen. Like I'm a prophecy walking. But I'm still the girl who catalogues broken pottery and gets nervous in customs lines.

They think I'm someone else. Someone made of starlight and stories. Someone powerful. But I still feel like the girl who tripped through a broken hallway and woke up in a world that shouldn't exist. The daughter of myth. A queen. A king. Death and life in one body.

No. That's not me. That can't be me. "Then maybe I shouldn't have come here at all."

"No," Raef says. The curve of his mouth is stiff for a smile, too fragile and frayed. "But you didn't come here, did you? You fell here. And we're all playing catch-up."

RAEF'S VOICE CUTS through before anyone else dares. "You can't stay here."

"No one said I wanted to," I mutter, keeping my eyes fixed anywhere but on him. My arms knot tight across my chest, jaw aching from holding back every word I'd rather spit. My skin still crawls like it's one size too small, stretched thin over something I don't understand. "You all are insane."

They ignore me.

Tris lounges against a carved bone post, tilting his head. "Then it's fortunate we've been making plans while you slept like a broken star."

The word *we* cuts through the haze, and my gaze snaps up, my stomach pitching. "We? Plans? They've changed?"

Raef's head tilts in a firm denial. "No, we still make for the Shadow Court. We move tonight."

I pull myself up, refusing to look as weak as I feel. "Why aren't we waiting until I'm stronger?"

"We don't have that luxury. You don't have that luxury anymore," Raef says. "You vaporized three of the frenzied. Every creature within twenty liorin felt that surge. There'll be more coming."

Tris folds his arms, gaze sharp. "And not just beasts. Courts will take notice. Whispers are already moving faster than we can. Some will want to claim you. Some will want to cut you open and study what leaks out. This is more of a risk now than it ever was before."

Well, that's a gut punch I didn't need today, or ever really.

Javi angles in until his shoulder brushes mine, a quiet barrier against the rest of the room.

A tremor runs through my voice as I speak my peace. "So, we're just walking into the lion's den?"

Raef's eyes don't waver. "Better my lion's den than theirs."

"But your father—" I start.

"Wanted you dead," Tris interrupted, with no particular softness. "Or worse."

Raef doesn't deny it. Of course he doesn't. That part was always clear, written in the way he watches me like I'm both a weapon and a liability. And maybe that should scare me more than it does. Maybe it does, and I'm too damn tired to flinch anymore.

"He'll test you," Tris adds. "Probe for weakness. But showing up together—united, bonded—might stay his hand. At least long enough for us to move."

There's something in his voice. *Us.* Not *you.* Not Raef. *Us.*

Something twists low, not fear this time. It drags slower and heavier, feeling suspiciously like trust. I hate that I even recognize it. Like my ribs don't get a say in how stupid I'm being.

"I don't like being a part of anyone's plan," I say quietly. "When is this all going to stop?" I whisper to myself. Javi presses a soft kiss to my temple, and my shoulders fall back down. The weight doesn't vanish. It shifts.

Raef's eyes hold mine, unblinking, like he means to nail the words in place. "You already are. Whether you like it or not. But I promise you this, We'll get you through it."

"And if you can't?"

"Then may the gods pity us all from their slumber," Tris mutters. "Because no one else will."

I clamp down on the stab, swallowing it back where no one can see. Let it scrape against the edges of my ribs. I cross my arms, pulse ticking too fast. They don't sound very sure of themselves at all. "So what's the rest of the plan? Is that all it is? Just march into the Shadow Court and hope I survive it?"

"No," Raef says, sighing. "We train you."

"Starting now," Tris adds. "Magic control. Sword skill. What to say. What not to say. You'll learn fast, or you won't last long. And that, my dear, is not an option."

My eyes flick from one to the other, waiting for one of them to break. I'm watching a game I don't know the rules to. "You sound like you've done this before."

"Survived tyrants?" Tris says, flashing a crooked grin. "A time or two."

"And," Raef says, dialing down his tone, "we'll train and stay together. I won't send you in unarmed. I swore I'd protect you. That doesn't mean keeping you weak. Once you master what we teach, we'll break off the binding."

Yeah, that one lands. Right where it hurts.

My heart lurches at the word. Binding. My choice ripped out from under me, tied to something I never truly agreed to. I didn't understand it then, and more, I still don't now. That ignorance feels like its own type of cage.

But his tone isn't cruel nor distant. It drags with something I can't name at first, and when I finally do, it makes my stomach turn. Regret. Hope. Things I don't trust from him. Things I don't trust at all. I don't know if I'm ready. I give barely a nod, enough to count but nothing more.

"Then we leave tonight," Raef says.

"Hope you like bleeding," Tris murmurs. "Training gets messy."

"Charming," I mutter.

But deep inside me, a small flame kindles. It's not hope. Hope is a fickle thing. When you need it, you don't have it, and when you don't need it, it's right there staring you in the face.

I SIT OUTSIDE the hut, right by the door. I've pulled my legs tightly to my chest, hoping my knees will help keep me together as the others prepare to leave.

The moons hang low and swollen above the trees, silver light filtering through branches that look more like bones than boughs. The air smells like burnt herbs and damp moss. There's still smoke in it, something cloying that clings to the roof of my mouth. My tongue tastes like ash and sugar. The witch's strange spells still cling to the corner of my mind like cobwebs I can't brush off.

I don't know how to sit still anymore. My muscles won't stop bracing, like they expect something to break. Maybe they're right because I don't know what I am anymore. Not exactly. But I'm not human. I can't deny that. I want to go home. I want to curl up in my mom's arms and cry on the couch while she runs her hand down my back and over my hair. But that's not an option, and it's a dream that grows fainter and further away every day.

I felt it when I pulled Javi back—like something in me had snapped loose, something wild and raw. A power that doesn't ask permission. Innate, Tris said. It answered to panic, to grief, and somehow… it worked.

I press my palm to my chest. It's quiet now, but not gone. It feels like something's awake under my skin, biding its time. The buzz is faint, but it's there, a low hum I can't scrub out. Not power, I don't think, it's more like a warning light that refuses to shut off, daring me to pretend it isn't blinking. I know I'll keep pretending until it blows up in my face.

Inside, voices drift through the open doorway. I don't mean to listen. But when the witch speaks, something in her tone roots me to the spot.

"She's too close to breaking," the old woman rasps.

No one jumps to fill the gap. It stretches, brittle, until Raef breaks it with a voice pulled taut. "The ring's holding. The binding serves multiple purposes at this point. My father's reputation behind me protects her from others, and the magic from my mother helps keep too much from seeping out."

"For now," the witch says. "But she's a tide you'll drown in. It cannot be only you. You know that now that you know who she is. She's destined for others."

More silence.

Raef speaks again, more quietly. "She saved him."

"She rewrote him with a touch. And she didn't even know what she was doing."

I flinch, on the inside. That line, 'rewrote him,' sticks under my ribs like a splinter I can't dig out. Yeah, that one's enough to ice me from the inside out.

"She'll learn," Raef says, but he doesn't sound certain.

"Or she'll burn," the witch answers. "And take the rest of you with her."

I shrink back into my shadow. They're not scared of me. They're scared of what I might become. They're not wrong to be. They're talking about me like I'm a storm that no one can steer. Like I'm already spiraling toward ruin. Like I'm not worth protecting.

Maybe I'm not.

I stand before I can hear anymore, boots crunching softly in the dirt. I need space away from the door and the voices inside, deeper into the shadows beyond the firelight. The cold settles on my skin, needling into me until that's all I can feel. I want it to numb me. I want something to feel simple again.

My chest aches perpetually. My thoughts are a snarl of too much. But one thing rings clear. If I stay, they'll keep bleeding for me, or more that I don't want to think about. I need to stay away from all of them. Or I'll get them all killed. This isn't about courage or power anymore. It's damage control.

It's time I make a plan for myself.

28

WHEN THE FOREST DECIDES YOURE NOT WORTH EATING

THE PATH WINDS BETWEEN TREES laced in silver. Frosted bark shimmers in the low morning light, catching where the sun cracks through the canopy. I catch myself cataloguing things, running my mind non-stop because that's what I do. It's normal, habitual, and comforting. Silver bark, lichen on the east side of trunks, and moss disturbed in patches that aren't from us. All useless data, but it grounds me. Leaves unfurl like velvet coins overhead, shivering though there's no wind. Each step I take makes the undergrowth whisper back.

The witch's hut has long disappeared behind the underbrush. Just a smudge in my memory now—thatch and bone and shadow. She didn't say goodbye. A bundle of salves got pressed into my hand with fingers that felt too light for what I've seen her do with them and she muttered, "Mind the thresholds."

Whatever that means.

The forest smells different this morning. Damp, earthy moss, bright peppermint, and something metallic curling in the air, setting my teeth on edge. There's a bite to it that doesn't belong. It's keyed up, straining like it's daring us to take another step. I know that feeling. I've had it since I opened the gate. Like the universe keeps tensing around me, waiting for my next mistake or even the next attack.

Raef walks ahead in complete silence. His boots don't make a sound. No snap of twigs, no crunch of leaves. He's a flicker of shadow moving steadily between trees, his coat catching every glint of light in dark rainbows. He hasn't spoken since we left. Maybe he won't. I have a big feeling we're back to what it was before.

I shouldn't care. But my eyes keep checking the gap between us anyway, measuring every step he doesn't take to close it. The silence hangs between us as heavy as his damned shadow. What I hate the absolute most is that I notice.

Tris walks beside me, hands behind his head, head tipped back to watch the canopy drift by. I can't figure out how he walks in a straight line because every time I try, I walk into him. He hums a tune I don't know, some lilting, careless thing. I can't tell if he's mocking the moment or sweetening it.

Javi brings up the rear, quiet but present. I can feel his gaze brush my back every few minutes—enough to know I'm still whole. He's the one that died, but I think he's as shaken to have woken up with me unconscious and bleeding everywhere. I'm not whole, not really. More duct tape and bad decisions than person right now, and everyone here knows it. I'm stitched together with pain and half-broken magic, and it's only a matter of time before the seams give. But stopping isn't an option. Stopping would prove I'm already in pieces.

I keep thinking maybe if I pretend hard enough, the cracks will glue back together. But my body remembers. It keeps the ache in every step and twitch. It keeps the magic humming low, a background noise I can't shut off. Each step sends an ache blooming in my legs. The bandages beneath my shirt are starting to itch, and the faint perfume of blood and crushed herbs clings to my skin like a second scent.

My feet drag forward anyway. If I open my mouth to ask for a break, I'll never hear the end of it. I would only prove what he's been saying from the beginning, that I won't survive here alone. That I'm a weak mortal with nothing to give but blood.

Javi must see it. It's not like I'm doing a good job hiding it. They're doing a much better job hiding whether they care. He falls into step closer, his back shifting against his shoulders, straps creaking, and I catch the scrape of his hand along his jaw. The beard he's been growing is uneven, a shade darker than his hair, soft at the edges. It doesn't make him look older so much as more stubborn. His mouth curves when he notices me watching, lips too soft and inviting for someone who's survived as much or more than me. He doesn't say anything right away, just brushes his thumb over the scarred leather grip of his pack strap, a quiet rhythm he always falls into when he's thinking.

The fact that no one talks weighs heavier than my legs do, but he starts talking, like he knows the thoughts flying along in my mind. His voice is low, a little rough, he could read audio books and take me to another world, and I'd welcome it.

"Want to hear a Greenwood tale?" he asks.

I wanted someone to talk, but me speaking is too dangerous. I'm not sure I can control what words will come out of my mouth. I can't do this without Mattie, and that hurts. I thought I was strong and independent, but what I realize now is that I depended on his strength so much more than I ever thought. I manage a half-shrug in answer, and he takes it as a yes.

"They called her the Mossbound Bride." His tone shifts into that almost lyrical cadence that comes with telling legends and tales that have been passed down over centuries around late night campfires. "They say she wandered too deep on her wedding day, chasing a fox with eyes like stars. The kind the old songs say were once messengers of the wild. She followed it past the last rowan trees, past the moss circles, into a place brides aren't meant to walk."

His eyes don't find mine; they follow the canopy, tracing silver bark and grey-tipped branches like he's telling the tale to the trees.

"The Greenwood doesn't give back what it takes. Except, this time...it did. Decades later, she stepped out of the trees, veil still on her head, gown still white. Not a wrinkle touched her face. But her eyes..." He lowers his voice, bending his head lower toward mine. "...older than stone. Like they'd been staring at roots and rivers long before we learned how to name them. Her hair dragged the forest with it, vines knotted through the strands, moss blooming with flowers no season claimed."

He runs his thumb over the strap of his pack as though marking the rhythm of what he's trying to say. Keeping the beat. "When she spoke, it wasn't with blessings or prayers. She whispered truths into children's ears, who would die, who would betray, who would love in secret. And every word came to pass."

Our path narrows, roots slick beneath my boots, but I don't interrupt. Javi's eyes stay on the trees, lips shaping the words with a reverence that makes me wonder how many times he's heard them before.

"The village couldn't bear it. Mothers said their children woke screaming, fathers said their sons walked to war because of her, lovers said their marriages broke before vows were ever spoken. So they bound her." His voice dips even lower, threaded with something almost like pity. "They poured sap over her until it hardened clear, wove songs around the coffin to keep her voice locked inside. A cage of glass and resin, singing softly."

He finally glances my way, though his eyes hold something distant, older than his years, though that's hard to determine because these males don't seem to age like I do. "They said it was for peace. Said it was for silence. But in Greenwood, everyone knows the truth. It wasn't silence they wanted. It was mercy for themselves. The wild had chosen her, the sleeping Gods, and the rest of them couldn't forgive it."

The canopy closes again overhead, silver bark gleaming in the weak light, and Javi's voice softens even more, a feat I didn't think possible. It's almost a quiet prayer now. "That's why Greenwood brides prick their palms with thorns and let the blood stain beneath their veil. A promise to the wild, 'remember me kindly, and I will not run.'"

He looks at me again, his sure, light feet never breaking stride. His lips part like the story hasn't fully left him. "The villagers feared her because she came back changed. Stronger. Not because she was lost." His voice is so warm, smoothing the edges of a sad story about a woman changed and scorned. "She walked out of the forest alive, against all odds, Rory. And no one could take that from her. You can still hear her whispers muted by resin and glass."

His hand brushes against mine, not pushing or demanding, a gentle reminder that he's still there, right next to me. "You've walked out of worse. And you're still here."

I huff out something that's almost a laugh. "Great. So I'm now a cautionary bridal tale. Guess all I'm missing is the veil and a fox with starry eyes...unless Tris counts?"

But I don't pull my hand away.

The trail bends east, and the trees thin. Light spills through the branches in wide, golden sheets. Too bright after days in the hush of shadow groves. I squint as the sudden bright light pierces after so much dim green and silver. It exposes me, like a rabbit stepping into a clearing where hawks might watch. What waits past the trees feels wide and watchful; it's an openness that makes prey nervous. Makes me nervous because that's what I am now, prey.

Raef pauses ahead, one hand on the hilt at his hip. He doesn't speak with his voice, but the set of his shoulders draws tight, like the world handed him a cue. The air follows, pulled taut. That invisible thread again. The one I'm starting to recognize before anything else.

Tris stops beside me, lips pursed. Even he's not smiling now. His deep humming has stopped. The absence of that careless tune makes the air feel strained.

I swallow against the dryness in my throat.

There are no bird calls here. No rustle of squirrels or stir of wings. Just the creak of my boots on damp roots, the soft wheeze of Javi's pack as he shifts behind me, and my own heart tapping too hard against my ribs. The quiet isn't peace. This is the quiet they warn you about on hiking safety videos that usually comes right before something awful jumps out. Horror movie rules 101, and here I am walking straight into it. Whatever waits past the next rise...it knows we're coming. And it has no reason to welcome us.

I tighten my grip on the strap across my chest. It's not going to save me from anything, but at least it keeps my hands from looking as useless as I feel.

"Raef," I whisper.

Javi's already gripping his weapon, muscles tight enough that I hear leather strain under his knuckles. He plants himself at my side like a shield, warm eyes locked on the trees. It's a look that says he'll cut down the forest itself if it blinks at me threateningly, or at all. I keep mine forward too, because if he's that focused, I should be worried.

I don't know what I feel exactly. I don't hear anything. I don't see anything. There's a weight on the back of my neck—primal. Like something's watching us from the dark. It's instinct that doesn't come from reason. It comes from evolution. From prey trying to outlive predators.

We stand there long enough for my legs to start itching to move, but no one does.

I'm breathing, technically, but it feels like I'm doing it wrong. My eyes burn from not blinking, and the trees aren't helping—they look frozen, like they're in on the joke.

Something moves beyond the mist.

The ring at my neck lights up like it's throwing a tantrum, searing against my skin. I stumble, catch myself, and huff out a curse. Great. Even my jewelry is trying to kill me too.

Tris tilts his head toward the trees. "It's close."

"Too close," Raef mutters. He's focused and ready to kill.

Whatever it is, it never shows itself. Its presence sinks into the ground, the bark, and the bones of the trees. I can feel it pacing, intelligent, curious; it already knows how it ends.

The forest keeps strangling the quiet until, all at once, it eases. Not because we scared it off. More like it decided we weren't worth finishing yet.

Whatever it was, it peels off, slow as you please. More like a predator passing over scraps. A wolf losing interest in prey that wouldn't fill its teeth. Which almost feels worse than if it had tried.

The pressure vanishes, but not the tension. It lingers like a footprint left behind.

Raef waits several long heartbeats, then says, "We move off the path. No fire. No noise."

"And then what?" I ask, trying to keep my voice from shaking.

He gives me his full attention, smiling. "Then you learn how to survive."

His smile isn't cruel, exactly. But it isn't comforting either, it's more like the Cheshire cat disappearing on Alice in the dark night sky.

THAT NIGHT, WE make camp in a hollow surrounded by stones. As Raef said, we don't risk a fire. Tris deigns to explain that the smoke would be an invitation to everything that wants us dead. The stones block the worst of the draft, but not the part that keeps stabbing my neck. Cozy doesn't even make the list.

Raef places a sword in my hands. Not my sword. That was too dangerous in my inexperienced hands, he says. I can't completely disagree considering. This one is leaner but somehow heavier. The glyphs etched into the blade shift faintly when they catch the fading light. I try not to look at them too long, but my eyes keep darting back like they're daring me to. They don't look carved so much as alive, twitching at the edge of sight, and it makes my skin prickle. A weapon shouldn't feel like it's watching me back. It shouldn't feel heavier than bone when it's supposed to be "lighter," like Raef says. Maybe it's me, maybe it's the magic, but the thought that this thing knows more about killing than I ever will makes my grip tighten—and not in a reassuring way.

"Magic won't save you in every fight," he says.

"No shit."

"So you start here."

I turn the blade over in my hands, the glyphs catching the last slant of daylight again. "What do they do?" I ask. "The glyphs. They're on every blade I've seen, but none of them look the same."

Raef glances up, faint surprise softening his usual severity. "They shouldn't. Each one's tuned to the wielder. Mine dampen recoil and balance weight—I don't have to think about the blade; it moves with me. Tris's glyphs are different. His channel the heat in his blood. The steel burns hotter and strikes harder the longer he fights."

He steps closer, watching how the sword sits in my grip. "You'd need something else. Glyphs that ground you. Anchor you when the magic spikes. It's possible your Atlantean blade is already made that way."

I trace one of the shifting marks with my thumb. "And Javi?"

Raef shakes his head, quiet. "I don't know. His blade isn't from any court I recognize offhand."

The glyphs shimmer again, and I swear I feel them hum against my skin. "Feels like it's breathing," I mutter.

Raef's mouth twitches at the corners. "Good. Then it likes you."

"So, they're sentient? What happens if they dislike you?" "In a manner of speaking, yes, the glyphs make them sentient. If they don't like you, they'll hurt. You cannot wield a blade that finds you unworthy."

He shows me how to stand, how to hold my weight, and how not to hack off my own toes. His voice is clipped into instruction, all muscle memory and correction, no softness. He nudges my elbow with the pad of his knuckle, the motion is small, but it lands in the places that still ache. I blink hard, taste metal, and the glade narrows to the scrape of his blade against mine and the way my ribs complain with every inhale.

I keep going because stopping would mean listening to every fracture inside me, and I'm not ready to hear that conversation out loud. I need this more than I need to whine about it, which is saying something.

Tris leans against a crooked tree, arms crossed, amused. "And after you're done playing with sharp things, we'll see if you can set fire to the sky."

I tilt my head enough to make it clear I'm two seconds from calling him an idiot. "What does that even mean?"

He tips his head, one eye glinting with mock solemnity, the other narrowing like he's in on a joke only he can hear. "It means I'm teaching you magic, little star. And I believe in learning through play, like the cubs."

My shoulders sag, and a sound escapes my throat that's closer to a dying mule than agreement. Still, I don't set the sword down.

Raef corrects my stance again, nudging my elbow with the back of his knuckle. "Stop thinking. Feel the balance."

The blade tilts off balance, biting toward the dirt as sweat slicks my palm. My arms shake like they're holding up a mountain.

"That's your job," Tris calls. "I'll make her think later."

I can barely lift the sword, and the fact that I'm still trying feels like the dumbest kind of stubborn. Every muscle in my arms is begging for mercy, but pride's louder than pain right now. Sweat clings to my spine despite the cool wind off the ridge, and my arms tremble from the endless drills. Raef has made me repeat the same swing, the same step, again and again until the world blurs to muscle memory and bruises. I stopped feeling my left hand three sets ago. I'm not sure I care, though. I have a sudden new appreciation for the knights and warriors I've studied and only dreamed of excavating.

"Again," he says. He doesn't even sound winded. One word, sharp enough to leave no room for argument.

I bite my tongue and obey, though every part of me screams to throw the sword at his smug face instead. The only thing stopping me is the tiny, infuriating part of me that wants to prove him right about me lasting this long. Pain blooms down my side, my old wound pulling, but I don't stop. Won't give him the satisfaction.

I train until my muscles scream, until my feet slip again and again and I hit the dirt. And then Raef walks away without a word. I want to scream and watch his pointy little ears bleed. Instead, I lay there for a beat, tasting dirt and fury.

Tris kneels beside me, offering a hand and a crooked grin. His silver hair falls forward, catching the light like it's in on the joke, and there's a smudge of dirt across his cheek that he clearly hasn't noticed or doesn't care about. His grin widens when he sees me glaring up at him, exposing his straight, brilliant teeth and alarmingly longer canines. It's like bruises and sweat are another form of entertainment. But it's his eyes that are the most alarming. Those violet storms catch on mine, bright and unbothered, like he's never doubted he'd outlast the world. And of course some part of me stirs at that, the same part that already reacts to Javi's warmth and Raef's impossible steadiness. Three of them, and me in the middle, bleeding and half-broken, still trying not to admit how tangled I'm becoming in all of it. And moving further and further away from my goal of finding a way home. I'm losing focus.

"You didn't fall," he says. "You landed. Mostly gracefully."

Javi appears with water and a worried brow, easing me to a seat and checking my bandages. "Maybe that's enough for today."

I take it, drinking greedily. The water tastes like minerals and something sweet, wild mint maybe. It's cold and clean, but not enough.

Javi hands me a bundle of dried fruit, his eyes warm, his fingers brushing mine a little too long. I pretend not to notice. I act like it's nothing, but the touch settles, small and stubborn, the way hope does when you don't want it. I hate that it lingers, dragging along my knuckle, and a stupid little lift skitters through my chest. I'm going to be the death of him...again.

But I actually managed to hold a sword without dropping it, which feels like an accomplishment worth framing. And I'm still standing. Metaphorically speaking, of course. My legs aren't on speaking terms with the rest of me in reality.

Tris, of course, hasn't lifted a blade all day.

"Lesson time," he says, tossing a pinecone-like thing from one hand to the other like a lazy juggler.

"Unless that pinecone is enchanted," I mutter, "I might stab you with it."

"That's the spirit," he says cheerfully. "Now, come here."

I stay planted, partly because standing feels impossible, partly because I'm petty enough to make him wait.

His lashes dip in a slow blink, mouth twitching like he's trying not to laugh. "Fine. I'll come to you, mortal menace." He plops down cross-legged beside me and sets the pinecone between us like it's some sacred relic. His energy is lighter than Raef's, but no less deliberate. It's a distraction and a dare all in one.

"Close your eyes."

"No."

"Do it."

I sigh and do. The insides of my eyelids are red from the lantern light. My fingers twitch in the dirt.

"Now," he says gently, "imagine warmth. I mean the kind that doesn't burn or break. The kind that steadies your breath when fear tries to take it. When was the last time you felt that, even scared out of your wits?"

The teasing is still in his voice, but it dips lower, slower, until it settles over me like hands just shy of contact. It brushes against me like the press of thin glass; one slip and it'll shatter.

I think of Javi's arms, holding me after I fell. Of Tris brushing hair from my face while I trembled. Of Raef standing guard close enough that I can feel him there, even when I can't see him. The press of Javi's heartbeat. The sound of Tris humming to himself while pretending not to care. Raef's silence, steadier than anything.

I don't say any of that out loud.

I mean to sound sharp, but it slips out thin, almost swallowed by the dirt between us. "I don't know."

"Try."

I take a large inhale—pine needles, moss, and the faint trace of lavender on my skin. When I open my eyes, Tris has that smug little curve to his plush lips, the kind that says he'll be insufferable about this later.

The pinecone sits untouched between us, and I shrug my shoulders. "What?"

Tris keeps smiling and jerks his head to the side. A torch, one of the tall ones that Raef planted earlier around the clearing, flickers to life beyond my reach. Blue and gold fire, soft as candlelight, blooms from the wick.

I go rigid, pulse hammering so loud it feels like the trees should hear it too.

The heat doesn't touch me, but I feel it anyway as it kicks open a door with my name on it.

Tris only leans back on his hands, a self-satisfied smirk stretching his lips. "There it is," he murmurs. "The little star burns."

Raef pivots from where he'd been pretending not to watch, his eyes locked on the flame, then on me. He keeps the same poker face, but his stance gives him away—back a little too straight, shoulders a little too stiff, like someone shoved a rod down his shirt. Like he's watching history repeat itself and doesn't know whether to be afraid or grateful.

I mean, I was supposed to light the pinecone...

THE NEXT NIGHT, the next glade opens like a wound in the forest—wide and quiet, framed by leaning stones thick with moss. Dappled light falls through the canopy in golden shafts, warm on my shoulders, the air heady with crushed leaves and distant wildflowers. The sweetness sticks in my throat, heavy enough to choke on. It doesn't fit in a place I already know is about to hurt me.

As expected, Raef skips the pep talk and chucks a blade at me. Real inspirational teaching style. I catch it—barely—and nearly drop it on my foot. My arms ache from the last session and stretch of travel in between, but I clench my fingers tight around the hilt. My palms are already raw. A fresh blister burns beneath my thumb.

"You've never held a blade," he says, flatly.

"I wouldn't say I never held one. I'm an archaeologist, for crying out loud. We like swords. I don't know how to use one...properly anyway."

He circles me once, his features flat and guarded, like he's already measuring where I'll fail. "Now you must."

Raef doesn't smile, doesn't even attempt to soften his demeanor. He circles me like I'm a puzzle he's already halfway solved, but by forcing pieces together that only almost fit, his eyes catch on every flaw—my stance, my breath, the angle of my grip, and my toes.

"Higher," he says. "No, closer to the guard. Your elbows are locked. You'll snap something. Did you forget everything from last night?"

I shift my grip, awkward and stubborn, sweat sliding down the back of my neck until it stings the edge of my collar. The sun creeps lower, pressing heat into my shoulders, sticky in the small of my back. I grit my teeth, push forward, and lunge, with more willpower than skill, but it's all I've got.

I swing wide. Miss completely. Of course. Try again, same result. I'm starting to feel like the world's most dangerous windmill.

"You're not strong enough to survive this world untrained," he says.

"I vaporized three monsters in the woods," I snap, blurting it faster than I mean to, like volume alone can make it less pathetic.

His blade meets mine midair—a lazy, sideways parry that sends my arm jolting off course. "You got lucky."

My glare sticks to him like my own personal brand. My heart hammers so loud I can hear it in my teeth. Every muscle aches and wants to move—to swing, collapse, howl—and I'm furious that I can't do all three at once.

Then, like laughter breaking tension, Tris's voice rings out from the shade. "That's enough punishment, dear Raef. She's not a soldier."

He leans against a stone at the edge of the glade, twirling a grape-like fruit between his slender fingers like he hasn't been watching—but of course he has. His silver hair catches the light like threads of starlight, pulled back into a messy bun at the nape of his neck. "You don't train fire by beating it down. You feed it. Let it dance."

Raef doesn't look at him. "Dancing won't help her when someone's aiming for her throat."

Tris rolls his eyes, steps forward, and plucks the blade from my hand. "But choking it will burn you both." He then bends and tosses me his blade with a wink. "Again, little star. This time, hit him like you mean it. Give the prince a proper bruise."

I catch his blade with one hand. It's lighter than the one Raef gave me, faster, and nimbler. The hilt fits my palm like it's been waiting. My fingers close around it, and something shifts, like balance finally found.

Raef's eyes narrow. "This isn't a game."

"Everything's a game," Tris counters, stepping back. "You don't know how to play."

I face off with Raef. He raises his blade again, stance rooted, steady, and unreadable as ever.

I move. This time, my footing doesn't slip. The weight of the sword moves with me instead of against me. My arm remembers the rhythm from his endless drills—turn, step, pivot—the ache fades into memory. The dirt feels solid beneath my feet. I don't think, I act. I strike.

Steel rings out as our blades collide. He parries again, but not as lazily. The faint rise of his brows sets a crease between them, drawing my eye to the sharp cut of his cheek and pulling at the faint scar by his temple. He's so controlled it's infuriating, but I catch myself staring anyway. I pivot, shift the weight, and come in at a different angle. It's not graceful. It's not clean. But I'm faster.

The flat of my blade smacks his side with a sound that's way too satisfying for how much my arms are shaking. He underestimated me. I freeze, a lump catching in my throat. Raef steps back, hand brushing the spot above his hip where I'd struck.

Tris whoops from the edge of the glade. "That's it! Did you see her face?"

I lock on Raef, grip slick on the hilt. My shoulders twitch with the strain, arms trembling like they're seconds from giving out, but I keep the blade raised. He won't get the satisfaction of watching me drop it first.

Raef doesn't bother with a glare or lecture. His eyes stay on me, steady and unreadable, long enough to make my grip falter. At last, he speaks, one word, cool and unyielding, "Again." There's no heat behind it, no insult. It's a command, carved clean as the blade in my hand.

But this time, I think, maybe, something else sits behind it. Approval. Or the beginning of it.

<h1 style="text-align:center">29</h1>

WHEN BLISTERS BECOME A BADGE OF HONOR

WE CONTINUE THIS PATTERN FOR days. Sword skill with Raef beating me until I can't stand, then Tris beating my mind apart with magic. I'm exhausted. Genuinely exhausted. The kind that settles behind the eyes and claws down the spine. Everything aches, even my will.

The air has gone lavender with dusk, soft light catching in the ripples of the stream. Crickets hum even and unhurried, or something that sounds like them. I sit on a flat stone near the bank, rolling my sore shoulders and peeling a flake of dried blood from my palm. The skin beneath is raw and stinging. I'd worn it open on the sword. The edge of the wound glistens, pink and angry. Like me.

"Should've aimed lower," I mutter.

"You did fine."

Javi's voice doesn't rise, yet it settles over me like he's closer than he is. I look up to find him crouched beside me, a waterskin in one hand and a clean strip of bandage in the other. He always finds me when I start to fray. It's becoming a pattern I don't know how to stop.

"I've had worse," I say.

"I'm well aware," he answers.

He dips the cloth, wrings it out, and reaches gently for my wrist.

"I haven't—" he murmurs, dabbing the blister with practiced care. "Watching you in the clearing...you don't quit."

His touch is careful, almost too careful, like he's trying not to set off another fracture. Truth is, the break's already there.

"I don't know how. It's an affliction."

He smiles, and it's not his usual lopsided grin. This one hangs back, quiet, almost shy. Hopeful, too, which is the part that makes me nervous.

He takes my other hand and wraps it next. His touch slips across my skin, light but certain, and it's enough to scatter every thought except him. The way he's looking at me, like I'm something worth tending. I want to pull away. I don't. I want to ask what he sees when he looks at me like that, but I'm terrified of the answer.

I let him. I shouldn't. But I do. I can't help it. Because for once, someone's touching me without wanting something in return. There's no demand in it, no expectation. It's touch that I need, not that I'm going to admit that to myself.

I had boyfriends back home, but this feels so much different. And maybe that's because lives are on the line and everything feels so much more intense, but—no. It's not that. He's not just that. There's a calm in him I didn't know I needed until now. A warmth that doesn't try to burn me up.

Behind us, the others move quietly. Tris lounges in the grass like it's velvet, his silver hair catching the firelight as he toys with a coin between his long fingers. Always watching. Always moving. Raef leans against a tree, long legs crossed at the ankles, sharpening a blade with methodical patience. He hasn't spoken much at all, but I feel him...them. The weight of their eyes. The silence between them feels full of choices they haven't made yet and others they already regret.

But something is different tonight. This silence between them isn't sharp. It isn't empty either. It's a hum, like tension paused mid-note. Someone rolled the dice, but they have yet to land.

I glance back, half-expecting he'd have moved. But Javi's still there, still holding my hand like it's the most natural thing in the world. Like I'm not a walking disaster waiting to happen.

His thumb drags over the inside of my wrist, slow enough to make heat spark under my skin. He doesn't let go. Neither do I. I tell myself it's easier that way, but the truth is I don't want him to. I should...make him, but right now, I'm tired of knowing better.

The fire catches in his eyes, warm with those flecks of gold and impossibly kind. There's no storm in him, only the bright, warm light that is Javi, nothing hiding in the shadows. And in that light, something soft and wonderful is blooming.

"You don't have to be strong all the time," he says quietly. "You can lean if you need to." His voice finds that part of me that still wants to say no, still wants to fight the very idea of softness in this realm. But I'm too tired to fight that, too.

The back of my tongue tastes like burnt coffee as the admission drags free. "I might."

"Then lean," he murmurs.

My shoulder eases against him, the fight bleeding out of me before I realize it's gone. The strength in his arm steadies me in a way I can't name. The noise of everything else fades—wars and grief and the weight of whatever I'm supposed to be. All that's left is the hush of water nearby and the steady beat of someone who's still here, holding me up when I don't know if I can do it myself. A boy with the gentle voice and too bright soul.

When I look at the others, Raef and Tris, I still feel that tether pulling between us, thin and strange. But I don't know what it means yet. Not the same. Not with the clarity I feel here. But there's a pull, and I'd be lying if I said I couldn't feel it growing. Three different men pulling at me.

But with Javi?

It feels like choosing.

And for now, I choose him.

WE SIT, HUDDLED together, and I lean as the sun hangs lower and lower. The light goes gold, then amber, then something bruised. A sky strung tight, like it might snap if I make the wrong choice here.

A twitch in his chest stutters against my spine when I press closer, like he wasn't expecting me to actually let myself fall. Honestly, neither was I. I should laugh it off and make some snide comment, but the truth is... I like the way he tenses, like holding me is both the best and most terrifying thing that's ever happened to him. It makes me wonder what it would take to let myself stay here.

I don't think I startle him. I'd like to think he's been waiting and hadn't dared to hope. Because I've been waiting, too, haven't I? For something to anchor me that doesn't come with a blade. Javi has a blade, but that's not all he has.

The fire behind us crackles. Tris gives a low hum—some half-song, half-thought drifting lazily into the night. Raef's knife scrapes softly over steel. They're close, but they've faded, blurring the edges in a world that's suddenly shrunk down to this single point of contact. The world has narrowed to the way Javi's arm curls around my shoulders, careful and warm, and the way his fingers find mine again and hold them like a secret. Like a vow. Like he doesn't know if I'll keep it or cut it loose.

"I'm sorry," he says suddenly, voice low. "If I'm—crossing a line. I just... I've been scared I'd never get to do this." There's a hitch in his voice that's almost shame. Like wanting me might be something he shouldn't admit out loud.

I tilt my face toward him, my forehead nearly brushing his. "Do what? Trip over me until I cave? You'll have to be more specific." I know exactly what he means, but if I say it first, it becomes real. And I'm not sure I'm ready for real. I need him to risk saying it out loud. Otherwise it's another trick my head's playing on me.

His eyes search mine.

"This," he whispers. A single word that drags a hundred others with it: hope, ache, apology. Things he'll never spell out, but I hear them anyway.

He lingers, his gaze snagged on mine. The gold flecks in his dark eyes catch the firelight, flickering like they're trying to decide whether to stay or run. His lips part, then press together again. He's holding back words that might shatter the moment. I can feel the question in the way his breath stalls between us and the way his hand tightens slightly where it rests against my jaw. I nod.

He shifts closer, enough that the space between us finally gives. His lips find mine, soft and careful, like he's testing if I'll shove him away. It's not some grand cosmic moment, not a kiss you'd etch into legend. It's human and real. And maybe that's exactly why it rattles me.

The kiss isn't pushy, only cautious. He's waiting to see if I'll break it off. His other hand lifts to cup my jaw, thumb barely brushing my cheek like he's not sure I'd let him stay. He's not asking for anything but the moment. He's holding the moment out like an offering, and I don't snatch it away.

I let him stay.

The kiss deepens, slow as a sunrise, and for a moment I let myself melt into it—into him. Into the promise of something that isn't survival or strategy.

When we pull apart, the silence still hums around us. But it's changed. So have I. Something inside me loosens. I let my head rest against him again. Close my eyes. And breathe.

30

BEING A PAWN WHILE PRETENDING YOU'RE A QUEEN IS MORE DIFFICULT THAN IT SOUNDS

T HE MORNING IS COLDER THAN the last. Mist clings to the ground in low, curling tendrils, softening the forest into a half-dream. It seeps into my boots, my sleeves, and down the collar of my shirt. Not biting per se, more like a stubborn hair, the one that keeps tickling your skin but is never there when you reach for it. The cold is a chill that lingers even after you've stopped noticing.

I sit on a fallen log lacing up my boots, fingers slow and sore from yesterday's training, but they still get the job done. My knuckles are swollen, the skin split in places, and every lace pull stings, but the shakes are gone. I guess that's what happens when pain turns into routine. Something I haven't faced much since field school.

Across the clearing, Raef adjusts the straps on his sword belt in his methodical way. He's never hurried in his movements, only in how he speaks to everyone else. In another world his incredibly methodical nature would make me wonder about OCD and other neurodivergent mentalities. But this world doesn't give labels like that. It watches the weight we carry and whether we wear it well.

He hasn't said a word to me all morning. Nothing since his last 'again' before he walked off and left me aching in the dirt last night. No nod, no glance, just the echo of his blade colliding with mine until my arms went numb. He hasn't looked at me, either. Which would be fine if I didn't keep noticing it. I'm an idiot counting the seconds in the silence.

But when I laugh too easily at something Javi says, Raef's hands pause mid-buckle, long enough to give him away. Not much, but I catch it. It's a tell he probably hates anyone noticing.

"Break camp," he says flatly. "We'll reach the Greenwood border by midday."

Tris stretches like a cat, flipping a silver coin between his fingers. "Should we pack our crowns and declarations of war, or will our charming faces do?" It's a good line, but no one laughs. The coin clicks against his ring in the hush.

Raef doesn't rise to the bait. He buckles his last strap and stands tall. "When we reach the Greenwood border," he says, voice clipped and cool, "we travel as bonded. No exceptions. Public displays must reflect that. Keep close and keep quiet."

He doesn't bother looking at me. The words hit like they've got my name written all over them, neat little cuts meant to remind me who's holding the knife.

Javi goes rigid beside me, and Tris's brow quirks like he's watching a play unfold. My face burns hot enough to match the firelight. It's not the lie that knots my stomach; it's how smoothly Raef palms it off. It's about how easily he makes it mine to carry.

"You're the one who said I didn't have to mean it," I seethe.

He finally drags his eyes to me, and I almost wish he hadn't. It's the quiet that you can easily read as tight rather than calm. His jaw ticks once. That's it. That ice he wears like armor.

"*I* don't care if *you* mean it," he says. "Magic does, and my father will." He turns his back and walks toward the tree line, barking orders to one of the scouts without waiting to see if I'll follow.

Like I ever had a choice.

I STAND BESIDE my pack, bent in two, fingers tugging at a loose strap, face still burning from Raef's warning. *Keep close and keep quiet.* No mention of names, but every pointy ear heard them unspoken. The bark of his voice still echoes in my head, clipped and cold and not for me—not really. It's for the others and the courts, all part of the game. I'm just the piece that keeps moving.

I haven't even looked at Javi since. I can feel him hovering, a weight at my side I didn't ask for. I don't have to look to know he's there. My skin already does.

Tris appears first, brushing past me with an exaggerated sigh, his bright hair pulled into a lazy knot. "Good gods, he's wound tighter than a deathroot vine," he mutters, loud enough for me—and most of the others— to hear. "You'd think someone kissed *his* betrothed."

I bite the inside of my cheek before managing, "Tris." My voice catches somewhere between embarrassment and warning. But he doesn't appear to care.

He grins, completely unbothered. "What? I'm just saying, if we're performing a romance for the realm, he might try acting less like someone carved from old bark."

I don't get a chance to answer him as Javi steps beside me, hands full of folded canvas. "Don't let him get under your skin," he says softly, eyes flicking to mine. "Raef's good at giving orders. Not so good at being—"

"Likeable? Emotional? Something more than a plank of wood used to bash things into your brains?" Tris interjects.

I try to smile, but it comes out a crooked, half thing. Because I'm still too raw. Still too aware of how many people heard that order and looked at me like I was a sealed document being passed up the chain.

Javi shifts the canvas to one arm and offers the other to me like I might need help with the pack. I don't, but I let him anyway. Because I need something to hold onto. Even if it's just kindness. Even if it's just him.

"You okay?" he asks quietly, like it's for me.

"I don't know," I admit.

To my surprise, Tris loops back around and drops a flat leather pouch into my hands. "Since we're all pretending to play nice, you should at least look the part. Fae don't walk into court empty-handed."

Inside is a comb carved from bone, sleek and pale, the teeth fine enough to snag if I'm not careful. It feels wicked and right all at once in my palm, smooth and cold as if it still remembers the creature it came from. Next, a bottle that glitters when I tilt it, gold swirling like molten sunlight trapped in glass. It's too pretty to trust, not in this place, but tempting at the same time. And then there's a pendant. It's a simple ring of dark wood on a black cord, worn at the edges like someone else's thumb rubbed it smooth over the years. When I lift it, it's warm against my skin, and not from the fire. Old warmth. Somehow I know it's Tris.

"What is this?" I ask.

"Distraction," Tris says with a wink. "A little glamour, a little tradition, and something to keep the court guessing."

"And a reminder," Javi adds, his thumbs brushing my knuckles. "That not all of us are playing pretend."

I look between them—Tris with his effortless poise and Javi with his open heart—and something in my chest loosens.

Maybe I am a pawn in someone else's game, but at least I'm not alone on the board.

THE FOREST CROWDS in as we climb, their trunks spiral like twisting spindles, and bark alive with bioluminescent veins that light the path in muted emerald and blue. Every so often, a branch moves with no wind, twitching like something has let go.

Ahead, the outpost gates rise from the roots themselves, tall, arching, and grown. They definitely are hand-built, but not in the way I'm used to.

Guarding them stand fae clad in green-glass armor etched in runes. The armor catches the light like mirrors and moss fused together. It's getting harder and harder to match what I see with anything I comprehend.

Raef walks first, his posture formal and detached. Ever the crownless prince in his element. The rest of us follow in intentional and ordered silence.

I reach up and adjust the pendant Tris had given me. The wood is warm now. I'd smeared a touch of the gold shimmer at my collarbone, and the bone comb holds my hair in a neat twist at the base of my skull. I look the part, or close enough. I doubt these people are expecting much from me. But I feel like a counterfeit coin. Dressed in gifts I didn't earn, marching toward something I don't understand. I'm not a weapon. I'm not a myth. I'm pretending I belong in a story that isn't mine.

"Don't speak," Raef tells me under his breath as we approach. "Smile. Nod. Let them look at you, but not inside you."

I squint at him like he's sprouted horns. "Inside me?"

He keeps moving, boots crushing soft against the path, eyes fixed forward. "Your power. Your thoughts. Your fear. Don't let them catch scent of any of it."

The space between us drags, heavy as wet rope, and all I can hear is the scrape of my own teeth grinding.

"Is that a thing that can happen?" I ask, voice flat. I'm most definitely afraid of the answer and pissed that I asked for it anyway.

"With you?" he says quietly. "Easier than breathing."

Why did he wait until now to tell me this can happen? I've been walking around with a hole in my pocket and only now noticed everything spilling out. He's been watching me bleed thoughts and emotions without realizing it this whole time.

I drag the knot in my throat down with effort, trying not to glance at the guards as we pass. What am I made of, that even silence betrays me? That even my fear glows like a beacon?

The gate looms, that armor glinting on either side. I keep my gaze forward, my spine straight, but my insides twist. What did it mean to be seen inside? How do you stop someone from sniffing out your fear like it's blood on the water?

I want to fold my arms over my chest. Cover my pulse. Turn invisible. But I can't. Because this is the part where I'm supposed to look powerful. Useful.

I pull down the cuffs of my sleeves again, running my palms over the wrinkles like that's going to fool anyone. My heart's still beating loud enough to sell tickets. Pretending I'm invisible feels a lot like standing under a stage light in my underwear.

One of the guards tilts his head, watching me too long. Another mutters something and touches two fingers to his lips, like a ward or a prayer. I feel like he's crossing his fingers in front of him hoping to keep the devil, me, at bay.

I hold onto Raef's orders, cold as stone. Keep your face smooth. Give them the nod. Lock it all down where no one can see.

So, I smile. Not wide, not fake. Just enough to say I see them but don't care. My head dips in something like a nod. I think. Or maybe it's a twitch. I have no idea if I pulled it off. All I know is I manage not to flinch. That has to count for something.

We make it past the guards, though every step feels like I'm balancing glass on my shoulders.

I don't let out the air in my chest until the green-glass glint fades from the corners of my vision. Even then, I keep my spine tight and my hands still. I feel like I've walked through a museum exhibit where the glass is one-way and I'm the artifact on display.

Inside the outpost, it's much quieter. An alert quiet that makes my skin itch.

Stone paths coil through arched doorways grown into trees. Light filters through leaves like stained glass. Noble fae in robes of feather and leaf watch from balconies above. I hear them before I see them, soft but intense voices behind lattice screens.

"Is that her?"

"She glows."

"If she's real, every court will want her."

My hands curl into fists at my sides. They don't sound surprised at all. They sound downright greedy. I'm a shard dug out of the dirt that proves their myths have teeth. A relic to catalog, trade, or steal.

Raef angles his head, just enough to murmur, "Eyes forward."

So I do. And of course, their eyes don't stop. They aren't watching, they're actively judging. Like I'm up for auction and nobody told me.

I can't tell if I'm being measured for a crown...or a coffin.

31

HOW TO BORROW NORMAL FOR AN HOUR AND RETURN IT BROKEN

THE ROOMS THEY GIVE US are carved into the trunk of a tree so wide, it could've swallowed a cathedral. The interior smells like wood shavings and peat smoke. Light filters down through glowing moss strung across the ceiling, casting everything in that soft green-gold light. It's beautiful, in the way old libraries and forgotten churches are beautiful—sacred and silent and not quite meant for me. Nothing in this world is. I keep stepping into places that feel older than my bones, older than my blood, and every time I wonder how long until they spit me back out.

Raef speaks briefly with the steward at the entrance, then waves us inside without a word. He slips away right after. How predictable from a male who lives on quiet and distance. Like if he says nothing, none of this will touch him.

I barely wait for the door to close before the air rushes out of me like I'd been holding it hostage. It tastes like moss and nerves. My jaw aches from clenching it too long.

"They looked at me like I was about to sprout wings and rip their throats out," I mutter.

"You might," Tris says lightly, lounging across the back of a curved bench. "Wouldn't be the worst diplomatic move."

I level a glare meant to burn him down, but he only throws me a wink, lounging there like sin made casual. The ridiculous part is that it almost works. That grin could probably charm blood from a stone—and yeah, maybe me, if I wasn't so stubborn. I'm regretting my five-year dry spell right now. I am not going there. I love reading why choose smut, but I don't want to become one...*right*?

While Tris sprawls in his usual cat-like grace across the bench, Javi closes the space between us without any theatrics, warmth replacing mockery. His voice cuts through the fog in my head like something meant only for me. "You did well. You didn't flinch. That matters."

"I wanted to." I wanted to scream, actually. To turn and run until the forest swallowed me whole.

There's that half smile again, small but powerful, the one that sneaks past my defenses before I can even activate them. "Wanting to is not the same as doing."

"Truth," says Tris. "I have wanted to rip many throats out. I've wanted your blood since I met you, but alas, I have not accomplished either."

"Excuse me?"

He stalks over and shocks me by pressing his face to my neck and inhaling in an exaggerated fashion. "You smell delectable, little star. I'm not going to lie."

I press a palm into his forehead, pushing as hard as I can to get him away from my still-healing neck. "Yeah...nope, that's not happening."

The absurdity of the moment hits hard enough to slice through the fog in my head. Leave it to Tris to make me laugh with my skin still on fire.

"Of course," he says, like he solved the riddle of the universe. I roll my eyes, but the corner of my mouth betrays me, tugging upward anyway. God help me, his smugness works.

"Did he really mean what he said?" I ask a beat later. "About people getting inside me?"

My voice is even and casual even though I'm anything but. If I sound calm, maybe I'll stay that way. But my hands curl tight around each other. I can still feel the stares like fingerprints on my skin.

Tris's expression morphs into something uncharacteristically serious. "It's not just a metaphor. Fae magic isn't always cast. Sometimes it's sense and the only kind of intention that matters. The older courts have seers, empaths, siphons, and mindmelders. If you let your guard down—if you let them feel you too clearly—they can read you like a book. Shift you. Even break pieces off just to see what makes you tick." His tone makes it worse, not better. Like he's describing the weather, 'There's a slight chance of rain with a side of mind-shredding.' Just another Tuesday for the fae.

Javi adds in a serious tone he rarely uses, "It's how the powerful stay powerful. Secrets aren't currency, they're armor. Weak minds are the perfect weapons."

I press my eyes shut, harder than a blink, fighting the burn behind them. Not because I'm close to crying, even though I should be, but because the thought of someone peeling back my thoughts like petals is enough to make my stomach pitch.

I scrape my teeth over the inside of my cheek, forcing the words out anyway. "So if I'd asked the wrong question, or smiled the wrong way..."

"They'd have seen the truth of you," Tris says, "and trust me, little star—you're not ready for that. When you're close to us and relaxed, we can help protect your mind."

Relax. That's a joke. My body is a knot, my thoughts a snarl. But I nod anyway like it's exactly that simple. Because what's the alternative? Curl up in the moss and hope no one peeks inside me again?

A SOFT CHIME sounds, like wind through glass, and the door swings open. Raef steps inside. No hello. No greeting of any kind. His presence changes the air. Great. The atmosphere drops twenty degrees just because he exists. Must be nice to carry your own personal storm cloud around. And I feel bad that he makes me feel this way. Like I'm waiting for a blow that never lands but leaves bruises anyway.

I straighten instinctively, spine stiffening as he crosses the threshold. Whatever the Greenwood steward had to say outside definitely didn't improve his mood. He looks composed, sure, but his jaw's too set, shoulders pulled to square. A man trying not to splinter. He doesn't meet my eyes, and that should make it all easier. It doesn't, though. It makes everything feel unfinished.

"We don't linger here," he says flatly. "I was hoping to give you more time to recover in some comfort—"

Tris, once again half-draped over the bench, lifts a brow. "Then it's good we've settled in so quickly."

Raef ignores him. "They've agreed to let us pass at dawn. Until then, we remain in the guest tier. That means this suite. Nothing outside this suite. No courtyard strolls, no straying from the three of us."

His gaze cuts to me, then slides away as quickly. Like it stings to look too long. It reads like self-flagellation, not command. He keeps his face turned because looking at me would be like reading the ledger of what he couldn't prevent.

"If anyone speaks to you, let me answer first. Especially you."

I bristle. "Because I might say something wrong?" The heat in my voice surprises even me. But I'm tired of being treated like I'm seconds from blowing everything up.

His voice stays level, though I can see the muscle jump in his jaw, every syllable forced through teeth that want to snap. "Because you might say something true. And truth, here, is dangerous."

I hate that he's right. I hate how often I forget the rules until they snap against me.

A pause stretches, fragile as old bone I know will snap if I breathe on it wrong. I don't know if I want to scream or cry or throw something.

Even Tris has the common sense to keep his mouth shut.

Raef nods toward the arching hall behind him. "The rooms are grown into the elder tree itself. They're private, shielded, and warded. Stay in them after dark. Lock the doors. Draw the sigils as instructed."

"And if we're hungry?" Javi asks.

"There'll be food sent up. Don't eat anything that sings to you. Or stares back."

"Charming," Tris mutters. "Truly a feast for the senses."

Of course he stares, because blinking would make him human. "This isn't hospitality. It's politics. We're guests of a court that wants something from us and would rather not pretend otherwise. Every court does. They want her."

He holds my eyes and it feels like the room grows smaller.

My throat feels tight. I want to say something cutting, something that will bite, but all I manage is a nod. Because I already know this. They want to own me. And Raef...he's the only shield I have in a world that measures power by how well you bleed.

He moves to leave, his coat whispering over the stone floor. "Rest while you can. We move with the sun."

The door eases closed with a muted click, sealing the moss-lit room in his absence. Raef's shoulders stayed rigid until the last second, posture too straight, all practiced poise. He's a man who will never admit he's frayed at the edges. And when the wood swallows him from sight, it's not only quiet that lingers. It's him. The faint scrape of steel still in my ears, the smell of leather and cold air clinging to the space he vacated, like he's left the weight of himself, his shade, behind on purpose.

Tris lets out a low whistle. "That boy could use a drink. Or a decade long nap."

I hold my ground, staring at the closed door, fists curled at my sides, as if sheer will might drag him back through it. The glow of the moss catches the edge of the pendant at my throat. I tell myself I'm not afraid. That I'm angry, that I'm tired. But fear hides in the cracks. In the way my hands won't unclench. In that way I already know I won't sleep.

32

WHEN IN DOUBT, BLAME THE TEA

THE DINING ROOM GLOWS GREEN; in fact, it drowns in it. The light seeps from the moss threaded through the walls, casting everything in a sickly halo. The walls are bark, but polished, lacquered, and inlaid with veins of gold that move beneath the surface like metallic sap. Shadows pool in the seams of the bark, but even they look tinted green, like this place doesn't allow real darkness. Even the chairs look like they've grown into shape; bark curls into curves, and moss forms plush seats. The table stretches too long for the four of us. Five courses, two wines, and three teas. All placed with immaculate care. The plates are thin crystal carved with runes I can't read. The food looks more like art than nourishment, petals that smoke faintly, meat that shimmers under the light, and a fruit that bleeds gold when cut. It's beautifully uneasy.

Raef hasn't touched a thing. Tris, of course, is sipping the red tea with the air of someone daring the drink to kill him. Javi sits close, not tense, but alert, like he might need to dive across the table at any second.

I'm halfway through some sort of candied root when I feel it. A presence at my shoulder. One of the servers, silent, setting a small bowl before me. Clear broth, with something pearlescent drifting in it. Then her fingers brush my shoulder.

The room fissures in front of me, a hairline slicing straight through my vision. It's not blurred, nor black. A fine, splintering line splits across the center of my sight—like someone has tapped my eye with a chisel and cracked it straight through. Pressure slams in next, inherently off, against the grain. A scraping, skittering force that slides under my skin, curls down my spine, and coils like cold wire behind my eyes. It's too deep. I want to scream. I feel her inside my skull like she's peeling pages out of a book that should be locked closed.

Get out, I think. *Get out, get out, get out—*

My shoulder jerks hard enough to rattle the chair, my knee slamming into the table's underside.

The table jerks sideways—no, I do. My body moves on its own, muscles seizing, head snapping back as if struck. The ceiling spins. The glimmering plates and shifting light blur together in a smear of green and gold. The table rushes up toward me.

Strong arms catch me.

Tris is suddenly there, one arm catching my back, the other gripping my wrist. "Easy," he says, though his voice is sharp-edged, taut with something dangerous.

She eases back, every step measured, like she's gliding instead of walking. Her face stays so smooth, untouched, and calm in a way that feels completely unnatural. But her eyes—her eyes gleam like mirrored glass, shining but completely empty on the other side.

"Get out," Raef's voice rips through the room, low and dangerous, already on his feet, blade drawn. His posture is rigid, one hand extended to me, the other gripping steel so tightly his knuckles are pale.

The air drops ten degrees. The other servers freeze mid-step, silks fluttering in the breeze created by the abrupt movement. A murmur passes between them, "Siphon."

The one who touched me doesn't so much as blink. She's the epitome of calm. Her posture stays loose, hands folded neatly at her waist, but her eyes gleam too smoothly, almost pleased with herself as they throw that eerie green light back at me. She offers a low, elegant bow, but the curve of her mouth makes it feel like mockery rather than respect.

"She glows," she says, voice like cracking sugar. "The city wakes. I only tasted what's already unraveling." She slips backward, the corner claiming her until nothing's left but the echo of her words.

Warmth drips down over my lip. I swipe at it, dazed, and stare at the smear on my fingertips, red, thin, barely more than a scratch mark of proof.

The cloth napkin vanishes from beside my plate, and Tris's fingers brush away mine with a tenderness that doesn't match the sharp line of his jaw. He presses the cloth gently to my face, his movements unhurried, almost careful enough to make me forget who he is.

"She got in," he says, voice like a blade dulled enough to hurt more. "I felt it. That wasn't a taste. She was digging."

My hand is still stained. A drop of blood clings to my knuckle, trembling. I stare at it like it might show me something, like if I look hard enough, I'll understand what she took.

Before I can wipe it away, Tris catches my wrist in one fluid motion and guides my hand up, my knuckle caught against the heat of his mouth.

His lips are warm. His mouth hotter. I feel the wet slide of his tongue and the gentle scrape of his teeth along my skin. A bolt of heat lances through my spine. Off. Too intimate. But, I don't pull away. I freeze, breath caught. My body, the complete traitor that it is, flares under the attention. My heart skitters.

"Tris." Javi's voice is clipped, tighter than his usual warmth. He fills my peripheral vision, one hand already half-lifted, like he'd been about to reach for me himself. But he pulls back, like nothing happened at all.

"Don't want to frenzy," Tris says quietly, a faint smile curving his lips. "Better me than someone less charming. Or less in control."

My jaw drops in the most unladylike and unsexy way. "That's all it takes? A drop?"

"Yes." His answer comes without hesitation. Tipping his head, he watches me from beneath his dark lashes, unreadable. "Then again, a breath can topple kingdoms. A drop? A well-placed drop can start a war."

I don't know what to say to that. I want to say something smart, something witty. But I still feel her in my bones. I still feel his mouth on my skin. I still feel like I might lose it. I swallow as my mind races. "Then why are there so many frenzied?"

His gaze darkens. "That," he says, almost tender, "is the big question, now isn't it?"

Javi takes the cloth napkin Tris dropped on the table in his haste. "She's not a snack."

"I know exactly what she is," Tris says, still watching me.

Javi drops to one knee, the band of his arm brushing mine as he reaches up, dabbing at the blood left under my nose with calm hands. His touch is gentler than it needs to be, his eyes darker than usual. "You okay?"

I manage a nod. It's the closest thing to honest I can make right now. It tastes like something I stole. But I need to say something. I need someone to believe it, even if I don't.

Across the room, Raef's blade scrapes against the floor, steady as a chisel working stone, as he shifts his stance. He's circling, measuring, adjusting, not restless so much as caged. I can feel the weight of his footsteps; my chest aches with it. He's doing everything but looking at me.

That hurts more. Like I've done something wrong by bleeding. He whips my emotions around in ways that don't make sense.

Tris leans closer, voice a soft murmur. "Someone let her in. She didn't slip in here without their knowledge. They altered the wards. They were testing her and us."

"I know," Raef says, finally—without letting me see his face.

I wait for more. An order. A plan. Anything. But he keeps walking the edge of the room like the perimeter might collapse if he stops moving.

"I don't know what she took," I say. "But it felt like she pried up the floorboards in my skull and left something loose and empty."

Now he turns. His eyes flick over the lineup: me looking like I lost a bar fight, Javi doing his best human shield impression, and Tris practically breathing my air. Raef's jaw locks hard, like the whole tableau personally offends him.

"Enough."

Just that. Neat and final, like a gavel dropping on my skull.

Tris lifts a brow, unapologetic. "Didn't realize you were watching."

Raef doesn't rise to the bait.

I don't feel like trying to talk to him anymore. My heart still thunders in my chest. My head throbs. They all look at me, but no one else asks if I'm okay. Because we all know I'm not. This place isn't neutral ground. It's not safe. The quiet starts to itch. Too many eyes, too much heat. I can feel the pressure building behind my ribs again, and this time it's not a seer clawing through my head—it's *everything*. The blood, the look Raef hadn't given me, the one he had, and so much more swirling inside.

"I need air," I snap, already rising.

Javi shoots to his feet so fast it startles me more than the question. His eyes are wide, already searching for something to fix. "Do you want me to—"

"No," I say sharply and immediately regret my tone. "I just...need a minute."

A faint line settles between his dark brows before he inclines his head.

I step out through the arched doorway, down the curling path grown from bark and woven vine. The hallway teeming with the life of the tree around it—moss glowing faintly, branches twisting overhead. Everything here is alive. And I don't know where I begin and the magic ends anymore.

I don't get far. Boots scrape behind me. I know the steps well.

Raef.

He doesn't say anything right away. He watches me. I can feel his eyes on my back. When I look back at him, for a second, his mask slips, hurt bleeding through before he slams the door on it again.

"I'm fine," I say, crossing my arms over my chest to hide some of the vulnerability I'm feeling. "You don't have to check."

"That's not why I came."

"No?" Heat climbs up my throat before I can stop it. "Then why not go back in there and keep pretending you don't care?"

A muscle ticks near his temple. "You think I don't?"

"You won't even look at me."

"I *always* look at you," he says, his voice a low rasp. "Even when I shouldn't."

Something in my chest skips, then stumbles. I'm...I have nothing to say to that.

He takes one step closer, then another, until the space between us feels taut, a thread pulled so tight it's about to snap. My feet are frozen to the path, but my pulse hammers against my ribs like it's trying to escape.

"You let them touch you." His eyes flick to where Javi's hand had been on mine, then back to me, dark and unyielding. "You let them close."

"They're my friends," I snap. "They're not just yours to order and use."

"And I use you, is that it?" He doesn't mean to say it. I can tell by the way his mouth presses shut right after. But it's already out.

I fold my arms tighter across my chest, this time in defiance, chin lifting high. "No. You put a ring on my finger and promised me to your father."

Silence. Thicker than the trees.

"I'm trying to protect you."

Part of me knows he means it—and part of me hates him for the way he did it. Because I didn't ask for protection like that. I didn't ask for any of this. And I'm so tired of everyone deciding what's best for me without letting me decide anything at all.

His voice drops. "I felt it when she touched your mind. I felt it, Rory. Like someone cracked open the earth beneath me."

I meet his gaze finally, and the sharp edge of it is gone. All that remains is fear.

Not for himself. For me. And that undoes me more than anything else could. Maybe that should've softened me. Maybe once, it would have. But not now.

"Do you know how many times you've said that to me?" I ask, my voice low and tight. "'*I'm protecting you.*' Like that makes it all okay."

His jaw ticks, but he says nothing.

I step forward, heat rising under my skin. "You say you're protecting me, but you won't talk to me. Won't trust me. Won't *look at me* unless it's to remind me what I'm not allowed to do."

"Because I'm trying to keep you alive."

"I'm trying to *live*, Raef!" My voice breaks on the word. "Everything and everyone I love are gone. Mattie is gone. And every time I think I've got a breath of air, you shove me back under the water."

He blinks and shifts back a pace, like I'd struck him. Good. Let him feel it. Let someone feel what I feel.

"You think I wanted this?" I whisper, shaking my head. "You think I asked to be a weapon or a symbol or whatever the hell they see when they look at me now?"

His tone scrapes rough across the space between us, every word heavy as steel. "No. I think you were dragged into a war none of us know how to win. And I think you scare the gods, even in their sleep, because you might be the only one who *can*."

I inhale sharply. His words are like rolling thunder—loud and low and impossible to ignore. My heart thuds in my ears as his hand twitches at his side like he doesn't know what to do with it.

It reaches out for me. Not like before. Not out of obligation or politics or any of the other stupid political reasons he always gave himself. This time his lips meet mine like he wants to.

Raef's mouth crushes mine, fierce, unsteady, and devastating. A storm held too long behind stone walls. His hand slides up the back of my neck, fingers threading through my hair with aching care, angling my face like he wants to memorize it with his lips. His other arm wraps around my waist and pulls me flush against him, and God help me, I melt like I've been waiting for this moment my whole life.

The kiss isn't soft. It's too much, too late, too everything. And I give in like I was made to break for him. I kiss him back. Because whatever this is, this jagged broken thing between us, I want it, too. God knows why.

My fingers curl in the front of his shirt. My knees nearly give out as my heart thunders against my sternum like it wants to reach for him, too. I feel it from the inside, flushed, gasping, spiraling.

When he finally pulls away—when the air rushes back in and the cold finds my skin—I sway forward like I've forgotten how to stand without him. Warm hands steady me as he presses his forehead to mine, I can't tell which one of us is breathing harder, faster.

"I didn't want to stop last time," he murmurs. "And I sure as strutting depths don't want to stop now."

My eyes flutter shut. I don't trust them to hold steady, because if I look up, he might see everything. And I'm not ready for that either.

He walks back into the glowing corridor as silent as ever.

I stand there, stunned. My lips tingle. My blood roars. Every nerve in me feels rewired, like the world tilted without asking my permission, again. I don't know if I want to punch him or pull him back, maybe both. My head's screaming that this is a mistake, that I don't need one more complication, but my body isn't listening. Every nerve is screaming for more. And yet I'm shaking. Wanting and warning tangled together so tightly I can't separate one from the other. All I can do is press my fingers to my mouth, pulse a thunderstorm behind my ribs, and whisper into the quiet—

"What the hell is wrong with me?"

Three of them.

Three of them, and every time they touch me, I crack open more.

God, when did I turn into such a slut for damaged men? I bite the inside of my cheek. The joke lands like a stone in water, with ripples and regret. But it's easier than crying.

How the fuck am I going to choose?

Why am I even thinking about choosing? I should be thinking about finding a way home and out of this godforsaken place.

33

DINNER ETIQUETTE FOR THE DOOMED

THE CORRIDOR LIGHTS SHIMMER BEHIND me, soft and green, and the taste of Raef's kiss still clings to my mouth. It shouldn't still be there. But it is. Stubborn as memory. Sharp as longing. God help me.

The tips of my fingers drift to my lips, uselessly. I don't know what I'm doing. What any of this means. But my pulse doesn't slow, and my thoughts are a chaos of silver, sea foam, and wildfire. Raef's voice. Javi's warmth. Tris smiles like he knows too much. It's like trying to hold three conversations at once in a language I barely speak.

The dining room has gone soft and hushed, but it doesn't feel empty. It feels loaded, like every chair and fork is waiting for someone to snap first.

Javi's on his feet, color high in his cheeks, jaw locked tight enough to ache looking at him. Tris sits, but only just, leaning half over the table, one hand curled around a glass that has cracked from the pressure of his grip.

Raef stands with his back to them both, like he's walked in and is already sorry he had.

"What the depths did you do?" Javi demands.

Raef keeps his lips sealed tight. His shoulders are tense, but his expression stays maddeningly neutral. Of course it does. That blank look again. The one he uses like a shield. The one I want to tear off his face and shake until something human breaks through. But he's not human, is he?

"She looks like she's been well kissed and stabbed," Tris says coolly. "Which one was it?"

"Stop." I raise my hand, palm out. No theatrics or volume. "No more, please." The air shifts, a subtle ripple I feel more than hear. Even Tris stops mid-smirk. I didn't mean for it to come out like that, but I'm done.

Three heads snap toward me. Great. Love being the center of attention. My stomach flips, but my heels stay planted. If I blink hard enough, maybe I'll look composed instead of like a deer in the headlights.

I don't know where to sit. What to do with my hands. The table is laid again—strange, elegant, and still somehow... erroneous. Flowers bloom over the bowls, curling like snakes toward the candlelight. The utensils are carved bone and silver, and the wine in the crystal cups is a deep iridescent violet, like it has been bled from dusk itself. Even the food looks dishonest. It's polished and perfect, something that belongs in a five-star restaurant. Something I picture finding in a sealed and cursed tomb and immediately regret touching.

I take the empty chair between Javi and Tris. I can't meet Raef's eyes as he slowly sits across from me.

"I need you to stop arguing," I say quietly, curling my fingers around the rim of the glass but not drinking. "Because I... I don't know what I'm doing. And I'm scared. And all of this"—I gesture between them—"it's not helping."

The words feel like blood drawn from my vein, that slow pinching pull. Exposing more than I mean to. But maybe that's what they need. Maybe it's what I need, too.

They're all silent, which is beyond disconcerting. I can feel Javi's gaze on me, soft, warm, and searching. Tris's eyes are bright and curious. And Raef?

Blank slate, as always. Except it's not anger in his eyes. Not this time. It's something deeper. Quieter. Like pity.

"I don't know what I feel," I say. "For each of you. Something's there. With *all* of you. And I don't know what to *do* with that."

Javi's the first to move, his hand finding mine, careful in that way that makes me want to laugh and cry all at once. Like I'm breakable. And maybe I am. This has to be the most awkward conversation of my life. "You don't have to do anything," he says. "Not yet. Not ever, if you don't want to."

Raef nods slowly. "I told you before—fae don't mind sharing."

I give him my best 'are you serious' glare. "Seriously, Mr Jealousy incarnate?" It's a weak jab. But I need humor like I need air.

Tris smirks around the rim of his glass, finally letting the pressure go. "Of course, some of us *prefer* it."

That earns him twin glares from Raef and Javi. But he shrugs and leans back, the cracked glass dancing between two fingers like it doesn't weigh a thing. "You're a high queen now, little star. Or will be. And we all know what that means."

I raise a brow. "Do *we*?"

He tilts his head, mouth curving, while Raef pinches the bridge of his nose. "It means you'll find bonds. Sometimes romantic, sometimes physical, sometimes loyalty only. But they run deep. They're powerful and loyal. They'll keep your power from running wild and anchor your crown when it gets too heavy. Those people? They're the council you'll lean on."

"She's not crowned yet," Raef mutters.

"Don't be tedious," Tris says. "She will be. And the bonds are already forming either way."

Javi glances down at his hand still over mine. A sad look on his face. I squeeze his hand in reassurance. His thumb brushes mine once, and my chest aches with the softness of it. With the weight of knowing I'm the one who might break something so gentle. He lifts my hand, curling my fingers over his and pressing his lips to my knuckles.

"I don't want to hurt anyone," I say, voice barely above a whisper. "But I'm already failing at that, aren't I?"

"No," Javi squeezes back. "You're trying. That's more than most."

Raef looks at me then—actually looks, not the polite prince glance he usually throws around. The unnatural calm that usually surrounds him, breaks. I see regret. Want. Something raw and unguarded because he forgot to lock the door before I saw inside. It guts me, because I didn't realize how much I needed to see him break that façade until he did.

"I kissed you," he says simply. "Because I wanted to. I think I make my stance clear. And I won't pretend otherwise. Not anymore."

Tris raises his glass. "About time, old chap."

I exhale, part laugh, part sigh, and push a piece of glowing fruit around my plate with the side of my fork. It leaves a streak of light like it's bleeding. Everything here is so dramatic, even the food.

"So this is normal, then? For a fae queen, who's human, to sit at dinner with three men she might be in love with?"

"No," says Tris, eyes gleaming. "But it makes for an excellent story."

Javi chuckles low in his chest. Raef even cracks the edge of a smile.

I groan and hold my face in my hands. My cheeks are burning. My heart is doing its best impression of a riot squad. But I'm still at this table, somehow. Still breathing. Still stuck with these three walking disasters and whatever the hell this is turning into.

Tris's warm palm rests on my shoulder. "You're not human, love, and technically we're males, as we're not human either. But the part about loving three of us and being with three of us—that's not unheard of. If that's what you want, then we'll work it out. The fates have chosen us for a reason."

There's a quiet but firm knock at the door. All three of their heads snap up at once.

Tris holds my face in his palm. "There is more to this conversation we need to discuss," he says. "Do not make any decisions before we do." His thumb strokes the line of my jaw, so gentle for someone I know is capable of incredible violence. The touch steadies me more than I want to admit, but it doesn't stop me from hearing the storm pressing at the door.

THE STRANGE FIRE in the hearth crackles, throwing shifting shadows across the polished bark walls. We linger after dinner. Not quite at ease and too unsettled to retreat. The air tastes like tension, aged and perfumed, like old wine left too long in the glass.

The room has grown crowded. Greenwood nobles filter in with the quiet tread of cats, dressed in threadleaf silks with accents that look like carved jade. Even I notice the specific locations of these decorations, covering important body parts. Like armor for a ball rather than a battlefield. They glitter like ivy, these beautiful and barbed fae. Their eyes are curious, but their smiles are the kind that belong on masks, plastered and fake.

A slender fae female in bark-laced robes lifts her goblet with a slight incline of her head. "Your pardon, my lady," she says to me. "For what transpired earlier. We are...unaccustomed to such breaches."

Her words slide smooth as honey, but her hands tell on her—grip too tight, knuckles pale. And she won't meet my eyes, like one glance might singe her eyebrows off.

The one with moss stitched into his collar nods, all dignified. "The seers shouldn't have had access. There will be inquiries." Sure. Inquiries. Not consequences. It's the wording politicians love because it doesn't mean shit.

Raef stands beside the long table, posture easy but watchful. "There always are," he says coolly. His voice is all silk and chill. He might as well have said, 'And they never matter.'

A thin male with ivy stitched into his sleeves tips a decanter, filling his goblet with wine so purple it looks toxic. He swirls it like it's fine vintage instead of nightmare fuel. "A toast," he says. "To the guests who survived our terrible hospitality."

A few chuckle, but it doesn't reach their eyes. I feel it more than hear it, that ripple of tension behind the laughter. It's not funny-ha-ha, but more funny-as-in-I-might-get-stabbed. Nothing like dinner and death threats to round out the evening.

Tris has taken up residence near the hearth, one leg draped over the arm of a moss-covered chair, his long, silver hair a loose, gleaming mess. He looks the picture of fae arrogance, serene, smirking, and untouchable. But I see the tightness in his jaw. The way he watches every move with his hands loose, but his posture locked, every muscle saying he's ready to move in a moments notice.

Javi sits next to me, his hand resting close enough to mine to feel the warmth without touching. That almost-touch tells my skittering pulse to calm, my shoulders to climb back out of my ears. I don't want to be alone in this room.

"Despite the…mishap…we're honored you've granted us rest here," Raef says after a moment. "It won't be for long."

"You carry heavy rumors," says an older male noble, his hair bound back in a braid streaked silver. His eyes flicking to me as he leans on his goblet. I don't think silver streaks in hair have anything to do with age here because the rest of him looks so young. "They travel faster than any steed." It crawls under my skin because it's not curiosity or admiration. He's trying to peel me apart piece by piece. Or size me up for the market.

"Then they're already out of date," Raef replies smoothly.

A faint ripple of laughter. A few more sips of wine. The game continues. And I recognize it as a game now. One I'm expected to play but don't know any of the rules or cards in my hand.

Across the table, a narrow-faced male with hawk-bright eyes doesn't bother to take a seat like the others. He lingers standing, weight tipped forward on his toes, glass dangling carelessly in one hand. "Tell me, silver one, what corner of the old courts do you crawl from?" His stare homes in on Tris, hungry, like he almost recognizes the shape of his face. "There's something…familiar about you."

Tris blinks slowly. "You flatter me."

This hawk-eyed male is relentless; the stem of his wineglass is balanced between two fingers, keeping the rim below his mouth like he might drink or bare his teeth, undecided. His gaze doesn't waver, pinning Tris as if the rest of us have vanished. "I know that face," he says, low and certain. "I *do*."

Someone else whispers, "Prince of the Ash Gates."

The name strikes like a sparking flint. The entire room stiffens. A woman, female, with vine work braided through her long hair—lets her goblet slip from nerveless fingers. It shatters on the stone.

"Sanguine filth," she says.

Shards glitter across the floor, no one moving to touch them. From the far end of the table, a voice curls through the quiet, hushed but cutting enough to slice skin. "The Blood Prince."

The room goes dead quiet. Even the fire looks uneasy, flames curling low, hunching under the weight of it all. My pulse stutters hard as my body braces for whatever comes next.

I feel my heartbeat in my teeth. I'm not made for politics. How the hell am I supposed to become a queen? My stomach turns. *Fuck my life.*

Tris doesn't move, not a blink, nor a breathe. But the lazy amusement does fade. What looked like boredom turns into something else. Ancient and cold, a side of him I've never seen before, and it's outright terrifying. The rest of the room may see a prince. Me? I know better. Princes don't look at a room like it's the Thanksgiving turkey that they're drooling to carve up.

"Didn't think I still had a court," he says, voice even, deceptively calm. "How quaint."

My tongue sticks to the roof of my mouth, every word I don't say disintegrating to dust there. II look to Raef, but he remains quiet, choosing to let Tris handle it apparently. But he watches them carefully. Letting this happen. Letting them see. There's a reason for it. I know there is. But it doesn't make it any easier. It doesn't make it make sense.

One of the nobles who had smiled at me earlier—a younger male with a scar across one cheek—backs away a step, eyes darting between Tris and me. "What are you bringing through our borders?" he asks. "What have you *bound* yourself to?"

Raef's jaw twitches. Still, he says nothing. A storm brews behind his eyes, but he holds it. I admire him for it, for the control that I will never have time in my mortal life to hone for myself. *Damn it! I can't believe I'm jealous of him of all people.*

It's Tris who moves first, rising with the slow elegance of falling silk. He doesn't bare his sharp fangs or lift a blade, but the room still jerks like someone dropped a torch into dry grass. Had I not seen him fight off a pack of frenzied, I wouldn't understand. But I did see. He's dangerous, but only if you deserve it.

He looks at the nobles like one might regard insects on a chessboard. "I left," he says, "before the crown could ruin me. Before it could hollow me out like it did my siblings."

When he looks at me, it's different. That tell-tale smirk is gone along with his usual game. His eyes feel too old and raw for Tris. Like he's letting me see something I'm not supposed to. I can't look away.

"I didn't think my name still meant anything," he says, nonchalantly. "But if it does—we'll use it."

Raef pushes to his feet, every move considered, like he's counting steps. His eyes never leave me as he circles the table, closing the space one heavy stride at a time.

The room goes still in that awful way that says all eyes are on you. I suddenly forget how to sit like a normal person and not a busted mannequin at a yard sale. I forget how to be anything but the girl who doesn't belong.

He stops in front of me, his face says nothing. Then, with the same deliberate grace he uses for every court ritual, he lowers himself, slowly, and kisses me. A soft press of his lips to mine. No heat. No apology. Just pressure and silence and something I don't know how to name. And I'm not sure I like it.

When he leans off to the side as he leaves, he pauses at my ear. "Let them wonder."

I'm positive every fae in the room did, including me.

34

How to Fail at Sparring, Drinking, and Feelings All Before Sunset

THE PATH OUT OF GREENWOOD snakes behind us, more like a bad scar than a trail. The light's fading, and so is whatever passed for a welcome there. My shoulders ache like someone's still watching, but maybe that's my brain replaying their stares on a loop.

The trees still crowd overhead, their bark streaked with lingering traces of green light, but it's fading now. It figures the welcome was never there. More like a stage dressing with fake smiles, careful words, and the politeness that cuts deep enough to leave bruises no one admits to.

I fall in behind Raef this time, not beside him. I'm not sure if it's for show or for silence. Either way, I let the distance grow. He doesn't look back. Doesn't ask. Maybe he knows I wouldn't have answered if he did.

Javi flanks me on the right, his shoulder brushing mine enough to remind me he's there. Tris whistles something aimless as he trails at the back, but even his steps feel more careful now. His eyes keep flicking toward the trees like he's waiting for it to bite. But his whistle has no real melody. Just sound to fill the silence.

None of us have anything to say. Not about the kiss. Not about the nobles' faces—hollow with fear when they recognized the Prince of the Ash Gates. *Two princes now? What crazy secret is Javi hiding from me?*

We're also not speaking about the way Raef sealed our political fate with a kiss before walking off like it meant nothing at all. My cheeks still sting from the memory of it. Not the kiss itself. The hollow silence after. The room was watching my every move. Judging. The way his mouth brushed mine like I was a line in a speech. A maneuver. A move on a chessboard.

That man...male... runs hot and cold so fast I'm getting whiplash. But , worse than that, I still want to chase the heat.

The trees start to give way, gaps opening overhead where pale light slips through, the sun cutting through the canopy in pale, fragile beams. A breeze sneaks in too, cool against my face, shocking me into pulling the cool air into my lungs, my first real breath since that dinner started. A small freedom. I could cry from the simplicity of it. It's light and air, so simple, but after Greenwood it feels like shaking off a weight that was dragging me down. I'm done feeling like the world is caving in on me. I keep saying that to myself because eventually it will stick and come true.

I glance sideways at Javi, and he's already watching me. I knew he would be. Steady, patient, like he's made a habit of catching me before I trip.

"You okay?" he asks softly.

No. "I will be," I say. At least I think that's what comes out. If I say it out loud, maybe that will make it true. Maybe I become real.

He nods and doesn't press. He never does because I think he can see right through me no matter what I say. His fingers twitch slightly, like he wants to reach for me and isn't sure if now is the right time.

Behind us, Greenwood slips back into the trees, watching, waiting, and far too quiet. It feels less like we left and more like it's biding its time.

RAEF TOSSES THE practice blade at me without warning. It spins through the air like he doesn't care if I catch it or get clocked in the face.

I catch it...barely. My fingers ache from cold, from the nerves, and from the sting of still-healing wounds. Everything hurts today. And I'm tired of pretending I'm not falling apart inside.

"This isn't for your ego," he says flatly. "It's for your survival."

Same old Raef, and here I thought we'd reached a turning point. I guess not. He makes it look like the kiss meant nothing. Maybe it did. Maybe it didn't. Either way, I can't stop spinning it over like it's some puzzle I'm supposed to solve. Which doesn't help when I'm supposed to be focusing on sword skill and not getting tossed on my ass.

The glade we stopped in was nothing like the quiet paths we've left. The earth here is dry and beaten. Stones ring the edge like ancient teeth. This doesn't feel like a nice little camp clearing. It's a place for violence. Or maybe I feel like violence. Maybe I want to hit something until the ache in my chest goes quiet.

Raef circles me once, then twice. His eyes missing nothing. I can feel him reading me, judging me. Looking for weakness like he always does.

I shift my stance.

He shakes his head. "Wider. You'll tip."

I move.

"Again."

Heat flares in my chest. "You know, you could say something helpful...even encouraging."

"I did. You just didn't listen."

Of course. Because god forbid he give me more than a scrap of kindness.

He comes at me. Fast.

Our blades clang—a sound that's started echoing in my bones. I barely manage to parry. My grip slips. My wrist twists. I stumble back.

"Better," he mutters. "Still sloppy."

"I'm not a warrior. I'm a scientist."

"No," he says, sword already swinging again, "you're something far more dangerous and far less disciplined." He spits it out less like a compliment and more like a warning label. Like I'm a problem he's stuck with, not a fighter he's training.

I duck. Swing. Miss. The edge of his blade kisses my ribs with warning. The pain sets off something new, magic twitching beneath my skin, buzzing in my hands like it's itching for a fight. It won't shut up. Won't sit still. Always pressing, like a second pulse I didn't ask for or want.

He sees it. "Don't."

"I'm not doing anything."

"Yes. You are." His voice is harsh, like I chose to lose control to spite him.

I fling the next blow harder than I mean to, losing control exactly as he's accusing me of. He blocks it easily, but I feel the vibration travel up my arms like lightning. My legs burn. My vision swims.

Wild, messy magic jolts out of my hands before I can even think about it. The air shudders, and wind tears through the clearing like it's been waiting for me to break it loose. Raef's blade is wrenched sideways as the burst hits him, not enough to injure, but enough to knock him back a step. Enough to draw a curse from his lips.

He rounds on me. "Magic isn't a weapon if you don't know how to control it," he snaps. "It's a liability."

My chest is tighter than ever, eyes burning as my hands won't stay steady. I feel like I'm unraveling, and he's calling it weakness. I've had everything thrown at me all at once over and over and over again, and he expects me to lie there and take it without complaint.

"I *was* trying to control it—"

"Try harder."

His words are worse than his hits. They hit something raw and burning, already split open. Something that is already breaking.

I throw down the practice sword. "Maybe if you stopped treating me like I'm already doomed," I say, "I'd stop acting like it." My voice shakes. I hate that it shakes.

I'm done. I walk off the field before I do something stupid, like cry in front of him.

I'd rather bleed.

THE GLADE GIVES way to scrub, then roots, then a half-collapsed log I drop onto with a graceless thud. It creaks beneath me like it might give out, which honestly feels about right. My fingers still tingle, my jaw's locked tight, and the practice sword has left a raw welt along my palm.

Magic isn't a liability.

I am.

I am the fracture in the blade. The spark that goes off in an illegal place. The problem everyone wishes they hadn't picked up.

The air smells like crushed moss and damp leaves. The wind whispers through the trees like it wants to say something but doesn't know how. Or maybe there's nothing there, and it's just me, trying too hard to make sense of the noise in my own head.

"Fancy seeing you here," Tris says, not startling me at all, which is surprising. It's like I already knew he was there, a tug in my chest cluing me in to his presence. He always shows up when I least want company. Or rather, when I need it most, I'm the one getting in the way of the things that will actually help me.

He holds a bottle by the neck, pale glass bathed in the gold-pink of the dying sun. His silver hair is loose tonight, falling around his shoulders in a way that looks annoyingly perfect. I didn't know I had a long hair fetish, but here it is. I find myself daydreaming about running my fingers through it.

I stare at the bottle. Because it's easier than looking at him. It's easier than admitting I'm one mistaken word away from cracking open. I realize that, right now, I'm barely holding it together, but I'm too proud to lean on the three people that are trying so hard to keep me together, both literally and figuratively.

He plops down beside me without waiting for an invitation. "The hedge witch gave me this. Said it was for 'moments of temper and truth.' You seem to be having both."

"I'm not drinking," I mutter.

"You're not?" he asks, uncorking it anyway.

I sigh. It comes out more like a slow exhale of everything I've been trying not to feel.

He pours two fingers' worth into a wooden cup and hands it over, keeping the heavier pour for himself.

Neither of us bothers talking at first, and I'm perfectly okay with that. The first sip hits warm and sweet, sweet enough to go down easy but with a burn that lingers at the back of my throat. It reminds me of a good scotch.

"You're your own worst enemy, little star. Always have been," Tris says at last.

"Raef is harder."

"Well, he's always been a blade with legs. But that doesn't mean he's wrong. He's worried. We all are. Why do you think he's taking so long to reach the Shadow Court? We should have been there a week ago."

A week ago, I hadn't kissed him. A week ago, he hadn't kissed me back like it would end the world.

I set the cup down. My fingers twitching toward it again before I can make them stop.

Tris tilts his head, studying me. Not with pity in his eyes, which would have been easier. I can see he understands. I don't want to be understood. Not right now. Not when I feel so jagged inside.

"I know what it feels like," he says. "When it bubbles up. When it burns. When it answers you before you're ready. Most of us, who still have some innate power, struggle with that in the beginning, when they manifest. Don't be too hard on yourself. It's partially controlled by emotions. Learn to regulate your emotions, and it will become easier."

I let the silence do the talking. If I open my mouth, the truth comes out, and I'm a coward. The truth is ugly. It's starting to feel like it owns me.

He rolls the cup in his hand, liquid shifting with the motion, though his eyes never shift from me. "I've seen what you can be, little star. When you're not stuck in your head. That scares me."

He keeps staring, so I stare back like it doesn't bother me. "Me too."

The corner of his mouth lifts, not his usual Cheshire grin, but something smaller and more intimate. "Good. It should. Power that doesn't scare you is the kind that gets everyone else killed."

I press my knuckles into my knees. "Do you think I'm dangerous?"

"I think you're becoming dangerous. There's a difference."

A long silence stretches. One I don't know how to fill but feel like it needs filling. The wind stirs again, catching my hair.

"Why are you training me?" I ask. "Truly?"

He leans in slightly, his shoulder pressing closer to mine, voice low. "Because if you're going to burn, I'd rather you knew how to aim the fire."

We're so close now, and still, I can actually take in his face, my eyes catching on the faint scar near his jaw, half-hidden by the light stubble growing there. At the way his posture never fully relaxes, even now. At the truth he doesn't clearly say. That he's scared *for* me, not *of* me.

"Thank you," I say, my voice as small as I feel right now.

He taps his cup to mine. "Drink, little star. Tomorrow, we might be bleeding again."

He might be right. He probably is right.

I drink anyway. It's a bad idea, sure, but at least it shuts me up for a second. The warmth slides down like a promise I didn't mean to make.

Tris watches me for a long moment. The humor in his eyes fading, that dreamy, distracted glint giving way to something far more serious. Too serious. He's about to put something heavy in my hands and dare me not to drop it.

"Now for the truth part. You're falling for him," he states.

I fix him with a look like he's lost his mind. "What?"

"Raef," he says. "And Javi. Maybe even me, though that one's a slow burn." His grin flashes quick, because he knows exactly how much trouble he's stirring. "But it matters which one you choose."

I want to laugh, but the sound won't come. I want to tell him he's full of it. But the problem is, he's not. Not all the way.

"Why are we talking about this again?"

"Because *you* need to know the rules of the game you're playing." Gone is the playful lilt. This is Tris when he's done joking. "Fae bonds aren't metaphors. They're magic. If you cross a certain threshold—say you rut with Raef while that ring is still under your skin—your bond becomes sealed. Final. The ring roots. The magic anchors. There's no untangling the threads without a steep price."

My heart trips over itself. That's probably what he wants. He says it so simply. The implication dripping off his words that I should've known all along.

I shove myself upright faster than I should, and the rush to my head makes the trees lurch sideways.

"And Javi?" I ask, biting the inside of my cheek. "Is it just Raef?"

Tris leans back on his elbows, eyes narrowing a touch. "There's no thread between you. Not like the one pulling at Raef and me. Not yet. Javi loves the human way—slow, sweet, stupid. Beautiful. He won't bind you unless you bind him back."

Something inside me sours. Because I believe him, every single word. That truth feels worse than any lie he could have told me, any sugar coating of what he thinks I should know.

My insides pitch like they're staging a revolt, the one my brain wants, and all I can get out is, "You're out of line."

"I'm trying to keep you from making a choice out of lust and lack of education that you can't undo." He doesn't rise, but his voice follows me like this tether he keeps talking about. "I told you once—power without direction is chaos. You think love is softer? You think that won't burn?"

"I'm not choosing any of you," I snap. "Not yet." *Not ever*, part of me wants to say. But that would be another lie, and even the thought brings a bitter taste to my mouth.

For once he doesn't look amused or dangerous, just raw, and it unsettles me. "You already are."

His words, his confession, sting, not because they're sharp and swung around like a weapon, but because they're right. They brush up against the part of me I'm pretending isn't there, the part that can't stop wanting, reaching, tangling itself into a mess I can't comprehend.

I whirl on my heel and storm back to camp—fists clenched, throat tight, the trees blurring at the edges.

The sunset's bleeding through the canopy now, and it feels like the whole forest is up in flames, watching me break and burn.

I don't know if I'm running from Tris or from myself. If I'm running away at all.

35

PUNCHING PRINCES AND OTHER BAD IDEAS

I MARCH INTO CAMP LIKE a storm on legs—barely thinking, just burning. Tris trails behind me, saying nothing now, thank the stars. The trees feel too close. The firelight too bright. Everything stings.

Raef looks up from where he crouches near the fire, one knee bent, blade halfway through a sharpening stroke. He doesn't have time to speak or react to the storm written all over my face.

I haul back and *punch* him. Knuckles to jaw. A sickening crack of bone against bone. The impact shudders up my arm, and pain blooms hot in my hand. It's not satisfying. It hurts.

"Damn it—*shit!*" I hiss, clutching my fingers as they throb. My whole hand screams. "God, I think I broke something—"

Raef staggers back, his hand pressed to his cheek, blinking like I'd clocked him with a baseball bat instead of bare knuckles.

Javi shoots to his feet. Tris doesn't move—just leans against a tree, arms crossed, watching like he'd seen this coming hours ago.

"You kissed me," I spit, still cradling my hand, "in that hallway. In front of everyone. You didn't want to *warn me*. Share the little tidbit about what would happen if we went further. If we gave in to that heat?" My voice is strained, jagged with all the betrayal. My skin still feels branded from his touch, and more so now, knowing how close I came without realizing the stakes.

Raef's gaze locks on Tris and then mine. "Why do you think I stopped and walked away?"

I stop dead, jaw slack. The fire spits beside us, the only one willing to make a sound.

"I stopped us before—" he finally says. "Because I didn't want to take your choice. But in that hallway—after everything—there wasn't time. And I wanted to. *Gods, Rory,* I wanted to." The raw edge in his voice slices through the heat in my chest.

"You should've told me what could happen," I say, every nerve raw.

"I know."

There's a hitch in his voice, quick and rough, and it hits me harder than anything he's said so far.

"I never wanted to bind you out of duty, or desperation, or the weight of politics." His gaze drops to the fire. "But I did want you to agree and quickly, so I framed it in a way to convince you. I knew if I kissed you again, it might tip the scales. I was selfish. I couldn't help it." The firelight dances across his face, but his eyes bore into me, pleading.

Behind me, Tris gives a quiet snort. "Fae instincts are like gravity. But this? This is what makes us dangerous." His tone is dry, but I hear the warning buried beneath it. The reminder that magic always has teeth.

I keep my eyes fixed on the fire, refusing to give any of them the satisfaction of a glance. I cradle my hand against my chest, the split skin over my knuckles throbbing in time with all the guilt and doubt floating through my mind.

Meanwhile, I wonder when exactly I'd become the girl who has three males in her head—and not a single answer in her heart. I used to be so sure of myself. Now I'm a storm pretending to be a girl, and I think I'm starting to believe my own lie.

I SIT ON the edge of the camp, far enough from the fire that its warmth doesn't touch me. The cold settles in, but it's better than the heat. The heat reminds me I'm still angry. Still ashamed.

I'm mad enough to cry but too stubborn to do it where anyone can see. Especially not Raef. Not now. I'll deal with the pressure cooker under my ribs.

Footsteps crunch softly over leaf litter, too careful to be Raef but also too steady to be anything hunting us.

I keep my eyes on the dirt at my feet. "If you're here to tell me I overreacted—don't."

"I'm not," Javi says. His voice alone a valve for the storm that rages in my chest.

He crouches beside me, careful not to touch me until I nod. Considering how they talk, what I've experienced, Javi's understanding of consent is shocking and lovely.

His fingers brush my wrist. Featherlight. "May I?"

I give him my hand, jaw clenched. The ache in my knuckles is nothing compared to the one lodged in my sternum. But it gives me something else to focus on.

His thumb skims over my knuckles. "You're lucky it's not broken."

"Feels like it is."

I need the flicker of warmth in his face, subtle but calming. "At least I can do something about little things like this." He places his other hand lightly over mine. His magic isn't flashy. It's not bright or loud. It seeps into me like sunlight filtered through leaves, a gentle, quiet, and kind breeze. A quiet heat pulses from his skin, steady and golden-green.

"There," he murmurs. "Good as new."

My fingers linger against his. "Thank you."

"For the hand?"

"For not asking questions I can't answer yet."

Javi's smile tugs higher. "Then I won't tell you I've already picked a side."

I fix on his face, waiting for him to take it back. "What?"

He leans closer, voice low and incredibly sexy. "Yours."

When he says it, it hooks under my skin, claiming space inside me I never meant to give.

A rustle cuts through the quiet, then another, closer. Instinct drags me to my feet alongside Javi. The night has twisted hollow, stripped of every birdcall and hum of insects.

Javi reaches for his blade. I feel them, something scraping along my spine.

"Frenzied."

They come out of the trees like shadows torn from the bark, moving with a speed that feels immoral and in numbers that turn my stomach. Their eyes catch the light, black and wet like obsidian, and their limbs bend in ways no body should. The stench reaches me first, thick with rot and undercut by the metallic bite of blood.

Javi is already moving, stepping in front of me with blade drawn, eyes scanning for the weakest point in the swarm. His stance looks steady, but I catch the tight pull in his shoulders that says otherwise.

I get my sword free, but it's messy and shaky, nothing that looks like the control of my companions. But I do it. It scrapes free with a whisper. My fingers protest, my legs shake, but my grip stays locked tight.

Behind me, Tris lets a curse slip. A raw anger that rattles the edges of his magic. Silver flashes as he sends a burst of some concussive force into the trees, hurling back the first wave of Frenzied like dolls dropped by a careless god. The trees groan, splinters flying. One Frenzied with too-long arms and a jaw unhinged on one side, slams spine-first into a trunk. The crack that follows is wet, splintered, and unmistakably bone.

Raef comes from the dark like a blade loosed from hell. His knives find flesh before I can blink. The Frenzied he cuts down lets out a scream that curdles the air, then collapses at my feet in a heap of claws and blood.

He doesn't waste air on words or lack of movement. He's a storm in motion, every strike clean and merciless, like the act of killing is built into him. In this moment, I understand why they fear him.

We move in orbit, separate stars pulled by the same gravity.

Raef's hand finds my shoulder long enough to shove me right. I duck, and his knife misses my ear by inches—striking something behind me. The creature shrieks. Something hot and wet splashes my ankle. I don't need to look to know it's blood, a lot of it. I'm also not giving myself the image to go with the smell.

"Left flank," he snaps. "You cover Tris."

It isn't a suggestion, and we both know it. I move as instructed, because dying here would be stupider than listening to him.

I pivot, heart hammering, and meet a Frenzied face-to-face. This one has wilder eyes and abnormally long teeth. There's no time to think.

I swing, the jolt of contact rattling up my arms as steel bites through bone with a crunch I'll be hearing in my nightmares. The Frenzied crumples before I can even catch my breath.

Another lunges, and my blade comes up a heartbeat too late. I can already feel how bad that timing is.

But Javi is there. A quick slash. A softer voice, "Watch your right, love."

I can't speak, so I nod. My throat's too tight. My mind too full, considering it the perfect time to realize how much I'm not cut out for this. I swing again.

Tris holds the center, face alight with malice. He spins magic like silk, weaving shields and bursts of energy with flicks of his fingers—artful, deadly. His feet don't move, but the battlefield bends around him. Like the magic listens before anyone else does. He's magnificent.

A scream shatters the rhythm as a Frenzied lunges too close, teeth gnashing and claws tearing through the air. It rakes across Raef's arm, and he hisses but never falters. Blood spills down to his fingertips, and he shifts the blade into his other hand, fighting on like pain is another opponent to cut through.

The fight builds around me, louder, faster, until it feels like I'm swinging to keep my head above water.

I don't know how long we last—seconds? Hours? How does one keep time while murdering their enemies? My muscles burn. My lungs drag fire. But I don't stop. I can't stop. Not while they still need me. Not while I still have breath.

The air tightens, prickling over my skin, and I know before I even swing that my magic is moving whether I want it to or not.

I don't mean to use it, but the moment my blade knocks one back, a shield blooms—silver and blue—from my hand. It catches the next strike, then shatters like glass. My own gasp breaks it. The impact rattles through my teeth. It's like being caught inside a bell's toll.

"Do it again!" Tris shouts.

But I'm already doing something else. I swing. Parry. Move between them, because this isn't just survival.

It's a mess, but it's our mess. Raef bleeding, Tris wild, and Javi steady. Then there's me, in the center of it all. I'm not waiting anymore. I'm not hiding. I'm here. I'm fighting.

The last of the Frenzied barrels out of the dark, all teeth and speed, like it can't wait to make me dinner.

Javi's blade is too far. Tris's spell hits wide. Raef reaches, but far too late.

Looks like it's my turn. No time for thinking, no chance to calculate. My body's already moving.

Steel rings against bone once more. Light bursts from my hands, not clean or controlled but violent, like it's clawing its way out through muscle and bone. It sears along my tendons, hot and electric, every nerve lit up as if my own body is the conduit and the punishment at once. My grip shakes on the hilt, but the blade keeps moving, driven by the current ripping through me. It's not strength. It's not skill. It's raw power forcing its way through my skin, and I can't tell if I'm wielding it or if it's wielding me.

The creature doesn't fall; it disintegrates mid-lunge—dust and sparks collapsing before either touches the ground. Ash hits the earth in a slow, spiraling fall. My blade hums in my hands. My whole body trembles.

The noise dies all at once, leaving only the echo of blades still rattling my bones while the clearing pretends to be peaceful and quiet.

I double over, dragging air into my lungs that won't seem to fill, my shoulders caving under the weight of it. The sword hangs heavy in my grip, lowered, while faint blue-silver light still curls stubbornly at my fingertips. I wait, half expecting someone else to break the silence, but no one does. The pause stretches until Raef steps forward, blood running down his arm, sweat darkening the line of his jaw, his eyes still cutting like blades.

He gives the smallest nod, a clipped motion that feels far more intense than warranted. A single motion that carries more weight than a speech ever could.

"Impressive."

That word shouldn't mean anything, but it means everything. It's only a nod and a simple, single word, but it hits right in the center of me, marking me, branding me.

I'm crying, and it's not the quiet, dignified kind. This is the shaking, ugly, and unstoppable kind. It's not about fear, not even the pain. It's every weight I've been dragging since the ship, the seer, and Atlantis, all finally snapping loose.

Tris gives a low, amused hum from where he leans against a rock, brushing blood off his knuckles. "Told you. She's fire."

In time, the other courts grew hungry.

They learned to drag mortals through the hidden paths between,

selling stolen days like coin,

weighing human lives against favors and power.

The Queen of Souls watched chains laid upon those

who had no names in their ledgers,

and the sea inside her began to rise.

-Book of the Atma, The First Age

36

A Beginners Manual to Mortification

THE RING WAKES ME BEFORE the sun even tries, throbbing in time with a heartbeat that isn't mine. A steady rhythm thuh-thumping on my finger. *Nothing creepy about that.*

I curl my fingers tightly, but the sensation doesn't fade. It thrums once more, steady and insistent, pulling on a string that sits barely under my skin. It's not painful, exactly, but more like a pressure that has a purpose. I don't know what that purpose is, but eventually I'm going to find someone who can tell me before I lose it completely.

I sit up slowly, careful not to wake the others. Javi lies close, one arm tucked under his head, the other resting loose against his chest. His breath is slow and constant, lifting his shirt enough to catch the faint rise and fall of muscle underneath. In sleep, the lines of his face are soft, his mouth curved the slightest bit like he's holding onto some private dream, a happy one. It's

251

unfair, the way he looks both strong and impossibly gentle at the same time. I have to tear my eyes away before I start inventing excuses to stay staring or curl up closer.

On my other side, Tris is sprawled across the moss in that careless way of his, silver hair fanned over his shoulder, lips parted around a soft snore. For once, he looks almost human, calm. The sight tugs at the corner of my mouth, nearly a smile. But the ring pulses again, hard enough to cut the moment short. No peace for me.

Across the fire pit, Raef watches me. He isn't hiding behind the usual mask this morning, his face, bare and worn, has shadows carved deep under his eyes from a night without sleep. His elbows rest on his knees, posture held like he's bracing against something I can't see. The firelight cuts across his cheekbones, throwing him into sharp places and shadow, more statue than male, but still too alive to mistake for stone.

I lift my hand slightly, the ring catching the gray light. It gleams like it's waiting.

"I didn't do anything to piss it off," I whisper. "If it's acting up, that's all on the ring."

Raef stays where he is, doing what he was already doing in a stillness that feels intentional, like he's waiting me out. The dagger rests across his lap, metal catching the firelight in a way that shows it's been cleaned but not too long ago. Blood rims the edges of his nails, dark and crusted, and I can't quite decide if I want the answer as to whose it is.

"It shouldn't do this," I add. "Should it?"

His gaze drops, not to the ring but to the skin beneath it, lingering like the metal isn't the problem at all. His jaw works, tight, like he's forcing something sour down his throat.

"I said it would bind *us*," he murmurs. His tone's got that loaded quality I'm supposed to decipher, but of course he doesn't explain it. "But that binding isn't passive. It responds."

"To what?"

"To danger," he says. "To distance. To doubt."

That flares hot under my skin, spreading until there's nowhere left to hide from them. I feel those three words more than I hear them. They echo in the hollow of my ribs, as if the ring's throb has synced with my pulse and found me lacking.

I rub at the ring with my thumb. "It doesn't feel like it's protecting me. It feels like it's watching me."

His reply is thin and restrained. "It is. In a manner of speaking."

The mist drifts in thick, curling around camp like it owns the place. The trees lean in too close, the branches crowding, slowly stealing all light and peace. Even the birds know better than to sing today. The whole forest feels like it's waiting for bad news. It's suffocating.

I fidget with what's left of the band like it might cough up answers. "So, what happens if the ring decides the bond isn't real?"

He finally looks at me fully. Startled by my question. He's not a prince now or a guard; he's Raef, caught holding a truth he clearly hates.

"Then it breaks," he says. "And so does the protection it offers you. The magic snaps back."

"Snaps back how?" I ask. That doesn't sound good or pleasant at all. Much less survivable. My stomach churns while my brain tries to fill in the blanks. Burned out from the inside? Exploded like a faulty battery? Some charming new way to die slow and loud? Of course, Raef leaves it vague, like vague is the way to comfort me, his own version of toxic protection by leaving the poor little mortal girl in the dark.

Raef flexes his jaw. "You'll feel it. The rest of the world might too."

I press a hand to my middle, like that'll stop the twisting inside me. "What happens to *you*?"

He waits, staring into the embers, hoping they'll speak something softer than what he's about to say. The fire is low, barely more than a whisper of heat. The glow clings to his light eyes, making promises with a single look while saying nothing and daring me to fill in the rest.

"I'm not the one the courts will come for," he says at last.

Suddenly this ring doesn't feel like a gift, or a shield, or even a curse. It feels like a timer. A fuse already burning, and I don't know how close we are to the end.

I TELL MYSELF I come for fever root. It's straightforward and something I can hold in my hands. It grows near water, and I need the quiet of the stream song more than I need the plant. My legs move without asking. My mind scrapes against the edges of everything I don't want to feel. My fingers tremble hours after the ring's pulse has gone quiet, like my body hasn't gotten the memo. Too much of me is on display, all the time, with nothing left to hide behind. When is all of this going to prove too much for my poor mind? When does the moment come when I finally break? Will anyone notice when I do? When am I going to cross that threshold, because I must be pretty damn close by now?

The world narrows to the smell of wet bark and moss, damp and rich, clinging to the back of my throat. Ahead, steam rises off the stream in pale ribbons, twisting through the branches like the water's reaching out to caress my weary skin. Edges blurred like the world is giving me permission to slow down, if only for a second. And stars help me; I almost do.

I meander along a bend in the trail and find him.

Javi sits on the edge of the shore, boots kicked aside, shirt tossed beside him in a careless heap. He scoops water into his hands and tips it over his neck, the stream sliding down his chest in clear rivulets that trace every line of muscle before dripping back to the stones. The sun catches on his skin, turning it bronze and wet, each drop glinting like it's got no business being that distracting. His shoulders roll as he bends forward again, easy strength in the motion, the ends of his shorter hair falling loose across his temple. It's infuriating how good he looks without even trying, all gold-lit, water-slick, and entirely unfair.

My mouth waters. His skin steams faintly where it meets the cool air.

"You okay?" I ask.

His hand slips, scattering water back into the stream, but he recovers quickly, turning with that crooked smile. "You tell me?"

I tilt my head. "What?"

Javi leans forward, settling his elbows on his knees like he's carrying something heavier than words. The usual grin is gone, stripped away along with the easy warmth he hides behind. What's left is plain honesty, steady and unflinching, and it hits me in the gut before I can brace for it.

"Since you brought me back...something's changed." He presses his hand flat against his chest. "It's like something's alive in me. Not just heartbeats. Something more. I dream in color now. I dream *you.*"

"You didn't dream in color before?"

"No. We usually don't. It makes it easier to tell what's real and what's sleep. Did you?"

"All the time," I say.

He takes a breath, eyes flicking toward the water, and the change is subtle but no less strained. His voice turns quiet in a way that makes me lean closer, like the words are meant only for me. Or maybe he's like me and afraid the truth will change shape if we speak about it too loud.

"Sometimes I wake up knowing things I shouldn't. Old songs I've never heard before. Languages I understand but can't name. I'm not scared of it— but I thought *you* should know."

"You share my dreams." I lower myself beside him, knees folding awkwardly, heart ticking louder than I like. The brush of his shoulder against mine is nothing, barely contact at all, yet it sends a ripple through me that leaves the air too tight to swallow.

"Is it...bad?" I ask.

"No," he says. "I don't think anyway. Just new. It doesn't hurt. It just doesn't make any sense to me. Your world is strange. What you do is strange..."

A smile tugs at my lips. "You mean my job?"

He nods slowly. "You dig up bones and broken things and treat them like treasure."

"They *are* treasure," I say, nudging him lightly with my shoulder. "They're stories. Forgotten ones. It's like...the world leaves behind puzzle pieces, and I try to put them together. Not for glory. Just so someone remembers."

Javi looks at me like I've grown a second head. Then, like, he wants to kiss it anyway.

"You mourn the dead by...digging them up?"

"Sometimes," I say, my voice catching in a way I can't quite hide. The ache curls inward, low and insistent, like it wants, no, demands, to be noticed. Mattie would have teased me for getting poetic and then made a better metaphor. I miss Mattie. I miss our conversations about history and the amazing people we've met throughout our work, both living and dead. I miss being known. Without magic. Without prophecy. Just...me. It feels good to talk about normal things for once. "But it's more about the living. Understanding where we came from. How we got broken in the first place."

He watches the current too long, the muscles in his throat shifting as he swallows something back, and then finally releases the words. "Maybe that's what you did to me."

"What?"

He touches his chest again. "Found the broken pieces and put something ancient in their place. You're the first soul reaper in fifty thousand years."

"But Raef said the gates have only been closed for ten thousand years."

"He must have been talking mortal years. Time passes differently between the two realms."

He glances sideways, watching me as I absorb yet another unbelievable tidbit of information. His hand, calloused and warm, lifts slowly, like he doesn't want to spook me. He tucks a loose strand of hair behind my ear, fingers brushing my jaw long enough to leave sparks. Every inch of me tenses in wanting.

"I don't care what that ring says," he murmurs. "I'm still yours. If you'll have me."

My mouth opens, but nothing comes out. The lump in my throat is growing and cutting off my air. My heart scrapes against my ribs, wanting to escape and leap into his hands.

So, I lean in a fraction more. Enough for his arm to wrap around my shoulders and pull me the rest of the way.

We stay like that, pressed close, wrapped in warmth and hush and things we can't name. His heartbeat presses against mine, and I swear it's mere seconds before they sync.

His lips find my neck. Not rushed or greedy. A slow press below my ear, then another at the curve of my collarbone. His hand finds my waist, firm, and mine curls into his shoulder, holding tight knowing I'll run if I let go.

My throat tightens, but his name still escapes, "Javi," barely more than a whisper, frayed with something I didn't want him to hear.

"I know," he murmurs. "We don't have to." But his mouth brushes mine anyway, featherlight.

The second kiss comes slower and deeper, and it unravels me more than the first. He knows I'll give in if he takes his time.

He tastes like the wild mint he's been chewing and something sweeter underneath. Something I want to taste again and again.

He's warm, safe, and a pull I don't have the strength to resist. And I don't. I'm falling.

His hand trails up my spine, taking its time wandering, until his palm cups the back of my neck. I arch into him as heat blooms low and liquid inside me.

Javi kisses me already knowing the shape of my hunger. Like he's dreamed it in every impossible color he can't put a name to.

My fingers find bare skin—his ribs, his waist, and the dip of his back. He's all warmth and tension, the shallow rise and fall of his chest matching the rabbit fast pulse underneath. He makes a sound low in his throat when I pull him closer.

Stars, I want him closer.

He kisses down the line of my jaw, his lips warm and firm, like we have all the time in the world. Like he doesn't care that we don't. His hand slips beneath the hem of my shirt, palm splayed flat against my spine. The heat of his skin seeps into me, and it's more than enough to stir that ache I keep pretending isn't there.

"You're sure?" he whispers, voice wearing at the edges.

I nod, dizzy with it all. "Yes."

Everything inside me pulls toward him, bright and raw. Javi's mouth is on mine again before I can think more, and this time there's no softness in it. There's nothing gentle now, only heat pressed hard against me, and a hunger that makes my body move before my brain catches up. His hands beneath my shirt shift, calloused palms skating up my ribs. I gasp into him, back arching, body bowing to his. He catches me with one hand at my spine, moving up to thread into my hair.

I feel reckless. That bright golden light curls up inside me, but I let it and don't fight it because he feels real. His kiss, his body, the growling sound he makes when I bite his lip.

"Strutting depths," he rasps against my neck where his mouth lingers, every word dragging the heat through me. "You're going to undo me."

I curl my fingers against his belt, holding there, wanting to feel the way his body answers even the smallest touch.

His breathing stumbles against my skin before his mouth drags lower, settling at the curve of my shoulder. "Tell me to stop," he murmurs.

I don't. His name slips from my lips, raggedly speaking everything I can't right now.

He leans in closer, lowering me with him until I'm stretched out beneath the press of his heat, the earth soft with moss and damp with shade, and the ground cool against my shoulders. Our hips align as he lifts my shirt and palms my breast. The moment stretches until my chest aches with it, every second strung out too long, heavy with wanting.

"Am I interrupting?"

I feel Javi still on top of me, his warmth holding but unmoving. His hand still under my shirt, holding my breast. My fingers curled around his belt, freezing halfway through releasing the knot.

Raef stands at the edge of the clearing, a dark arched brow raised, with an unusual smirk lifting the corner of his mouth. His eyes—*his eyes*—glitter like ice cracked in a glass of water.

"We need to chat," he says. "Compose yourselves, please." He saunters a few steps away, every line of him smug. Interrupting us was the highlight of his day.

Javi leans his forehead to mine, trying to slow his breathing. "Strutting depths, that bastard."

I let out a shaking laugh. "I'm going to kill him."

He grins. "Get in line."

WE HEAD HIS way, my stare sharp enough to cut. Javi trails a step behind me, close enough that I can still feel where his hands had been, and stars, that doesn't help.

The heat of his touch still lingers at the small of my back, but neither of us speaks first.

Raef remains braced against the tree, one arm still loose at his side, the other smoothing out the lines of his coat. Like a cat who already knocked the glass off the table and is waiting to see if anyone noticed. The loose arm braces against the tree, coat ruffled in a way that's beyond relaxed for him. The very picture of smug.

"You decent?" he asks mildly. "Or do I need to stare pointedly at the trees for another minute?"

Javi coughs and runs a hand through his damp hair. "We're settled."

"Didn't mean to ruin the moment," he says at last, voice low and far too even. "But the border doesn't wait, and I figured I'd rather be the one to interrupt...than Tris or the scout with an Iron crest and a sharp tongue."

My face burns. I fold my arms tight across my chest, a flimsy shield against the heat rising everywhere else. Mortification is an ugly heat, and Raef is pouring gasoline on it with every word. "You couldn't have shouted from the trail like a normal person?"

"I could've," Raef agrees. "But then I'd have missed the way your knees gave out.

Javi coughs into his fist, very deliberately not laughing. I don't bother to answer. Because if I do, I might say something I'll regret, or something he'll enjoy, or both.

"Mm, you're wrinkled," he says, staring down my shirt.

"Thanks for the fashion critique, your timing's impeccable."

Raef's mouth twitches like he might smile. "I don't care what you do off the road," he says, pushing off the tree and brushing moss from his sleeve. "But when we cross the hardline, we do it as bonded."

He pins me with that look, calm on the surface but hard enough that it makes my skin prickle. The wind lifts his black hair, catching the edge of something serious beneath the smirk. "Eyes will always be watching, and some of them hostile. Some curious, but none of them stupid."

I nod, but something must show on my face, because he adds, more gently this time, "I'm not asking you to lie. Just to remember who's supposed to have the claim."

"And if someone calls our bluff?" I ask.

Raef's glance flicks to the wards ahead, still glowing low between the trees. "Then I'll make sure it's not a bluff."

He looks back at me, something unreadable beneath his words. "The ring does half the talking already. All we have to do is not contradict it. Besides, I enjoy kissing you as well. I bet I can have you weak at the knees in half the time."

My cheeks warm to epic levels. Javi tenses beside me. Raef notices, of course—he notices everything. He tilts his head thoughtfully. "You can kiss her later, you know. After the border."

The only thing that makes it past my lips is a flat, "What?"

He shrugs. "Just not while someone might sketch it into a report."

Without waiting for a response, my mouth hanging wide open, he strides back toward the edge of the wards, coat catching on the wind; our conversation decided it was over, grew wings, and left.

The nerve. The absolute royal nerve.

I see it. The curl of a smirk he doesn't quite manage to hide.

That dirty rat bastard.

37

A Step-by-Step Guide to Being Measured Like Livestock

T HE MOUNTAIN SWALLOWS THE SKY. Jagged cliffs loom on all sides, sheer slabs of iron veined stone rise in veiled tiers, the bones of the realm laid bare. It's beautiful in the way a knife is beautiful. Snow doesn't fall in flakes here; it drifts in slow petals, like ash from some ancient fire long dead. Each flake gleams faintly as it passes, catching the light from blue torches set into the mountainside. They burn without smoke, without true flame, flickering cold above wrought-iron sconces carved in the shape of women bearing spears, hammers, and axes. *I wonder if any of them are watching me. I hope not.*

The sudden change in atmosphere when we crossed the ward line caught me off guard. I was not expecting a shift from a warm summer to cold and snow. Raef was, of course, and pulled a warm coat out of nowhere, resting it over my shoulders like the doting fiancé he's playing. It smells like him. Forest and steel and something darker underneath. I try not to inhale it in too obviously. I made sure to master my thankful worship face, and he almost broke and laughed. I like this version of him. A lot.

We cross a narrow bridge highly suspended over a chasm that screams with wind and darkness. It's the same stomach flip I felt balancing on a scaffold over a half-excavated cistern, knowing one loose stone could send me tumbling. At least scaffolds creak before they betray you. This bridge stares back in judgy silence.

The stone is slick beneath my boots, not with ice, but with moisture leaching up from the deep, warmed by the ancient earth lurking beneath. I focus on my footing and don't look down. Definitely don't look down. The wind claws out of the chasm, carrying grit and damp, like the mountain's trying to remind me it's older and louder than I'll ever be. It's alive. Of course, the Iron Court lives somewhere like this. Somewhere that tries to scare you before you even knock on the door.

Raef walks ahead, posture rigid. Tris keeps pace, cloak whipping around him in the wind in a dramatic way that I know he enjoys. In my world, there's no way Tris would not have been king of the drama club or, at the bare minimum, king of the Renaissance faire. I follow behind them, Javi at my side, close enough to touch if I need him. I don't, not yet. But I won't pretend his warmth isn't welcome.

The bitter, relentless wind screams through the peaks, dragging veils of snow in its wake. I pull my coat tighter, boots crunching over frost-laced stone. The cliffs part, a dark mouth opening in the stone, waiting to swallow us whole. Not literally, of course. But the path curves, and the fortress comes into view—half hidden in shadow, half carved into the sheer face of the mountain, a part of the rock long before anyone thought to call it a court. My legs slow, moving like molasses in January, as my brain tries to decide if it's in awe or dread. Considering my experiences so far, this beauty always comes with teeth. Well-sharpened teeth.

It's austere. Towering walls lined with iron, their seams radiant beneath the surface like veins under thin skin. Bridges arch across deep chasms, delicate-looking but forged from blackened steel. Torches burn in sconces shaped like talons, casting a pale, bluish light that doesn't flicker or warm.

The glow is all exposure, casting the stone bare and merciless. Nothing here softens the edges. Nothing here lets you forget who's in charge.

Above the gates, snow clings to the stone like lace. Balconies jut from the cliff face like ledges, surrounded by more veins of iron and quartz.

Figures stand along the walls, watching. Strong-shouldered, shorter than any fae I've met so far, but no less powerful. Their cloaks are trimmed with fur and laced with shards of brilliant stones. Their hair is twisted into thick braids entwined with wire, leather, and quartz pins. Their eyes follow us like we are thieves already caught in the act. I straighten my posture automatically, then hate myself a little for it.

When the outer gates grind open, the sound is like a glacier shifting. It rattles through my chest, heavy enough to feel like it's shaking something loose in my ribs. When it fades, one figure is left standing inside the gate.

She's as still as the stone that bears her name, arms folded across a chest clad in burnished steel and slate. Her braids hang like banners, heavy with rings of bone and blackened gold. She looks young the way most fae do, but there's nothing soft about her. Her face is honed hard, every look a reminder that stone doesn't need age to crush you. If someone told me she punched her way out of the mountain at birth, I'd believe it.

Raef steps forward and bows, one arm across his chest. "Matron Varaka Stoneveil. We seek safe passage over your borders."

Her pale eyes barely glance at the others. Me, she studies like a problem she already knows the answer to, and I'm not sure I want to hear her conclusion.

"This is the girl," she says, her voice like rock cracking under weight. Not a question. Not awe. Frank. I once asked why I'm a 'girl' when I'm a grown woman. Raef laughed at that statement. Tris was kind enough to explain that all humans are too young to be anything but children. Our lives are too short to ever be considered mature. I didn't argue at the time, but I'd like to. Our lives are shorter, so perhaps it's more that we mature faster than they do. We have less time to grow up enough to learn to survive.

Raef lifts his chin and squares his shoulders, his posture sliding into that perfect court formality. "Yes."

She graces me with all of her attention. "What the mountain gives, it tests. You want shelter and passage, girl? Then you'll face our stone, as these younglings did long ago."

I swallow. The air feels thinner here, colder, steam curling out of my mouth with each exhale. *How old is she if she considers my companions younglings, or children? On second thought, I don't think I'm mentally prepared to deal with the idea that they've all lived centuries already.*

Tris dips closer, the heat of his mouth brushing my ear, the words coming out nothing but cold. "They don't care how charming you are, star. They care if you can stand when the mountain tries to break you."

"Not helpful," I tell him out of the corner of my mouth.

Even though she phrased it like it's optional, I don't think it is. Varaka turns and walks into her fortress without waiting for my answer. Which, honestly, I wasn't going to give out loud anyway. Not while I'm still pretending I'm not terrified. *Show no fear, right?*

We follow, me frantically looking at my friends as they nonchalantly sign me up for some test without a word and without my consent. They don't even look at me. Cowards. Gorgeous, ancient, smug cowards. This is not how you earn my affections.

The halls swallow sound. The stone drinks it down and gives nothing back. Archways wind through chambers lit with that same blue flame, flickering against walls etched in deep, ancient runes. A cold magic. Not cruel, but unmoved by kindness.

I get the feeling I could scream in here and no one would care.

This is the Iron Mountain. They don't care who I am or what others have said about me. Only what I can prove.

THE CORRIDOR NARROWS as we continue our descent, the stone darkening with streaks of iron so thick they shine like vessels. It's like the mountain has a bloodstream, and we're heading straight for its heart. The cold slides in deep, settling thick and immovable, daring me to last longer than the last idiot who tried. I want to wake up from this nightmare instead. Preferably somewhere warm. With coffee.

Nobody says a word, which is probably for the best because my voice would echo back and mock me.

The guards who flank me wear armor that looks carved from mountain rock itself, etched with jagged glyphs, yet another strange written language. Even their breathing is silent, as if they've trained the sound out of their lungs. I'd find that impressive if it weren't so deeply unsettling.

We emerge at last into a vast hollow carved into the heart of the mountain. The chamber is circular, domed, and impossibly tall, shaped less like a hall and more like a room meant to let voices carry. Light filters down from crystalline shafts overhead, caught and multiplied by mirrored walls that refract torchlight into dancing fragments. Pretty. In the way a predator's lair might be. Shadows move like specters, disjointed and strange. It's a stone angler fish dangling pretties for unsuspecting prey.

These new fae line the tiered benches in layers, mostly women, all armored in what looks like slate and iron-threaded leather. But it can't be slate; that would make terrible armor. It must be some new alloy designed to look like stone while still protecting them.

They sit like statues, unsmiling, watching, and judging. *Of course they're all watching me. Why not make this even more humiliating?* Nothing like falling on your face or vomiting on your own shoes in front of a huge crowd.

At the highest seat, set back into a jagged alcove like a throne of broken rock, sits the Matron. She's now in robes of deep green with metallic filigree, her throat wrapped in an iron torque. Her eyes are pale as snowmelt and as merciless. One hand rests on a scepter of twisted ore; the other cups her chin as if I'm already disappointing her.

"Thessa Fireknot," she commands. The name hurtles across the chamber with a crack, and I search the crowd with frantic glances trying to find who she's called and prepare myself, but no one moves.

Instead, a figure steps forward from the shadows at the arena's edge. A woman, wide-framed with flame-bright copper hair, dressed in slate grey robes that fall like dark water around her. Her features are unlined, but there's a weight to them, a permanence, like stone that's been polished by centuries. She's all long bones, and her narrow eyes are surrounded by lashes of pale silver, giving her a sharp, strange brightness. But her skin is marked with hair-thin filaments of iron that trace her face in elegant arcs, disappearing beneath her jaw and sleeves like living circuitry.

Some kind of shaman, maybe?

Her voice is low, but it carries in a way I don't expect. "The girl must step into the ring."

No one speaks up, not even Raef, and the silence settles over me like a guilty verdict. It feels personal, as if everyone here agreed I'm expendable and couldn't be bothered to say it out loud.

"What the hell, guys?" I snap at them as quietly as possible.

Raef stands to the side, jaw clenched, arms crossed over his chest. His face is passive but still cold in a way that belongs to this place. When his eyes meet mine, it's not comfort I see. It's preparation. Like he already knows if I'll survive or won't. Either way, the gears are turning.

So, I move. I don't appear to have any choice at all. *Well, fuck you too, buddy.*

The sigils on the floor glow as I near, etched into a stone circle the color of storm clouds. They pulse faintly, not blue but something darker, like ice-cold iron, a color that makes your teeth ache looking at it.

I step inside.

When my first foot lands, a low, hum rises beneath the floor, low and eerie, like something's using a tuning fork somewhere deep in the mountain. It's not sound exactly. More like a vibration that climbs up my spine and settles between my ribs.

A ring of symbols flares outward in a snap, locking me in with a wall of cold white light. Every instinct screams at me to back out, but there's nowhere to go. Sound vanishes. The crowd fades into a blur. No more judging stares. Just me and whatever horror they've dug up for entertainment. I push the air out of my lungs, but it thins before it reaches my lips. The air is here, but it's... still. Trapped. It's not free for me to take anymore.

The mountain recognizes me; an old presence is staring straight through my skin. Maybe it thinks it knows me. Maybe it's mistaking me for something I'll never be, and that's terrifying. The stone shudders beneath my feet, twice, heavy as a thumping, scared heart. Then the light rips away, and the room drops into black.

38

HOW TO DROWN ON DRY LAND

TIME QUITS STUTTERING, AND REALITY slams back like a door I thought was locked.

It smells like salt and cheap ramen. Not moss or iron of magic. It smells like home.

Warm sun slants across the deck of the boat, and everything is too bright, too good. It isn't fear that makes my knees nearly buckle, but a hope that feels like a dagger dressed in pretty colors. Hope doesn't feel like healing. It feels like poison.

Mattie's laugh echoes off the railings. God, I haven't heard that in—

He's there. Standing a few feet away, wind tossing his shaggy curls, grinning like a devil. He's holding two steaming cups of ramen, like the night we stayed up cataloging pottery shards until dawn. It smells exactly right. The grease. The salt. The paper cup warping under heat.

"Thought you'd want the good stuff," he says. "Mystery meat flavor. Only the best for your goat stomach."

I choke on a laugh. It spills out anyway, raw and ragged. I reach for him, tears spilling down my cheeks unbidden. I don't care if it's a trick. I want one more second. One more taste of before.

His fingers close around my wrist, the heat of him bleeding into my skin until the illusion feels real enough to hurt. To tear apart my insides.

"Mattie," I whisper. "You're—"

"Right here," he says, his smile easing into the one I used to get across excavation trenches, all sun and secrets. The wind tosses his curls, his eyes crinkling at the corners in a way that makes my chest cave in. His fingers press steadily into my wrist, grounding me where I shouldn't be grounded. "I always was."

The fog is thinner here. The sea is calm. The sky is perfect. But a whisper curls beneath it. A current I know too well. One that pulls, not freely drifting. I can feel it more now than I could that day, the magic creeping in on us.

The deck creaks, not like it used to, but with that groan I know too well.

Mattie's hand tightens, a fraction too long, a fraction too tight. The hairs on my neck rise, instinct prickling in warning.

My eyes dart to the railing, searching the edges where the dark likes to gather. Where I know it will be. Nothing yet. No shifting black. No curling shapes. But I know better than to trust the stillness. The shadows always come.

"Do you remember what happened next?" he asks, still smiling, still holding my wrist. "Because I do."

It feels like something's cinched tight around my ribs, stealing the air. "This isn't real."

He tilts his head as if studying me, strands of blond hair falling into his brilliant blue eyes. They're too bright. There's no warmth there, only terrible certainty. "Sure it is. You made it real. The moment you let go."

The fog instantly swells thick around me, heavy enough to taste. The tang of metal cuts through the brine, copper slipping over salt. Blood. I can't see it, but my body knows it's there.

I wrench back, but Mattie's grip doesn't budge. "You didn't jump back for me. You didn't scream until I was gone. What does that say, Ror?"

My nickname in his mouth feels criminal. There's nothing neutral or friendly in it. It's an accusation hidden behind a smile.

"Stop it."

"You *let* me die."

"Stop—"

The sea lurches. Screams crack through the illusion. The ship *splits*, and I see them again—those glowing amber eyes. Kya's blood on my hands and knees. The coil of something too long, too slick, slithering across the deck.

Mattie's smile is gone. Now he looks like he did at the end. Eyes wide. Terrified.

"You said you'd always be there," he whispers.

I scream as his face bloats, skin sagging into a gray-blue mask. The sound tears out of me, wordless, nothing but a ragged attempt at '*no.*'

Magic flares from my chest—gold and white, laced with grief, searing the false world apart.

Glass explodes, light burning through everything. The boat, the sea, Mattie—gone in an instant. I slam down hard, stone beneath my knees, cold and unyielding. I barely feel it.

I scream again, hoarse and wordless, until it scrapes my throat bloody. Until the sound fades to nothing. Until it's me, sobbing into the emptiness, gasping for air that won't fill my lungs.

No air. No boat. Just me and the truth. Mattie's gone. Dead. It keeps happening over and over until I can't tell where it started, but it always ends with me letting him go. And I'm still here. I always am.

I claw at the mirrored floor like I can dig my way out. Like I can crack the illusion and find him beneath it. My nails scrape the iron-veined stone. Blood wells. I don't stop.

"Stop it!" I shout to the chamber, to the test, to myself. "That wasn't fair! He didn't deserve—"

My voice breaks. I curl in on myself, forehead pressed to the floor.

"I would've traded," I whisper. "You should've taken me. He was innocent."

Silence creeps in, crawling over my frayed nerves.

The runes beneath me flicker once—then pulse.

Cold. Indifferent.

"Trial Two begins."

39

How to Accidentally Make a Monster... Maybe and Other Poor Life Choices

T HE MIRRORED CHAMBER DOESN'T WAIT for me to recover. My knees ache from where I collapsed. My hands shake. My throat is raw, scraped clean by screams that still echo in the hollows of my body. I can still feel Mattie's fingers around my wrist. Still see the shape of his face when the light broke him apart.

The sigils beneath me flare white-blue—then vanish. In their place, a second ring ignites, tighter this time. No space to move. No place to run. Every muscle pulls tight, as if I'd be able to run away. Like I'd try, even knowing it's useless.

A heartbeat later, the light shifts—warping the mirrors, rippling the world into a heat mirage on stone. The chamber inhales again. It's not air filling the space, but pressure, thick and crushing.

I'm standing. Not by choice—not really. The chamber lifts me; I'm a puppet on strings, magic brushing over my spine, commanding muscles that haven't stopped trembling. My joints creak. My skin buzzes. I want to collapse again, but I can't. The mirrors pulse.

Javi sits cross-legged in the center of the mirrored floor, shirt torn open, the faint glow of a mark over his heart shining more intensely and then fading to almost nothing over and over. It looks less like an injury and more like something alive, feeding on him. Something ancient has its hooks in him, and I put it there. But his eyes are wicked. They're too still, and when he speaks, his voice is his and not. Layered with something indescribable.

"You didn't ask," he says.

I take a step. The stone beneath my feet hums. "Javi?"

His head tilts vaguely, a too-slow motion. "You just did. You laid your hands on my chest and poured the storm into me, and now I dream things that aren't mine."

The ring sitting against my chest pulses.

A shadow hangs at the corner of my vision, patient as a predator.

He rises. His body stutters—one frame Javi, the next a stranger with my eyes, then Javi again. The light above flickers with him. I want to look away, but my eyes won't move.

"You made me into something new," he says. "Something hungry. Do you know what lives inside me now?"

"I was saving your life." My voice sounds too small in this place. It barely makes a dent.

"And did you? Or did you crack something open?"

The mirror ripples.

Reflections of the moment repeat. My hands on his chest. My screams. The flash of golden light explodes from my palms. Repeatedly. A terrible crime caught in endless playback. Each loop worse than the last. Each one showing more magic than control.

"Did you give me something?" he asks, softer now, voice almost normal again. "Or did you take it?"

My legs give out, dumping me onto my knees.

"I didn't know." My voice breaks. "I didn't know what I was doing, just that I couldn't let you die. I didn't know it could change you. How could I know?"

He kneels in front of me. A hand lifts toward my face but never touches. His eyes flicker—from gold to brown to something else. Something I can't name. But maybe I made it.

"Then own it," he says. "Because it matters. Because I matter."

I press my hand to the runes on the floor, palm flat. The burn races up my wrist.

"I don't know what I did. If I did, do you think Mattie would be decaying at the bottom of the ocean instead of being here by my side? Do you think I wouldn't have done the same for him, my best friend? I let him go. I let him die. He didn't deserve what I dragged him to. It's my fault he's dead," I whisper. "It's my fault." Slow tears drag warm trails down my cold cheeks. "I couldn't let someone die for me again. I will never pretend it doesn't matter. It matters. You matter, and I'll figure out my magic. I swear it."

Javi vanishes. The marks fade from the floor. And I'm alone again.

40

Step One Dont Become a Villain· Step Two Repeat Step One

THE ROOM SHIFTS AGAIN. Of course it does. Because God forbid I get a second to breathe between the torture. I'm beyond tired of this. Tears spill hot down my cheeks. I'm not even wiping them away anymore. Let them fall. Let them see.

No crack of light. No sudden fall. Just the sensation of being *peeled*—layer by layer—until the air bites at my skin. Until thought itself goes thin. Something is sanding me down to the bone to see what's underneath.

The mirrored chamber steadies around me, but it's not the same. The quartz is gilded now, touched with veins of gold and black. And in the center of the ring, *she* appears.

Me. But not me. Not anymore.

She wears a crown that looks forged from ruin—spikes of metal that curve like antlers, studded with glowing gems of an unknown origin. Her gown flows like liquid flame, gold licked with obsidian. Her hair falls in dark waves down her back, and her eyes—my eyes—gleam like star fire. Cold. Impossibly cold.

High Queen Aurora.

She stands in the center of the chamber, perfectly still. Someone could strike me down right now, and her image would still be the one that would haunt me. The quiet around her isn't empty; it's certain. Every inch of her radiates a version of me who never hesitated. A version of me who said yes to every hard thing and never looked back.

"So," she says—my voice, layered with something older, something cracked. "You've come to see what you become."

It takes effort to force sound past the lump in my throat. "You're not real."

"I am *inevitable*." She tilts her head, her smile brittle. "And you should thank me. You survive. You win."

"Win *what?*"

She spreads her arms, and the chamber ripples outward—scenes flaring like visions in glass. Ashes where forests once grew. Empty thrones. Broken crowns. People kneeling. People running. A world reshaped by a hand that glows like mine.

"Everything."

Bile stings at the back of my throat. "At what cost?"

Future me steps closer. Her feet don't echo on the stone. I mean, why not? She doesn't need footsteps. She doesn't need anything or anyone. She's already won.

"You think you get to lead without bleeding for it? Without becoming the blade they need?"

"I don't *want* to be a blade."

"Then you will break. Or worse—*bend.*" Her tone snaps, edged with energy that's meant to wound me. "You're still clinging to softness. To excuses. To the lie that you can love them all and lose nothing."

She circles me with the patience of someone who knows I can't run. "You think they'll stay? When they see what you become? You think they'll love the queen who burns cities to keep them safe?"

A shiver slips through before I can stop it, her gaze locking on the weakness. Why wouldn't she see? She's me. Just...less of a mess. Less afraid. Or maybe there's more. She's more.

"You think softness is a weakness," I say. My voice is hoarse but strong, even though I'm broken. "But I've *seen* what happens when you close every door. When you turn pain into armor and forget who you are inside it."

Her crown catches the light. Her expression doesn't flicker. She doesn't blink or flinch, and I hate her for it. But I press forward anyway.

I close the space between us, my voice splintering under the weight of it. "I'm not a crown. I'm not a weapon. I'm me." I choke on the words, my voice breaking in a sound I can't hold back. "I'm the girl who held her best friend's hand as long as possible as the sea took him forever. Who gave a piece of herself to save someone else, not knowing what it might cost.

"I still dream of him—Mattie. I still wonder if I shouldn't have held on tighter. If my letting go damned him. If saving Javi makes me something I didn't ask to be, or him into something wrong."

Future me stays quiet, eyes on me like she's waiting for me to crack first, to prove her point. "I hate that I can't fix it," I whisper. "That I'll never know if it was right. But I won't stop feeling it because it hurts."

I wipe my face on my sleeve, breath hitching in hiccups. I'm shaking again, but I don't back down. Not this time.

"Because feeling is what makes me *real*. It's what makes me *me*.

"I have doubts," I admit. "All the damn time. I've been afraid. I still am, but I won't cut out the parts of me that feel too much, that love too hard. That *hope*. Life is too precious to waste on emptiness and pride."

Her lips part—but nothing comes out. No clever retort. No cruel jab. Only silence.

Golden magic sparks at my fingertips, restless and alive. Not because I command it, but because I stopped pushing it away. Because it's mine.

"I'll bleed for the people I love," I whisper. "But I will not become you. I may not know yet what it will cost me. But I will pay it. I know what it takes, and I'll carry it all. Every death. Every choice. Every thread of power that scares the shit out of me enough to test me.

I don't want to break the world."

Her silence drags long enough that I end up filling it myself.

"But I will, if I have to. I will save those who don't have the power to help themselves, but not without care."

The dark queen's mouth opens, but no sound comes. Her image cracks—fracturing along the edges like porcelain.

"I *will not* become you," I hurl the words and my hands together, power crackling off my skin. She shatters in a burst of golden light. Into dust and all the things I refuse to be. The sigils go still, and the mirrors fade as the light fractures with a snap of pressure behind my eyes. Something let go of its hold on me.

The stone floor firms beneath my knees.

Now, I am falling—

The chamber splits open with a sound like ice cracking underfoot. Cold air rushes in, stinging my wet face as the amphitheater comes into view again—clearer than I remember, veined with frost and iron. Light glimmers in from above despite it feeling like days have passed.

I stumble.

Javi surges forward first—his face a wreck, eyes red-rimmed, tear tracks frozen along his cheeks. His hands are out before he reaches me, like I'll slip away the second he lets go.

Behind him, Tris stands stiff and pale, jaw clenched so tight his teeth must ache. Raef hasn't moved from his place, but his hands are curled into fists, and his eyes—his eyes are wrecked. Gutted.

They saw it. *All of it.*

The trials didn't only test me—they displayed me for everyone to see. Every scream, every weakness, every broken piece. My grief for Mattie. My terror over Javi. That aching, dangerous question of what I'm becoming. The rawest parts of me, stripped bare.

Their eyes are wet, red-rimmed, their faces cracked open in ways I've never seen. No words come. It's all the weight of them looking at me, the broken pieces that we might not be able to fix. Like I've walked out of my own funeral.

They move at once, a blur of arms before I can track who reached me first. Suddenly I'm wrapped in warmth—Javi's arms cinched around my waist, Tris's hand at my back, and Raef's palm cradling my cheek like I'm something delicate and precious.

"I'm okay," I rasp. "I—"

But I'm not. My nose is bleeding. My hands won't stop shaking. My magic surges under the surface like a live wire, still hot with grief and rage and something too big to even think about right now.

A quiet scrape of boots echoes through the chamber. The matriarch descends from her high seat above the amphitheater. Her robes drag, the cloth pulling along the ground with a sound closer to chains than fabric. Her face gleams cold and otherworldly in the blue torchlight. A circlet of hammered silver crowning her temple, a simple piece like you'd pull from a Celtic barrow, stripped of everything but weight and age.

She stops before me. I'm waiting for her to judge, to tell me I failed miserably. She looks me over like a merchant inspecting a blade and smiles.

"You are not meant for this world, girl," she says, the words smooth and final, a judge delivering a sentence. "You were made to break it."

No one moves. Perhaps they're all as shocked as I am right now. We're all having to process what she declared on my behalf. *I think I passed...*

With a turn, her voice suddenly bright, projecting to the crowd, she declares, "Let us eat and celebrate the return of the High Queen of the Atma!"

41

WHEN A GUEST, DONT WAKE THE WYRM. BUT ALSO, DONT CHOKE ON THE STEW.

THE GREAT HALL OF THE Iron Court is carved into the mountain next to the amphitheater. Thank every god still listening. I don't think I would have made it any further.

Its ceiling is high and domed, held by ribbed iron columns that glitter like frost on a field. Stone and light take the place of tapestries and flowers, the silence broken by the clatter of bowls and the low murmur of voices.

We sit at a long, low table set in a semicircle near the fire pit, this one warm and burning some dense black fuel that smells like the peat fires of Ireland. My place is slightly elevated now. Not a throne, but not nothing. It's strange to be set apart without being crowned. To sit one step higher and still feel like I don't belong here. Because I don't, and I don't think I ever will.

Maybe that's the point of it all. I'm human and think like one instead of a power hungry fae.

The Matriarch watches me from her stone seat with that same unreadable smile. I don't meet her eyes. I'm too tired to stand, too wired to sleep. The food—god, the food—doesn't help.

It's strange. Root vegetables soaked in brine and charred over mineral-rich flame. Paper-thin slices of cured beast I've never seen before, but that melts against my tongue like fat, salt, and fire. Some kind of fermented berry liquor that tastes like winter caught in glass—sharp, then warm, then gone. Steam coils from bowls of a thick, rust-colored stew that smells of marrow and spice. I eat slowly. Each bite tastes like it came from deep underground—earthy, dense, humming with history. It's strangely pleasant.

The others are close. Tris sits on my left, lounging as usual, as he has no bones, but his eyes flick to me every few seconds, checking. His hand never quite leaves the chair at the curve of my shoulder, his fingertips grazing my tunic every so often. Javi's on my right, eating with quiet appreciation. His thigh presses into mine under the table. Raef... Raef is across from me, watching like a general tallying battlefield wounds. His plate is mostly untouched. But he hasn't looked away once.

We don't talk much at first. But the mood is different. Light instead of heavy, not quite cheerful, but not broken or bleeding either. I'll take it. At least it's different.

"I thought the chamber was going to split open," Tris mutters, swirling the dark wine in his cup. "And honestly, I'm not sure you didn't break it."

"Maybe she did," Javi says, nudging my knee with his. "Wouldn't be the first thing she broke in this realm."

The familiar banter settles under my skin, easing the tremor in my hands. Raef doesn't speak, but when I glance his way, he gives me a slow, almost imperceptible nod. The kind that says he saw everything, and he's still here. I didn't scare him in the slightest.

Around the room, nobles of the Iron Court begin to drink more freely. Their laughter is clipped and gravel-deep, but it's laughter all the same. One of them—a taller woman with a tattoo down the side of her face that glows when she raises her cup—offers me a curt salute. A heavyset male with silver rings on every finger and in each ear lobe nods with what might be approval or wariness; I can't pin it down.

Somewhere deep below, a low sound rolls through the stone. A long, slow groan. Something old and large shifting in its sleep.

The sound roots me in place, my spoon halfway to my mouth, and a few of the nobles go still with me. The laughter dies mid-note, leaving the hall hollow.

"Thronvaldir stirs," a young noble with silver dust still clinging to his braids mutters. Every voice dies entirely.

"What was that?" I whisper, turning toward Tris.

He's already still, wine forgotten in his hand. "The mountain," he says softly, "or what sleeps beneath it."

The noble nearby, on the left of Raef—with iron rings in his nose, thorns in his ears, and scarred knuckles I wouldn't expect on a council member—answers my deeper questions without asking. "Thronvaldir," he murmurs. "They say he was the first to claim this place. A worm the size of cities, born of molten ore and stone. The Iron Court never killed him. We built around him."

My mouth goes dry. "And he's...alive?"

Tris's smile doesn't reach his eyes. "They say he only stirs when something important happens."

The sound fades slowly, leaking into the cracks in the stone.

The nobles resume eating, but a few cast wary glances toward the dark corners of the hall, as if listening for more.

The Matriarch doesn't speak until her plate is empty. Then she stands, eliciting a hush over the hall.

"A queen must bleed," she says, raising her cup, "but not alone."

A quiet hum of agreement moves through the room.

She looks at me, not unkindly. "Eat. Rest. Tomorrow, you walk through the ancient paths with our blessing and our support."

My fingers tighten on my cup.

Blessings and support.

I don't fully trust the words, but I feel them settle anyway. Heavy. Real. Like weights laid in my hands instead of shackles fastening around my wrists.

Did I earn us an ally?

Across the fire-warmed stone, I find the Matriarch. She doesn't smile this time. She nods.

Yes.

What happened in that chamber was more than survival, more than another trial. It feels like the beginning of something real. Maybe the closest thing I'll ever get to respect in this realm.

Raef is the first to break the silence of my group, his voice quiet but confident and maybe even proud. "You didn't pass the test. You won them over."

There's something unguarded in his expression, something that might've been admiration if we weren't both so tired.

Javi exhales a low breath beside me, like he's been holding it for days. "The Iron Mountain," he murmurs. "They've always been old, always been silent. But tonight, they stand with you."

"They'll stand back and watch," Tris mutters, though there's no bite in it. "They always do. But if she declared you High Queen in front of her people...that's something. That means she's staking her name on you and your power." He glances toward Varaka Stoneveil with a flicker of unease. "She wouldn't have done that lightly."

I lift my head until his eyes catch mine. "So, what now?"

Raef leans forward, his voice steady and sure, which I need right now. "Now we start counting allies instead of losses."

A silence settles between us. Full of possibility. Of something taking shape. Outside, the wind howls beyond the stone. Inside, waits warmth, food, and the flicker of something like hope.

The wine lulls my head, and sleep crawls closer. The others drift into easy conversation, debating which court might move next and what paths we'll take through the mountains.

I settle deeper into the chair, the stone at my back, heat at my sides. Tris is still at my shoulder, Javi's weight solid beside me, his knee still pressed to mine. Raef across the table, unblinking. The room hums with voices, but it's the nearness of them that lets me close my eyes.

42

EASILY TRAVEL FROM CELEBRATION TO TARGET PRACTICE IN ONE NIGHT

THE STONE WALLS OF THE mountain's guest quarters glow faintly as the enchanted torches cast cold blue light that seeps into every little seam. The air tastes of iron and cold, the mountains chill clings no matter how many furs they pile on the beds. Outside, snow whispers down the cliff face, brushing constantly against the shutters like a lover's caress. Inside, is muffled silence. The fire in the corner has burned low, embers glowing a faint red, creating more shadows than heat. Everyone else sleeps, sprawled across pelts and blankets, their breaths even and slow. The entire chamber is resting.

Everyone except me, that is. The quiet is suffocating. You'd think a nice quiet night would make sleep easier, but the quiet makes my mind race and think on all the things that have happened and could still happen. I've never had to fight with anxiety before, and I have a new understanding and sympathy for anyone who deals with this day in and day out.

I lay on the furs, eyes wide, pulse still erratic. My body stopped shaking hours ago, the wine lulling me. But my mind won't be still. The harder I try to rest, the faster they come. A flood of thoughts, all bad, none useful.

Across the chamber, Tris sits up on the windowsill niche, one knee bent. Awake now and humming another unfamiliar tune. It's not lullaby-soft or cheerful. It's wistful. I imagine the tune to be more for trying to remember and forget at the same time.

His silhouette is dark against the pale glass, silver braids trailing back from his temples catching torchlight enough to gleam. He hums like the melody belongs to someone else, and he's keeping it alive a little longer. He's always humming. I don't expect to recognize any of the tunes, but I can say they rarely sound like the jigs, reels, and ditties you'd hear in a tavern. They sound more like scraps of sound that never stop. I don't know if it's habit or if he's trying to keep something out by filling the silence. I heard once that humming helps control stress by resetting your nervous system. Maybe that's it. Tris hums to keep himself calm.

I watch the rise and fall of his shoulders, and somewhere between one slow blink and the next—

—I slip.

A city rises before me, luminous and impossible. Towers of coral glass spiral into the sky, etched in living runes that pulse in time with my own heartbeat. Each beat throbs in my chest because the city knows me—somehow it is me. Bridges sweep like crescents over wide canals, the water lit from beneath in shifting bands of blue and silver, its reflection breaking against the stone with soft, endless ripples.

The air is thick with the scent of salt and jasmine, heady and cloying. It coats my tongue, sweet and briny all at once. Chills race across my skin because I know this. I remember this.

White petals fall from nowhere, spiraling like snow, but warm when they brush against my cheek, dissolving before they touch the ground. I catch myself holding my breath, half expecting to wake, but also afraid not to.

Everything is too perfect. The perfection is so polished it hurts to look at. All the colors sing to me because they're the colors I've put together my whole life. In my bedrooms, my school art projects, and even my doodling in college notebooks. It stings behind my eyes, because this is memory that I don't remember living.

At the center of it all, she waits for me, anchored to the terrace as the city rises around her. Tall. Regal. I know she commands without a throne or a crown. Her hair falls in a curtain of moonlight, silver threads braided through until it glimmers like spun metal. Her skin shimmers faintly, alive in a way that says the light belongs to her and not the torches and sconces on the walls.

Robes of sapphire silk spill to the ground, pooling around her bare feet, so fluid they move like the water around us, every fold pierced with pinpricks of starlight that flare when she shifts.

And her eyes—her eyes are mine. Not in color, but in every other way possible. The shape, the weight, the way they see straight through me. She's a version of me stripped of hesitation, built to rule, to burn, to last. Looking at her is like staring in a tinted mirror, one I spent the last few weeks avoiding.

She reaches for me, and her mouth moves. Only one word. "Aurora."

The sound crawls under my skin, setting my ribs buzzing and my teeth aching.

I bolt upright, gasping. My hand flies to my chest. The pendant Tris gave me pulses with faint silver light, the ring against my chest on fire.

"Rory?" Javi's voice is rough with nagging sleep, breaking low in the back of his throat. He pushes himself up on one elbow, blankets sliding from his shoulders, hair sticking up at odd angles. His eyes blink against the bare light, still heavy, but the second they find me, the haze clears. Concern flickers there as he searches my face for answers, for injury. "You okay?"

My throat works around a swallow, too tight. I give a quick nod before the truth drags my head the other way.

He shoves the blankets off and pushes upright, tension snapping through his shoulders. "That place—the glowing towers. Did you see it too?"

A stone rolls in my throat, making me cough to loosen it as I lock on his face. My mouth incapable of shaping more than one word. "You—?"

He nods. "She said a name. Aurora. Who's Aurora?"

Across the room, blankets rustle. Tris shifts upright in the window's glow, Raef drags a hand down his face, and Javi glances over his shoulder toward them as if bracing for something obviously bad.

I look down at my hands, then up again. "Me. That's me. Aurora Darling."

Nothing comes at first, so my tense shoulders trying to clean out my ears seems like overkill. They all stare at me as I stiffen like a statue, bracing for a sting that never comes.

"I hated it," I add. "Growing up. It always sounded like a name you'd give your sweet little, perfect porcelain doll. And there were a lot of Disney princess jokes, which you wouldn't understand, but take my word that they were ridiculous. I started going by Rory when I turned thirteen."

Tris's voice comes soft, gentle, as if he's offering me a place to set something heavy down. "And the dreams?"

"You too?"

He nods. The blue firelight casts faint shadows across his high cheekbones. His expression is hard to read. But something flickers in recognition.

I look to Raef, and I don't even have to ask; he nods too.

"I've had them since I was a kid. Of the city at least. The woman is new. I thought it was my imagination."

A long silence follows.

Javi breaks it. "It's not imagination anymore."

No. It's not.

WE BREAK OUT at first light, the mountain sky bruised with gray. The aftertaste of celebration still lingers on my tongue, with smoke from the peat fires, salt from cured meat, and sweet wine that burned going down. Outside the great gates, the air is raw and thin, stinging my lungs with cold. Snow crunches under our boots, brittle and loud in the quiet that follows us everywhere. The firelight and laughter of the hall feel miles away already, sealed behind iron doors. Out here, it's only rock, frost, and the weight of everything waiting for us beyond the mountain. Because I know every day brings us closer to Raef's court, and I don't like the idea of that anymore.

The Iron Matriarch waits for us at the gate, a wall of guards braced at her sides, their armor a patchwork of hammered silver and fur. Their spears gleam in the cold, unmoving. It reminds me of the guards in London, where everyone tries to get them to break form and move. She's as still as they are, if not more so, and I think I would prefer raised voices. Her face gives nothing away, but the air around her is colder than the wind spilling down the pass. She's upset, but I don't think it's aimed at us. I hope not anyway.

Her silver-lined cloak whips and snaps in the wind. The runes along her sleeves flicker, pulsing with stone-deep magic.

"The Sea Court has already sent assassins," she says without ceremony. "We turned two away a week past from the outer wards."

The word "assassins" lodges under my skin, and my chest clamps down like it's trying to keep the air inside my lungs because any new air might be poison. My kicking pulse doesn't help its efforts at all. They're already this close. Already looking for me. Because it must be me. Who else would they come for?

She studies me too long, solidifying my own thoughts. Her eyes narrow, only a little, like she's weighing something she doesn't want to share with me. "One of them looked...familiar. It struck me only after the trials." She tilts her head, her long braids brushing over her shoulder. "Perhaps it was a trick of the mountains' magic. But be cautious, High Queen."

I hear the faint creak of leather as Raef shifts behind me. I can easily picture the tension pulling tight in his shoulders. I know Tris is next to him, and I can hear nothing there, which is as telling. I don't have to see them to understand they don't like this news at all. I don't like this news. I hear the stiff inhales and subtle halting of movement, and I don't need to be a psychic to interpret any of it.

"A queen must bleed," Varaka adds, voice rising. "But she must also survive. Go now. You have our blessing."

She turns, cloak snapping once in the wind, and strides back into the fortress without another word. The gate drags shut after her with a grinding groan of old metal and finality. The sound echoing against the cliffs like a closing verdict. The wind suddenly dies in the pass, cold air suspended and biting in my throat. Then it breaks loose, shrieking through the gap, high and piercing, a cry that doesn't sound like weather at all. It claws down my spine in warning, a voice from something old and buried deep in the stone around us.

I have so many questions, but I have learned that this isn't the time, but the need for answers is eating away at my insides. I hold my tongue until we're well down the trail, iron-rich rock giving way to dry forest.

Tris steps forward, long fingers locking around Raef's arm. He keeps his voice quiet, but even I can hear the edged steel in it, "It's time to stop dallying."

Raef arches a brow. "You think I'm—"

"I think we need to go straight to the Shadow Court," Tris cuts in. "Your father won't wait forever. Yes, he'll be a problem, but the Sea Court is hunting her."

Raef glances behind us, toward the mountains. "They won't dare cross the Iron borders. We still have time to prepare—"

"No," Tris says, his gaze as cutting as his tone. "But they can cross the Iron Wards, and the second we step beyond them, we're exposed. We've wasted enough time pretending this is still a game. Your father is a problem, but the shadow borders are impenetrable."

Raef chews on his decision before spitting it out. Weighing something in his mind, his jaw shifts.

At last his chin dips, a single deliberate motion. "Fine. No more delays."

He faces the horizon, where the land fractures into ruin. Behind us lie stone halls and stone-choked peaks; ahead, only shadow. My boots crunch over stone as I blindly fall in step. Which is so unbelievably stupid.

43

So You've Entered the Land of Secrets... Now What?

THE PATH CLIMBS LIKE IT regrets the decision, mirroring my own apprehension with a crooked scar cut into the mountain. Every turn whips back on itself, switchbacks that grind upward with no railing, no mercy, only a long drop yawning at my side. My boots slip against pale marble slick with mist, the stone uneven enough to keep me watching my steps instead of the sky.

On either side, the cliffs bear their wounds. Rock split ages ago, jagged seams running deep, the fissures blackened with the mountain's blood because it never got the chance to heal. Thin veins of obsidian glint like this congealed blood in the cracks, catching the weak light and throwing it back in muted shards.

From deep inside of these splits comes a sound I don't want to name or think about, with its low tone that almost passes as a whisper. It's not an echo because none of us are speaking. It's a deep murmur that coils under my hearing, tugging like a language I should understand but can't quite grasp. The hair on my arms rises, even under the pressure of my sleeves, because I feel like the stone is leaning in to listen for my answer.

Mist bleeds from the crevices, slow and methodical, curling like smoke that can't quite get up the energy to rise. It slips across the marble path and sinks into the grooves etched there, filling them line by line until the patterns almost glow, faint and wet, veins lit from within. For a second I think they're ornamental, another court's idea of decoration, until the shapes tilt in that recognizable fashion. They're script.

Not the kind I know or have seen here before. Not any kind I've studied. The lines bend in ways language shouldn't, at least following the linguistic rules I'm familiar with.

The ground drones beneath our feet to the point it feels like I'm balancing on a guitar string. I wonder if the humming is coming from sacred spaces, long forgotten, and they're trying to get someone to remember them. The land of this realm is desperate for someone to remember the old ways and the old magic, that innate power that Tris has told me about.

I flex my fingers at my sides, resisting the urge to reach for someone. Tris, Javi, even Raef, but no one says a word, and the silence presses in; the mountain testing how much weight I can carry before I crack. It's not a lot. I'm well past my limit already. I'm pretty sure I passed that a week ago when the Iron Matriarch told me assassins were on my trail. Every day my shoulders climb higher, I hear things when nothing's there and sleep is a figment of my imagination.

Ahead, the walls of the court loom, bone-white marble streaked with black, the stone mottled like an old scar that never quite healed.

I don't like the quiet up here. I don't like that even my thoughts feel too loud.

Below us sprawl the court's nearest fields, but there's no green, no crops. Instead, the earth is carved into training rings, circles laid out like a mosaic, each filled with bodies moving in perfect synchronicity. Dozens of fighters advance and retreat as one, blades flashing in unison, too synced to be chance, too exact to be human ease. It looks less like sparring and more like someone wound up their toys and set them loose.

Blades catch the light and vanish again, a staccato of silver arcs, but not a sound follows. No ring of steel, no grunt of effort, not even the scuff of boots in dirt. The mountain swallows it all, pressing heavy against my ears until it feels like the ground itself drinks noise, hoarding it all for itself. It's wrong. It's like watching a fight behind bulletproof glass, the volume cut to nothing, every strike perfectly clean and rehearsed.

And it's not only soldiers. On the fringes, veiled spymasters gesture to runners who slip away without sound as well, their footsteps swallowed like the rest. Children guide sightless beasts with ropes tied to delicate fingers, their pale eyes unblinking as they move in patient, practiced lines. Artisans crouch in clusters, silver veins hammered into blank masks braced between their knees. The clang of metal against metal never reaches me; I have to imagine it. Each mask shimmers briefly, then dulls; the metal is tasting what's been fed into it, deciding whether to keep it or spit it out.

There's no daily rhythm of life here. No shouted orders, no barking dogs, no scraps of laughter to break the monotony. Only bodies in motion, mechanical and exact, every gesture absorbed into the still, choking air. It's the same unease as stepping into a room that's been deep cleaned, polished, scoured, and stripped of the messy signs of living. Scrubbed of sound and emotion. This place has been sanitized of anything human and alive.

It's different from what I've seen of this court already, but at the same time, it's the same. Fields had stretched wide and bare, the soil dark as ash with furrows that looked like some beast clawed the landscape. Thin figures worked in silence, bent-backed, long shadows carrying more weight than they do. Clothes hang in tatters, patched and re-patched until the fabric looks more stitch than cloth. Their faces were hollowed, eyes dim, not the wide, wild hunger of starvation, but the gray glaze of people worn past it. They're not starving, but not living either. It's like the field is feeding on them instead of the other way around.

There was no laughter, no barking dogs, or children's voices. Just the hiss of wind brushing through rows of withered stalks that should be golden but are gray and brittle, snapping under the touch. It's not a harvest; it's a graveyard.

I hate how easy it is to stop seeing them. One glance, and my brain tries to move on. These people are the kind you're not supposed to remember, but I want to. I need to.

Many homes are built into the narrow, steep cliffside, shuttered with stone slats and doors painted in deep purples and blackened green bark. Moss creeps across everything, but it's dark, almost black. Some windows have no glass, only gauzy curtains that move like spirits. Everything here is shadows and death. I can't for the life of me figure out how this place birthed Raef, someone stoic but still full of life and light.

By the time the road narrowed to the staircase and path of marble and obsidian, the silence was already a heavy weight on my chest. This wasn't a court of spectacle like those I've experienced already. This was a kingdom that whispers you into compliance.

Raef walks ahead, back straight, his jaw set more than usual, which I didn't think was possible. His posture is princely, but there's a stiffness to it, the kind he never wore in the other courts. His fingers brush his sword belt once, then again.

It's not fear; I can tell that, but he's bracing for something, and that makes the nerves crawling up my spine dig in harder.

Tris draws up beside me. "Welcome to the land of secrets," he says under his breath. "Try not to inhale any, they curdle."

Javi doesn't laugh at his jest. He glances skyward, squinting. "Even the birds don't fly here."

He's right. The sky above the court is unnerving. Nothing moves, not wings or even the drift of clouds. There's only a pale silver-blue, flat as glass and as fragile looking.

"No," Raef says, "The only birds that dare to live on this land keep to the forests. The only things you'll see flying in this sky are dark reptiles."

"You have dragons?" I ask in awe.

"In a manner of speaking," he says with a small smile.

At the next bend in the path, the guards wait. They stand motionless on either side of a black arch that grows from the stone. Their armor is like polished obsidian trimmed with white steel. But it's their faces that make me falter—because they don't have any.

Each one wears a mirrored mask, polished to a high sheen, flawless as glass, and yet iniquitous. Each mask reflects all of us, but the movements are off by seconds. One shows me already stepping forward when I haven't moved. Another reflects me with my head turned, watching something behind me, even though I'm still facing forward.

It's unnerving.

"They wear your reflection," Raef says without looking. "But only if you're worth seeing."

At first, I thought he was being cruel. But then I notice Javi's mirrored self moves in perfect sync. So does Tris. But one sentinel... its mask shows nothing. Just blank marble surroundings. And the moment I notice, it shifts, a little, so I can see myself again. My reflection wavers, tiled and stretched until it looks mistaken in a way that makes my skin crawl.

My stomach turns. Cold creeps in behind my ribs, some window left open inside me letting in the bitter breeze.

As we pass the next figure, one of the mirrored faces tilts its head.

I don't reciprocate, but my reflection does.

Air snags hard in my throat as I stumble to a halt. The mask throws my reflection back at me, but the face staring out isn't mine in the way a mirror should be. The eyes glint sinful, bright and calculating in a way I would never be. They're too cold to belong to me, even that future me from the trials. My mouth curls into a smile I'm not making, and I touch my lips to be sure. I look away quickly, and now my pulse won't settle. It's the same jolt I think one would get when a stranger calls your name before you've introduced yourself.

I turn away, catching Raef watching me sidelong. "They choose what to reflect," he says. "Some say they show your truest self. Others say they can show you what you fear becoming."

"And which is it?" I ask, throat dry.

"Neither—most of the time. Mostly they show your intentions, your next moves. Increases success in battle, but only if they deem you a danger to the court."

Danger. Right. So, I guess the creepy smiles are their version of applause.

I swallow hard and keep walking behind him.

The arch doesn't swing open the way a gate should. It yawns, slow and soundless, swallowing us whole. It receives us; that's the only word for it. Not like we're guests being welcomed, but like the stone has already decided what we are. Offerings perhaps, or specimens, something to be catalogued and kept in a glass case.

The staircase spills out ahead, each step unfolding from the last like a sprung mechanism. Polished white marble gleams under the torchlight, but it never feels bright. It feels sterile and clean, the way bone looks after it's been boiled down to nothing but surface. Veins of obsidian streak through each tread like frozen lightning, dark and jagged against the white.

Mist coils up from the stone, thin tendrils brushing my ankles, an ethereal tongue tasting my skin. My boots slide a fraction on the damp, and my gut lurches with the sense of being led somewhere I won't climb back from. Even without Raef's tension, even without Tris's warnings, I'd know it. Anyone with even the slightest bit of intuition would know this place is wrong in all senses of the word. Light doesn't soften the edges. If anything, the brightness makes the shadows lean in sharper, waiting for their moment.

Courtiers line the path on either side, a gauntlet of preternatural stillness that grates against my ears. They don't move. Don't blink. Not even their chests move as proof of life. They stand in rows, dozens of them, draped in layered silks and cloaks the colors of ash, bone, and night. The fabric doesn't rustle or shift with the draft. It hangs heavy, funereal, like shrouds waiting for their bodies.

Every face is hidden behind a mask. Not the polished, mirrored ones we passed earlier. These are worse. Feathers curl upward like antlers, catching the torchlight in a shimmer of brittle sheen. Filigree twists into thorns that look sharp enough to break skin, and the longer I stare, the more I wonder if they would. Some are carved from stone and look heavy and cold, others from bleached bone, the hollows dark as eye sockets. A few are so fine they seem stitched from shadows themselves, edges blurring under my focus. I catch a glint of mirrored glass, a flicker of enamel, a spark of something like teeth where no mouth should be.

Not a single face is real, and that claws at me. A hall full of people, and not one expression I can read. Not one human marker to anchor me. Just masks watching, silent, waiting. My skin crawls like I'm the only one here who forgot to dress the part.

The only sounds are our footsteps. Even those feel like a mistake; sound itself doesn't belong here, we're intruding.

I reach for Raef without meaning to, a brush of fingers against his sleeve, but he steps ahead, spine straight, jaw set. His posture is perfect, but I feel it. The tension. Like every muscle is braced for a blow or another test.

Something cold touches the palm of my hand. I jerk until I see what caused it. A copper ring, thin as wire, presses into my palm by a silent attendant in gray. No explanation. No greeting. Just a gesture and a stare. I would guess this is the first test, assessing how well I take it. It slides over my knuckle with unnatural ease.

"They'll remove it once the king speaks," Raef whispers.

"So, we're not allowed to talk?"

"Apparently, at least not until you're acknowledged."

That same attendant sidles up next to Raef's ear between us, "Light finds you well, I trust, Prince," he says in barely a whisper.

"And may yours keep you safe, Dante," Raef returns with practiced formality, his lips only moving enough to get the words out.

"The river tithe came short again," Dante whispers. "He'll blame it on the girl and make a spectacle."

"Shadows take it!"

Raef is obviously upset about this news, but now isn't the time to ask, even if I think I can, which apparently I can't; I've been magically muzzled.

I force the swallow down, my throat raw, but I don't want to show my hand. The air is thick with perfume, a sweetness with sour notes underneath, cloying enough to take any hunger I was feeling away. A tang of metal clings to my tongue, coppery. I might have bitten my own lip, but I didn't notice any pain. My skin feels too tight. One step, then another. I don't dare speak. I don't dare breathe too loudly.

There's something in the silence. A static-like hum, like surveillance on older phones. And the moment I think it, one of the masked courtiers tips its head, a fraction. Enough to make my skin crawl.

Another courtier breaks the line. She steps forward, graceful and sure, robes rustling like dry leaves. Her mask is carved from some pale wood, inlaid with tiny pearls. Her hands move first, a slow, elegant bow. Deep. To *me*.

I open my mouth without thinking. Forgetting the ring. Forgetting the rules. But nothing comes out. My retort hits enamel and stops.

The woman straightens. Her mask tilts slightly. Enough for me to catch a glimpse beneath—sharp cheekbones, lips painted black-blue, and eyes the color of pressed gems.

A second figure leans forward, this one younger, draped in silver lace with gemstone pupils that catch the light and fracture it. They *mouth* something to me.

I don't catch it. I don't need to. I see the way their gaze lingers on my throat. The ring. The pulse beneath it.

It's not curiosity. It's assessment. Like they're measuring how tightly the leash fits.

Raef moves closer. Not touching, not claiming, but close enough to prove to them that he's there, at my side, and I'm his. Staking his claim. Saying '*mine*' without uttering a word.

Whispers drift on the wind like falling ash, but no lips move. Not that I can see them anyway.

"Starborn."

"Sea-lit."

"Nightmare Queen."

All I can think is, they're not wrong to be afraid.

I don't know who they should be afraid of.

44

SO YOUR BOYFRIEND'S FATHER HATES YOU, NOW WHAT?

THE DOORS DON'T SWING AS much as unclench, the stone jaw deciding it's done holding back. The hinges are well oiled, the great maw opening to welcome us to dinner. And apparently that's me. At this point I feel like every step I take adds another letter of my name signing a contract I didn't get to read.

A wave of cold hits us, sharp, dry, and metallic. Fade, or their winter hits harder in this court than in the damp chill of Greenwood. But it's still feels like the instant before a blade strikes. My lungs flinch, pulling in shallow breaths that I try desperately to hide. It tastes of the iron of magic and copper, as if the very threshold of the court has been salted with old blood. It's a scent and taste I've become very familiar with...unfortunately. The stone under my boots is still slick with a thin sheen of condensation, and every step sends up a scent of frost and something chemical. My skin prickles like tiny static shocks brushing against me in waves, a warning in a language that my body remembers easily enough. The hairs on the back of my neck stand, my instincts on high alert, having been honed to prey animal levels since the ship. I don't think this cold I'm feeling is only the weather. I think this court exhales cold, keeping you off guard, testing what crossed its teeth.

Light spills from within, but it isn't warm. No golden glow, no welcoming hearth-fire. There's the cold gleam of polished obsidian that throws my reflection back in dark, fractured shards. Silver sconces hang in equal measure that are home to flames that barely move, so little that at first glance I think they're paper parlor tricks.

This is not a place built to welcome. It's a place built to judge, each line of stone carved with the weight of decisions already made. And I'm walking straight into it. I thought I'd experienced imposter syndrome before, but boy was I mistaken.

I wish I could say I walk in tall, proud, and powerful. I don't. My spine straightens, yes, but that's stubbornness, not courage. I'm only refusing to hunch over as the air presses heavier the farther we go. My fingers twitch at my sides like they're looking for something to grip.

And if they are judging? Fine. Let them write it down. I've never been good at pretending anyway.

Every step bounces off the walls. I can feel the eyes behind them. Behind the veils. I can feel expectation crowding the ceiling like smoke, waiting to see what I will become.

Raef doesn't reach for me no matter how badly I want him to. I'm not on my own, but I am at the same time. The strain shows in the set of his shoulders, in the way his breath comes as shallow as mine. Chest held tight like he's bracing for impact. I catch it in the twitch of his jaw, the way his hand hovers too close to his sword before he pulls it back. Not reassuring in the least. He'd warned me this will be a fight. He didn't say how many would smile while as they worked to break me. I won't let them. If they want to see me crack under their polite cruelty, they'll have to watch me stand first. If they want to see me snap, they'll have to work a hell of a lot harder than they think.

The throne room is split down the middle, not in architecture, but in temperament. One half rises toward a carved dome open to the gray sky, where beams of silvery light stream through narrow arches to strike the floor in rigid lines. The other half sinks into shadow. Stone columns, half-shrouded tapestries, and cold marble that drinks light instead of reflecting it.

The division runs straight through the floor, a seam of contrast so distinct I'm scared to walk over it. One side glimmers in distraction. The other...watches, hushed and waiting. The whole place is a nightmare dressed as a cathedral, beauty arranged with the sole purpose of unsettling visitors.

At the end of it all sits a throne.

It's not shaped like a chair. It's jagged and angular—more like a seat hacked from a fallen tree whose roots fossilized into crystal. The veins running through it pulse faintly red, like magic that's gone brittle and refuses to die. There are no cushions. No signs of softness. Because apparently comfort isn't for kings here. The edges look like they'd cut anyone foolish enough to sit too long.

The male who sits there isn't what I expect either. Handsome, devastatingly so, in the way some ancient statues are handsome with those perfect angles. His dark hair is swept back with care that says he's never broken a sweat in his life. Cheekbones sharp enough to chisel with, and a mouth carved for power, not kindness, the edge of his lips so stark I would be afraid to kiss him out of fear of losing my own to their blade.

He doesn't wear a crown; with his mere presence, it's an unnecessary doily. Power clings to him the way dust clings to a bookshelf. What he does wear is stranger. A thin braid of shadowy twine coiled behind one ear. It glints faintly, barely perceptible in his dark hair, the way an artifact never ends up in a burial by accident. A mark of something. Rank? Ownership? Whatever it means, no one else in the room wears one, so the message is crystal clear. Which means I'm supposed to notice it. Which also means I hate that I already have because I fell right into his clutches. He wants me to puzzle it out while he sits there watching. And damn it, it's working. My brain is already cataloguing possibilities like I'm back in a trench piecing together grave goods. I hate that he's somehow using my instincts against me, especially when we've never met before. He's turned my own way of seeing the world into part of the show. Which makes that little thread less of a symbol and more of a leash I've already tugged on by accident. And he knows it. While I'm busy decoding the thread, he's already assessing me.

His eyes catch mine, and the braid stops mattering. Raef's eyes are light, pale, and storm-shot, always edged with control, as he rations how much of himself he lets anyone see. That makes so much more sense now. This male's are black. Not like a void or ink. More like the obsidian that surrounds us. They're slick and gleaming with so much packed into one stare.

Suddenly I'm an artifact on display, a collectible. A curl at the corner of his gaze feels like a hand on skin that I didn't invite. A leer, dressed as appraisal, that leaves me wanting to scrub it off with sand and salt until my skin is red and raw. He's measuring me up, for sure, but he's enjoying what he sees. It's disgusting.

His mouth curves into a perfect, symmetrical, museum-ready smile, and it's rotten. The curl of the lips you see on tyrants that's flawless on the surface but poisoned underneath.

"So," he says, voice smooth as honey spilled over razors. "This is the girl who set the city aflame."

I open my mouth—and feel the copper ring tighten around my finger.

The short laugh that comes out of him rolls low and even, the sound of someone too sure of his own power to bother raising his voice. Unsurprisingly, it doesn't reach his eyes; if anything, it makes them darker, more intent, as he enjoys how uncomfortable it makes me. The sound slides under my skin in a way that leaves me wanting a scalding bath to burn it off.

"Still silent. How dutiful."

His gaze flicks to Raef, who stands beside me like a blade barely sheathed. That perfect mask he always wears has slipped. Enough to show the tension beneath. His father sees it; he savors it.

I see it too. The twitch in his jaw. The way his knuckles flex once before curling into fists at his sides.

"My son brings me so many gifts," the king says, still watching me. "Most of them are broken. Some of them, bleeding. You are...neither. How curious."

He rises from his throne in one fluid motion, no strength wasted because he doesn't have to work at it. How fae of him. Every line of his body says he's in control of the pace of the room, of me. There's no rush, but no hesitation; he moves with the certainty of someone who knows the ground will move to meet him. His lithe form descends the dais because it belongs to him alone, and I feel each graceful step like pressure settling in my chest.

My body tightens, except for my bladder, muscles locking before I can stop them triggering my fight or flight instincts. I've leaned too far over the edge of a drop, and I'm flailing a little as gravity decides which way I'll tip. Raef holds his own at my side, shoulders squared, jaw rigid in a dangerous stillness should it break, and I think he's close. Javi shifts behind me, like his body's ready to move whether his mind tells it to or not. And Tris, he goes the other way; I can feel him melting back into the shadow of the column near him, watching with a stillness that's all calculation. Which is somewhat empowering, giving a little more strength in my spine.

The king stops two paces from me. Close enough to smell something like ash and sandalwood, but with a sharper note I can't figure out.

He doesn't touch me. But he looks at me like he already has. "I wonder," he murmurs, "what you'll be worth once the mask comes off."

His gaze dips. To my hand. And the ring. Not the copper silence band—but *his* ring. Raef's. The one I can't remove. The one still pulsing faintly with magic that knows me now and claims me whether I like it or not.

The king stills, and before I can react to anything that's happening, his hand snaps around my wrist. The movement is clean and practiced, like someone grasping a delicate instrument they know for a fact won't break under this pressure. His grip isn't crushing, but it's absolute with no room for give or take. Heat flares against my skin in a way that makes me flinch inside, not from pain but violation, like the contact of his skin has branded me without leaving a mark. It feels beyond wrong. I have a sick certainty that even if he lets go, I'll still feel him there.

Raef moves as fast. His hand shoots out, fingers curling around the king's wrist. A quiet clash of skin against skin. Stillness snaps tight.

"Let her go," Raef says, his voice flat and serious. The hair along my arms lifts at the edge beneath it.

The king's eyes never leave mine, but something in them fractures, the way mirrors do right before they shatter. That smile—perfect, placid, poisonous—holds firm, but I can see the fury thrumming beneath it. It pulses off him in waves, barely banked.

"She wears your ring," he says, soft enough to be lethal.

"She does."

"And you didn't ask my leave?"

Raef's jaw locks. "I didn't know I needed it."

For a heartbeat, nothing moves.

The king releases me with a snap of his wrist, as if my skin has bitten him. I stumble back half a step before I catch myself. My wrist throbs from the mere memory of his grip. It lingers like frostbite, invisible but dangerous.

He turns, a fraction, and murmurs, "You never did know much, did you, my son?"

For a heartbeat even Raef goes rigid, and not in a confident way. His jaw locks so hard his cheeks look like caved stone, and his shoulders tighten enough for me to catch it even if no one else is meant to. His shift ripples outward anyway. I feel it in the sudden quiet and see it in the way the courtiers lean ever so slightly forward, like wolves scenting a wound. Even though he doesn't flinch, the room knows he's been struck.

The king ascends the steps again, robe trailing behind him like a dark promise.

"Come," he says without looking back. "Let us begin the reckoning."

The courtiers bow as one, fluid and flawless.

Raef's stance hasn't changed; that's how shocked he's become, realizing something, reading something in the room that I can't.

My hand...still burns where his father had touched me.

I have looked into the eyes of the male Raef never wants to become. I'm not sure which one of them scares me more. Because if Raef is the blade, then this king is the forge. And fire always leaves its mark.

"CUT ME TO glass," Raef says under his breath as he guides our group off to the "light" side of the room to the left of the dais.

"What?" I whisper to him as the copper ring slides off my finger. I've apparently been acknowledged enough now.

Tris is the one to whisper in my ear, "The king intends a spectacle just for you. He intends to show you why you should obey without question. It's a demonstration for his people, that he owns you and you aren't a threat."

My stomach coils. I know that tone. I've used it before, digging through bones, uncovering something I wasn't sure I wanted to see.

"Come now, you four, follow or suffer. You're the special guests after all," the King says, swiftly turning beyond the dais to a door in the back.

"Whatever you do, Rory, do not get ill. That's the epitome of weakness," Raef whispers to me as we proceed.

"What do you mean get ill…Raef? What exactly are we heading toward? … Raef?"

He doesn't answer, his eyes pleading with me as he stretches out an open hand, asking for my own. I take it hesitantly. The burns left by his father are cooling with our touch. His hand is steady, but I can feel the tremor hiding beneath it. That alone terrifies me more than anything else that's been said.

Tris sidles up to Raef's other side. "He tried, with that touch, to enter her mind. I kept him out this time, but we won't be that lucky again."

What?!

Raef nods, a succinct gesture that says the conversation is over. Well, he better mean for now.

The door spills us into an amphitheater, and my instincts bristle before my eyes even adjust to the change in light. Alarm bells, loud and insistent clang in my head. It's carved into the cliffside like a scar—narrow, tiered, lined in veiled black stone that drinks the light. No breeze stirs. Even the sun above is dimmer here, as if shadow has crept into the sky itself. Shadow clings to the edges of the pit, patient and waiting, and I can't shake the sense that the mountain itself has closed around us, shutting off any chance of escape.

Raef hasn't spoken since the throne room. Neither have I. Not even when he leads us to the edge of the viewing gallery and motions for us to sit.

They call it the Reckoning. "Ceremonial justice," the courtier that bowed earlier whispers. "A reminder of consequence," he adds, like it's something sacred to them; the whole court is about to bow their heads for a prayer. But there is nothing ceremonial happening.

The word "reckoning" makes me think of balance, of weight against weight, of truth tested on a scale. There's nothing balanced here. No ceremony I can see. It's a pit carved for blood and sport, and masks waiting to watch it spill. The word, here, tasted like ash all dressed up to hide the rot underneath. What follows only proves my feelings and intuition are spot on.

Three prisoners are brought into the pit below. Their feet are bare, chained, and bloodied from the drag across jagged stone. No one whispers their names. No charges are read aloud. But as they stand there trembling, the masked court begins to file in around us, silent and smooth, like oil poured across marble.

Movement ripples through the court, and there he is, King Selmire Noctarion. He doesn't need a crown to announce himself; as I surmised, the arena bends around him without one. He doesn't bring any guards, which is stupidly arrogant or equally terrifying. A predator doesn't parade protection when it knows it already owns all the teeth.

The only ornament is that coil of shadowy thread wound behind his ear, glinting in the low light as it carries meaning everyone else in the room already knows. His smile is even worse than before. I didn't think that possible. A half-formed expression carved by acute practice, not emotion. It's the smile of a serpent before it strikes. My stomach knots, because I can't tell if it's for me, Raef, or the whole damn court.

He steps into the center of the amphitheater. No sound accompanies his movement, no rustle of fabric, no click of a heel.

"You have all chosen," he says, quietly, "and now you will know the weight of those choices."

He walks to the first—a woman with silver braids and veins blackened by something. "This one," he states, "spoke a name not hers to speak during Veilfast. A name buried. A name we do not touch."

He doesn't raise his hand. Doesn't cast a noticeable spell. The sound of her scream rips through the pit, high and raw, making my teeth ache.

Shadow blooms from her mouth. It's not smoke; even from this distance it looks like thick, black threads, glistening. They pierce through the skin of her lips, drag through her tongue and her cheeks, sliding deeper until the dark silk vanishes down her throat. Every inch pulls sound out of her, not muting it but unraveling it, scream by scream, until nothing is left.

She collapses, choking on silence, and my whole body jerks; those threads snagging me too. I can almost feel them dragging over my own mouth, phantom lines stitching tight across my teeth. My jaw locks against it, clamping so hard it aches; it's trying to keep the magic out by sheer force. The taste of copper sparks in the back of my throat anyway, either from my own tongue or her ghost blood.

I keep inhaling slowly through my nose, remembering Raef's words. Don't puke, don't puke, don't puke. The words beat with my pulse, so ridiculous, but better than focusing on the wet scrape of those threads.

Bile climbs my throat anyway, hot and sour, and I clamp down harder. My eyes sting. God, if I lose it here, if I crumple in front of this court, they'll file me under weak before I even finish retching. Part of me wants to look away, to pretend I didn't watch a woman's voice get torn out of her like a string from a spindle. But I can't. I've spent my whole life staring at ruins where these types of punishments happened hundreds, even thousands of years ago, the stone and metal that's left after they broke themselves—but witnessing it for myself? This is breaking in real time. I can't stop seeing it.

Selmire moves to the second—a gardener, they say. Someone who tends roots. The King says his roots whisper with foreign, banned magic.

The man's shadow begins to move. It slides outward, peeling from his heels like oil on water. My stomach lurches before it even touches him.

The darkness strikes; tendrils wrap around his arms and his legs, yanking him to the stone. His back arches with the pull, tendons standing out in his neck as he screams. We all do, maybe. Except the court. Except Raef. Except the king. So, it's just me, but since no one looks, perhaps it's all in my head.

His shadow flays him alive. It shears across his skin, strips of darkness slicing flesh into ribbons. The tearing is wet, sticky, and worse than anything I've ever heard. His magic peels with it, threads of light sucked out and shredded like overripe fruit left too long in the sun. Rotten sweetness.

The stench hits me next. Burnt copper, bile, feces, something charred that coats my tongue as if I swallowed ash. My throat heaves. I gag, hard, doubling into myself, but I don't dare let it out. Tris's hand presses two fingers firm against my thigh without looking at me. He's trying to anchor me; I can feel it. I claw at the edge of my seat instead, nails splitting against stone I can't afford to let go of.

The third, God, he's a boy. Young. Terrified.

I wrap my hand tighter in Raef's hold. Grasping his arm with my other hand. I can't watch this; I can't.

"You must," he says softly. "I'm sorry... I'm so sorry." His voice sounds older in this place. Not like Raef-the-prince or Raef-the-warrior. Like Raef-the-survivor.

"Deserter," the king says. "Or perhaps dreamer. You ran from your conscription. From your place. So, I offer you a choice as I'm feeling lenient today. You may thank the Atma Princess."

The boy sobs, and everyone looks at me. Their masked faces don't move, but I feel it, like they're peeling open my soul.

"Serve me," Selmire continues, "as a shadow-bound. Your name, gone. Your will, mine. Or bleed your truth here."

The boy shakes his head. Whispering something I can't hear.

Selmire smiles. Then he raises his hand.

A blade appears. From nowhere. It shimmers, silver, curved, humming like it drinks the light.

He slits the boy's throat in one fluid motion. Not quick. The blade drags deep, carving from one side to the other, prying the neck open like a book I never want to read again. Blood spills faster than my mind can keep up, hot and bright against the cold, pale stone. I can't tell if I'm choking on air or bile.

"Oh God." Tears well in my eyes and spill over. I gag once, twice. Raef grabs my hand with his other so he can trace slow circles along my back. I can feel Tris's light touch on my thigh.

"Breathe through it, love," he says. "It's almost over."

But I can't feel my legs. My ears ring. The taste of copper is in my throat, and it doesn't belong to me.

Blood pours into the grooves of the stone floor. The amphitheater drinks it.

The sound of the child's blood is interrupted by a ripple of clapping, almost dainty. No cheers or shouts, just the crisp patter of palms meeting. Like an opera had ended. Like nothing monstrous had happened at all. They applaud like murder deserves proper etiquette. I think I hate them. I think I understand them. And that scares me more.

My stomach turns. My hands are fists.

Tris's eyes have gone glassy with fury. Raef stares ahead. Blank.
This is his home. Now, it's mine too.
I need to open that damn gate again.

45

A Practical Guide to Not Vomiting at State Dinners

I EMPTY MY STOMACH THE moment we're out of sight. Down a narrow corridor behind the grand atrium, I brace one hand against cold marble and let my stomach empty into a basin carved with wings. The wings are chipped. One feather broken clean off. The water inside is rust-stained. It doesn't look ceremonial. It barely looks used.

They don't help. Nothing about this place does. The stone holds the screams like echoes. I can still hear them. Thread pulled through flesh, a throat opening like a piece of fruit.

I wipe my mouth with the back of my hand. No one says a word. Not Raef. Not Tris. Not Javi, who offers me a flask of something that tastes like herbs and steel. It burns enough to remind me I'm still here. Still in this body. Still in this court of nightmares. Still inside a story I never wanted.

But there's no reprieve. Not here.

"That was a boy, a child," I seethe.

"I know," Raef says, cradling my face in his hands. "I'm sorry, Rory. You should never have had to watch that. I'd hoped… I hoped we would have had some time to prepare you before seeing his cruelty."

"He offered him leniency on my behalf?"

"No," Tris says from behind us. "He offered that boy a fate worse than death. The king would sully his mind, trap him inside, and take over his body, where the boy would be witness to unimaginable cruelties committed with his own hands and have the power to do nothing about it."

My stomach lurches again. This time, I manage to hold it down. But the bitter taste of bile doesn't leave.

"Oh God…" I whine. "He offered to do that on my behalf?"

"It's purely political," Raef says. "He's sullying your name before you can show the people who you are."

Before I've even found out who I am.

A steward appears moments later, expression blank, voice too smooth. "The feast awaits."

Of course it does. This court doesn't take a break; it pivots onto the next mediocre thing. Cruelty in, silk out. That's how they function here. Like lungs that only work if fed blood first. And they have the audacity to call the Frenzied animals. The screams of the dying don't fade; they get lacquered over with candlelight and silver platters.

Everyone accepts it as normal. It's the natural rhythm of life. This isn't a new concept. Civilizations have built their beauty on the bones of the dead for eons. Now that I know what I know, maybe they learned that from the fae. The Aztecs with their altars still sticky when the feast drums started. The Romans paraded the condemned through marble arches before tossing them to beasts, all while vendors sold wine and honey cakes. Egypt's banquets for the gods, perfumed halls that reeked of incense while slaves bled in the sand outside. It's always the same story: a people dressing their horror in ceremony so it looks like culture instead of cruelty.

Now, I'm not studying it from a distance of time and decay. I'm sitting at their table.

We're led into a banquet hall that shouldn't exist in a place like this—too grand, too radiant. It's someone trying to wallpaper over a dungeon with opulence. The long table glows with candlelight caught in red crystal, the light fracturing into ruby shards that dance across the walls. Silver vines curl across platters of golden fruit, carved meats, and pastries that glisten like lacquered gems.

It smells like cinnamon, roasted meat, and lies. Thick enough to cling to the back of my throat, sweetened with honey glaze and something rich and creamy.

The atmosphere hums with a low, constant murmur, the rustle of silks, the faint scrape of silver cutlery, and the measured gulps of wine.

Heat radiates from the torches, seeping into the skin at my neck, but the marble under my palms is cold as a tomb slab. The two don't balance; they press against me from both sides.

I've never wanted to eat less in my life. Considering I've been presented with chocolate-covered bugs. I'd take the bugs. Any day. At least they didn't die screaming.

The Shadow King lounges at the head of the table, a vulture dressed in velvet. His smile is back—sleek and soft, like none of the carnage matters. He looks sated already. Not from the feast spread before him, no, he feasts on fear.

"Ah," he says, lifting a glass. "The honored guests arrive, and not a minute too soon. You'll forgive the...opening acts. They do so love their theater." His voice licks across the table like smoke from a burning library, quiet, choking, carrying ruin under its sweetness.

My seat is too close to his. Every bite I don't take, he notices. I feel his gaze like a brand against my cheek. He's waiting to see what cracks first, my appetite or my nerve.

"To the girl who lit the city aflame," he says, voice silken and strong. "May your fire never dim."

I don't drink. I can't. The wine gleams like blood in glass, and for one sick second I picture it spilling over the stone the way his victims' did. If I swallow that, if I let it in, I'm not sure I'll ever get the taste out.

Raef does. His throat works once, hard, and his cup hits the table louder than it should.

The king's eyes flick to mine. "Do you remember your mother?"

I freeze, fork halfway to my mouth, the slick fruit I had speared sliding off the tines and splattering on my plate. What kind of question is that? Of course I remember my mother. I haven't been here long enough to forget her face, her voice, or the smell of cheap coffee in the mornings. But the way he asks twists under my skin. He's testing for something and not truly interested in my answer.

"I hear blood calls to blood." His mouth curves, all white teeth and perfection, but no warmth. He's a predator preparing to bite. "And some bloodlines," his gaze lingers too long on me, "are more flammable than others."

My necklace thrums against my sternum, answering his call. I always told myself it meant nothing, a trinket left with me from birth. Since coming here, I'm beginning to wonder if that was ever the case.

Tris leans forward, eyes narrowing. He's not angry. I'm not sure I've seen him angry before. His mind is spinning a mile a minute, but I don't know what he's calculating. Is he picking apart what the king is saying? Or is he planning an attack that would be foolhardy at best? Next to me, Javi's hand tightens on his knife until his knuckles pale. He's not thinking strategy. He's thinking defense. I can feel the tension radiating off both, two different responses to the same threat, and neither one makes me feel safer.

The king sees it all. Watches us like a scholar watching insects. We've been dissected before the meal's even begun. He hasn't spilled a single drop of wine while doing it.

The silence after the king's words stretches long enough to suffocate. Tris relaxes again and reaches for his goblet. He doesn't raise it high, just enough.

His words are steady and intentional, each one measured like he's done this before. "To the dead queen of the Shadow Court," he says. "May her fire burn longer than the one who tried to snuff it. May her mercy and kindness live long in her heirs."

A heartbeat passes. Another. Around the table, courtiers freeze. The tension is a string drawn so tight I could reach out and pluck it. He doesn't say her name, but everyone seems to know exactly who he speaks of.

I glance at Raef, but he's still. His jaw is tight, his hand curled beneath the table into a fist. The only sign that anything's off is the ring on my finger tightening. Is it warning me or mirroring him?

The king's smile doesn't falter. It stretches a fraction more, the way a blade looks longer when it tilts its edge into the light. "A touching sentiment," he says, swirling his wine. "Though I'm afraid shades have no place at a celebration. We feast for the living."

His voice is too smooth. The silk of it stretches over something sharper. Blood-slicked.

Tris tips his goblet back in blatant defiance. I follow suit even though the smell of it alone makes my stomach clench. The bitterness hits my tongue like a bottle of ink. I choke it down, steadying my hand on the stem of the glass, daring him with my glare. He wants me to show weakness, to gag or grimace, to prove I'm not good enough. I won't give him that. Not now. Not ever.

"We have much to prepare for. My son will marry at the next moons, during Fyrfall."

I sputter into my wine, and it burns up my nose as I cough and nearly choke on it. Across from me, Raef goes rigid, his knuckles whitening against the stem of his untouched glass. Tris's lips part on a hissed word I barely catch over my own noises.

That doesn't sound good at all.

The wine scorches down the wrong pipe, and my heart follows it. The next moons? How long is that? And what does he mean by marry? Because I have a feeling our definitions are vastly different.

When the trade in stolen lives swelled beyond bearing,

she broke with the courts she once held in balance.

With her consorts and her Sanguine king,

she shattered the meeting place of realms

and called the tide to swallow its door.

The Gate that had fed on mortal fear

sank beneath a storm of her making.

Not for crown. Not for conquest.

For the mortals who had never given consent.

-Book of the Atma, The First Age

46

PRELIMINARY STUDY OF STAR-FORGED CAGES

THE FIRE'S TOO BIG FOR the size of the room. It's loud and hungry, but I sit close anyway. The heat bites at my face, a poor trade for the chill lodged under my ribs. Every chamber in this cursed palace is built to impress, not to provide comfort: marble walls veined like frozen lightning, obsidian floors polished so bright they throw my dark reflection back at me in shards. It's beautiful, sure, but that fragile beauty of silken petals that bruise when you touch them.

The air tastes of iron and smoke, the way old cathedrals do when the candles have burned too long. Despite the warmth, my breath fogs near the edges of the room. It's not a large room, and the fire is large, but for unknown reasons, the heat doesn't reach the edges. I lean forward, elbows on my knees, trying to let the heat soak through the ache that still lives in my bones.

The copper silence ring sits where I left it, catching firelight on the table's black surface. It's so misleading and so delicate to be a weapon, and yet that's exactly what it is. Or was. It looks so simple, like something I unearthed from a burial years ago, some simple jewelry bestowed on a chieftain's wife. I will never look at a simple piece of jewelry the same again, because even without the magic, it can mean so much more than decoration for a finger or a neck. It can weigh so much more on the soul. I hate it. Hate how it glints, flaunting its curse. Hate that my skin still feels it, phantom tight, a chain, a manacle to keep me silent.

There's no doubt in my mind that if I had been born in another time, I would have been a loud and obnoxious suffragette. But if what they're all implying is true, I *was* born in another time. Somehow. Born long before human women fought for their voice in the United States. I've been trying to wrap my head around how that was even possible and failing miserably. Between the claims of Raef and Tris and even Selmire and my dreams, nothing is adding up. Two plus two is still coming to five. If my dreams aren't dreams but memories, I was a child, not an infant, but my parents adopted an infant thousands upon thousands of years after the ruler of Atlantis was killed. None of this makes any sort of sense, even when you take out the magic and all of the things here that don't make sense anyway: floating streams, mind readers, siphons, vampires, purple meadows, and murder grass.

The quiet scrape of old hinges slices straight through my racing thoughts. I don't need to look away from the fire to know who it is. The air shifts a certain way around Raef, something I recognize now. It's cooler and heavier and carries the scent of steel and pine. I keep my eyes on the fire, pretending its crackles are more interesting than whatever apology he's rehearsed.

"I was wondering when you'd remember where I live," I say, my voice dry enough to blister anyone's hide.

My snide commentary doesn't bait him into speaking, but that's not surprising. The silence stretches, thin as wire. He crosses the room with steps soft against the obsidian, even, and not minutely close to careless or relaxed.

His coat hangs open, the edges dusted with ashes and grit, the faint scent of cold air and steel following him inside. His shoulders aren't squared for battle this time; they're bowed, weighted with something I know he won't share with me. I can see the tension settle through him. He very much looks like a man who's practiced holding himself together and is now realizing I'm watching the cracks.

He's cataloguing each movement, each tick, like he's afraid the wrong sound might set me off. He's not mistaken. What he doesn't realize is that his mere presence has 'set me off.'

"You're in shock," he says.

"No shit," I spit at him. "No, actually I think I'm more furious."

"I told you—"

"No...no, you don't get to pull any I-told-you-so bullshit," I snap some more, pointing a very stiff finger at him. "Not this time. You told me nothing but vague 'my father sucks' nonsense. You prepared me for nothing. I walked in here blind and foolish, and he wiped the floor with me."

I'm so tense my hands are clenched into shaking fists. My chest so tight it feels like my ribs might bruise from the inside, but my mouth doesn't stop. If I stop, I'll fold in on myself, wet paper incapable of keeping itself open. It's either lay into him or shatter, and I'm so done with shattering, done with picking myself up from the rubble like some fragile artifact that no one dares touch. I keep pushing the words out, each one a strike of a pick against stone, carving out space to breathe in a place that wants me small.

"Rory—"

"You should've warned me," I whisper. "About the executions. About what this place is."

He stays standing even though there are multiple places for him to sit and relax. Rigid as the marble walls around us. He's not indifferent; he's controlled, and it costs him. He holds himself rigid and plants his feet acting like motion would break something—me or himself.

"I never wanted you to see that," he says finally.

I laugh, a quick, crazed thing slipping out of my throat. "Too late, Raef. I saw firsthand what your father calls justice. A woman silenced, a farmer literally torn apart, and a boy killed for crying and being scared. Tell me how that's ruling. Go on. Tell me how great fascism and dictatorships are. Because they haven't destroyed kingdoms and countries for centuries back home. Does he hand out crowns for cruelty here, or is that just a family perk?"

The muscle in his jaw jumps. I want to hit something as my blood continues to boil and steam.

"You knew it would happen. You knew what he'd show me, and you still brought me here," I add, voice trembling with anger, exhaustion, and betrayal.

I stand, pacing to the curtained windows. "What did he mean about my mother?"

His mouth opens, then closes again as he shifts his weight. He at least shows me enough courtesy not to start lying, but I'm giving him no room to even try.

"Don't you dare lie to me or give me vague answers and if you even try that 'you wouldn't understand' or 'not now' bullshit, I swear on everything you hold holy, Raef Noctarion—"

"She was Atma," he says quietly. "Not Sea. Not Greenwood. Not Shadow. Older than any of them."

I turn to face him. "What does he mean 'blood calls to blood'? He acts like he knows."

Raef's jaw tightens. "He *believes* you're descended directly from the High Queen. The one who ruled with the Atma, who closed the gates of Atlantis, before the walling of Fyrala."

My mind blanks for a second because I already know the numbers don't add up; I already surmised this was the answer I would get. "But she's been dead for—what, ten thousand years?"

"Closer to fifty thousand years here. Ten thousand in your mortal years."

"That's impossible."

"I agree." His eyes drop to the floor for a moment, then lift again, darker than the firelight should make them. "But impossibility doesn't matter here. Belief does."

He seems to settle into the conversation, releasing a deep sigh. The fire paints sharp lines across his face, cheekbone, and jaw, the muscle working there like he's chewing on something bitter. "And if he thinks your blood carries hers... he'll do anything to control it.

When he meets my eyes, the distance between us hums with static. "He already tried to invade your mind. Tris had to block him."

My hand lifts instinctively to my temple, my fingers pressing against the pulse that flutters there. It aches now, dull and ghostly. I can picture it like a bruise blooming beneath the skin of my mind. I didn't feel him in there when he tried it, and that makes me sick all over again. The idea that someone can crawl through my thoughts without me knowing, without even a flicker of warning, makes my skin feel creepy, like I'm wearing it inside out.

I ignore the scariest part of that confession. "He thinks she's my mother? My birth mother?"

Raef meets my eyes, solemn, the static crackling between us still. "In his mind, yes. You have her eyes, he says. Her presence from the few portraits that continued to exist after her execution."

"He wasn't even *alive* when she died. He can't know any of that."

"No," Raef says. "But some of his spies...his seers...they see the echo of her in you. And that's enough."

I back toward the fire, toward the only light in this damned place, and sink into the low chair again. Everything hurts. But more than that, everything feels too big. Too far gone to fight. Everyone is two steps ahead of me, and I'm crawling to catch up.

I get up and return to my pacing; I can't sit. There's too much energy boiling in my veins, enough that it makes my voice jagged. "Is that what you think I am? A threat? A mistake you bound yourself to?"

"No." His voice is too low and too vulnerable for my current condition. "I think you're the only thing he didn't plan for, and that scares him."

I hold his gaze with my own. I don't know whether I want to scream again or crawl into his arms and disappear. I settle for doing neither. I burn in silence.

He doesn't push to continue, reading the room well. I'm sure he was trained his entire life to do that. Our breathing syncs close enough that I can't hear the difference while the fire hisses and cracks.

I fix on those sounds, bracing an arm against the mantle, hanging my sore head while I stare at the flames in some sort of meditation. I think it's my focus on those normal sounds that clues me in to the fact that we're not alone anymore; the introduction of the creaking hinges is far more noticeable in the silence.

Tris strolls in first, shirt untucked, hair windblown like he walked out of a romantic poem or a Jane Austen movie. Javi follows, calmer, but with that quiet fire in his eyes. I didn't hear them knock either. I thought they were princes, nobles. Did no one teach them to knock before entering someone else's room? Is that not something that passes as proper in this world?

"They assigned you rooms?" Raef asks tightly.

"They're across the palace," Javi replies. "And haunted by smug silence and decorative trauma."

Tris throws himself onto a couch. "We're sleeping here."

Raef pinches the bridge of his nose. "That's not safe."

"Neither is leaving her alone," Javi says. "She doesn't belong in a place like this."

"I'm standing *right here*," I snap. My voice cracks like flint against stone, sharp and cutting. Any calm I'd achieved moments ago has flown out the window on the back of an albatross.

Tris raises a hand in mock surrender. "Noted, starfire."

Javi's expression softens. "We're not leaving you, Rory. You already saw what this court does to people."

Raef sighs. "He'll punish you."

"He'll have to get in line," Tris says lazily. "Now. What did we interrupt?"

"Fyrfall," I say, wanting to move on to the next insane topic of the evening.

Javi frowns. "The meteor storm?"

I'm not amused, and make sure he knows it. "Explain."

Tris's mouth stays in a flat line, no trace of his usual grin, and that makes my heart drop down to my intestines. "Not just that."

Raef leans forward, hands braced on the table. "Fyrfall marks a moment of alignment—when the stars, the old gods, and the laws of magic synchronize every twelve years or so. For one night, as the stars fall, the gods, the fates, and all the powerful beings listen. And anything bound then, any vow made, remains unbroken—forever."

My tongue sticks to the roof of my mouth, a useless thing, not that I have anything to say, but it's dry as bone. The one time I need words, I need to fight the nonsense and chaos, my body says, 'nope.'

Tris decides to chime in and clarify, not that it's needed. I understood well and good what Raef was trying to say. "Any vow. Any oath. Any tether forged under Fyrfall becomes cosmic law. You could tear the world apart, little star, and it still won't break."

Javi sits closer to me as I fall into the cushion next to him. "That's not a wedding. It's a sentence."

Raef meets my eyes, the concern and the guilt an open book for anyone to read. "He knows what it means. That's *why* he chose it. He wants us shackled. Not just publicly. Not just politically. But in the bones of the realm itself. He's punishing me."

I swallow hard. There's so much implication in what he's not saying that it's hard to even process what does come out of his mouth. "Even if I say yes now..."

"You can't take it back," Raef finishes.

I look to Tris, and he stares back. "You'd be his forever. Not Raef's. Not yours. *His.* The king may not wear a crown, but he forges his power, his throne, from chains."

Javi's fingers find mine, a quiet bridge across the chaos in my head. His skin is warm and steady where mine trembles, solid in a way that nothing else in this place feels right now. "We won't let it happen. There's got to be another way."

I don't trust the promise, not really. But the contact is an anchor I need right now, not that I'd admit it out loud. His thumb moves once, slow against my knuckles, and the simple pressure steadies my body better than any spell or vow. The fear's still there; I don't think it ever won't be, not until I get home, but it finally has somewhere to go, so I'm not buzzing along the surface all the time. It's not smothering the spark inside me that's been fighting for air.

Raef's face doesn't change, making it obvious—no other way exists.

His voice is quiet when he finally speaks. "It wouldn't just bind us together, like the ring. It would change you. A bond like this seeps into everything—your magic, your choices, your name. Even love doesn't matter.

It would be written into the stars. Literally into both of our eternities, the afterlife."

I can feel myself hyperventilating. Javi wraps his arms around me, trying to hold in my fear, my soul, my everything. "Then why did you go pale when he said it?"

"Because I know what it would cost you," he says. "Because I know what it would cost *me*."

Silence stretches.

Tris finally murmurs, "He's dressing it up like honor. But this...this is how tyrants build cages. How they control people. Create fear and conflict and reward those loyal with more cages they can't escape from."

The fire snaps behind us. I'm too raw to react even though my mind noticed.

"So that's it? We don't even have to have sex? He can make this permanent because of some crazy meteor shower and circumvent everything?"

"If we'd wandered around another week, we could have—I didn't think, Rory. I didn't make the connection. It's my fault, and I cannot express how sorry I am to have put you in this position again." Raef says, kneeling in front of me and taking my hands.

The silence doesn't last as my brain kicks back in...somehow. It's like surfacing from deep water, lungs full of panic, but finally catching air.

"It's not just the when," I murmur. "It's the how. Right? You said intention doesn't matter much here."

Raef's eyes meet mine, a flicker of something there—hope, or desperation. It's hard to tell the difference. "What are you thinking?"

"Clever girl," Tris says softly, the glint in his violet eyes beyond admiring.

Javi leans forward, brows drawn. "So...we bury the danger in the phrasing. In the wording of whatever vow you take. Building loopholes?"

"We have to be careful enough that the king doesn't detect what we're doing. That's the hard part," I say, finally feeling some hope for myself. It isn't much, just a thread, but I cling to it like it might unravel the whole trap.

Raef smiles. "No, it won't be that hard. Shadow Court marriage isn't a public spectacle. They're private. Intimate. Which means we can choose whatever words we want. No one else will hear but us and the stars."

"We vow alliance," I say. "Not ownership. We vow mutual protection. Not magic sharing or stealing bondage bullshit."

Tris tilts his head. "But the stars might not accept half-measures. Fyrfall magic isn't interested in nuance."

"No," Raef agrees. "But it *is* literal. If we word it precisely enough—tie it to time, place, specific intent—we can give it limits." He looks like he's thinking out loud now. Like the idea is forming faster than his fear. I like this openness, it feels like a truce, like a true partnership blooming instead of whatever it was before.

Javi nods. "What if the vow you take expires? 'Until the storm ends' or 'so long as the Shadow Court stands' phrasing?"

Tris smirks. "You could lace it with misdirection? 'I vow to remain as yours as you are mine.' A perfect mirror—useless if either side breaks."

The idea clicks into place, clean and simple, a puzzle piece slipping exactly where it should be. "Like a spell with a backdoor."

"Exactly," Tris says. "But subtle. Too subtle for a narcissist drunk on power to notice."

I finally drag in a full breath, the first one since he showed up and started dismantling my evening. It burns a touch going down, but at least it's air. The weight bearing down on my shoulders doesn't lift, but it shifts, becoming something I can carry, at least for while.

We fall into silence again, but this time, it's different. The air isn't weighted with fear—it's charged with cunning.

"They'll be watching," Javi says. "Your father, the courtiers, but they won't hear what she whispers."

"Then we whisper well," Raef says. He gives a small, grim smile. "We make the vow. We survive the night, and we leave with the stars bent to *our* shape. I'll have to consult with someone, but this could work."

Tris raises an imaginary glass. "To the woman who outfoxed the constellations. Who rewrites the stars."

He says it like a toast, and now I can look to our future without flinching. That little ember inside flares a bit more.

And for the first time in weeks, I feel something more than dread.

I feel ready.

47

How to Carbon Date Your Trauma

WHAT THE BOYS DON'T TELL me is that Fyrfall is in two days. What they do tell me—Raef, Tris, and Javi, all in their own clipped and hovering ways—is to stay in my suite while they handle *things*. None of them define *things*. None of them admit they're nervous. But they hover like they expect the walls to bite me.

So, I spend the morning encased in silk, stitched into by half a dozen seamstresses who murmur in yet another language I don't know. The room smells of starch and hot wax, and their needles flick like insects, with the steady hiss of thread through fabric that's starting to feel like snakes hiding in the brush. The oldest of them hums softly, a tuneless sound that grates like nails on a chalkboard. The youngest keeps her head bowed, dark braid swinging forward to hide her face, fingers trembling whenever they brush my skin. Another has eyes clouded white, blind maybe, and yet her needlework looks the best out of all of them.

The gown begins at my collarbone and ends in stars—literally. Glittering beads of spell-fused glass that twinkle whenever I shift. The skirt moves like water, but darker and colder, and every time I shift, it sighs. They tell me the shadows are *trained*. That if I wander too far from Raef during the ceremony, they'll tighten like vines.

Charming.

They don't mention what happens if I run instead of wander and I let my imagination run wild. Because the fact that they don't tell me anything about running says all I need to know.

By midday, I'm done pretending I can sit still. The air is too heavy, and the constant silence is like a bedfellow that's far too polite. The damn torches on the wall burn bright but give off no heat, feeling fake, like everything else in this place. It's fake, all of it, and everyone is fake. Like mean girls times a thousand, and I'm starting to lose it.

The second gown they stitched stays on, clinging to me like a second skin. I can't tell if I'm wearing it or being worn. The fabric's too fine, too tight, it was intended for someone with smaller lungs and fewer options. Layers of silk and satin tug at my shoulders every time I move, whispering against themselves like gossiping teenagers. The seams itch, the collar pinches, and whoever designed this thing clearly never had to sit down in it.

By the time I try, the bodice presses so hard I can feel my pulse in my ribs. The scent of starch and perfume clings to me, heavy and sweet enough to make me regret lunch. My skin feels trapped inside it, like it's being wrapped for display. Give me a pair of cargo pants and a t-shirt, please. My thoughts start pacing the same way my feet want to. I need space. I need air. I need—

Raef left a rune-locked charm on the door. A soft chime sounds if I cross the threshold—so he'll know, they'll all know. I cross it anyway. I press my fingers to the seam, daring the alarm to stop me. It doesn't. The door opens like it's been waiting. Like it agrees. I can't breathe in here.

The halls outside my suite feel alive in the worst possible way. They're not full of people, plants, or animals alive and moving. The air moves when nothing's there, brushing my neck like a set of frisky fingers. The stone under my soft slippers vibrates low, as if something big and buried is saying hello. Mirrors line the walls, but half of them lie. One ripples when I pass, twisting my reflection until it looks like someone else. Someone I don't want to meet alone in a dark alley, much less here.

This place doesn't feel like a home. I'm the smudge that doesn't belong and needs to be wiped away.

I wander past veiled courtiers who don't speak. Past statues that weren't there a moment ago. Past a corridor I swear led to the library, now ending in a stairwell that disappears into fog. Every step feels like a mistake, but turning around would be a bigger one.

I should go back. There are no windows here. The light comes from veins in the stone, emitting a strange silvery glow. I walk without direction through hushed halls and chambers where the air itself feels like a dare.

Just when I feel utterly and completely lost, I find it. A portrait room— or mausoleum—I can't tell which. Oil paintings hang in intentional disorder, some old enough to have cracked beneath their lacquer. All loom, both grand and severe, meant to remind you who holds the power here. None of them have name plaques. It's all faces staring down from their gilded prisons, daring you to forget they were ever human. Then again, I guess they were never human.

The silence here is different. Not heavy like grief, not cold like the hallways. It's reverent. As if this chamber remembers what the rest of the palace tries to forget.

A young woman stops me cold. Pale as starlight, with dark hair coiled like silk, her eyes light as frost. They're Raef's eyes. Not similar, the same.

My mouth goes dry. I don't know her, but something inside me reacts like I do. Like I've seen her standing in moonlight. Like she's always been there, behind the veil of dream.

My heart skips around in my chest like a giddy schoolgirl.

There's power in this canvas. Something ancient curled in the corners of her painted smile. I take a step closer, then another, so we're practically nose to nose. It's not that she's beautiful. It's that she's watching. I don't think she's ever stopped looking for what she left behind.

"She's been watching since these walls were soft," says a voice behind me.

I spin so fast my heel scrapes the floor. My pulse trips over itself before I even see where he is.

A figure stands half in shadow, tall, robed in a soft gray, fingers ink-stained and clasped neatly. His voice is quiet but not unkind, with the soft lilt of an accent, which automatically sets off alarm bells in my head. A curtain of pale hair falls past his jaw.

"I did not mean to startle you," he adds, bowing slightly. "Few come this way. Fewer are meant to."

His presence doesn't scream danger, but that doesn't relax me, not in this realm. He moves like a ghost who hasn't decided if it's haunting you or helping.

"And you are?" My voice comes out steady despite the shake to my legs. *I should have stayed in my room.*

He smiles, and it's genuine, and that makes my heart skip a beat. "Emrys," he says, placing his right hand over his heart. "I am the king's archivist and researcher."

Archivist. That explains the ink and the semi-creepy silent demeanor. The careful posture, like everything he does is a footnote. I should be asking more questions. I should be backing away, but I don't. Because somehow, I think he's the first person I've met here who might tell me the truth. It's a feeling in my gut, and I learned a long time ago to trust that feeling. It has yet to steer me wrong, well except with the creepy cat-bat thing, but that wasn't my fault.

He stands with me in the silence, letting the moment stretch. Letting the weight of that portrait settle on my shoulders like a second skin.

"She had his eyes," I say aloud.

"No," he replies. "Raef has hers."

I glance at him. He's right, of course, but I can't catch the extra meaning behind his words, just that they're there.

He's watching the painting, but there's something in his posture—like reverence, even quiet mourning.

"Tell me," I say.

After a long pause and a deep breath, "She was not meant for this court."

His voice is quiet, almost a whisper, as if speaking louder would wake something that should stay sleeping. He doesn't want our conversation overheard. Noted.

"Her name is gone now. Forbidden, as you've seen, but once, she was a light in this dark place. Soft. Too soft, many said, but she never bent. Not to the cruelty. Nor the shadows. She smiled at monsters and kissed maids on the forehead. She grew herbs on windowsills and sang to the palace cats."

He breaks off, his throat working once before he forces himself steady again. Whatever he was about to say tastes sour on his tongue.

The image he paints pierces me, this queen who tended cats and kept her spine straight while monsters circled. I can see her, clearer than any painting. Not a queen. A woman who chose kindness anyway. Someone I would have liked, I think.

"Her marriage to the king was arranged before she ever stepped foot into the valley. A gift from the Greenwood, some say a binding made to stave off war. She bore him sons. Twins. Something beyond rare among the fae. The bloodline was secured, and with it, his attention...vanished."

My hands curl at my sides, nails biting into the flesh of my palms. There's something visceral about hearing her life reduced into a transaction. A woman's usefulness and worth can easily be written down to dowries and bloodlines and political leverage. I've studied enough civilizations to know arranged marriages weren't always cruel. Sometimes they meant survival, unity, even peace and close family ties. But this? This sounds like ownership disguised as alliance. Like every story carved into a temple wall where the queen smiles while her cage is gilded.

"He took lovers," Emrys continues. "Publicly. Viciously. He made her watch sometimes. Caged her with his own desires. She said nothing. Not out of weakness, but out of pride and dignity. She raised her sons with care even when he turned them into weapons."

"That's disgusting. I mean, some people like it, watching others, but I...to make her watch him fuck someone else—"

The words spill out before I can stop them. Crude. Unfiltered. But true. It makes me sick. It makes my skin crawl. It makes me think of how he looked at me across the throne room, like I was already his favorite game.

He shifts his feet a fraction, the only sign that the story was taking a cruel turn.

"And then...she fell in love."

No.

"No one knows with whom. A courtier, perhaps, or a warrior, or maybe a mage who tended the ancient runes. It doesn't matter in the end. What matters is that he lit that light within her again. Quietly, but real."

My heart thuds. Because I know that feeling. The sudden spark in a dead place. The rebellion of hope. It's the same pulse that hits in the middle of a long, relentless, boring dig, when the dirt gives way to something ancient and impossible, when you realize the past isn't gone, it's buried and waiting further on. It's dangerous, that kind of hope. It tricks you into thinking you can breathe again, that maybe you're not trapped after all. I've felt it recently. It always costs something.

"The king noticed. Not much escapes him. He broke her maid's mind to find the truth—the one she trusted most. A terrible, cruel death for the queen's oldest friend. She fought him herself. Her mind shields were stronger than most. But they were bonded... and even love doesn't guard forever."

I stagger back a step, that quiet, agonizing truth hitting hard. A life destroyed not by swords, but by slow violations. By possession and betrayal. I don't realize I'm shaking until Emrys touches my wrist. Just a brush of his calloused fingers.

"He wore her down. Most say she broke under the sorrow. That she slit her own wrists with an Atlantean blade. That the grief took her." He looks me in the eyes. "But some of us...know better."

He waits, the expert storyteller, as he lets that sink in. As the tears form in my eyes.

"He took her mind, and then he slit her wrists for her."

The room tilts some. My pulse thundering in my ears, but everything else fades, like I've fallen into the stillness between layers of earth. Not one place, but not yet the next either. My brain tries to catalogue the horror of it, to name it, but all I can manage is the shaking in my hands.

My voice comes out raw. "That's terrible. No one stopped him?"

"There was no one left strong enough to try. Not then."

We stand there a long time. Sharing air and remembering a woman I never knew—but somehow recognize in the ache behind my ribs.

"She wasn't like the rest of them," I whisper.

"No," he agrees. "And that worried him more than any sword ever could."

A silence blooms between us, thick with things unspoken. The light in the chamber shifts slightly, casting the portrait in a cooler shade.

"He's doing it again," I murmur. "Trying to destroy what scares him."

Emrys tilts his head slightly, studying me the way one might study a page half-burned but still legible. His next words come slow, "You've seen the way he looks at you."

I nod. "Like I'm already his. Like my choices don't matter."

"Then you understand the danger and the power."

It takes an embarrassing amount of effort to make my voice work, to sound like I'm asking about history and not ghosts. "What happened to her sons?"

His expression falters. "One obeyed him. The other resisted, but you already know this."

I turn back to the painting. The woman stares back at me across time, unbowed, unbroken, even in paint.

"He won't win," I say, voice low. "Not this time."

Emrys doesn't smile, but his eyes soften. "Then you must be clever and crueler than you want to be. Because power here doesn't move for kindness and light alone. The darkness is strong and buried deep."

I nod, even as my throat tightens. Because I know he's right and because the shadows have already started whispering my name.

I follow Emrys through a narrow corridor that smells of vellum and time. The library's inner court is tucked deep in the stone, where the dust is thicker and the walls hum softly with old, untranslated runes.

"You're not like the others," I say.

Emrys smiles a soft, sad smile. "Because I don't bare my teeth at strangers?"

"That's part of it," I murmur, returning his soft smile.

"No fangs. No veils. No politics." I ease down onto the bench beside him. "It's nice to meet a scholar with secrets instead of knives. I've seen enough blades to last me a lifetime," I add quietly. "Especially the ones disguised as smiles.

There's a legendary Emrys in my world, you know."

"Ah, yes, he's a wizard, I believe? One that somehow ages backwards?"

"You know of the stories?" I'm shocked but pleased to have a conversation that's on this side of normal by my standards. "I wonder, now, if perhaps the inspiration for those tales of wizards and kings with magic swords were inspired by the fae. Maybe Merlin or Emrys was a fae, someone with real magic, and the aging backwards is a detail of his eternal youth that morphed over the centuries?"

"Or perhaps he could shapeshift and appear in different forms?" he says, a glint in his eyes.

"There are fae who can do that?"

"Indeed. Perhaps I can suggest some reading material while you are here to help you catch up?"

"That would be greatly appreciated. Thank you."

He glances at me, then reaches into the folds of his robes. "I found something of yours, I think," he says. "It called to me."

He pulls it free of his robes with a care usually reserved for relics. My phone. Intact. The screen glowing in sleep in the dim light, so absurdly human it physically hurts.

My brain scrambles for logic, for an explanation that doesn't exist. "You—how did you—?"

My voice breaks halfway through the question. Because this is impossible. This is mine. This is from the life I've left behind, the one I can't look at too long without feeling like it'll break me.

"I can't make it communicate across the realms," he says. "But I remember old tech. Dream metals and logic stone. I gave it a tether. You'll be able to charge it now. In moonlight. Magic doesn't mean we're lazy and lack technology. Hold it again. Listen. See. Feel a bit of home."

I take it from his hands like it might turn to dust with a simple touch. I certainly will. This is a lifeline and a curse at the same time. It's heavier than I remember, edges biting into my palms. The weight isn't real. It's everything it carries. Every message, every photo, every version of me that didn't have blood on her hands. Memories settle in behind my ribs, bruising.

My thumb brushes the screen, and it blooms to life. A single breath escapes me. Ragged and shaky. Too much and not enough. I touch the rainbow flower, and there they are.

My parents, my apartment, the framed fossils in that museum hallway in Dublin, and—Mattie.

We're both grinning, muddy and triumphant, half-buried in rich Irish soil beside a Neolithic hearth. My laughter is frozen. His arm is slung around my shoulders. It's blurry, but only because of my watering eyes. Perfect.

The ache hits before the smile can. A sucker punch straight to the chest. My hand trembles as I lift the phone closer. I can still hear the joke he was telling. I just... I can't remember the punchline.

My chest cracks open. It crawls up my throat and floods behind my eyes, bringing the taste of salt and metal. My head throbs, my teeth ache, and I can't tell if my lungs still work.

"He's got a kind smile," Emrys says, peering gently over my shoulder.

I nod, even though I can barely see. "Yeah. He always smiled like that. Even when he was mad. Even when everything was falling apart."

My voice shakes, and the sniffles start. "He was my best friend."

"Was?" The firelight catches the ink smudges along his knuckles and the edges of his fingernails, on the faint silver threaded through his hair. The torches make his skin look almost translucent and so soft. But not his eyes; they're sharp and see too much, reflecting someone who's catalogued as much grief, if not more than my own.

I tell him. Not all of it. Enough about the ship and the fog, when Raef's warriors cut the crew down. Mattie dragging me toward the rail. The monster from the sea coiled around him like he belonged there instead of with me.

"He pushed me away," I whisper. "And then he was gone."

Emrys doesn't offer pity. He doesn't say he's sorry. Doesn't pretend to understand. He listens. Like someone who knows the shape of loss and won't try to sand it down into something different, something softer and easier for him to deal with.

Instead, he studies the photo. "He doesn't look dead."

My brain trips over his statement; I'm afraid I'm done processing for the day. "He was alive when this was taken."

He nods like that was a given. "Yes. But here, portraits dim after death. The eyes fade. The color leaches. Like the eyes when the soul leaves the body."

He lifts my phone, gaze unreadable. "This...still shines."

My heart stutters. I look again, and he's right, or maybe I've lost it. It's a backlit screen; it will always shine. But the colors glow faintly. It's Mattie. Whole and bright. Laughing like the world hasn't ended yet.

"I guess," I choke on something trapped in my throat, "I guess it's different with photos, digital things."

It's a weak deflection. A lie I want to believe. Because if this means what he thinks it means. I can't believe it. Because then Mattie is alive somewhere, and I abandoned him. Then everything changes. Again.

I can't stop it. The tears come fast, blurring the screen. The past tucked into my palm. A whole world in pixels.

"I don't think I'll ever smile like that again," I say.

"You will," Emrys answers quietly, an arm around my shoulder as I cry. "But not the same way. You're not the same person anymore. We all change every day; that's part of living. Without change, we die and fade instead of grow."

He rests his hand near mine as I grip the edge of the bench, not touching—anchoring me back in the now. A steady presence, a soft gravity. For once, the silence doesn't crush.

"Here, we find new ways to hold on. And sometimes...new reasons to try."

48

THE ART OF TELLING YOUR FIANCE HIS DAD'S A PSYCHOPATH

THE HALLS FEEL COLDER ON the way back. It's like the walls know what I learned. Like they heard Emrys speak of the dead queen with reverence and regret and now hold their silence like a knife waiting for my punishment.

I wind my way back through unfamiliar corridors, past shifting walls and doors that weren't there before. My fingertips trail along the wall as I walk, it's slick in places, ridged in others, with a subtle vibration much like the floor. My steps echo off the walls despite the soft soles of my slippers. The palace is alive and I don't like the sound of it at all.

I round the last corner before my suite and catch the end of a conversation. Reflex takes over and I step back into the shadow of a column, the stone cool and gritty beneath my fingers. The obsidian glints in the low light.

The king's voice cuts through the hush. "She has her mother's eyes."

A second voice—a woman, low and clipped—answers, "They all have, in one way or another."

He hums. "But none of the others made it this far."

"She's...different. Even the court feels it."

"Let it feel what it wants." Neither of them says anything, at least at a volume I can hear for a good chunk of time. "This one's worth watching. Worth breeding if nothing else. There's power in her."

I hear the sounds of their feet against the stone floor, getting softer as they move further away.

I don't take another breath until the silence stretches long enough that my heart stops its marathon pace.

When I push open the door to my rooms, the suite is dimly lit, the curtains drawn. The silence here is heavier, thicker than the shadows, which is saying something. My phone is still warm in my hand as I perch myself on the edge of the bed, thumb brushing over Mattie's face, my parents, and the field dig in Galway. A music file from my old playlist hums to life in my ears.

More secrets. Now the comment about being the lucky one to survive takes on meaning that makes far too scary sense.

Tears trail slowly down my cheeks and onto my dress. Not the kind that rips from your chest—but the quiet, aching kind. The kind that feels like drowning under fogging glass. The slow drips of condensation meandering down its panes.

I don't remember curling up. I find the weight of the sheets, my phone against my chest, and Mattie's grin staring up at me from the lock screen. His smile a ghost light in a room full of smoke. A reminder of something solid when everything else feels hollow and empty.

That's how they find me. The door opens softly, someone having greased those creaky hinges. I don't lift my head to look. I know it's them, but I also don't care.

Tris swears quietly enough I know he didn't want me to hear. Javi crosses the room in three strides and sinks beside me, one arm coming around my back, and the tears start again. Raef lingers at the threshold—frozen.

I feel the way he watches me. Like he's afraid of what he'll see, or maybe of what he won't.

"We shouldn't have left you alone," Tris says at last, voice low and rough. "Not in this place. We've been looking for you everywhere. For the first time in my centuries of life, I was terrified."

"She wasn't alone," Javi mutters. "Not genuinely. But love, ghosts don't make for happy company." His fingers brush the phone.

I finally lift my head and look at him, Raef.

He's unreadable again—mask locked into place, eyes shadowed in a way that has nothing to do with light. It's not armor. It's evasion, and I've had enough of it.

I push myself upright. My voice comes out raw. "You could've told me."

Raef doesn't pretend to misunderstand. "Told you what?"

"That your court is a graveyard. That your father is planning a ceremony to bind me for eternity or at least to breed. That there were other wives."

Behind me, Javi goes still; the rhythm of his chest against my back changing. Tris's jaw clenches, a muscle ticking in his cheek. He's already counting all the ways this will end badly and not for me or him. This thought causes my mind to stray even more. *How do I know these men, males, so well already that I can read his mind from his facial expressions?*

"I chose to marry once," Raef says quietly. "To make a point. To defy him."

"And she died."

"Yes."

"And the others?"

"I never touched them. I never wanted them. But wanting has never mattered much to the Shadow Court. I watched them all die by blade and poison before ever reaching home."

My grip tightens around the phone. A tremble working its way up my arms.

I stand slowly, phone still clutched in my hand like a weapon. "And me, Raef? What am I? A symbol? A power play? Another way to challenge an overbearing father?"

"No," he says gently, and I can't tell if he's being genuine or condescending. The restraint of him shakes like a rubber band on brink of snapping. "You're the only thing I ever wanted for myself."

The confession stops me, but only long enough for my brain to catch up.

"Then why didn't you warn me about exactly how much trouble I was in, both before the betrothal and being betrothed to you? So many fucking secrets!"

"I didn't want it to be real yet," he says, hoarse. "I wanted more time." He sounds almost young when he says it. Like someone trying to hold back the tide, the high tide of everything he knows is coming. That something is threatening that small bubble of happiness he built...again.

"You think time is going to save me from this?"

"I think you will. You don't need anything or anyone to save you but you."

His words are meant to flatter. To empower. But they hit dishonestly. Like he's still handing me the whole mess and calling it a compliment.

Raef steps forward, slow, and for the first time, he looks tired. Not the kind that sleep fixes, but soul-deep, bone-fractured tired.

"I didn't mean to lie," he says. "In actuality I never lied—"

"You minced words, or gave non-answers; that's the same thing."

"You're right, and I was selfish. But I didn't know how to tell you the truth without watching you run. And that...that would break me." There's a crack in his voice that makes it hard to hold onto the anger. But I cling to it anyway. It's all I have left to shield myself.

"Then maybe you should have trusted me to be smart enough to stay."

A twitch cuts through his composure, enough to show I hit where it hurts. I guess even princes have tells.

"You think I'm weak?" The laugh that follows sounds more like a snarl. "You think I can't handle the truth? I've been through worse than your father's theatrics and brutal power plays."

He opens his mouth, but I'm already pacing, my feet landing hard with each step.

"I was top of my class at seventeen. First published paper before I could legally drink in my world. Five years in a row I was nominated as the youngest rising archaeologist on two fucking continents. I've excavated tombs with nothing but a flashlight and nerve, argued with men twice my age, and made them eat their degrees."

Tris lets out a low whistle. Javi watches me with something like awe.

Raef stands in shock.

I round on him. Pushing my index finger into his remarkably hard chest.

"You think you're protecting me by hiding things? You're not. You're just making it harder. You're telling me I'm supposed to be a queen, but God forbid I be treated like one. Like I deserve to know what's going on. Like I have a fucking say about what happens to me!"

The silence that follows is brutal.

Raef's jaw flexes. Tris smiles brightly with his whole face.

"I don't think you're weak," Raef stutters.

"Then stop treating me like glass." I don't wait for Raef to answer; I don't give him time to—there's nothing for him to say. "I've survived monsters. I've bled on court floors and kissed boys I'm not allowed to want. I've broken into ruins with my bare hands and outrun cave-ins with a map drawn in charcoal. I've held the dying and buried the dead. You think this—" I gesture around us, at the palace, the politics, the ever-watching eyes "—is the first time I've felt hunted?"

I laugh, and it's not pretty. It comes out cracked and feral.

"This place whispers like it's trying to break me. And maybe it will. But not like this. Not by your silence. Not by the way you keep standing in front of me instead of *with* me."

Raef looks like he's been struck. But I'm not done.

"You want a queen? Then treat me like one. You want a weapon? Try forging one without lying to it."

I step into his space, chin lifted, fists clenched.

"Because here's the truth, Raef. I've fought for everything. *Everything*. And I'm *not* afraid of becoming powerful. I'm afraid of becoming *small* in someone else's story because they take mine away."

The silence after that is loud with unspoken truths. My chest is heaving. My hands are trembling, but I don't step back. I'm not scared; I'm furious.

For a long second, no one utters a word.

Tris breaks the silence in his epic fashion, "Stars, I love it when she's feral."

I glance over, startled—half-laughing, half-unraveled. "Tris—"

One step, then another, and his hands are on either side of my face, like they've done it a hundred times in his head. His eyes flick over mine—checking, asking, daring—and then his mouth crashes into my half open lips like he's run out of patience and permission both.

It steals my balance, burns hot and full of all the things we never said. I taste salt, figs, and that impossible *almost* that's been buzzing between us for weeks. I kiss him back like I've been waiting for someone to meet me on the edge of a cliff.

And he does. My knees go weak. His touch pins the world back into place, at least for a moment, and that's enough for now.

When we break apart, his forehead rests lightly against mine.

"For the record," he breathes, "you're the most dangerous thing in this court."

I grin. "Took you long enough to notice."

Javi crosses his arms, looking at Raef, yanking his attention from my swollen, red lips. "You going to answer her now, or are we all going to keep pretending you've had a good plan this whole time?"

Raef swallows hard, forcing his next words through his teeth. "You want the truth?"

"Yes," I say, back to snapping. He's very good at bringing out the worst in me. "All of it."

He's watching me, gaze cool as storm-wrought steel. Pale eyes unreadable, the gold flash still there but less. Except for the tight line of his jaw and the twitch of his fingers near his side—like he's holding something in with effort.

"Good," he says at last, voice quiet. "I was beginning to wonder if you'd choose *anyone*."

Great. Add that to the list of things I wasn't ready to feel today. I swallow the sting before it shows on my face. He doesn't get to see me bleed because of words today.

"Don't do that," I snap. "Don't pretend you're above this. You could've told me everything. You could've fought me. But instead, you let your father treat me like—"

"I *am* fighting," Raef says, losing all composure and feigned resilience. "Just not the way you want." His tone changes, fractures. For the first time, I realize he's not withholding to punish me. He's withholding to protect something fragile in himself.

"You think this is about how?" I shake my head. "You think I care about which of you fights cleaner? I care about the fact that I'm out here bleeding in front of the whole damned court and you're still hiding in the shadows."

Raef looks at Tris, at me, at the still-glowing phone clutched in my hand.

His shoulders drop, the fight leaking out of him like a tire that rolled over a nail.

"I'm not hiding," he says. "I'm preparing."

Before I can stop him, before I can ask what the hell that even means— he walks out, not looking back. The door clicking behind him and the silence he leaves are colder than the palace halls.

I'm left here, tangled between heat and heartbreak, with Tris beside me, quiet now, but smiling that irksome smile of his all the same.

"We're getting married tomorrow night, and I still know nothing about him that I haven't learned from other people."

Tris sighs. "I'll go talk some sense into him."

I nod numbly, but my eyes stay fixed on the door. On the giant space he left behind. The cold ache inside me grows.

49

HOW TO FIND YOURSELF BETWEEN HEARTBEATS

THE HALLWAY OUTSIDE THE ARCHIVES feels too bright. Torchlight throws neat gold squares across the floor, all innocent looking. It isn't. Word travelled fast after that dinner that we'll take our vows at Fyrfall. It's not a threat anymore; Selmire announced it to the council and sent out the invitations.

Raef knew we needed help. We have our theory, but we need someone to verify the magic and our suppositions. We need Emrys.

Emrys picked the location hours ago, the south laundry supply closet, third turn past the dye vats. It's the only room in the palace you can seal all the way—no listening stones, no witness wards, no clerk behind a wall taking notes.

We move at the edge of the crowd after the council breaks—enough bodies to hide in, not enough to slow us down and miss the very small window we have. Raef sets the pace. Javi marks turns with his hand like he's counting cards. Tris listens intently for bells that mark something.

As if he's reading my mind, he says, "The steward swaps out lanterns at quarter past the hour, exactly."

"So we're trying to sneak in between spying ears," I say.

"Precisely."

We cut off the main hall into the servants' run. The heat drops away; the air smells like lye and damp stone. A pair of novices pass with a basket of folded linens and don't look up. Good.

"Remind me," Javi says, keeping his voice low, "why this box and not the nice reading room with chairs?"

"Because the reading room reports to the throne," Raef says. "This one reports to mildew."

The door Raef presses isn't a door so much as a panel that pretends to be a wall. He palms the edge, finds the give, and we slip through into a storage closet that smells like old soap and oil.

Shelves climb to the rafters, full of coils of rope and a cracked barrel marked SALT. Bundles of herbs hang upside down like bats. Dust lifts when we move and tries to make a scene of it.

Emrys is already inside, wedged on a stool as part of the inventory this whole time. He's got chalk on his fingers and ink on his sleeve. He doesn't look up when we enter, obviously expecting us—he keeps drawing a neat ring on a slate shard with a tick mark at the north point.

"Close it," he says. His voice perfectly normal, no drama or tension from the sneaking around.

Javi presses the panel back into place. It seals with a cough of air.

Tris taps the jamb with his knuckle, counting softly. "Footsteps pass this hall every eight to ten minutes. They change the lanterns at the quarter hour. We've got...seven minutes."

"And a ward to keep them out," Emrys says. He looks up at me. "Your palm."

I hold it out. He sketches a quick loop over my skin—chalk that feels so normal, cold and grainy like a sandy riverbed. The mark flashes once, instantly fading into nothing.

"Speak," he tells me.

"Speak what?"

"Anything."

I clear my throat. "This room is mine."

The other chalk lines I didn't see him draw answer across the room: a soft pressure in the ears, like the world cupping its hands. The faint murmur of the corridor dies. Raef shifts beside me, his hand tapping the shelf once, careful. Javi tests the panel again, making sure it's latched.

Emrys nods, satisfied, and flips the slate toward us. On the ring he's drawn, he marks four points with quick taps. "You asked how to make the words behave," he says. "Listen once so I don't have to repeat it while we run."

Raef's jaw works, but he keeps quiet.

"Plain version, for you, Rory," he says, and I nod with a smile. "Magic takes the exact words you say and enforces them. Not your feelings. Not your intent. Your words."

He looks to Raef, which is great since I'm not the only one who's learning here. "Say 'by my hand,' and only your hands are bound. Not hers. Not anyone else's."

"Tie a vow to Fyrfall and it gets tougher—more force behind it—but it's still breakable. Breaking costs blood. The bigger the promise, the bigger the price." He taps the mark at north. "Rings are different. A ring makes a tether. It points. Useful for finding. If you try to tear it loose, it snaps back and hurts the one yanking."

I glance at my embedded ring. It sits calm and vicious on my finger, a pretty little cat pretending to nap.

Tris leans in, resting a hip on a shelf. "So we can work with phrasing. Intent doesn't matter?"

"Right," Emrys says. "Intent is for gods and gossips. The magic isn't a mind reader. It's a clerk. It files what you say and enforces it to the letter. The trick is writing a letter that says what you mean without saying what you mean."

Javi exhales. "So all the vows are grammar and syntax."

"Grammar with teeth," Emrys says.

Raef folds his arms, then stops himself. "If I swore 'by my hand I won't harm,' then—"

"Your hands are out," Emrys says, and I have no idea what he means. "Your mouth is not. Your orders in that case are... murky."

Tris tilts his head. "No 'by my word' in the phrasing?"

"Did he say it?" Emrys asks.

Raef's mouth goes thin. "I wasn't planning on it."

"Then your word won't be bound," Emrys says. "But don't get cute. If you start directing too much, he'll know what you're doing. It's a fine line you're all planning to walk as it is.

I rub my palm where the chalk marked me. It's stopped feeling cold and starts feeling like a splinter, which I take as meaning we're running out of time. "If someone—hypothetically—wanted to cut a ring's tether without dying, how would they not do that stupid thing?"

"Don't pull," Emrys says. "Unhook." He sketches two tiny links and a pin between them. "You follow the thread to the anchor, you lift the pin. You do not yank like a fisherman with a snag, unless you want the hook in your own throat."

"And if there's no pin?" Tris says.

"Then you have to make one. Blood for blood. A cut that counts enough to fool the ledger." He sets the slate on a crate. "I don't recommend trying that during Fyrfall."

The lantern outside the panel hisses. Glass clinks. Tris flicks his fingers. "Three minutes," he says.

Emrys digs into a pocket and brings up a twist of twine and a brass tag. He tosses it to Javi. "Hang that on the outside latch. If someone tests it and hears the tag, they'll assume 'occupied' and move on. They're all cowards. They prefer paperwork to confrontation," he says with a wiggle of his brows. I guess that's the fae version of a sock on a doorknob.

Javi slips the tag through the seam and lets it dangle. The panel looks like a wall again, but a very guilty wall with a sign on it.

Tris notices my thoughts straying. "Okay, simplify this talk, she's lost. What do they say at Fyrfall so it doesn't trap her?"

Emrys taps the slate ring. "Build the vow like a form. Five boxes: who, what, where, how long, and exclusion. Keep each box small."

Raef taps a finger along his chin, pacing along the short space we have. "If we're forced to vow a marriage at Fyrfall, how do we make it political only? He wants to breed her."

Emrys, having an answer for everything, says, "Say 'I take her in title only' and spell out the limits. For example, 'no claim to her body, magic, name, or will.' Add 'no compulsion by mine or any proxy.' Add 'her existing bonds and future choices remain hers.' That blocks any attempt he might make for control."

It's Javi that voices all my concerns. "Can he still twist it?"

"Only if you leave gaps. Don't say 'protect' unless you define from what and by what means. Don't say 'obey' at all."

Javi's mind is working overtime as he frantically tries to think of every question before our time runs out. "Selmire will try to expand the scope."

"So you limit where it applies: 'within the hall of witnesses' or 'within the borders of the Shadow court.' If they drag you south tomorrow, the vow won't travel with you," Emrys says, erasing another tick on his circle. There's only one left now.

Raef meets my eyes. "Say it all back."

I do. "Title only. No claim to body, magic, name, or will. No compulsion by him or proxy. My bonds stay mine. Witness at Fyrfall, not bound to it. Duration short. Harm limited to 'by my hand,' with my leave if I ask for defense. No orders that make us his hand. No tether to the ring, which stays separate. Scope stays in the hall or the court. No obeying. Make it end at sunrise or on a breach."

Emrys gives one sharp nod. "If you word this vow correctly, it's one that holds them, not you. Think hard on what you'll say, but keep it simple because you'll have to memorize it."

With that he erases the last tick on his circle, and sound returns.

JAVI KNOCKS ONCE, then lets himself in when I don't answer.

I don't turn from the window. The city below is too quiet. Even the stars look like they're hiding tonight.

"I brought tea," he says, holding a pristine porcelain cup.

"I hate tea."

"I know. It's wine."

That gets a smile. A tired one, but my lips curl anyway. I take the cup and let him stay. Let him sit beside me, hip to hip, his thigh brushing mine, steady and warm, his presence a tether in a world that keeps slipping sideways like my dress. The silk I wear feels too thin, too formal, like it belongs to someone else. This isn't me. Not the old me anyway. But the new me? That remains to be seen. I'm not sure I'll ever prefer silk dresses to dirt encrusted boots and holey jeans.

"You look like you're about to bolt," he says after a long silence. "You won't. But I can feel the tension in you."

"I don't know who I'm going to be tomorrow," I say. "And I'm starting to forget who I was before."

Javi was quiet for a moment, thinking. "Then, tell me."

"Tell you what?"

"Mattie, your parents, the house you grew up in. Tell me what made you. Tell me so I can remember for you."

That breaks me. Just tiny crack. I look down at the wine in my hand like it might steady me. It doesn't, but Javi does, and I still don't know what to do with that.

I lean against him and let the words come. About my mom's humming and the ash trees outside my bedroom window. About Mattie's stupid fake accent and how he made every dig, no matter how boring, feel like an adventure. About the time we both cried over a broken pot we weren't even sure was from the right century.

By the end, I'm crying again.

My tears don't seem to bother him, as in make him want to run away like a lot of other guys. He doesn't look away or find a way to fill the silence. Instead, he cups my face and wipes the tears away with his thumb. "You're still her," he says. "And she's still in you."

His mouth finds mine before I can speak.

It's not like before. Not sweet, nor careful. It's all heat and hunger and something fraying at the edges. All the things we've shoved down, bleeding to the surface.

I climb into his lap. His hands grip my thighs, then slide higher. Fingertips dragging up my hips like he's relearning the shape of want. The silk slides off my shoulder like it was never meant to stay on.

"I don't know if I'll ever get to choose again," I whisper against his mouth.

He kisses me like that isn't even a question. Like the answer is already yes.

Clothes come off in pieces. His breath hitches when my fingers trace the scars on his ribs. Old wounds. Faded stories. I want to know all of them. I want to make new ones, better ones, with him.

My mind stutters when he whispers my name, a sacred word, as he carries me over to the bed.

His magic brushes against mine, soft, glowing, aching. I let it. Because tonight, tonight we aren't royalty or weapons or pawns. We're us. I don't want to feel anything but *this.*

"You sure," he asks, his voice thready and weak.

"Stop talking," I say, taking over the kiss.

My fingers tangle in his hair, not to pull him back, to pull him closer. I need to be closer.

Javi groans softly, the sound vibrating against my lips as he kisses me deeper, hungrier. His hand curls beneath my thigh, lifts, shifts me under him, breath rough as it ghosts over my jaw. His mouth claims mine like he's starving, like he's been waiting for permission he never thought he'd get again.

The mattress shifts as he leans over me, one arm braced beside my head, the other sliding beneath my back to draw me up into him. Our bodies align—hot skin against hot skin, hearts pounding.

"You don't have to stop," I whisper, my voice already gone to ruin.

His mouth moves over my jaw, my throat, tracing fire across my skin. "I'm not planning to."

Fingers trace my ribs, reverent and slow, but with a building urgency that makes me gasp. He kisses the hollow of my throat, my collarbone, then lower, feather-light, then firm, like he's tasting the future in every inch of my skin.

I arch into him, legs parting instinctively, and he settles between them, careful but bold. I want this, need this. I need to feel something normal.

I guide him. Not because I'm unsure, because I want this right. I want *him* right. Every line. Every breath.

The ring on my finger pulses once, silent, watching. I don't care. For now, the court means nothing. No marriage. No war. It's me and Javi, and the little sounds that leak out as we drown in each other.

Wrapped in his arms, I stop thinking. I stop aching. I let myself want. Let myself burn. Let myself explode with the stars.

His name leaves my lips like a spell, and mine leaves his like a prayer. We fall. Together. Not shattered. Not broken. Finally alive.

I feel like a woman, not that scared little girl.

Not an heir. Not a weapon. Not the king's pawn.

Javi saw all of me and stayed. I finally let him in, all of him.

50

Ways to Keeping Smiling While the Sky Falls

A WEAK SUN EDGES UP and throws broken gold over the sheets knotted beneath us. The air still smells like him, all salt, skin, and something warm like cinnamon in autumn.

Javi is still asleep, one arm curled around my waist, the other tucked under his head like he didn't mean to fall that deeply. His mouth is slightly open. His hair mussed from sleep and other things. His skin is warm where it presses into mine.

There's a faint mark on his collarbone—me. A bruise. I trace it lightly with one finger. That's my only move; I don't dare move more. I could if I wanted to, but I don't want to break the stillness—the peace.

The war hasn't touched this room yet. Not the marriage. Not the court. Not the curse of stars binding themselves over our heads. Just quiet. Just this.

His hand twitches, then tightens. A sleepy murmur stirs at the edge of his lips. "You're still here," he whispers.

"Where else would I be?"

He blinks a few times before his gaze finds mine. His eyes open slowly, brown and full of golden light. "Anywhere. Gone. Changed."

I turn toward him, brushing a thumb beneath his eyes. "Not yet."

A silence blooms, comfortable for once. He strokes a finger down my spine, light as feathers. "You're warm," he says.

"You're clingy."

His smile bends sideways. "Only because you're trying to escape."

I lean in, tucking my nose against the curve of his throat. "Not trying very hard."

He shifts, enough to gather me closer, arm sliding under my neck, a hold you don't use unless you plan to stay.

We stay like that for I don't know how long. Until the sun hits the far wall. Until the light touches the gown standing in the corner. Until memory starts to return like a slow, cold tide.

The sound of distant bells tells us the court is already awake.

"Do you regret it? Us?" he asks, his voice muffled in my hair.

I don't answer right away, and he doesn't press.

"No."

A pause stretches between us, long enough for the morning to ease in. The air tastes faintly of ash and apple wine. His thumb draws idle circles against my hip, steady, unthinking, like his body remembers comfort even when his mind doesn't. I feel the pulse beneath his skin and can almost hear my heartbeat syncing to his.

"Do you?"

He kisses my forehead. "Never."

THEY'D LAID THE table like it mattered. Fruit carved into flower shapes. Steam curling from silver teapots. Bread still warm, butter melting in slow golden streaks. Honeysweet, shadow melon, cuts of firebird ham, and folded eggs steeped in starlight.

None of us touch it.

I stand by the balcony doors, arms crossed, watching the wind drag mist over the valley below. The fractured cliffs cut the horizon like broken teeth. Even the wind sounds haunted today, much like myself. I wonder how many bodies are buried in those cracks, or if the bones are left to bleach like everything else in this court. Maybe they don't bother burying what they break here. Maybe the mountain takes it.

Tris leans against the balustrade beside me, sipping from a teacup he didn't fill. It was mine. "Nothing like a feast before an execution," he says. "Very civilized."

Javi elbows him in the side as he sidles past. "It's not an execution."

"Not yet."

Javi comes to my side instead of responding, slipping his hand into mine. His palm is warm where mine isn't, the heat sinking through skin until I can't tell which of us is warmer. I hadn't realized how cold I'd gotten until I felt him.

"You don't have to wear that dress," he says, nodding toward the corner where it taunts me, waiting like the promise we haven't made.

"Don't I?"

The shadows stitched into its hem shift as if listening. Like they know something I don't. Like they're already hungry for it.

"It's just a dress," I say.

Raef stands a pace apart. At the edge of the room, not quite facing the table. His hands are tucked behind his back; profile his usual unreadable but somehow still different.

"I didn't sleep," he says quietly. His voice is hoarse, as if it rubbed against too many thorns last night and didn't heal. Under his eyes is smudged, accentuated by his tight jaw. That strange stillness again—like he's bracing for something. He already knows he's bleeding for it.

"I noticed."

He doesn't apologize. Doesn't explain. That hurts. I used to think his silence meant comfort. Now, I know it can also mean surrender or guilt.

Tris exhales dramatically. "Maybe we run. Say to hell with the courts and the stars and the vows. Take her hand and make a break for the eastern wilds. Marry her under a Moonbloom tree; it'll be poetically romantic if also predictably doomed…"

Javi smiles lightly. But he knows that it means nothing to me and remembers to explain Tris's overture. "The petals of the Moonbloom tree only open at moonrise. They are said to only grow from the burial sites of star-crossed lovers. The bark is also faintly luminescent, adding another romantic touch." He turns to Tris again after finishing his explanation, and I can't help but think about how romantic Tris is under all that blood and violence. "She'd still be a queen."

"Then she can damn well reign with moss in her hair and dirt on her boots."

I don't laugh, but I want to. God, I want to. Just for a second. To prove I still can. Because he knows this isn't me. That the silk and crowns aren't me. I'm meant to be dirty, wearing boots, and exploring, not cooped up in tight dresses and dainty slippers where I can't move.

Raef speaks again, killing the moment. "There's no running from Fyrfall."

Outside, the wind screams through the marble teeth of the valley. A sound like a warning bell.

The food on the table steams. Unbroken. Untouched. Like an offering no one dares accept.

ONE MOMENT, I'M staring at the untouched fruit on the plate in front of me; the next, a familiar voice cuts through the thick silence.

"I brought you something."

Emrys stands inside the doorway, robes dusted with frost from the courtyard's shadows, hair pinned back in the careful, quiet way of scholars who don't need crowns to be dangerous. He looks like winter, cold at the edges but soft and steady at the core.

Raef stiffens. Tris doesn't bother hiding his surprise. Javi, at least, offers a small wave. "I thought you kept to your tower."

"I'll leave it for something worthwhile," Emrys says.

He steps closer and places a small object wrapped in midnight cloth onto the table between us. It's no larger than my palm. The cloth looks as soft as a moth wing, but as I lift it, it carries an unexpected weight.

I pull the folds back. A charm rests inside—silver wire twisted and coiled around a sharp stone of black-blue glass. The wire is braided into an intricate pattern. Each knot shimmers like a highly polished crystal.

"She said you might need this," Emrys says, nodding once. "The Iron Matriarch sends her protection. Not every promise is a loud one."

Raef narrows his eyes. "From the Iron Mountain?"

"She said the shadows eat careless queens. And she's not in the habit of letting her allies rot."

I swallow the knot that's been sitting in my throat all morning, fingers brushing the edge of the stone. It stings on contact, a prick of pain. Recognizing its target, I guess.

"Is it...a ward?"

Emrys tilts his head. "As far as I can tell, it's a blade against unraveling. Keep it near your skin. It will sting if it's working."

"And if it fails?"

He doesn't answer. No one wants to think on that option. Just offers me a soft look, too kind for this place. Kindness here feels like rebellion or a trick.

"You should know," he adds, shifting his weight, "there are stirrings near the eastern borders. Greenwood is tightening its patrols. Someone crossed without permission. Left something or someone bleeding."

The word "bleeding" makes Javi tense. His fingers twitch near his belt, even without a weapon attached.

"They think it's the Sea Court," Emrys continues, voice low. "Small movements. Testing for cracks, but a shadow passed through my tower last night. One I didn't summon."

That chills me more than the stone in my hand even though I don't actually know what it means. The charm stings in my palm, a jab like working clumsily with a needle.

Raef's voice goes tight. I wonder why I trust Emrys while he does not. "Why come here to tell us that?"

"Because your father won't." Emrys meets his stony gaze, calm and unafraid. "And she deserves to know."

I stand slowly, still holding the charm. "Thank you."

Emrys gives a small bow, more respectful than court appropriate, and glances once at my gown, still draped and waiting. "You look like her, you know."

"Who?"

He doesn't answer. He turns, robes whispering over the marble, and leaves me with the charm, the cold, and a question that refuses to leave. The door shuts behind him with a sound like finality. Or a beginning. It's too soon to tell which.

51

SURVIVE BEING SEWN INTO SOMEONE ELSES STORY

1 STAND BAREFOOT ON A polished pedestal of obsidian. The seamstress doesn't speak as she circles me, nor do the three others trailing behind her like silent shadows. They don't need to speak. They communicate in tugs, gestures, and the snip of shears that never quite touch flesh but come awfully close.

The gown hangs from a suspended frame above me, veiled in moon-pale gauze and threads that shimmer black-blue in the torchlight. When they lower it, the fabric slithers over my shoulders like smoke spun into silk. It moves like it has a mind of its own.

It's like wearing a secret. A very old, very dangerous secret.

"There," the seamstress murmurs at last, pulling the back tight. "The shadow knows your shape now."

I'm not sure what that means, but it doesn't feel like a compliment or a good thing.

The sleeves are sheer, embroidered with inky constellations. The train pools behind me like a dark tide. It whispers when I move, layers of glamour and stitches magically woven into the seams. Starlight has been caught here or sacrificed. Maybe that's their talent, their magic. They can snatch stars out of the night sky and trap them in fabric.

One of the assistants adjusts the open neckline and then pins something sharp in place behind my ear, and my shoulders jerk.

"Still," the seamstress snaps.

"It bit me," I mutter.

"As it should."

The bodice cinches tight. I can barely breathe. Not from the pressure exactly, but from the weight of it all. I can breathe, technically, but it feels like the gown's making sure I remember who's in charge.

This isn't a dress.

It's a literal binding.

A promise stitched in secrets and silk. The seams feel like they're spelling something in a language I don't speak yet.

A courtier lingers nearby, watching too closely. She wears a mask carved from black bones and feathers dipped in oil. When she speaks, her voice is rusted nails wrapped in honey. I recognize that voice.

"Death," she says softly, "was once dressed this finely."

My jaw clenches. "Is that a compliment?"

Her mask tilts. "You'll find compliments are often warnings."

The seamstress gives a satisfied nod. "It's done."

I turn to the mirror—and barely recognize the woman who looks back.

No—not a woman

A bride.

A queen.

My dark hair has been drawn back in intricate braids, pinned with obsidian thorns and thin chains of starlight silver that shimmer like constellations. Strands have been left free to frame my face—too soft, too human for this court, and somehow more defiant because of it.

My face looks older. Not by years, but by edges. The kind grief carves when you aren't looking.

The dress is shadow-shaped, they tell me, the epitome of style and grace here. It's strangely magnificent. The bodice clings below my collarbone, not quite modest, not quite daring—made to draw attention without offering any warmth. Threads of silver dance like phantom fire through black fabric that shifts as I move, making the crystal stars shimmer and dance.

The sleeves are sheer, ending in cuffs that wrap around my wrists like restraints disguised as grace. The train behind me is huge and pools like ink, and I realize it doesn't reflect the light in the room. It reflects something deeper. As if the fabric remembers the starlight that made it and refuses to forget it or release it for anyone else to enjoy. It feels like stepping out of a myth. Like the tragic story where the bride is always so beautiful before she dies.

A weapon dressed in elegance. Somewhere, under all of it, a human heart beats too loud for this place.

I never felt less like myself.

Or more beautiful.

THE PALACE IS eerily quiet. Not the heavy, watching silence of the formal court, but waiting, a tense pause. The kind that comes before a fall. Even the torches burn lower tonight, creating more shadows to spy with.

I find Raef alone on the high balcony that faces the jagged valley, the veil of mist thicker now, laced with gold from the setting sun. He doesn't turn when I step beside him. Doesn't speak. He stands there, arms braced on the stone railing, wind threading through the loose strands of his long, dark hair like it belongs more than I do. He looks like he was carved into the stone itself. He's part of this place but still set apart.

We stand like that for a long time. A stillness that says everything and nothing.

Then I ask it. The burning question. "Do you regret it?"

His knuckles flex on the railing. Such a small motion that tells so much. "Bringing me here," I clarify. "Choosing me? Any of it?"

Still no answer. Just the sound of the wind between us and the faint hum of magic in the stone.

I look down at the fractured land below, where nothing grows and everything waits. "You could have kept your distance. Followed orders. Bound yourself to someone more suitable. Less...impossible."

Raef exhales. Not a laugh, but almost. Like he's surprised I still don't understand. Like it hurts him.

"I've made a thousand mistakes, more even," he says. "But you were never one of them."

His words draw my attention, so heartfelt and honest, I can't help meeting his eyes, heart in my throat. "Then why do I feel like you're always one step out the door?"

His eyes find mine, silver catching the last of the dying light and then that flash of gold. And for once, they don't look like armor. They look tired. Soft and raw. Like someone who's bled and mourned in silence too long. Like someone afraid to ask for what he wants.

"I'm trying not to want what I can't protect," he says.

"That's not an answer."

"No, It's not."

His hand lifts like he means to touch me, then drops. A brush of knuckles at my side. Nothing more. But my skin hums where it almost was. Because he and I were always almost. Almost honest. Almost safe. Almost something more.

But it's enough to make something in my chest ache.

"I don't know how this ends," he says. "But if it's the last calm before everything breaks—I want it with you."

I don't move. Don't speak. I want to. I want to reach for him. I want to say something reckless and real. But if I do, I'll mean it. If I mean it, I can't take it back.

But maybe I want that too. And maybe that is the scariest truth of all. Not the war. Not the vows. Not even the court's watching eyes. But the way he makes me want to stay.

52

HOW TO SAY 'I DO' WHEN YOU MEAN 'I DARE YOU'

THE BELLS RING AS DUSK settles into night. Low and deep, as if rung from within the mountain itself. It's a sound that sinks straight into your bones and settles there to live.

The courtyard is already filled with light. Not candlelight, not torchlight, but starfire—threads of celestial flame arcing across the velvet sky, the first signs of Fyrfall blooming overhead. Meteors streak the heavens in silence. The stars watching us all.

King Selmire stands in the hallway, draped in silk blacker than shadows and trimmed with starlight thread. No crown. No guard. Just a half-smile that splits his handsome face like a crack in polished glass.

"I hope you've dressed for the occasion," he says mildly. "There's a bit of a chill in the air tonight."

Raef steps between us, blocking him. "The ceremony's inside; I'll fetch her a cloak after."

A hum vibrates in the king's throat that's not music. No, I've heard that same tone from scholars before they pry open tombs they shouldn't.

"Yes," Selmire says. "But the court awaits tonight. Under the stars. Where all can bear witness to your devotion." He tilts his head. "And your obedience."

I step forward, disbelief curdling fast in my throat. "Public?"

He turns to me with a predator's charm. "Of course, girl. What union hides in the dark, if not a shameful one?"

Raef's body snaps taut. "That's not our way."

"Ah," the king sighs, touching the wall like it's a spine he can pluck. "But you are marrying a *High Queen*. Tradition bends to history."

Raef steps forward, fury in every movement. "You break your own customs."

"No," the king says softly. "I rewrote them. Don't dally." He walks out the door without another word.

The silence he leaves behind feels like a blade pressed to my neck. I feel lead settle in my gut, heavy and fast, but I can't stop it. "Fucking cock-sucker son of a—"

Raef's hand claps over my mouth before I can finish. His eyes locked on mine, pleading.

The king only glances with one eye over his shoulder. "The other monarchs are already arriving," he says. "They want to see the girl who lit the city. Who bears a starborn name. They want to see if she'll bow...or burn."

He turns without waiting for a reply. "Twilight falls, don't be late."

The door shuts between us with a whisper that feels like a sliding guillotine.

Raef still hasn't moved. Neither have I. But then he pulls me close, slow and shaking. His hands land at my waist like he's holding me together. And for this brief, agonizing moment, it's just us.

His voice comes through rough and cracked. "Rory." He presses his forehead to mine. "We only have a moment, but Fyrfall has already started."

He cups my face with one hand, his eyes shining. His other thumb brushes the place where my pulse betrays me. When his voice comes, it's low and raw, like it costs him everything to give it.

"I wanted you before the stars marked you. Before the ring. Before the city lit and the courts took notice. Back when you were a scared woman who knocked me off my balance." He laughs once, broken. "Who told me to go to hell and meant it. Who told me, repeatedly, she wouldn't marry me until this hell froze over.

"This mortal hell you speak of has been a frozen tundra since the first time I laid eyes on you."

He smiles, but it cracks.

"And I loved you before I had the words to name it. Before I knew the meaning of the fire in my chest. Before I knew what loving you would cost."

My eyes widen, and my whole body forgets how to carry air.

His fingers slide down, catching my hand, careful, almost trembling, and lifting it to his lips. The first brush of his lips is light, barely there, but it steals every thought I had left. His breath is warm, his skin cold, and the contrast burns. It's not just a kiss. It's a promise pressed into my flesh.

"I don't have a crown. I don't have peace. I barely have a name that isn't cursed. But I have *this.*"

He places my hand over his heart. His pulse thunders beneath my palm. Unrelenting. Unafraid.

"I vow—before the stars that bind, before the gods who sleep, before every cruel eye watching tonight—that I am *yours*. In ruin. In fire. In the absences between the thumps of war drums. Yours when the bond is forged and when it frays. Yours if the sky forgets our names. Yours even if you walk away."

His voice shakes now. But he doesn't let go. "I swear this, not because they asked me. Not because they demand it. But because my soul won't let me do anything else."

My vision blurs. The stars overhead streak silver and violet across the sky, but I can't see them. Only him through the tears running hot down my cheeks.

Raef leans in until his forehead rests against mine, breath a whisper on my wet cheek.

"They can take our choices. They can chain us to the sky. But they will never take *this*. The truth of you in my arms. The truth of us—before the gods ever wake to watch. I make this vow to you. You will know only love in my arms. You will know only truth from my lips. I will worship you to the end of my days. Of this you can be sure, no matter what happens."

And in that stillness, in this vow, the world softens. Just for a moment. Just for us, until he sweeps open the doors.

I HAVE NO idea where he's leading me. My feet follow the pressure of him pulling me along, but my mind hasn't travelled beyond what happened. Those words keep replaying, looping over themselves until they don't sound real anymore.

No one talks like that. Especially not him. And yet, I know he meant every single word. I felt it in the way his voice broke, the way his pulse kicked against my palm like it was ready to jump out of his chest into mine.

His thumb keeps brushing my knuckles, a small, steady rhythm that tells me two things: that he meant it and that he's not leaving my side. I don't want to believe him, but belief arrives anyway. I'm not swooning, but I'm damn close. Who wouldn't be? I feel like he took a bone and set it back where it belongs. It hurts, but it fits... perfectly.

The corridor feels warm. My veil, attached to my shoulders rather than my head, lifts and settles behind me with each step, my hem whispers, and thin slippers slide over cold stone. The walls shrink down to three things: his hand, my steps, and the faint thrum of the ring. I'm not ready for the crowd. I'm also not letting go.

We reach the threshold. The low bells roll up through the floor. Night waits outside, bright with falling fire. He looks at me once, and I nod—words fail me—and we step out.

I doubt this courtyard has ever seen this many living souls.

Raised tiers carved from obsidian and pale stone climb the cliff's edge like a broken amphitheater. Courtiers draped in black and silver stand shoulder to shoulder, their masks faceless and gleaming. No whispers pass through them. Not a cough. Not a word louder than the wind. They're statues made of silk and tension. An audience of ghosts still warm with judgment.

At the highest ledge sit the kings and queens who have bothered to answer the Shadow King's call.

The Iron Matriarch stands like a pillar outside the great Parthenon—draped in hammered steel and crimson thread, her face painted in ash. She meets my gaze, and her expression doesn't falter.

Beside her lounges a king crowned with thorns and coiled in petals, his eyes like honey caught in fire. Another wears sea-glass armor that steams faintly against the cold—his fingers dripping with rings carved from shell, bone, and pearl.

There are more. Too many to name. Too many watching. I can guarantee that none of them are here for love and romance.

Above us—the stars bleed light. The meteor storm has begun in earnest.

Silver streaks tear through the dark like cosmic tears. Each one feels like the sky's coming apart at the seams. Like they cut something invisible on their way down. Like they're slashing holes in the veil between what was and what comes next.

Raef stands at my side, holding my hand. We wear no veils. No moonlit chamber. No mirrored candles. This isn't a veil binding. This is now a display, a performance. A spectacle created to control and display the king's power.

The king stands above us, cloaked in shadow silk and pride. "Before these gathered courts," he intones, "we witness a bond that shall not be broken. A marriage forged not in silence, but in power."

Guards flank Tris and Javi behind the altar stones—boxed in, as if they might object. Their faces are still, but I can feel Tris's rage humming across the stones. Javi's tension curled in his fists.

I might have, too, if Raef hadn't slipped his hand into mine. Made those vows. The only tether I have in a ceremony built as a trap. He doesn't look at the crowd. He looks at me and only me.

As the thread of shadow-dyed silk is looped once...then twice... around our joined hands, Raef leans close and whispers so only I will hear, "This was never the ceremony. This is a cage. But I would still walk into it—if it means walking beside you."

As the final loop tightens, Selmire speaks—smooth, deliberate, ritualistic words designed to sound ceremonial but hide a noose underneath.

He's not stupid enough to make this sound like more than an alliance through marriage. No one here would believe that nonsense, but it's a noose nonetheless.

"Repeat after me: Before the gathered courts, beneath the stars that see all things, I bind my will and my magic to the Shadow Crown. My strength is the realm's. My life, its shield. My love, its offering."

He's not binding us to each other; he's binding me to the crown itself, to the King, to him. It also sounds like he wants to use our emotional connection to feed the court's power, creating a siphon disguised as romance. And even worse, use us as his shield. This is worse than I ever could have imagined.

I start to hyperventilate at this point, seeing exactly what's happening with the understanding that it's probably much worse than my understanding allows me to comprehend.

Raef, knowing his father's trick, cuts me a quick look—the "trust me" kind—and repeats the words with subtle alterations as quietly as possible, bending the vow's meaning, and there's nothing Selmire can do about it without making an embarrassing scene. I'm sure Raef will pay for it later, and that's something I have to process another time.

His thumb brushes against my knuckles, a silent warning or a plea to pay attention. His jaw ticks with the effort of pulling this off. "Before the gathered courts," he echoes, "beneath the stars that see all things…"

His eyes have never left mine, but he changes his glance for a heartbeat that holds a whole conversation.

Pay attention.

He changes those words, "…I bind my will and my magic *for the realm unbound.*"

Selmire's eyes narrow, but he doesn't interrupt. He doesn't dare let the other courts see that his son defies him.

Raef continues, each phrase softer. "My strength is the realm's. My life, its shield. *My love, my own reckoning.*"

I don't think the crowd hears the changes. Or maybe they do and don't dare or care to react. The stars do, I feel it—the air bending.

The King angles his body to me, staring me down. His smile is all teeth. "And the bride?"

It's a command disguised as a question. He's daring me to defy him too.

The silk glows between my fingers, waiting to devour whatever I feed it. I can feel Selmire's magic pressing close, invasive and cold, trying to get into my mind and shape my words for me. But Raef's thumb circles once over the back of my hand, small and steady, and that's enough to push him out.

I look up at the sky instead of Selmire. The meteors fall faster now, streaks of molten silver ripping the heavens open.

"Before the gathered courts," I say, my voice rough but sure, "beneath the stars that see all things, I bind my will and my magic…"

I stop. This is the moment of truth, and Selmire presses harder against my mental walls, pushing thoughts of Shadow Crowns loud into my mind. The pressure mounts behind my ribs like something about to break.

I drag my eyes back down to Raef. To his pale blue eyes staring at me with so much emotion flickering past like those old animation flip books. All the noise goes silent.

"… for the realm unbound."

I keep going. "My strength is my own. My life, my choosing. *My love— my reckoning.*"

The final word burns. Literally. The silk flares white-hot, light arcing up my arms, searing the pattern of stars into my palms before vanishing. The smell of smoke and ozone fills the air.

Selmire's smile falters, only slightly, but enough to taste a victory. He tries to recover, voice smooth and political but tighter at the edges. "So be it," he says. "The vow is made."

A torch is passed. Not to the king, but to Raef. He holds the flame between us.

I can feel the silk tense, like it knows what comes next. Like it remembers every vow it's ever burned into flesh.

But Raef doesn't burn it right away.

Instead, he raises my hand to his lips. Kisses my knuckles. And *then* lets the fire touch thread.

It catches instantly. The silk flares once, blue, then violet, then silver, and vanishes. Like it never existed. A bond swallowed.

Gone.

The stars above us seem to pulse in time.

Raef exhales shakily beside me, eyes on the sky. The meteors streak overhead like the heavens are bleeding light.

If Selmire meant to cage us, he's the one trapped now—watching as the stars he tried to command turn their faces toward us instead.

A crackle of magic sweeps through the gathered crowd.

It coats my skin like frost. Soaks into my bones like blood. A vow written into the heavens. A bond neither of us can undo. Not even if we wanted to.

53

LEARNING TO LEAVE AT DAWN AND PRETEND ITS A VACATION

MUSIC RISES LIKE SMOKE, THIN and strange. It coils through the arches and spills down the polished marble like something alive. I close my eyes and let it thread through me. I wouldn't say it's entirely enjoyable, but it does drown everything else out. It gives me something else to focus on. The scrape of silver on porcelain, the whispers of silk, the stares I can feel like teeth against skin.

In that high, I replay his words. Raef's vows were damn near perfect. Shaking and raw. Fractured at the edges, like he didn't expect to survive saying the words out loud. They were real. It wasn't spoken to a crowd as some part of a performance or ceremony or tradition. He gave it to me and only me. Not because he was told to, or because it would gain him anything, but because he wanted to promise me something under those stars.

I still feel it, where his hand closed around mine, where his lips brushed the inside of my wrist. So much truth in so little time. More than he's ever given me before. Everything he's been holding back. Something that makes this moment bearable, even as everything else feels staged and laced with paralyzing venom.

I haven't told him what that vow did to me. How it cracked something open. How, for the second time since I crossed into this world, I felt wanted in a way that had nothing to do with power, or fate, or usefulness. Just me. If I think too long about what it means, I'll fall apart. So I don't. I don't think about getting home, because that feels so far away now. I let the music fill that space instead.

Dancers spin, masked and gliding, their shadows more animated than their limbs seem to be. The air shimmers with illusions. Light bending around marble columns, turning them into hourglasses of gold and ash.

I sit beside Raef at the head table. Our table of honor and prestige. The newly bound. Queen in name. Pawn in practice. Still carrying his promise like a second heartbeat.

Food has been served—quail glazed in crisp, caramelized syrup, dark fruit bleeding on silver trays, and cups of wine that glitter like amethyst. I haven't touched a thing. Neither has Raef. He also hasn't let go of my hand.

Not once.

His grip is steady, but there's something brittle beneath it. Like he's holding on because letting go might crack him open. For once, I think the infallible Raef needs me to steady him, and I don't know what to do with that other than let it be. Maybe that's all I need to do or think.

I can feel him radiating fury beside me. But I keep my gaze forward. Blank. Distant. Survive. Survive.

My stomach coils tighter with each toast, each polite nod from courtiers who wore funeral masks to a wedding.

High Queen of the Shadow Court, my ass. I feel like a relic in a glass box. Something to look at. Something no one expects to last or expects far too much more of what hasn't been voiced.

Across from us, Selmire stands again, arms wide, smiling like a shark about to swallow a priest. "Let us not only celebrate the bond we've witnessed tonight," he says, "but ensure it flourishes," he stares me down, "and fruits."

Chatter passes through the room. Chairs scrape closer, fabric whispering as they edge toward the table.

"To that end, I gift the bride and groom a fortress of their own. Seacliff Watch. High above the Black Coast. Ancient and empty...until now."

Gasps sound throughout the large room. Polite ones, but Raef stands so fast his chair falls over backward, returning the room to sudden silence. It makes me jump as it breaks the king's performance. In this court, no one breaks character, but Raef did.

"That's outside the spine ward," he says, tightly. "Beyond the deep runes. You want to send her *outside* the wards?"

Selmire doesn't react at all. Surprise, surprise.

"If the bond is true, no harm will touch her. You seal the bond, gain access to her power, and put an heir in her belly. If not," he shrugs, "then we'll mourn yet another wife of yours. Either way, I win."

My stomach turns, and I'm even happier I haven't touched a bite of food. The grape-like fruit on my plate looks like bruises. The meat like blood. I'd thought the vows ended it—the risk, the weight of what touching him would mean. But the king's words make it sound like the rules have changed or there's another layer that Tris and Raef 'forgot' to mention. The ring and the oath tie us in a way that makes my magic something he can reach if we ever cross that line. And all I can think is—this isn't a honeymoon; it's a funeral march.

The trap still clicks into place despite everything we've done. Not a gift. A test. A gamble.

Raef's face is white with fury, but he refrains from saying anything more damning. There's nothing he can say; even I know that. We're powerless.

I grab his hand, standing myself. He pulls his glare from his father, and he must read my feelings on my face because his own instantly softens. I try my best to silently tell him, 'We'll figure this out. We'll make it work. Together.'

For now.

WE LEAVE AT dawn. There's no parade or fanfare. No guards lined in gold and obsidian to make a spectacle of it. Selmire made it clear: he wants Raef to seal the deal, breed me like a broodmare, and strip me of the distractions that make me dangerous. As such, Javi and Tris were forbidden to join us. Not as guards or witnesses. Not at all.

So, it's Raef, me, and a silent escort of half-trusted riders, and the weight of vows wound tight like chainmail beneath my skin. It's beautiful but feels like a trap dressed up in gold and grace.

Javi and Tris stand beyond the gate, armed and glaring, waiting there as my last link to something solid and good. "We'll watch the court," Tris says, jaw tight. "Watch the king. Don't get comfortable or do something you'll regret."

Javi steps close and presses something into my palm—an old token of some sort. "If anything happens," he says, "anything at all—you scream through this. I'll hear you."

My fingers close around it, and his around mine. I pull him in, a brief, hard hug that says what I can't. Then Tris. The same. It's all I have left to give without coming apart.

Leather creaks as I swing into the saddle. The horse snorts, his warm breath brushing my knee. He shifts under me as I grab the reins. It's been years since I've ridden anything that wasn't for a dig or an escape. My legs remember faster than my head does.

Emrys also waits outside the gate. He hands me a book, old, bound in soft black leather. I check the spine to see what he's given me, but there's no title pressed there to read.

"For when you forget who you are," he says softly. I don't say thank you. I clutch it tight. If I try to speak even those easy words, I'll lose any composure I have left.

The gate groans shut behind us. The world narrows to hoofbeats and fog. We ride. Past the first hardline. Past trees that drip with ash and damp. Past moss-wrapped stones full of memory.

Then—two figures step from a cairn, cloaked in green and grey.

Javi and Tris. Waiting. Somehow already ahead of us.

Tris's jaw is set, but his eyes are soft. "We only have a moment."

Javi walks up and takes my hand in his, pulling me from my horse and holding me to his chest.

"I wanted to see you," I whisper. "Before we were too far gone."

"You're not," Tris says. "Not yet."

I twist so fast my head spins. "You're going to come?"

He shakes his head. A flicker of grief crosses his face, fast and heart wrenching. "For now, we will watch the court. Keep track of what shifts. What stirs. What he plans. As best we can, anyway."

Javi leans in, pressing his forehead to mine. "Be safe, little star. If he so much as—"

"I'll light him on fire," I say.

I mean it. Every word. He almost laughs. Almost.

Tris kisses my temple quick and careful, because we still have an audience of armed riders who don't speak but know what it means to watch a woman be held like this.

Raef doesn't interrupt. He doesn't rush me. He waits a few paces ahead, glancing over his shoulder once to meet Tris's eyes. Something silent passes between them.

Before I ride on, I look back once more.

Two men I love standing in the fog, swallowed slowly by trees. I do love them, somehow. Somehow in this short amount of time they've wormed their way into my heart. An organ I thought to be permanently broken five years ago.

I don't cry yet. I'm proud of that.

But in the silence between heartbeats?

This feels a lot like goodbye.

54

HOW TO LOSE A PRINCE, AN ARM, AND YOUR MIND IN UNDER A MINUTE

R AEF AND I RIDE THROUGH shadowed forest, the two of us now. Our small escort turned back at the second hardline, which we both found to be a curious order from the king.

The trees begin to thin. Pines give way to a mix of ash and stone, their roots clawing through pale soil like they're trying desperately to hold on. Needles crunch under the horses' hooves, brittle and dry. The wind picks up, carrying the scent of dust and something burnt, like lightning struck a tall tree recently. Raef glances over at me. "You haven't said anything in over a liorin."

I shrug. "I suppose I'm still digesting the part where your father referred to me as breeding stock in front of six monarchs."

His eyes drop to the path, mouth tightening as the horse sidesteps under him. "You weren't meant to hear that."

"No?" I lift my chin. "Was I supposed to be too busy glowing in the starlight to notice?"

He exhales, slow and controlled. "He's testing you. That's what he does. Presses until something cracks, and then he finds a way in."

"Oh good," I snap. "Let's just hope it's not into my uterus."

That earns me a shocked glare from him that melts away as fast as it came. I let out a quiet snort, almost a laugh.

Another moment passes in silence. There's obviously something he wants to say.

He shifts in his saddle, the stiff leather creaking. "Did Javi give you a contraceptive tonic? Yesterday?"

No wonder he hesitated. I pull back on the reins, the horse tossing its head at the sudden check. "Excuse me?"

His focus doesn't waver. "Javi. Did he provide you with a tonic? After you two..." He doesn't finish the statement, only shakes his head toward me like an embarrassed twitch. I am loving his discomfort.

I tip my head, watching gleefully as the muscle ticks in his cheek. "Yes, he did. Not that it's any of your business."

"It is unfortunately," he mutters. "What color was it?"

"Red. Why the interrogation?"

"The red ones only last a month."

I narrow my eyes. "Again, that's a non-issue. It's just you and me here for who knows how long, and it's not like we can..." I gesture vaguely to the embedded ring on my finger. "You know. I'd rather not be bound twice. Not to mention the glaring omission on your part about accessing my magic after a romantic evening of flesh games."

He clears his throat, the faintest flush rising along his neck as he fixes his eyes on the trail ahead. The reins slide through his fingers once before he catches them again. "There are workarounds."

I stare. "I hate you."

"No, you don't." He smirks.

"Shut up." But my ears are burning. I can feel my cheeks heat like a sixteen-year-old virgin. "That's something I've been meaning to ask," I say.

"Now's as good a time as any, since we're finally alone. If we ever did... you know. You'd get access to my magic? Neither you nor Tris mentioned that before when we had this little conversation. You only said it would make our binding permanent, which is now a moot point."

His smirk fades. The horses slow. His horse tosses its head, impatient. He steadies it, still not meeting my eyes. "It would," he says at last. "The vows made it inevitable. Our bond would form, a stronger one, which would connect us in a way that would let me, whether you wanted me to or not. At least that's what the stories say. I wouldn't want to take it. Look at it as a part two to the bond. The one we have now is rather strong, but completing a soul bond is even more so."

I stare at him, however. "Sounds dangerous."

"It can be. It's a primal connection that no one understands anymore. It hasn't happened in a very long time."

"And the whole workarounds thing? What are those?"

He sighs, telling me he doesn't believe what he's about to say. "It requires control. Separating...the act...from emotion. It's possible, in theory. If neither person feels enough to open the pathway for the soul threads to find each other..."

"And that's supposed to work?"

"I don't think so," he admits quietly. "I think some can take the emotion out of it; they often do. I don't think we... I can."

We crest a bend in the path, and the light shifts, like it's being filtered through a gossamer veil. The cliffs to our left rise sharp and broken. To the right, a sheer drop vanishes into mist.

Raef's horse halts.

"I don't like this," he mutters.

I open my mouth to agree, but my view tilts sideways faster than the words that were already on my tongue can come out.

The trees to our left warp like heat haze—and then figures burst from the distortion. Hooded, heavily armed, and fast.

Raef wheels his horse toward them, blade half-drawn. "Stay behind—"

I never hear the rest.

The ground beneath my horse's front hooves crumbles. A stone gives way with a sickening crack. My body lurches. Weightless.

"Raef!" I scream.

He twists in the saddle, reaching. I catch a flash of gold in his eyes, the sound of leather, and a harsh gasp—then his hand is gone, swallowed by light and motion.

Magic shoves through the space between us, a hot wind laced with copper and what feels like shards of glass. An illusion? A barrier? Since when is wind as hard as a wall?

He vanishes in it—yanked sideways by something unseen. His shout back to me is swallowed whole.

I fall. The path disappears entirely as all I can see is rock and mist as the ledge tears loose. Earth and gravel cascade down with me. My horse screams, a raw, panicked sound—a crazy thought enters my mind as gravity defies itself because that sound is familiar, almost identical to the cave trolls in my favorite movie—then silence as we both plunge into the fog-choked abyss.

The wind in my ears pulls me back to my sudden reality along with the stone filling my mouth and my name—torn from someone's lips and lost in the fall.

55

How to Die Trying and Fail Beautifully

I WAKE TO THE TASTE of blood in my mouth and something sharp grinding in my arm.

The sky is a dull bruise overhead. Everything else is stone and ash and shadow. I'm on my side in a shallow pit, half-buried in scree. My ears ring. My head pulses in sick, uneven thuds. I try to breathe, and pain lances through my ribs—hot, splintering. I think I scream, but it's soundless, air and agony.

The world is distant. Like I've fallen out of it, and I'm still trying to claw my way back. My fingers twitch against the earth. Wet and sticky. Blood.

The ground shifts again. Not sideways like before, just unsteady. Tilting. Like I'm still falling, only slower now.

I roll onto my back. Wrong move. My vision sparks, whiting out.

I have to get up. I have to find Raef. I push to my knees. One leg folds under me. My arm—gods, my arm is broken. Not just broken, splintered. Bone juts through skin above the wrist, slick and pale in the dying light.

My stomach heaves at the sight, bile burning the back of my throat. The world around me tilts hard, a gray rush at the edges of my vision, but I catch myself before I hit the ground. Somehow, I stay up. I have to.

Breathe. Just breathe. Slow through the nose, out through the mouth.

I whisper a word, half-formed. A healing one, maybe. One I've heard Javi use. But it dies in my throat, useless. My magic doesn't come. I feel nothing of that now-familiar tingle when I need it the most.

I'm too human. Too hurt. Too far from anything that could save me. I'm alone in a place that wants me dead.

I bite down a sob and brace with my other hand, dragging myself upright. Each breath is a battlefield. My ribs scream. My vision tunnels. But I get my feet under me.

My right leg holds, barely. The left sends a bolt of pain through my calf and up behind my knee—twisted, maybe sprained.

I stagger, but I'm moving.

Each step is a gamble. My chest catches on the sharp hitch in my side, ribs grinding. Blood runs stickily down my arm. The world around me tilts and sways like I'm back on that damn hell boat.

One step.

Then another.

It's not the effort of walking on a sand beach; it's like I'm waist deep in the waves, but they're lava, hot and melting.

The trees are few and warped, black moss hanging from them like torn cloth. The air smells wet and sour, but that might be from me. Behind me, something shifts, slipping in the gravel. I'm being followed.

Footsteps? No. Lighter than that. A slip of sound from whispering leaves. Like something watching me, herding me.

It can't possibly be anyone or anything I want to see right now, so I keep my damn mouth shut.

The light breaks ahead, a tiny glimmer of hope. A clearing, or what's left of one, half-choked in fog.

I stumble toward it.

"You fall well, darling."

My heart stops. That voice. That voice doesn't belong here.

I turn so slowly as every muscle screams in protest.

He steps from the edge of the mist like it parts for him. Tall, with those wide shoulders I always admired. Brown hair neat as ever, too neat for this place. He's not dusty or bloodied. He can't be real.

But he is.

"Remington," I breathe. The name feels foreign in my mouth. Like I'm coughing up bones I buried years ago. Wait, because I did. I buried him years ago. Not literally, because they never found a body to bury.

He smiles like it's a joke with the best punchline. Like I've said something clever. "It's been a while."

My brain refuses to catch up. For a moment, all I can do is stare, my vision pulsing at the edges. He looks exactly the same. Like time forgot him. Like grief was a fever dream I never woke from.

I shake my head and immediately regret the motion. "You're dead. You died. They said you died." I hear the crack in my voice and feel it vibrate through every shattered bone and every unanswered prayer.

"No." He studies me the way he used to study maps, dispassionate and certain. But he smiles, a cruel tilt of one side of his lips, like the words taste sweet in his mouth. "You just stopped looking."

My stomach twists. A part of me splinters, and the sound it makes is deafening. "This isn't real."

Because it can't be. He disappeared five years ago. One night, without a word, without a trace. I searched. Called. Cried. I dreamed of him until it hurt to sleep. I dreamed of him for months. When I finally stopped dreaming, I buried the grief deep enough to pretend it wasn't rotting me from the inside. When I stopped dreaming, I started blaming myself. That I wasn't enough to keep him.

Now he's here, whole. Untouched. Wearing that same goddamn smirk. I want to scream. I want to run. I want to sob until the earth splits open and swallows me whole. Make it end. Make it stop.

But he's here. Standing in a stony fae forest like he belongs in it. Like he always did.

"Oh, it's very real." He steps closer. I don't retreat—can't. My legs are trembling, half-useless. My fingers twitch for a weapon I don't have.

His gaze drops to my arm, to the blood soaking my side. "You're in rough shape," he says softly. Almost kindly.

That voice. That tone. I remember how it used to soothe me. Now it curdles in my veins.

"Go to hell."

He chuckles. "Already been."

Another step.

I force my chin up. "Why are you here?"

"To offer you a choice." His voice is smooth, low, and easy. It's disgusting. "Come with me now, Rory..."

He lifts two fingers, gesturing to himself, like I'm a dog he expects to follow.

"...or I give the order to end your little love triangle. All three of them."

Time stops. No, it doesn't stop; it cracks down the middle. My vision whites out at the edges again, but not from pain this time. I'm angry. I can't believe any of this. It's the burning kind of betrayal.

"You're lying."

"Am I?" He glances over his shoulder into the dark. "Raef's stubborn. Tris, he bleeds the prettiest. Javi? He'd beg, not for himself. Never for himself. But for you? Always."

The room we shared. The letters. The way he touched me. The way he whispered my name like it meant something. The memory of it all burns away any guilt I ever felt over this man. It was all part of his grand plan. Was any of it real? No, it wasn't. It couldn't have been. Just another male, another damn fae prick using me as a pawn in their own story.

"You wouldn't—"

"I would." His smile fades. "This was always going to happen. Though, I didn't expect you to make it this far on your own."

I lurch, fighting the urge to vomit on his pretty boots. Or scream. Or combust. I feel pain and flames. This is all because of him, and my head hurts too much to try and figure out how. But I'm here, in this realm, because he wanted me to be. Of that I'm certain.

The grief curdles. Hardening like lead in my belly.

He didn't die. He *left*. He didn't vanish. He *betrayed* me.

My pulse pounds so loud it drowns out everything else. I'm shaking. I don't know if it's fear or rage or blood loss. All of the above, more like.

"What do you want from me?"

"Everything," he says. "But for now, your feet and your silence."

He holds out a hand.

I don't take it. Not yet. Not ever, not again. But gods help me, I nod. Because I don't have a choice. Not right now. Not with my arm shattered, my magic silenced, and three lives hanging in the balance. But that doesn't mean I yield. Let him think I've surrendered. Let him think the fall broke me. Let him think I'm still the girl who cried herself to sleep when he vanished five years ago.

But I'm not anymore. I'm still here. Still breathing. I remember the burn of saltwater in my lungs. The way Mattie was dragged under. That was his fault. Mattie is his fault, not mine. I think of the way Javi pressed a token into my palm and whispered promises he meant to keep. I think of Tris's kiss on my temple. Raef's voice cracking when he made his vows. They are not bargaining chips. They are the reason I will survive this. And I will crawl through fire and ash if that's what it takes.

So, I nod. I follow. I bite down on the scream in my throat and swallow the blood in my mouth.

But I'm planning. Counting every step. Every thump of my still beating heart.

Because if Remington Bristol wants everything...he's going to learn what it means to lose.

The courts howled.

They named her traitor, gate-breaker, oath-breaker,

and vowed to scour her bloodline to its last ember.

Only then did danger find what they did not yet know she held—

a child born in secret, between tide and flame.

So she hid the girl as she had drowned the Gate:

not by burying her,

but by unwriting every name that might lead the hunt.

—Book of the Atma, The First Age

56

The Art of Bleeding Gracefully in Front of Strangers

I FOLLOW HIM. I do. Each step is a dare against gravity. Pain sparks like flint up my leg and blooms hot and wet through my ribs. My arm hangs useless at my side, slick with blood. The world keeps sliding in and out of focus, and still—I follow.

Remington doesn't look back. Just walks, like he knows I'll come, following behind like a little puppy dog. Like he's done this before.

My throat burns. The words claw their way out anyway. "Did you ever love me?"

He stops.

So, I say it again, louder. Harsher, enunciating each syllable so I'll know he understands. "Was any of it real? Or was that part of the plan too?" This time, he turns his head. Just enough for me to see the smirk that curls the corner of his mouth, that familiar mouth, like this is some private joke. "What do you think, Aurora?"

My voice shreds into pieces. "I think you vanished," I hiss. "You left me grieving. For *you*."

He shrugs, dismissing me and all my feelings. "Grief builds resilience."

Something inside me splinters again. I want to hit him. I want to scream until my ribs shatter. I want to claw his perfect face until he bleeds something real.

"Why are you even here?" I whisper. "What are you in this realm?"

He turns to fully face me; it feels like a mask is peeling back.

Remington Bristol. The boy I once loved. He looks the same, but too much. He's sharper around the edges. His hair is still parted like he walked off a glossy prep school brochure, but his clothes are wrong. Not human anymore with sweater vests and brown slacks. They're tailored, high-collared, in a dark fabric that catches light and doesn't let it go. His boots gleam. His skin is unmarked. The little scars I'd memorized while in his arms are gone. A figment of my imagination. He doesn't look like someone who's been surviving in a strange and dangerous world. He looks like someone who's been *waiting*.

"Because this is my home. I belong here."

I reel. My knees threaten to fold again.

"Back there?" He lifts a lackadaisical hand in the direction of my entire life. "That was a cost. This?" He lifts his arms like he's showing off a stage. "This is skin. This is power. This is everything I'm due."

The air stirs, uneasy. Even he notices it. I suppose that makes sense because if I notice in my state, his pristine state means he already has.

Remington stiffens. His hands drop slowly to his side.

A low growl ripples through the trees, like thunder given feet. The mist parts, and something moves inside it.

I see eyes first—green, sharp, wild. The rest of him following, massive, fur streaked in charcoal and silver, paws silent on the moss. A wolf, too big to be natural, too obviously intelligent to be an animal.

It doesn't snarl. It doesn't lunge.

It steps between us, facing Remington. Protecting me.

Remington doesn't move. But he chuckles.

He's batshit crazy. How did I not see that before?

"Well," he says, backing away, voice low. "Looks like someone still thinks you're worth protecting."

He meets the wolf's stare. "I thought you left this territory when *she* died? Interesting. This isn't over."

And then he's gone, like he was never here at all. The moment he vanishes, my legs give. I crumple to the earth, pain screaming through my side. My broken arm hangs limp, soaked in red.

The wolf doesn't approach right away. He stands and watches out of reach. He decides to step closer, one careful paw at a time. Lowering his head, he sniffs at my bloodied shoulder. His nose brushes my cheek.

I don't jerk away or feel any fear. I don't know if it's because I don't have the energy or my body knows something I don't. Something deep inside me knows I'm safe.

He exhales in a puff of foggy mist. Then he turns. Pads a few steps forward. Stops. Looks back.

The meaning is clear.

Come.

My body trembles, every limb on fire—but I move. One step. Then another.

I follow.

Again.

THE TREES BLUR together, tall shapes stitched with moonlight. I trip more than I step, my feet dragging, ribs catching with every attempt at inhale, thorns piercing my muscles. I feel like I'm drowning all over again.

The wolf moves ahead in silence—fluid, powerful. He stops when I fall behind. Waits. Watches. Never speaks. Because why would an animal suddenly start talking to me?

That silence wrecks me right now more than words could. Though, after Remington's voice, smug, cruel, but so familiar, it's a mercy. A balm I didn't know I needed. No questions or commands. His patient presence is sorely needed.

At some point, I stop seeing the forest.

There's pain. The incessant throbbing in my skull and the slick, too-wet heat of blood down my fingers. The cold creeping into my chest. The night goes on like it forgot to let the sun out.

I smell water. Moss. Wet earth that's been disturbed.

The wolf pauses at a low rise. Roots twisting above a narrow stone mouth, half hidden by ivy. A cave.

He ducks inside without looking back.

I follow, stumbling through the threshold, and my eyes adjust poorly to the lack of light. I pitch forward, catching myself on my knees, vision dimming at the edges. I breathe through my teeth, fighting to stay conscious. Every inch of me screams. My body wants to give in. My heart doesn't know how.

The air inside is cool and wet, but still. It doesn't bite like the wind outside. The stone walls cradle the dark. There's a stream somewhere—just a thin trickle—but it sounds impossibly loud.

I press my good hand to the floor. Moss. Dry, somehow. My blood soaks into it like ink into dry paper.

My lashes flutter. My pulse skitters.

The wolf steps around me, except he's not a wolf anymore. One breath, fur, the next, flesh. A lot of flesh.

The shift doesn't startle me. I'm too far gone. Some part of me registers it, some deeper, older instinct that doesn't need eyes to recognize magic.

A male kneels beside me.

He's tall even crouched, with hair dark and curling near the shoulders, the tips of his pointed ears peeking out of the damp waves, and his eyes still glow faintly green in the dim. His skin is streaked with soot and pine needle scratches, but his movements are gentle and careful. His scent wraps around me before he does: ironstone, cold water, crushed pine.

He smells like a place I haven't been, but maybe always wanted to go. It's peaceful. Reassuring.

He reaches slowly. Wrapping a cloak around my shoulders, pulling it tight around my shaking frame. He eases me upright enough to wedge moss beneath my back, supporting my weight when I sag. His hand is warm and calloused, and it lingers at my back until I stop swaying.

The warmth seeps in slowly, fighting the cold that's been nesting in my ribs. For the first time since the fall, I feel safe. He doesn't want to use me. Somehow I know that. He doesn't seem to want to break me or claim me either.

I should ask him who he is. Why he helped me. What he wants. But my lips won't form words. Instead, I whisper nonsense. Fragments of thought. Apologies I don't remember thinking about. Names that slip from me like water from a cracked cup—Raef, Javi, Tris—broken syllables I can't explain.

The tears follow without warning. Salt and silence. I think I'm apologizing for all of it. For trusting the wrong person, for what it cost, for still being here when I shouldn't be.

He never speaks. But he doesn't leave.

And that, somehow, means everything.

57

BEFORE HER LIGHT FADES

I BOLT UPRIGHT IN THE dark, heart hitting hard against my ribs. For a moment, I don't know why—until the heat sears through my wrist.

The token. It pulses, sudden and violent, wildfire under my skin, taking the air straight from my aching lungs. The bed, the walls, even the air feels erroneous.

Then I hear it. Not with my ears—there's no sound in the room but my own ragged breathing. But still, I hear it.

Rory screams.

Not just in pain, but in terror. A sound that rips from the soul when the body knows it's falling and no one's there to catch it.

Cold drops through my stomach.

"Tris," I rasp, already fumbling for my boots.

He's beside me in an instant. No groggy blinking, no sleepy confusion. Just stillness, alert and immediate.

"What was that?" he asks.

"She screamed." I cinch the the laces with shaking fingers. "I felt it."

Tris reaches for his own boots, eyes on mine the whole time. "Through the token?"

I nod. "She's hurt."

He pauses—a second too long—and fear crests through his gaze like it might spill over.

We haven't said it aloud, not even to each other, but we've been living in her room for days. Because it still smells like her. The lavender from her soap, the faint ember scent that clings to her clothes, and that strange flower that I can't identify. We haven't been ready to let it go. Not when we didn't know when we'll see her again.

This was no hum of fear through the veins; it's a scream. I can't bear the thought of being too late.

"We need to move," I say, grabbing my coat, not caring that it's half inside-out. "Now."

Tris doesn't argue. He grabs his sword and a pack with shaking hands. His mouth twitches like he might say something, then shuts. It's too late for words.

We don't wait for guards or permission. We move through the halls in complete silence, slipping from the Shadow Court into the dark. And I pray to the sleeping gods, to my ancestors in the stars—harder than I have in years—that she's still alive when we reach her.

We find them near the bend in the path—what's left of them.

The first male lies near the rocks, armor scorched so badly it's cracked at the seams. His face is turned toward the sky, eyes open, lashes dusted gray with ash. The air stinks of burned leather and skin, thick enough to taste. His blade's been fused to his palm—fingers curled tight even in death.

A female sprawls a few feet away, her hair singed to the scalp, bow snapped clean in half beside her. Her throat bears the mark—two interlocked circles, seared deep and shining faintly red, like it's still feeding on the last of her magic. Tris kneels long enough to look, his brow furrowed, then pushes on.

A rustle cuts through the silence. Another fighter staggers from the trees, coughing on smoke, sword trembling in his grip. Tris moves fast. Steel meets flesh with a single, muted sound, and the male folds without a cry.

Movement to the right—a boy this time, barely grown, trying to run.

The boy bolts for the trees, half stumbling, half sprinting. He can't be more than sixteen, barely old enough to be considered grown. His armor hangs loose, stolen or inherited. The panic in his breathing is louder than his boots on stone.

Tris moves before I can speak. A flash of silver light arcs through the smoke, clean and fast. The spell hits mid-stride. The boy seizes, then drops, limbs folding in on themselves. The smell of burnt metal and hair hits me before I reach them.

I slow, pulse hammering, and crouch beside what's left of him. His eyes are open. Unfocused. The mark burns at his throat, the twin circles carved deep and still glowing. Whatever bound him didn't only command, but it also consumed. That is a hefty price to pay.

"Don't," Tris warns behind me. He knows what I'm thinking.

I press a hand to the boy's chest anyway. No rise. His warmth fading with an echo of a heartbeat that isn't there anymore.

"He was a child," I murmur.

Tris doesn't deign to argue with me. He's already moving on, scanning the trees, magic bright at his fingertips, searching for the next threat.

Smoke drifts between us, thick with heat and ash. I pull my hand back, wipe it on the dirt, and stand. My stomach twists, but there's no time to stop. He's right.

There's no time to question them, even if we could. No time to wonder who sent them or why. Not when the forest still tastes like burnt magic. Not when the very air feels wicked.

I barely register the carnage.

Because I see *him*.

Raef.

He's on his knees, hands bound behind his back by glowing bands of hardened light—tight and bright, forged from magic, angry magic.

His head hangs low, blood smeared across his temple. He twitches like he's trying to shake it off, but his muscles are trembling, overworked. Panic and rage spill off him like waves of heat. He looks like a star that's crashed into the earth. Cracked, scorched, still burning.

When he lifts his face and sees us, we're looking into something fractured and broken.

"Where is she?" his voice is raw. "Where—where is she—gods, she—she *fell.*"

He jerks hard against the restraints, veins bulging, muscles straining until the cords in his neck stand out. The bands flare, white-hot, spitting light and the sharp scent of scorched flesh. His wrists blister under the glow, skin peeling where the light touches—and still, he pulls harder.

"I couldn't reach her. They dragged me back, they pulled me away, and the ledge—it broke. She screamed—Javi, she—" he chokes. "She screamed, and then *nothing.*"

"I know." I keep my voice soft and gentle. I drop to my knees in front of him, ignoring the blood and the tremble in his limbs. "I heard her too."

"She's dead." His voice shatters. "You didn't see it. You didn't see—she fell. That drop—no one survives that. Especially not her. Not even—"

"She's not dead," Tris says sharply.

Raef twists against the bonds, light flaring, smoke curling from his wrists. "You don't know—"

"The bond hasn't broken," Tris snaps, stepping forward and crouching low. "You'd feel it if she were gone. You know that."

Raef stops thrashing.

One second. Two.

I watch the words dig into him—like they don't land so much as claw their way inside. His breath comes faster, shallow and ragged. His whole body shakes.

My chest tightens. This is Raef unraveled. The one none of us ever get to see. The one who never lets go because he can't—that's what his father wants and needs, to gain control. We must fix this; we can't let that happen.

"But she's hurt," he whispers. "She's hurt and frightened. I can't feel her right. I can't—*find* her."

Tris presses a hand to his shoulder. "We will. Raef, you can't break, not now, not here. Not where your father can find you. Get yourself together."

Raef refuses to meet his gaze. His head dips forward. "I felt her slip. Like she was being pulled into something. I didn't know if it was death or—" He chokes on the word.

I reach for the shackles. "We've got you. And then we'll get her."

Tris moves in fast, fingers already working through the air like he's sketching invisible runes. His magic has never made any sense to me, the things he can do. But I also never prodded or asked for an explanation. I don't need to poke the bear to assuage my curiosity. I trust him implicitly, and that's all that matters in the end.

"Hold still," he says tightly.

Raef doesn't. He thrashes again, his body jolting forward, the bands of magic searing brighter across his wrists and upper arms. The smell of scorched skin hits my nose, and I lurch forward, but Tris doesn't stop or even stutter in his action.

He mutters something quiet—short, clipped, and old. His fingers splay open and twist sharply.

Those shackles of light resist. Light rippling through them as the sound climbs into a raw, metallic wail.

They're made of something binding and invasive—blood-forged, maybe, or reinforced with bone ash or oath-metal.

Tris shifts his stance, presses both palms down flat toward the binding now glowing a searing white-blue. His magic pours into them like molten steel.

"Javi, brace him," he says through his clenched teeth.

I drop low, arms bracing Raef's chest, holding him steady even as his body bucks with pain.

Light splits the air with a crack sharp enough to sting my ears. Heat flashes across my hands, even through Raef, then the bands shatter—magic bursting outward in a rush of white and sound. The glow dies as fast as it came, leaving the smell of lightning and burned skin in its wake.

Raef collapses into me, and I nearly fall back under the weight. He's fever-warm and trembling uncontrollably.

"I should've held on," he mumbles. "I should've pulled her with me. I should've—"

"No," I say fiercely. "You're going to help us get her back. That's what you're going to do."

I say it like a command. Like a prayer. I need him to believe it, because I need to believe it too.

For a second, he stares at me—red-rimmed, hollow-eyed.

He nods.

We run.

WE FOLLOW THE scent of blood and pine sap down into the ravine. It's not easy. The slope is brutal, littered with broken rock and clawed earth. Something massive came through here; paws the size of plates pressed deep into the mud. A wolf, too big to be a regular forest dweller—this is the print of a shifter, an ancient one from the size of it.

Raef spots our clue first. "There," he says, voice hoarse. "That shape— it's leading somewhere."

We move fast and quiet, slipping between root and stone, following the path carved by a creature we don't know but desperately want to trust.

Raef exhales sharply—relief mixed with disbelief. "He got her out."

"He?" I echo.

Raef moves on. But beneath the wolf prints we can all see and smell Rory's trail. Flecks and drops of blood, a torn scrap of cloth snagged on a thorn bush. A footprint where she must have staggered. The print isn't clean. It drags at the heel.

She walked after the fall. That should be impossible. The healer training I received tells me what that far a drop does—bones shattered, lungs crushed, blood pooling where it shouldn't. It would be hard put for a fae to survive that fall, not without immediate help. Not without strong healing gifts within moments. But a mortal? Never in my wildest imagination is this possible. But there it is. Her blood on the stones, her prints dragging forward. Proof she stood up when reality says she couldn't, she shouldn't. A part of me wants to believe it's her strength, but the rest know it's something stranger.

"She's stronger than we thought." My thoughts seep to the outside, to the others.

"No," Raef says. "She's not. She's too stubborn to die."

Tris drops to another set of prints—booted, but larger, clean, and pressed deep into the damp earth. The stride is longer and confident. Lighter than Raef's, heavier than Tris's.

Tris's hand hovers above the print, fingers flexing once before curling into a fist. His magic dims, the light at his knuckles snuffing out. "These aren't hers." I could strike him for wasting time stating the obvious.

Raef crouches beside him, narrowing his eyes. "No." His voice is low and bitter cold. "I know that boot heel, that symbol."

My stomach drops when I see it: two entwined circles. "Remington."

He doesn't deny it. Just stares at the tracks like he can burn through the earth with fury alone.

"They were together," I say. I feel the words scrape the inside of my throat like broken glass.

Raef's whole body stiffens. "That means my father has something to do with this."

"You don't know that," Tris says.

"Don't I?" Raef snaps. "He's been whispering in my father's ear for forty years."

"Well, he didn't take her," Tris adds quickly as we move. "The prints diverge. See? She follows the wolf. He walks away."

Raef's fingers twitch once, then still. The muscle at his temple jumps, a pulse he can't hide. "If he touched her—"

I cut him off before the rest can leave his mouth. I can't let myself picture it—his hands on her, her afraid. The thought alone claws at something deep and feral in me. My stomach turns, heat crawling up the back of my throat. If I see it in my head, I'll lose what little calm I have left. Each step feels heavier now. The air thickens with damp and moss. Everything smells like her. Blood, sweat, stubborn life. Her blood is in the soil now, faint, but there. A smear on bark. A drop on stone. Tris follows it like breadcrumbs in that story about the lost children my nan used to tell me, and Raef barely keeps himself from shouting her name.

That is when we find the cave.

Tucked into the hill's base, half hidden by ferns and ivy. A stream trickles nearby, threading the silence with a sound of calm. The scent hits us all at once—pine, stone, blood.

"She's here," I say with a sigh.

Raef rushes in first. I'm only a heartbeat behind him.

Rory is slumped near the back wall, curled in on herself like a dying ember. Her hair is matted with blood. Her skin—gods, her skin is gray. Her arm is twisted beneath her, the bone punching through where it never should. Her breathing is shallow and amiss. Worrying to a level I've never felt before, and I pray to the gods I never feel again.

Raef drops to his knees beside her. He presses his forehead to her chest like if he listens hard enough, her heart will answer, like it will fix itself from our mere presence, and I can't help but foolishly hope the same thing.

I can't move. My body forgets how. My heart has stopped completely. I kneel on her other side and take her hand—what's left of it. The unbroken one. It's cold and damp. Clammy.

"Rory." My voice breaks around her name. "Rory, we're here."

She doesn't move. She doesn't know we're here.

A sound lodges in my chest. So small and hopeless. I'd scream if I had anything left. I don't know what to do. Where to even start. The damage is staggering. She shouldn't be alive. How is she alive?

Tris pushes me out of the way, panting. He peels back the cloak and places his palm gently on her ribs. His magic glows faint and green against all the blood.

"She's bleeding internally. Two, maybe three, ribs have collapsed inward, puncturing a lung. Compound fracture in the arm. The ankle's swollen—possibly torn. Her pulse is erratic. And..." He exhales. "Her magic's locked down. She's not healing."

"Then *heal* her," Raef growls.

"I'm trying," Tris snaps, his voice tense with the fear that's racing through all our blood. "But she's fading. If Javi wakes up and helps me," he glares at me, "we can stabilize her for now. That's it. We need a healer."

The cave narrows to the rise and fall of her chest, to those shallow breaths. My body feels locked, caught somewhere between disbelief and dread. Tris's words sink in and break something loose inside me. I lurch forward, dragging air into my lungs even though it hurts to breathe so deeply. I press my palm to the back of her head. Not because it helps, but because I need the contact. I need to anchor myself to her warmth, even if it's slipping. Blood dampens her hair, tacky under my fingers; the little warmth left is the only thread holding me together.

Raef leans back and drags both hands through his hair. His knuckles are raw from where the spellbinds burned them earlier. He stares at her like he's watching her fade already, like he can't unsee it.

"Don't do this," I whisper, leaning in closer and brushing her cheek with the backs of my fingers. "Don't leave us like this. Don't go where we can't follow. The stars don't want you—not yet."

Something shifts beneath my hand, a faint tremor, the smallest pull of deeper breath. Her lips part, rough and bloodstained, a whisper catching and dying before it finds sound. The air leaves my chest in a rush. It's barely movement, barely anything at all—yet it feels like the world stirs with her.

Raef's words stutter in his chest. He folds over her, hand splayed flat above her heart. "She's still in there," he whispers.

Tris is already casting again, this time stronger, reaching deeper. The magic seeps into her skin like sunlight through snow.

"We need to carry her. Move her now. Right back to the keep."

I nod, fast and frantic. I don't even wait for orders from the others. I lift her carefully as Tris wraps a glamour of warmth around her chest. Raef steadies her broken arm.

We run again.

This time, it feels like we're racing death itself, because we are. We're slowed down carrying her, but our legs will move faster than hers ever could all the same. The guilt I feel at the glimpse of happiness moving at our normal speed again after weeks with her is almost my undoing.

THE SHADOW COURT gates open as soon as we're seen, or perhaps even before. They knew we were coming. They were waiting.

Raef carries her in silence—bloodied, limp, her head against his chest like a broken doll no one knows how to fix. Her hair sticks to his shoulder.

Her arm dangles, memories flashing of bodies I once beheld that never came back.

No one stops us, but everyone watches.

The guards at the gate go still. Two of them bow their heads—not to us, to *her*. The torchlight flickers across their faces, catching on the hard line of their jaws and the uneasy set of their mouths. One presses a hand to his chest while the other murmurs something I can't hear even with my fae hearing, a movement of lips only. Word travels fast in this place, but not faster than we do. Every face we pass flickers with something close to fear. The corridor is otherwise silent except for the scrape of our boots and the wet sound of blood dripping from Raef's sleeve.

I don't know if they're afraid for her or of her.

By the time we reach the healing halls, whispers have already spread.

"She's back."

"She fell."

"She lived."

But they don't know what she looks like yet. They haven't seen the truth of what survival costs.

A male in embroidered shadow silk steps into our path, one of those nobles who's never bled for anything or anyone, and smells faintly of spice and ink. His sleeves shimmer with spell thread as he lifts a jeweled hand. His gaze flicks from Raef to the precious bundle in his arms, and for probably the first time in his long life, his confidence falters. "What happened out there?" he asks, eyes flicking to the blood soaking through Raef's sleeve.

None of us bothers to answer. The look Raef gives the male is colder than winter steel. It says, 'Ask again, and you'll join the earth she almost vanished into.'

The healing hall is empty and echoing; the few healers on duty recoil as we enter, a cluster of robed figures smelling of herbs and singed sage. One drops a bowl of fresh tinctures, glass shattering across the tile; another grips the edge of a cot so hard her knuckles blanch. Even the oldest among them, the one with silver braids and hands stained from years of poultices, goes still when he sees her. "That should've killed her."

Tris growls, "Then maybe you should count your blessings and get to work to keep it that way."

Raef doesn't let go of her until a bed is cleared and the spellwork begins. Even then, his hands hover at her hair, her shoulder, like if he doesn't touch her every second, she'll vanish again.

He's coming apart quietly, and I despise, because I don't know how to come apart quietly. I want to scream. I want to punch the stone walls until my fists split. I want to do something. Anything.

Tris murmurs quiet instructions to the experts. He looks steady on the outside, but I know him; I know his blood is boiling in his veins. There's magic at his fingertips again—he won't stop until he's spent everything. The glow of his spell light flickers across her face, only adding light to how pale and bloodied and too still she is.

I stay in the corner. I'm afraid if I get closer, I'll fall apart too. Because if I touch her, I might feel the truth I don't want to name.

I watch the way her chest rises. Still shallow. Too shallow.

It's wide of the mark. All of it. She should be cursing us for hovering. She should be fighting the healers, cracking jokes to cover the pain. She should be awake. She should be—

I can't feel her through the token anymore. Not even a spark. Not even a whisper of her heartbeat against mine. Just the cold space where she should be.

For the first time since she barged into our lives with mud on her boots and questions in her eyes, I think I might have been too late.

58

BEFORE SHE WAS RORY

Rory

1 FLOAT.

That's nice.

Or maybe I'm falling again. It's hard to tell, because the sky is below me and the sea is above, and both feel like they're made of glass. There's no up or down. Just the weightless ache of almost remembering something important.

I try to move, but I have no hands.

I try to breathe, but I have no lungs.

Still—I *know* this place. It smells of salt and jasmine. It tastes like memory long gone.

Atlantis.

Not the shining city from stories and memory. Not the gold towers or singing fountains. No—*my* Atlantis is bones and ruin. Streets half-swallowed by the tide. Statues cracked down the middle like broken spines.

Lights still flickering in the deep, like stars that drowned and forgot how to rise. Lost souls. I know it, but I don't know how I know it. But they're people that were forgotten and betrayed.

I drift through it.

Doors open and close without touching them. Murmurs slide through the walls. Names I don't know—except I *do*. They taste familiar. Like lullabies buried in bone. Like bedtime stories I forgot to believe.

A child runs past me, barefoot. Her dark hair flying behind her. She doesn't look back.

A voice follows her. Not a stranger's.

My mother's.

Soft. Laughing. Then more urgent. Calling something I can't make out.

I try to turn. I try to find her.

There she is.

Standing in a garden of stone and silver flame, wind twisting her skirts. She's blurred by light, but I feel her hand close around mine; the ring, my ring, sits gracefully on her finger.

"You were born for more than survival," she says.

My throat aches. My soul aches. "Why didn't you tell me?"

"I did," she says, almost smiling. "You just weren't ready to listen."

The garden darkens. Water rushes in from nowhere, rising and hungry.

"What am I?" I ask her.

Her eyes have an eerie inner glow.

"A key. A storm. A question the world forgot to ask."

The tide takes her away.

I'M FALLING AGAIN.

Down through stars and the silence of the night. Through heat and ache and the taste of blood.

But it isn't silent, is it?

A voice, real this time. Distant, muffled, and achingly familiar.

"Rory," someone says. "Rory, please..."

Light tugs at the edges of my vision. I swim toward it.

I want to surface. I want to stop sinking. But some part of me still isn't sure what waits above.

I keep drifting. So tired.

The water fades, but the sensation of weightlessness doesn't. It's like being suspended between choices. Between worlds.

I see flashes now. Not of Atlantis—but of before.

A cradle carved of obsidian and pearl. A lullaby sung in a language I know but don't speak, and somehow understand.

Māteris humei, thugatēnŕōs, thalassa phōsion kalyptor. Euprenos komē, nausēa choruses, agapē krataiōs, mē lypeis.

As a mother sings to her daughter, the shining sea is your shelter. Sleep softly, dream in gold, my strong love, do not weep.

Asteris phōsioi luei hē, thalassa phylaxei kalē. Thugatērūs, komē chrusea, euprenos komē, nausēa chrusea.

The stars above will guide you, the sea below will guard you. Daughter, golden heir, sleep softly, dream in gold.

Māteris phōsios, thugatērūs, thalassa chrusea kalyptor. Euprenos komē, nausēa chrusea, agapē aiōnos, mē lypeis.

A mother sings to her daughter, the shining sea is your shelter. Sleep softly, dream in gold, my strong love, do not weep.

Eurpenos komē, nausēa chrusea, thalassa phōsion kalyptor. Aurora.

Sleep softly, dream in gold, the shining sea is your shelter. Aurora.

The name coils through the dream like silk through fingers. It glows. Warms. Hurts. It's mine. Was mine. Before the world cracked open and someone tucked me into a skin that doesn't fit, a life stitched together with lies and longing.

There are new voices now. Councilors. Mothers. Lovers. One of them says, "She'll break it."

A different voice replies, "No—she *is* the breaking."

A third says, soft and certain, "She'll choose better than we did."

Each voice pulls through me like a thread yanked through old fabric. I don't know if they're right. But I want them to be. I want to be different.

The vision bends and ripples. Pulls apart like a book dropped in water, its glue softening the binding, pages floating away.

Hands.

Real, warm hands. With fingers pressing gently to my chest. The warmth of someone kneeling beside me. A voice trembling above my ear.

"Rory, please. Come back."

I speak, but my mouth won't move. But something inside me reaches for it. For the voice and the world I almost lost. The one I'm finally ready to face.

There's light again. But different. Dim. Steady. Torchlight. Not stars.

Pain returns like a tide. My ribs, my arm, my head. I'm not weightless anymore.

I'm home.

59

WHAT I COULDN'T HOLD

Raef

SHE'S BEEN STILL FOR TOO long.

The healers say she's stable. That the fever is down. That her breathing has evened out. That the worst is over. They don't know her.

She doesn't stay still. Not even in sleep. She flinches when the wind rises too sharply. Kicks off blankets. Talks in her dreams. Once, she plastered me in the ribs with her small but formidable fist. This stillness isn't peace and healing. She's lost.

I sit beside her, elbows on my knees, hands clenched tight enough to hurt. My knuckles ache, nails cutting half-moons into my palms, but it's the only way to stay still. The air smells of herbs and metal—blood that's been cleaned but not forgotten. The faint sharpness of healing salves clings to her skin, clean and sterile and very much not her.

Her skin has color again. Faint, but it's there. A fragile flush along her cheekbones that looks borrowed from someone living. The bandages are fresh and clean, a stark contrast against the bruises that mar her pale skin.

The room hums with silence, perfect and contained. Even the candles burn quietly, their flames flattened to thin gold threads. The longer it stays that way, the louder my heartbeat gets, until it's all I can hear.

I should feel relief. I should take the stillness for mercy. Instead, it feels like waiting for a storm that has been hovering over me for years, biding its time. Every part of me strains toward her, reaching through that dim thread of the bond, desperate for warmth, for anything.

And in that emptiness, I feel it—the faint pressure at the back of my skull, a familiar coldness threading through thought sliding along that frantic bond. A voice that isn't voice, patient and waiting. My father never pushes when the walls are strong. He waits for the cracks, and this bond punched a hole in my entire existence.

I clench my fists tighter. Pretend it's exhaustion, fool myself into thinking I'm not losing ground.

The bond feels different.

Not broken—thank the gods. But faint. Quiet where it should burn. A thread instead of the flame. It feels like someone poured cold ash over the tether that used to anchor me. Like something vital is missing, and I don't know how to find it.

I've lived my whole life trained to hide every flicker of emotion. But when I felt her vanish from my senses on the cliffside—like someone tearing the still beating heart from my chest—I broke. I don't know what I said. I don't remember how long I screamed.

I do remember the silence after. The moment I stopped making sound and realized my hands were bleeding. That I'd clawed stone. That Tris and Javi were calling my name and I couldn't answer.

She doesn't move. She hasn't moved for hours. Not even her eyes twitch in the healing sleep. Her hand lies curled on the blanket, fingers twitching now and then like she's lost in something far away and can't reach it.

I—I sit here like a child at a deathbed, waiting for the gods to change their minds.

I've been called prince, general, and heir. But even I couldn't stop her from falling. I couldn't hold the cliff. I couldn't hold her.

Now the only part of her that feels real is the guilt rotting in my chest.

But she proves me wrong at every turn.

A sound catches in her throat, thin and fragile. The smallest gasp, like the world remembering how to breathe through her. Her lips part, cracked and pale, and the faintest tremor runs through her shoulders. Her head shifts—barely toward me.

My entire person stills. Every muscle I own locking. The air becomes so heavy, charged, waiting with an intensity much like myself. I fear moving even a fraction, afraid I'll break whatever fragile thread pulled her back.

Her lashes flutter. Once. Twice. She opens her eyes. Not fully. Not clearly. Enough for the light to find them—and for me to see that she's looking at me. Not through me, not past me, but at me.

Something inside me buckles. The air leaves my chest in a ragged rush, and the noise that follows is half laugh, half sob. The walls around my thoughts crumble before I can stop them. All that control, all that armor—gone.

I don't think she sees me. Not yet. But her gaze settles—like a ship drifting home to a ruined harbor.

I lean forward, afraid to touch her, afraid she'll slip away again if I move too fast.

"You came back to me," I whisper.

Not knowing if she hears it—only that I need to say it before I shatter. And I break quietly, because she's here. Because she came back. Because I don't deserve it, and I don't care.

I would give anything to keep her here. Even the last pieces of myself.

With that thought there's a flicker at the edge of my mind.

A whisper that doesn't belong to me. Not yet a voice, but something older, colder, a door waiting to open. A crack in the wall I built to keep *him* out.

Uproar gave way to war.

Her consorts died before her. One by one.

Loyal to their horrid end.

The Sanguine turned on their own king.

And still, she stood.

Alone on a shattered throne,

sea salt drying on her lips,

she watched those she chose—

her council, her beloveds—

dragged from her hall and cut down

by the courts she once held in balance.

—Book of the Atma, The First Age

60

Healing in a Room Full of Liars

Rory

THE VOICE FILTERS THROUGH THE fog gripping my mind. I follow it, but the dark clings to me like wet cloth. My body is a distant thing. Every breath scrapes like stone grinding against stone.

I can't remember where I am, or why I hurt so much, but I remember *that* voice.

Raef.

The name steadies something in me, cuts through the void. I follow it—slowly, through the dark. My lashes drag open. The light is dim, wherever I am, but it's warm as it flickers. It's that strange faelight. The kind that clings to the walls like it owns them, whispering against old stone, crawling through every crack and shadow. It hums under my skin, familiar and wrong all at once.

The ceiling swims into focus—arches etched with curling inlaid lines that catch the faelight and scatter it across the walls like liquid gold. The pale stone radiates cold, old as bones, and the air tastes metallic, like after a spring rainstorm. I know this place before the name even forms. I'm back at the Shadow Court.

I'm alive.

The thought feels unreal. Feels like disbelief. Like I cheated something ancient and cruel. Like the pain is proof that I shouldn't have made it back.

The rest of it hits all at once.

Pain.

A tidal wave of it.

My chest aches, like someone caved it in and then tried to stitch it back together with frost. My arm is a furnace. My mouth tastes like metal and ash. A noise tears loose from my throat—hoarse, broken, halfway between a gasp and a curse.

Raef's face snaps into view—closer now. Eyes wide, his mouth moving once like he's about to speak, then shuts again, lips catching on the edge of a word that never makes it out.

He says my name. Like a prayer. Like he thought he'd never get to say it again. It takes me a few seconds to realize it's not another dream.

"Rory," he breathes. "You're here. You're really—"

He doesn't finish. He presses his forehead lightly to the edge of the mattress, like he can't trust himself to look at me too long.

Someone else moves behind him, a quiet scrape of boots, the low hum of fading magic. Tris. His face is all sharp edges and shadows, skin pale under the faint green light still clinging to his hands as he pulls them down his cheeks. The air around him smells like burnt sage and dirty laundry. His shirt is rumpled, sleeves shoved up to his elbows, and veins traced with the last glow of a spell that he refuses to let die out. He looks like he's been awake for days.

Javi—god, Javi—sits on the floor, knees drawn to his chest, holding something in his hands. The token. His lips are moving, barely audible, like he's been talking to me this whole time. He doesn't see me wake. Not at first. His voice keeps going, soft and frantic. A lifeline in the dark.

They're all here. And the look on their faces—grief, shock, love—makes it real in a way the pain didn't. I survived. But it wasn't clean. It wasn't easy. They paid for it as much as me.

I speak, but the only sound I manage is a broken croak.

Raef looks up instantly.

"Don't—don't try to talk," he says, voice cracking. "You're okay. You're safe. We've got you."

I don't believe it yet. Not fully. The world still feels like a dream collapsing around me. But their faces are real.

I'm still here.

For now.

I MEASURE TIME by the sound of Raef's breathing. It's the only thing in this place that doesn't change. Slow, steady, never quite restful. He sleeps in the chair beside my bed. Boots planted, arms folded, always angled toward me like he's waiting for something—attack, confession, collapse. He hasn't left since we came back. Not even to sleep properly. Not even when I beg him to. He keeps a blade within reach. I saw it once, slipped under the folds of his coat. He thinks I didn't.

Tris shifts in and out of consciousness on the settee near the hearth, a book balanced on his chest. He pretends he's reading it, but I've watched him turn the same page three times without blinking. He checks on me when he thinks I'm asleep—his fingers skimming lightly across my wrist, casting little pulses of diagnostic magic strong enough to make the inside of my skin tingle. He never says anything. Just sighs, like he's afraid the results will change. Every time, Tris exhales in relief. Every time, he does it less loudly.

Why isn't Javi doing this? The healing. He always has before.

Javi doesn't rest at all. He paces like something's chasing him. Sometimes I hear him talking, muttering to himself, sharp bursts of words too low to make out. The sound of his boots grinding across stone has become its own rhythm, a heartbeat layered under mine. Lately, he's started standing at the door. Just standing. Like a guard. Like he's daring someone to come in.

Sometimes I catch him staring into the dark like he sees something there I can't.

They don't leave me alone. But they can't keep everyone else out.

The visitors begin two days after I can sit up on my own. They aren't healers or officials and definitely aren't family. Courtiers, by the look of them. Too much silk and perfume they use to hide the stench of fear. They smile the way people do when they're waiting to see if you bite. Something has fundamentally changed. They knock without urgency, bow without sincerity, and speak without saying anything at all. They bring things—gifts, they call them—velvet boxes with wax seals, tinctures in blown glass, cloaks I'll never wear, and sugar-paste flowers that wilt the moment I touch them.

They never stay long, but they never come alone. One or two at a time with their servants, always cycling. I don't know who sends them. Raef never says. The others act like it's normal, like it's expected, but I see how Javi narrows his eyes when they linger. I see how Tris scribbles names when they leave, etching them into the margins of old letters. I see how Raef's jaw tightens, barely, whenever one of them speaks too softly, too kindly, or too close.

They call me a miracle, but they look at me like I'm a weapon someone forgot to bury. I'm starting to wonder if they're waiting for someone to give an order.

The magic is helping me heal. That's what they say. The breaks have closed; the worst of the swelling is gone, but my skin feels too tight. My bones ache in weather that doesn't exist. The inside of my chest still stings every time I breathe deeply, as though something in there never quite stopped cracking.

Sometimes I wake in the middle of the night with no idea how I got upright. Sometimes I speak in languages I don't remember learning. Twice now, I've dreamed of Remington's voice, but when I open my eyes, it's Raef watching me like he heard it too.

One of the old healers—the one with the green thread in her braid—disappeared yesterday. No explanation. A new one arrived this morning.

He's quiet; I like quiet. He also seems competent, but he won't look me in the eye.

He touches my arm without asking first. I see Raef's hand twitch toward his sword.

No one talks about it after. No one explains the big deal.

I've started watching the shadows more closely. Because I know what it feels like to be hunted now. And I know what it feels like when something presses against your mind from the inside. I know who's hunting me.

This time, no one's bothering to hide it.

RAEF DOESN'T SLAM the door when he returns, but the way the latch clicks—sharp and final—makes my shoulders twitch beneath the blanket. He walks across the room in brooding silence with clipped precision and lays something flat and folded on the edge of the table. Every emotion he has is locked behind his teeth. His movements betray him, though. The stiffness in his shoulders, the way his jaw moves like he's chewing through something bitter. I've seen this Raef before, many times.

I file those details away. The king cracks him in small, invisible ways. I need to learn where and how.

"Was it him?" I ask, though I don't need to. The black seal on the summons this morning had smelled faintly of scorched moss and old copper. My sense of smell is through the roof now, and I don't know what to make of it. Raef burned the letter in the fireplace after only one glance, but the scent lingers in my nose, haunting me.

He also won't look me in the eye. "It was."

"And?"

Raef shrugs off his coat and hangs it too carefully on the wall hook, as if the act of straightening it can somehow restore the balance of the world. "He wanted a report."

"That's all?"

He turns his head to acknowledge my location, but not enough to meet my eyes. "It's never just that. He's under the impression that, despite your condition, an heir should already be on the way."

The truth lands on its own without venom. Just cold inevitability. Like weather, the storm you see coming from miles off but still can't outrun. Even though we've been through this before, there's a moment where I can't so much as move a finger.

My ribs ache from the effort, from the swell of something sharp and rising in my chest—revulsion, fury, shame. It doesn't matter which. They all blur at the edges. I stare at him, but he won't look at me, and that's worse than if he had delivered the line with a sneer. At least then I can scream. At least then I can strike something. But either way, I can start to calculate.

But this? This quiet? The practiced indifference? That's what power looks like in this court. I need to remember that. To use it better. It feels like confirmation. That somewhere, in some poisoned ledger, my body is already accounted for. A future asset. A broodmare in pretty silk.

"I see," I say. My voice doesn't crack, which is impressive to me, but it's close. "Should I be grateful he waited until I could walk again?"

Raef shifts his weight like he's absorbing the verbal blow like a sponge. He still won't meet my eyes, damn him.

That silence stretches thin between us, finally breaking with a bitter laugh that I don't realize is mine.

"Tell me, was that a part of your report?" I ask. "Did you let him know the status of my womb? Or just note the color of the bruises?"

That's what pushes him over the edge. His gaze flicks up, earnest and pained.

"Don't," he says.

"Don't what?" I lean forward, biting past the pull of healing muscle. "Don't ask questions about how my life is being planned without me? Don't mention that the only reason I'm still breathing is because your father finds me *useful?*"

"I'm trying to protect you."

"You're failing."

The words hang in the air between us. I bite my tongue before I throw out more cruel words at someone who doesn't deserve them. I hate how much of me wants to take them back. I hate more that they're still true at the same time. No matter how many times I tell him we do this together, he insists on hiding things from me.

He pulls his shoulders back, his hands pulling at the chair back he's been bracing on, scraping wooden legs across stone. The sound grates like a saw against bone.

"I'll have someone bring your tea," he mutters, and before I can say anything else—before I can decide whether to throw something at his back or beg him not to go—he's already gone.

I watch him leave without moving. I'm not still too hurt, but I need him to think I'm still fragile. Because I need to learn what game his father thinks he's playing.

I'm once again alone in a room full of ghosts that haven't died yet.

I FEEL TERRIBLE. Not in the 'I'm still healing' way, but in the 'I just used Raef as my verbal punching bag' way. I don't regret what I said, but I regret how much of it I used to wound instead of warn. He still hasn't returned, and it's been hours.

I walk the corridor. The healers had cleared me for movement two days ago, but I hate how heavy my limbs still feel, how I drag slightly on the left side like a ship with a cracked hull. The cane Tris gave me clicks softly over the stone, echoing louder than I think it should, announcing me like a threat.

When I reach the archway to the longer corridor, one I used to walk daily without thought, I find it blocked. Two guards stand shoulder-to-shoulder, unfamiliar armor gleaming in that clean Shadow Court way. The sigils on their shoulders are crisp, slashed through with silver runes that glint whenever I look too long.

"I'd like to pass," I say, keeping my voice steady.

The guard on the left doesn't even bother to look me in the eye. His armor is awfully bright for a male on night duty, the black enamel polished to a mirror. His voice is predictably flat and practiced, with that authority that hides behind orders. "You're restricted from this wing."

"Since when?"

The second one steps forward enough to make it clear he enjoys following orders as well. His voice is smoother than the first, trained, and almost polite. "Since King Selmire's decree," he says, lowering his chin a fraction. "For your safety."

I stare at him. "This hall was safe enough for me a few weeks ago."

Neither of them bothers to respond, their duty done. The first one adjusts his grip on his spear. Not enough to be threatening. Just enough to remind me he can. Just enough to show me they're not used to being questioned.

I nod slowly and turn back the way I came. But I count the runes on his shoulder. I note the angle of the door behind them. I file it away, piece by piece. As I reach the corner, I hear one of them muttering something. I don't catch the words. I don't bother to ask. Next time, I will. And next time, I won't come unarmed.

I turn the next corner—and stop so quickly I slip on the smooth stone. The air changed, and I was too distracted to notice. The faint and haunting faelight dies like it's been smothered, and considering who I see in the hallway, it makes total sense.

Selmire.

Standing alone at the junction like he was waiting for me. Okay. I can do this. How do you block a mind... build a wall to keep someone out. They said to mind my emotions. Center my thoughts. Build an impenetrable wall of nothing.

He's alone, shadow silk glinting at his cuffs, eyes too dark to be called anything but bottomless. He looks me over, not with hunger or pity, but calculation. I can do the same, buddy. I'm a variable he expected to have solved by now and hasn't. And I find that after everything, I'm not afraid of him.

"Good afternoon, Lady Aurora," he says, smoothly. "You're walking well, considering your fall."

My fall, like he didn't have anything to do with it. It was all a clumsy accident. I keep my expression bland. "I'm told I'm very stubborn."

"A trait shared by most wild animals," he replies, lips curving faintly. "They tend to bite when cornered, instead of running like they should."

I smile. A small one. Not one that shows teeth. The kind that says, 'I see you. I know what you're doing. And I've started thinking for myself.'

"Careful," I say softly. "You might start sounding concerned."

He chuckles, genuinely, I think. "Only for the future of my court. And my bloodline."

"Then maybe you should stop trying to poison both."

That makes something flicker behind his eyes. But he doesn't rise to it. He steps closer instead.

"You've always been clever," he says. "But cleverness alone won't save you, child."

"No," I murmur, this time showing teeth as genteelly as possible. "But it makes the game more fun."

He studies me—really studies me. And I see it. A flicker of unease. The faintest tightening at the corners of his mouth.

He inclines his head, enough to be mocking. "Welcome back to the court, your Grace."

I'm left standing in the corridor, pulse steady, spine straight.

One piece moved. The game has begun.

61

PLAYING THE PAWN WHILE LEARNING THE BOARD

THE TRAY ARRIVED LATE THIS evening. It was supposed to be delivered at dawn—broth, a few fruits, and water laced with restorative tincture. When Tris lifts the lid, the steam is long gone, the fruit half-rotted at the edge. He stares at it like it has personally offended him.

"This is unacceptable," he mutters, grabbing the tray with both hands. "No, strike that. This is a message."

Raef, still seated at the hearth, says nothing. His fingers have been idly running a whetstone down the edge of one of his knives, but they stop now, held still in his lap.

"I'll return it myself," Tris snaps. "Let them see exactly who sends it back."

Javi starts to rise, but Tris waves him off and is gone before either of them can argue.

423

I stare at the untouched water glass until Raef quietly reaches out and moves it away from me. It's a small gesture but speaks volumes. It's protection and awareness. Quiet proof that my fears for my well-being are founded.

The next morning, a girl I've never seen before slips into the room, balancing a stack of folded linens against her chest. For a maid, she doesn't have a smudge on her apron. Her hair's braided tight, not a strand out of place, and she smells of rosewater and ink, not soap.

She doesn't ask permission, simply crosses the room with practiced ease, and says the east wing will be more comfortable. "Better light," she chirps, setting down the linens like she's offering me a gift. "More warmth."

"Who sent you?" I ask.

"Lord Selmire's steward."

"She's not going anywhere," Raef says from the edge of the balcony, the curtain covering the door hiding his presence. The girl jolts like she's been caught stealing silver, the linens nearly slipping off the table in her haste. She hadn't seen him there, or maybe she hadn't believed he would intervene. Color drains from her face so fast it's almost impressive.

"I was only told—"

"She stays."

His voice isn't loud. It doesn't need to be. She backs out fast enough to trip on the corner of the rug, and the linens never leave the floor. But her eyes linger. Calculating. Memorizing. Reporting.

The door closes behind the servant girl with a sharp click; Raef walks out onto the balcony.

He's half shadowed behind the velvet drape, the tension still coiled tight in his spine, his hand flexing once, twice, like he's working something out of his palm. I hate that I put tension there. I hate more that I can't seem to stop.

"Raef," I say, my voice soft, pleading. "Wait."

He pauses and draws the curtain aside and steps fully into the room again. The firelight catches the edge of his profile—drawn tight, blank in the way that people are when they're trying not to break. But he doesn't turn away when I reach for him.

"I shouldn't have said what I did before," I murmur. "About you...failing. That wasn't fair. I was a complete bitch."

He says nothing, but he's listening. That's enough. It's more than I deserve. But less than I want.

"I'm angry," I say. "And I don't know where to put it. I'm scared, and I'm sick of feeling watched, and I'm not handling any of it well. Not after the ambush. Not after—" My throat tightens. "Not after him."

That gets his attention. His gaze snaps to mine.

"Him," he echoes. "You mean the male in the ravine."

I nod once, slowly. "Remington."

Raef's mouth flattens. "You said his name in your sleep."

That surprises me, but I suppose it shouldn't. I've been dreaming too much. Letting things slip. Letting too much show. I'm not made for politics; I've got too big a mouth and no filter. But maybe I need to become someone who is. Because this is the second time someone has tried to move me like a piece on a board, and I'm getting tired of pretending I don't know how to play.

"It's worse than that," I say, my turn to not meet his eyes. "I knew him in the mortal realm," I say, voice barely above a whisper. "We... I knew him. Before. Before I ever came here. We were—" I look down, playing with the edge of the blanket in my lap. "We were together. For a while."

Yet again, he says nothing in response, but it's not in anger or indifference. I can feel his eyes on me. He's waiting for me to finish.

"I thought he was dead," I say. "He disappeared. One day he was in my bed, the next he was gone without a note or a by-your-leave. And then I saw him again on the Blood Plains—a glimpse. I told myself it was stress. Delirium. But it was him."

"What does he want?" Raef asks. He straightens slowly, the tension in his shoulders drawing tight as wire, but at least I'm not the cause this time. His voice is quiet and kind; that's how I know.

"To take me with him." My hand curls tightly, fingers digging into my palm. "He said if I didn't, he'd have his men kill you. Kill Tris. Kill Javi. All three of you. He gave me a choice, but it wasn't one."

Raef is quiet for a long time. I'm ashamed. I shouldn't be. But I am. Because I survived, and it still feels like a failure. He chooses to move quickly and kneel in front of me, his hand resting over mine.

"You should have told me...us," he says.

"I know. I didn't want to make it real. In case you haven't noticed, I struggle with my new reality." And I didn't want to show them how easily I could be broken. But I guess I wasn't, not really. I should have died. I overheard the healers say it when they thought I was sleeping. I shouldn't be alive after that fall, never mind back at this court getting healed.

His fingers shift, curling more firmly around mine. His warmth seeps into my skin like a heated brick at the foot of the bed, steadying where the rest of me still trembles, at least on the inside. "It was real," he says, voice low, rough at the edges, "the moment he threatened what's mine... The first strutting time."

I lift my eyes to his, startled, but not by his words, it's the look in them. There's no cold calculation there. No political strategy. Just Raef—furious and afraid and *here*, kneeling before me like I'm the only thing he wants to protect in a kingdom full of knives.

"You can't say things like that," I whisper.

"Why?" His thumb brushes lightly across my knuckles. "Because you'll start to believe me?"

"I already do," I admit, and it comes out like a confession. Like surrender. Not the helpless kind, but one I choose. The kind that I can build armor from if I have to.

He exhales, and the sound is almost a tremble. His forehead drops to the back of my hand, briefly, like the weight of everything we haven't said finally presses him back to earth.

"I won't let them take you," he says again, softer this time. A quiet promise between the two of us.

"I know," I breathe.

And I do know.

Because Raef doesn't make promises lightly.

He also never kneels without a reason, and yet the prince of the Shadow Court is kneeling at my feet.

If I'm outplaying a king, it won't be alone. It'll be with fire at my back and Raef, Tris, and Javi at my side.

62

HOW TO RUIN A PERFECTLY GOOD MORNING WITH PARANOIA

I WAKE WITH A HEAVY intake of breath. The taste of metal on my tongue and the memory of falling still trapped behind my ribs. Something else lingers too, a ghost note of a song, one I shouldn't remember. A voice not mine humming low in my bones.

Raef's arm is around me. Warm and strong, it curves under the edge of my back where the pillows failed. His chest rises steadily against mine, the heat of his bare skin flush along my side. His body is a wall of muscle—scarred and solid and unforgiving—but around me, he holds still. Careful. As if afraid of bruising what's already broken.

I don't remember falling asleep like this. I don't remember being pulled into the cradle of his arms, his hand curved loosely over my hip, warm air soft against the crown of my head.

But I don't want to move.

The fire has burned low, casting the room in flickering amber and indigo shadows stretching long across the floor. I shift slightly, enough to see him better in the low light—his brow furrows even in sleep, dark lashes dusting his cheek. There's a line along his throat at the join with his shoulder, pale and raised—an old scar, almost hidden beneath the curve of his collarbone. Almost deadly. I haven't seen it before. Haven't been close enough or at peace enough to truly study him this way.

My fingers itch to trace it. To ask what gave it to him. To learn the map of every wound he carries and what they mean. But something on the far wall catches my eye.

A shape. Still and tall. Just beyond the ripple of faelight that hovers near the arch.

Broad. Upright. Watching.

For one single heartbeat, every muscle in my being freezes solid.

Not Remington...

Not a dream.

The air gets suddenly thick with worry. It's like something is trying to crawl under my skin. I smell iron and cedar, bitter moss. My fingers twitch for a weapon I don't have.

Him.

Selmire, or some illusion of him. Some phantom meant to look like him—because it doesn't move. Just stands there, shrouded in silence, made of shadow and menace and knowing.

I jolt as the meaning of this finally wakes my mind, sucking in a breath too fast. Pain shoots through my ribs like hot needles. Raef stirs against me, mumbling something sleep-heavy and unintelligible, his arm tightening as if to protect me from whatever has startled me.

When I look back at the wall, the shadow is gone.

I push off the mattress with shaking fingers and swing my legs over the edge, ignoring the way the floor spins beneath me. Raef's hand brushes my back, confused and half-awake.

"Rory?" he murmurs.

"I thought I saw someone," I say, already moving toward the door. "I just... I need to check."

He doesn't stop me. But I hear him rise behind me, barefoot, quiet, a warrior even half-asleep.

The hall beyond is empty. There are no guards standing watch or servants bustling around. A faint kiss of enchantments crawling along the baseboard was unsettled at being disturbed. The air stinks faintly of sulfur and old iron.

I touch the stone with my fingertips. It hums mistaken, like a harp out of tune. Some part of me aches to follow the phantom deeper, to know where he went. To know if it was him.

Raef reaches the doorway and stands behind me, shirtless, hair tousled, shoulders backlit by the dim flames of our room. His voice is gravelly. "You think it was him."

I nod once, throat tight. "But that's not possible, right? Tris's ward would—"

"Tris's wards fade the longer he's gone. He's been sending them both on frivolous missions to keep them away from you. Less distraction, he says."

"He has spoken to me," I whisper. "Just once. But I feel him. I feel him everywhere."

Raef doesn't answer, wrapping his arms around me tightly, pulling me against his chest. I sag into him, letting the heat of his skin ground me; the steady beat of his heart chases the shadow from my pulse.

"You're not alone," he says, voice barely above a whisper. "Not while I breathe."

I don't relax with that knowledge. I press my cheek to his chest, eyes open wide awake. My mind turning over the image of that figure in the dark, silent, watching, certain.

He wanted me to see him.

Now that I have... it's my move.

63

A Lesson in Controlled Burns

The courtiers send flowers now.

These aren't ordinary blooms; they come from gardens that never see the sun. Petals slick with magic, stems that bleed silver sap when cut. They smell faintly of honey and wood smoke, and the scent sticks in the back of your throat, aching if you breathe it too deep.

One sits on the bedside table, a pale blue thing that vibrates in its vase, its petals turning to follow me whenever I shift under the blankets. Another, deep violet and edged in frost-like crystals, withers the instant Javi walks past. Its leaves curl in on themselves like little fists, only to unfurl again once he's gone. Raef doesn't say anything before plucking it from its vase and dropping it into the hearth. The flames catch fast, green at first before burning clean.

They're not gifts. They're messages. Like a corrupted version of the Victorian language of flowers. I smile anyway. Thank the courtiers. Tilt my

431

head just so. Let them think I'm weak enough to need soft things. I need to do something. This not doing anything while they plot and take steps is driving me batshit crazy.

It's easy to pretend I'm still fragile. I am, but not in the way they think. My body is mending by inches. My magic still knots in my chest like it's afraid of itself. But my mind? My mind is razor clear. And I've decided to use it.

Raef doesn't know yet. Tris would see too much. Javi would stop me. So I keep the game mine. For now. It's easier this way, to carry the danger quietly, to keep the weight tucked behind a smile. They all want to protect me, but protection and freedom don't live in the same room. I'll take the risk if it means the choice is mine.

This morning, I asked the steward for a gown.

Something court appropriate. Nothing extravagant. Just enough silk to pass as cooperative. I watched the request ripple through the staff like a dropped pebble in dark water. When it reached the king, I have no doubt he paused and smiled.

Good. Let him. Let him think I'm coming to heel. That the fall knocked the rebellion out of me. That I've learned my place. Let him look away, even for a moment.

Because when he does... I'll cut his legs out from under him. How... I haven't figured out yet, but I have time for that.

He sent another tray today. Tris intercepted it before it reached me and pretended not to notice the ash dust folded beneath the cloth napkin. One of Selmire's little symbols. A calling card. A dare. I'm sure it was for Raef, a silent message, a warning, but I know it too.

I bit into the apple anyway. The skin split with a nice clean sound, crisp to the core. Sweet at first and never bitter. My tongue tingled, waiting for the burn that never came. I didn't die. Shame. Would've saved everyone the trouble of pretending I'm safe.

Today's healer is new again. This one's even older than the last, with gray hair and a limp. He doesn't speak unless spoken to. His magic is gentle but curious. He lets his fingers linger too long. Not in a lecherous way. He's measuring. So, I give him something to measure.

I flinch on purpose. Gasp once when he presses near the fracture that no longer actually aches. When he apologizes, I smile weakly and say, "It's not your fault. I'm still so sore." Raef warned me not to lie, but beyond a slightly bitter taste in my mouth when I do, nothing happens. My magic does nothing to retaliate and I'm still here.

He nods. Writes something down. I don't ask what. I already know because I gave him what to write.

Tomorrow, I'll be even paler. Even quieter. Maybe I'll tremble, once. Let him report back that I'm breaking in the right direction.

When the time is right, I'll break in the only one that matters.

The king wants me watched. So be it.

Because I'm watching right back. I've studied enough strong women. I am not a well-behaved woman, and I very much plan on making history, even if it's not in my own realm.

I TELL THE guards I'm heading for the library. Which is technically true. I pass through it on the way.

The Shadow Keep's lower halls are a labyrinth of stories and old stone, paths worn smooth by power and time. The healers cleared me for short walks, so no one's the wiser. They also didn't specify where I could walk.

Selmire's study isn't marked, but I don't need it to be. I find it by scent. That same metallic tang of scorched moss and copper, like blood left too long in the sun. The guards at his door eye me with the vague discomfort of males who've been told not to stop me but desperately want to.

"Lady Aurora," the taller guard murmurs, bowing. His tone's all starch and discomfort. It's totally forced. He doesn't want to be at this door today, right now.

I knock once.

"Enter," says a voice behind the oak.

The study is lit with a single enchantment globe, low, silver, and pulsing softly like a heartbeat too slow to be human. That light pools across the desk, catching on ink stains and rings from half-drained goblets. Papers litter the massive desk in elegant disarray, the handwriting precise even in chaos. The air at least smells clean, of cedar and old ink, but is thick with the hush of magic that hasn't settled. Behind it all, in a high-backed chair carved with serpents and stars, reclines Selmire, as if he's been waiting for me since the beginning of time.

He doesn't rise in respect or smile. His eyes watch me cross the threshold like he's watching a predator enter a den that once belonged to her. Appropriate, I think. Either that or I've managed to become far too arrogant. Which is also a very distinct possibility.

"My lady," he says smoothly. "To what do I owe the pleasure?"

"I was hoping we could speak privately." I shut the door behind me, quietly, demurely. I'm a sweet, innocent, stupid little girl after all.

His eyes narrow. "You are... unchaperoned."

"I'm not the one who needs a chaperone," I say.

That earns me a flicker of a smile. Brief.

I don't sit. He doesn't invite me to.

We study each other for a long moment.

"You've recovered remarkably," he says. "Almost as if you've remembered what side your survival depends on."

"I never forgot," I murmur. "But I did have... clarity. In the ravine. In the dark."

His head tilts. "And what did you see in the dark, child?"

"I saw your face."

He stills.

"Not a vision or dream. You were in my room." I step forward. "Last night. Watching."

There's a pause, but no denial.

"I'm told the faelight can play tricks on mortal eyes."

"Oh no," I say, slow and soft, "it wasn't the light. You stood right there. In the arch. Just long enough to catch the end of a moment."

"Then perhaps you dreamed it."

I tilt my head and smile like I'm humoring a child. "Did you enjoy the show?"

He stiffens in the shoulders. That's how I know I've hit home.

"There was no show," he says, cold.

I sigh. "Aww. Too bad. You must've come too late."

The quiet stretches thin, and I think I might have taken it a step too far. Miscalculated him.

He rises then. Slowly. He's not angry; I've piqued his interest. He steps around the desk and comes to stand a hair too close, the old stone humming around us.

"You are clever," he says. "I wonder if you always were, or if the pain sharpened you."

"I wonder," I whisper, "if you're always this obvious, or if you've grown sloppy."

Something dangerous flickers behind his eyes: admiration and want, desire and lust. He's been playing alone for too long.

I may have played my role too well. The air is being sucked out of the room at a rapid rate.

"You should be careful what games you play."

"I'm already careful," I say. "You're the one who came uninvited. It's not my fault if you see something you don't want to. Or, maybe you're more upset that you missed it. You want me bred, but maybe you want to watch more?"

He smiles. It's the worst thing he's done in days. It's a smile that makes the room feel smaller and the air go sour. I wonder what Mattie would say to me right now. Would he laugh at my audacity or look at me with that quiet, disappointed sort of pity he used to reserve for liars and thieves? I'd take either, because it would mean he was still here. Plus it would wash this taste out of my mouth.

"I do hope you're as fertile as you are fearless," he murmurs, voice low. "It would be such a shame to waste all this fire." *On my son,* his eyes tell me as they move down my body.

I'm thoroughly disgusted, but I walked right into this one and will get myself out of it. It's not the game I wanted to play, but I can work with it. *I think.* Thank God for all those theater electives.

"I'm already burning," I say softly. "And fire spreads."

I walk out before he can fire off his best retort.

Let him stew in that. Let him *wonder.*

She called the tide to drown the Gate,

to end the buying and breaking of mortal souls.

In the chaos that followed,

she buried her child where no court could reach—

between the realms the Gate once bridged.

She lived long enough to see her court fall for it.

—Book of the Atma, The First Age

64

THE ART OF PLAYING PREY

THE LETTERS ARRIVE AFTER BREAKFAST. Not that I'm eating much. The broth's gone cold on the table, skin forming over the top, sealing itself shut. I'm curled on the lounge beneath the window, wrapped in a blanket that still smells faintly of smoke and herbs. The morning light slants through frost-laced glass, scattering across the dark stone floor in fractured gold. Dust drifts in it, slow and mesmerizing. My ribs still ache when I shift off center, but I can move on my own now. Sit. Think. Worry. Too much of all three.

Javi is the one who picks up the first envelope. It slid under the door, tucked into the space between polished stone and the fur of the old rug. No seal. No wax. No sigil. His name written in tight, nearly perfect script is the only blemish on the pristine parchment.

He turns it over, once, then again. There's no magic on it. No enchantment. It's plain parchment, folded with a precision that reeks of bureaucracy pretending it isn't a threat.

He scans the letter once, twice, the paper crumpling where his fingers tighten. A muscle jumps in his jaw, something I expect in Raef, not Javi. The vein at his temple pulses, slow and furious. He doesn't utter a word, but the air around him shivers in heat like the anger is leaking out through his skin.

"What is it?" I ask, already dreading the answer.

He doesn't answer me, tossing the letter toward the fire hard enough that it skids across the stone and lands against the grate. The embers hiss, and the parchment curls slightly in the heat. He stares at it like he's measuring how far he can push before it catches.

I push myself upright, ignoring the small throb in my side. Tris beats me to it. He moves fast, faster than I can on a good day, muttering something to himself as he crosses the room. The letter's still half on the hearth when he snatches it up, fingers brushing the heat in an 'it doesn't bother me anyway' move that I find irksome. *Typical*, I think, sinking back before I tear something open. Always first to fix things, even when they're already on fire.

He unfolds the parchment with a flick of his wrist, the edges obviously still warm from the hearth the way he pinches at them with the tips of his fingers. Javi's hand twitches, but Tris starts reading it aloud before he can stop him. "Required presence requested at the Border Keep of the Ninth Verge. No signature. No date. No details."

My mind stalls, then stutters forward again. "Where the hell is that?"

"It's a cliffside ruin," Tris says, frowning. "Uninhabited, grossly unimportant, and completely unreachable this season unless you're trying to die in an avalanche."

Javi doesn't sit. He hasn't sat all morning. He's wearing a groove into the rug, pacing tight circles between the window and the hearth, the walls almost visibly closing in on him. His boots whisper against the stone, soft and unending. I've been watching him since I woke in the healing house—how he never seems to rest, how this new edge in him never dulls. Every line in his body is coiled, ready to fight something he can't see. "It's bait," he mutters, more to the floor than to us.

Raef speaks from the corner, arms folded, cloak still damp from his earlier absence. "It's pressure. If you go, you're being moved off the board. If you refuse, you're being insubordinate."

I look at Raef. "Did your father send it?"

"Of course he did."

Another knock. This one light. Polite. A folded letter slides under the door with a soft hiss, catching on the rug once again before settling. Wax seal, black.

Tris picks it up and groans. "You have got to be jesting."

"What now?" Javi mutters to the floor again.

Tris breaks the wax, skims the contents, and then reads aloud in a clipped, mocking voice.

"Your expertise in recent healing procedures renders you uniquely suited to assess the eastern court's crisis protocol. Transport will be arranged. Immediate compliance preferred."

He tosses it to the side like it's wet trash.

"So," he says, turning to Raef. "We're being separated. Surgically. All wrapped up and tied neatly with a bow. Do we even have a plan going forward? Or are we simply avoiding the obvious problem? You sure as strutting depths will not be putting a pup in her belly, so, what are we waiting for? What's the plan? Or are we letting him take the reins and hoping for the best?"

Raef doesn't deny it. His silence is confirmation enough. The sound of it fills the large room, louder than any shouting could, heavier than all the excuses racing through my mind. Everyone seems to. Be waiting for someone else to fix it. For a council decision, a decree, a bloody miracle. Anything but action. And I'm starting to realize that's how Selmire wins—he doesn't have to strike first. He scares everyone and waits for hesitation to make it easy. Even Raef, with all his titles and power, sits there like he's carrying the whole court on his shoulders and can't move without breaking something sacred. Maybe he can't, and that's the point. Maybe he doesn't have as much power as I thought he did. Whether magic or political, but I find that hard to believe.

I watch them argue. Watch Javi pace harder, Tris lists contingencies, and Raef says nothing at all. They all know what's happening, and they're trying to make it sound like strategy when it's already too late for that.

"They won't actually force you to go," I say, mostly to reassure myself.

"No," Javi replies, voice flat. "They'll just make it impossible to stay."

"Raef?" I look to him because I have to believe he'll stop this. He's always been the barrier between me and the worst of his father's games.

He stares past us, not truly seeing, his focus somewhere behind the walls. His shoulders stay locked too high and still; he's bracing for a hit that hasn't come yet but he knows will but won't share with the class.

"You're being pulled too, aren't you?" I ask, quiet now.

I feel the truth shift around him. The way the air changes. The way something invisible coils tighter at the edge of his magic, dragging him toward a center he's trying not to serve.

And like that, the room I've come to think of as safe feels smaller. Like the walls are listening. Like the ceiling is already lowering, inch by inch. Like a trap that's already triggered and almost closed.

A flicker of panic rises, but I barely feel it. I breathe. I think. Because this is what he wants. Not Raef, Selmire. He wants me isolated, unprotected, and unstable. But why? For what purpose? He's trying to box me in, but you don't box in a storm.

I tuck that thought away, quiet and powerful. A blade slipped into a sleeve. Let him think I'm panicking. Let him think I'm breaking. I wonder if he's trying to force me into Raef's arms or his? It's that thought that sends a fierce chill up my spine.

I glance at the others, at Raef, still bending under the weight of a name he never asked to carry. At Tris, who is already making a list in his head of what to pack. At Javi, pacing like a caged animal with no door left to break out of.

They all see the move for what it is. They don't know what to do next. But I do. Or, at least I'm starting to. If he wants to play chess, I'm done playing with pieces; I'll become the board. Because I don't live here, I didn't grow up here, and I don't know what to be afraid of, and maybe that's a strength, not a weakness.

The next time I see the king, I'll smile like I don't see the snare around my feet, and I'll set one of my own.

65

Out-Monstering the Monster

I WAIT UNTIL THE OTHERS are gone. Raef's been called to an emergency council meeting, Javi is stalking the outer halls like he might burn the walls down with his pacing, and Tris is muttering something about needing a stronger tonic.

Only then do I slip the note into the steward's hand.

Not the king's steward, his assistant. The one who delivers tea that's always too cold and scrolls that never have seals. The one who lingers a moment too long in doorways, eyes always a bit too blank.

I don't need to ask who he reports to. The way he moves in that too quiet and unnaturally smooth way already tells me he's practiced at disappearing. I've also seen the same blank eyes on courtiers and corpses. It's always the loyal ones who look that empty.

"You'll deliver that?" I ask, sweet as anything.

He nods, lips pressed tight and disappears like fog under the heel of a boot.

The letter is short. A single line.

If he's going to watch, he might as well listen. Tonight. Private solar. No guards.

— Aurora

The stone still holds the day's warmth against my bare feet, a nice embrace under the thin rug. The fire burns low, fragrant with herbs and dark wood, smoke curling sweet in comfort when it should be warning me to stay sharp. Velvet shadows pool in the corners, softening the edges of the room. Light skims the silk drapes and catches on the glass decanters, turning them into small, watchful eyes. Everything is coming together perfectly for what I have in mind this time.

The hinges sigh. A shift in the air, and I know he's here. I keep still, eyes still fixed on the glass in my hand. Movement would break the illusion, and tonight, illusion is all I have left that's mine.

The hush that follows him is enough for me to know exactly who it is. The latch clicks softly behind him, and the air thickens like honey poured too slowly. I remain exactly where I am, half-reclined on the cushioned bench beside the window, one leg draped lazily over the other, a spill of skin bared through the high slit of the silk gown I chose on purpose. All my drama classes are coming in very handy. Who knew I'd ever have to act promiscuous? Mattie would be giggling uncontrollably right now.

The dress is deep wine-red. Drapes like water and falls like blood. It's downright perfect and something I would never wear with a sound mind.

He stands for a moment in silence, perhaps surprised I didn't greet him. Perhaps savoring the view, which I don't think on too much, or I'll shiver on the outside as much as I'm cringing on the inside.

I sip from the crystal cup in my hand; it's not wine, I need my head clear, but it's fruit and frost, something from the mountain groves.

When I finally glance his way, I let my gaze move slowly, deliberately up his form.

He's dressed in black again. Naturally. The male probably bleeds ink to stay on brand.

His eyes crawl up my bare thigh.

"Your Grace," I say lightly.

"I received your note," he replies, his voice rich with amusement. "How... bold."

"Or bored." I turned the goblet between my hands, watching the way the light bends through the glass. "It's hard to tell the difference these days. What with you sending everyone else away."

"I'm told you're still healing."

"Is that why you came?" I ask, tracing the rim of my goblet until it sings a low, brittle note. "To check on my condition?"

"I came," he says, "because you seem to think I should be here to listen."

I smile slowly, sipping without answering. Let the silence gather, sweet and dangerous.

"Sit," I say at last, gesturing toward the chair angled across from mine. "Or stand," I say when he doesn't move. "Either way, you'll want to hear this."

He remains standing.

So, I lean back, silk shifting over my thigh, pulling tight over my breasts—what it covers of them—and watch his eyes trail behind it. "There's been a breach in your guard rotations. Near the outer rim."

His mask holds, but his eyes narrow, giving me the briefest glimpse of a cornered animal. "That's a bold accusation," he says, voice smooth enough to hide the bruise I just left.

"Not an accusation," I say sweetly. "A fact. I have nothing to do but watch these days. It's one I can prove. Or I could, if I were motivated enough."

"And what would motivate you?"

"Protection," I say. Then add, "Freedom. And perhaps a future not shaped entirely by your obsession with heirs."

There it is—the pause, the flicker. A tiny fracture in the marble mask. I almost want to applaud.

He steps forward, eyes darkening as they sweep from my face to the leg I don't bother to cover. "You're too bold for someone who owes her life to my court."

"I owe my life to the three males who nearly died getting me back." I take another sip. "You just want what's in my womb, or rather what could be."

He studies me. "And you would give it away so easily?"

He walks slowly, circling like a man accustomed to owning any space he enters. His gaze doesn't bother with pretense. It flicks to my thigh, the vast dip of the gown's neckline, and the curve of my collarbone.

"You enjoy being watched," he says.

I have to work very hard at not gagging. Bile claws its way up, and I force it back down. Disgust has a sound, and I can't afford to make it. So, I inhale slowly through my nose and think about how easy it would be to open his throat instead. A blissfully psychotic and dark thought, especially for me.

"Who doesn't?"

"And yet," he says, eyes narrowing, "you've aligned yourself with my son."

"I've aligned myself with survival," I reply, tone cool. "Raef happened to be in the right place at the wrong time."

"Interesting," he murmurs. "But not exclusive."

He moves closer until I can feel the warmth of his vile breath against my cheek. He's testing boundaries, taking my measure like a craftsman inspecting a newly forged weapon. I hold my ground. He won't find what he's looking for.

"I already have three males orbiting like moons," I say. "Drooling might be a strong word, but only slightly. What's one more?"

He tilts his head. "I don't share."

I laugh, a slow, velvety sound that curls between us like smoke. "That's a pity."

His jaw tenses. His stillness is precise and controlled, but I struck something. I let the moment stretch, then rise slowly, letting the silk glide over my skin. I don't bother to adjust the hem or neckline that's now barely covering my left nipple. Let him look.

"You know," I say, taking one slow step toward him, "you showed up rather suddenly again last night. Standing inside my room. Watching."

"Raef was still inside me," I say, soft but unflinching. It's a lie, but only if I truly intended it in the physical way I implied. Raef is always inside me, just not that way. He's in the ache under my ribs, in the warmth that answers his name before I can stop it, and in the strange quiet that settles between us when everything else turns to noise. "Did you enjoy watching?"

"There was nothing to see, again," he says coldly.

I smile. "Aww, always a little too late."

He takes one step forward. I don't move. I want him to see that I'm not afraid. That whatever power he thought he held over me, I can bend as easily. I can feel his sickly touch on my mind, trying to find a way in. Trying and failing because my males have taught me how to build my walls, not that you have to teach an archaeologist how to build walls, my mind is a broch.

I turn my back on him, walking slowly back toward the window. "Thank you for coming," I say, casually now. "You've given me so much to think about."

"You enjoy playing games," he says from one step behind me.

I let the smile fade from my lips. "No, your Grace. I just learned how to from the best."

He steps even closer until I can feel the little hairs on my neck fluttering. "You forget, when I win, the board doesn't survive."

"And yet," I whisper, looking over my shoulder to meet his eyes, "you still came when I called."

He leans enough for his lips to graze my ear, his hips and obvious arousal pressing against my lower back through the too-thin fabric. "Enjoy your little rebellion," he murmurs. "While it lasts. *Someone* is putting a pup in that belly one way or another."

He straightens, turns, and walks out like he still owns the room.

That voice, his voice, wraps around the edges of my spine like a chain already half-locked. I don't move until I hear the click of the door shutting. Even then, I stay still. If I move too fast, I might break something. A glass. A chair. Myself.

The chain he left behind is still tightening. Not real, but the echo of his breath where it shouldn't be, against my skin, the sick pressure of those last words sinking into me.

Someone is putting a pup in that belly...

Yes, someone, but who? Have I played too far, and does he think he'll be the one?

My fingers curl against the stone edge of the hearth. I stare at the velvet drapes, the polished tray, and the untouched tea. Everything is perfectly arranged. Everything is slightly off.

He won that round. I stepped too far. But he also thinks fear is the same thing as surrender. I saw the look in his eyes when I turned to face him. When I didn't flinch but smiled.

That's the difference between us. He plays to dominate, but I'm playing to outlast.

At least now I know the shape of the game. I am done waiting for someone else to set the rules.

My stomach turns. I should tell them. Tris, Javi, even Raef. They deserve to know how far I'm willing to go. How close I'm standing to the edge. How I invited the monster into my room and let him think I might enjoy it. Might enjoy him. The thought of him touching me makes the juice in my stomach vinegar.

Except if I tell them... they'll stop me. They'll fight for me. They'll bleed for me. And he'll use that against me.

Selmire doesn't need weapons. He has people. Leverage. Blood ties and old vows twisted until they choke. He'll find the cracks in anyone who cares too loudly.

No—I can't tell them. Not yet. Not until I'm sure I've found a way to beat him at his own game.

66

How to Properly Thank Someone for Admitting They'd Do It Again

MY LETTER ARRIVES AT DUSK the next evening. Not with fanfare or a summons—a quiet knock, a bow from a servant in silver and pearl, and a scroll sealed in wax the color of deep tidewater. I don't need to lift it to know where it comes from. The scent curls off the parchment before anyone touches it. Ocean brine and lilies, cold and sweet like perfume on a dead body.

Tris catches it midair before it can touch the table. He frowns, lifting it closer to his nose. "There's trace magic on it. Faint, heavily glamoured. And—salt wound. Clever."

I don't ask what any of that means. I reach for the scroll.

"Don't," Raef says, softer than usual, almost openly caring.

"I'll read it," I say, already breaking the seal.

The wax crumbles under my thumb like wet sand. The parchment unfurls in a slow, dramatic sigh, the ink looping across it in long, graceful strokes. It's overdone and hides poison behind politeness.

To the honored Shadow Court and its present guests,

We acknowledge the unfortunate actions of certain rogue elements within our waters, which do not reflect the values of the Sea Court. We regret the distress caused and extend our assurances that those responsible will be disciplined.

In the interest of harmony, we ask for mutual discretion regarding this matter. The presence of destabilizing influences—particularly those of ancient, uncertain origin—may further agitate already delicate accords.

We trust you will take the necessary precautions, given the ancient legacy you may yet attempt to claim.

With tides eternal,

High Minister Thaleia, on behalf of Her Deep Grace.

Tris leans back in his chair, lips curled with disdain. "That's not diplomacy. 'Those responsible will be disciplined.' Strutting depths, do they think we don't know that their little prince is responsible?"

"First off," I snap, already rounding on Raef, "I would never refer to Vaeryn as 'little.' That male is huge. Second," my voice rises, sharp and sudden, "you never told me the scary, cocksucking sea bastard that came to look down his nose at me is the one that killed Mattie!"

Sound drains from the room, leaving only the hum of too many thoughts colliding at once.

Raef turns, slowly. He has this look of someone trying to hide in plain sight. "Because I didn't know."

"You knew who he was," I accuse, words shaking now. "You knew he was Sea Court elite. You said nothing when he stared me down like I was something half-formed."

"I didn't know he was responsible," Raef says, "not until after the fact. Not until it was too late."

"You sure you're not protecting your dear cousin? That's what he called you, right? Cousin?"

"They're circling," Javi says, breaking the tension with that low, even voice he uses when something's about to snap. "Getting ready to strike, or claim something before someone else does."

Raef moves back to the window, but he doesn't look out. "It's a threat," he says, "wrapped in apology. They're warning the other courts without declaring war."

Tris speaks what everyone else is afraid to, "First, your father sends us away in the morning, and now the Sea Court sends thinly veiled threats. You think this is a coincidence?"

"No," is his only response.

I'm still staring at the line burned into my eyeballs.

Given the ancient legacy you may yet attempt to claim.

I walk to the fire and feed the letter to the flames.

No one tries to stop me.

67

EVEN IF YOU ARE THE KEY, YOU CAN STILL BE LOCKED OUT

MY ROOMS ARE DEAFENING.

Turns out silence can be louder than three big fae arguing. Who knew? The quiet pulls at the seams of the room until it feels thinner now that Tris and Javi are gone. They had no choice. None of us saw Selmire hesitating in the least about killing them if they refused. I think he wanted them to refuse. We considered all leaving entirely and finding shelter elsewhere, until the missive from the Sea Court.

Their absence feels heavier than their presence ever did—like my room forgot how to breathe without them. Or maybe that was just me. I'm not used to this kind of quiet. Not here, where the walls have always whispered, where tension fills the air like mist. Because without them, I'm the only one left to play the game. I'm still learning the rules. Not that I told them, but now that it's not even an option to tell them, I feel lost.

I slip out while Raef is distracted with yet another council summons. No one tries to stop me. No one sees me leave.

The Shadow Court's halls darken the deeper you go. The walls draw closer together; light sinks into the stone. What begins as polished obsidian becomes stone veined with silver and runes that flicker when your eyes pass too quickly over them; you can only see them at the edge of sight. The air changes too, getting thicker, which alone isn't unusual; it's more normal than the rest of this place. It's touched with the dry nature of old dust and the tang of magic that's been sitting here longer than most of us have been alive.

I tell myself I'm walking to clear my head, but that's a lie. I'm looking for something. Leverage to use, a way to escape. Maybe memories buried deep inside.

Emrys's books are partly to blame. He's been leaving them where I'll find them—old volumes bound in cracked hide, written in half-dead tongues that make my teeth ache when I sound them out. At least he's nice enough to also provide me with the appropriate lexicons. They talk about the kingdom before the Shadow Court, before the air smelled like smoke and iron. Back when light still lived in the stone.

One passage mentioned a door. Not just any door, but *the* door—one built before the first war came from outside, when something crossed the realm that shouldn't have. A seal, a gate, depending on who was writing. Every translation twists it differently, but they all agree on one thing: the door is here somewhere, dating from before the shadows took over.

My fingers graze the wall as I round the next corner. The stone is cold, then warm. Then pulsing, faint and steady, like a heartbeat. Light curls under my skin in response. The old magic, I have found, beats like a heartbeat. I don't think everyone hears it, or feels it, but I can.

There, carved into the arch of a narrow hallway, is a ring of glyphs. I don't recognize the script, but it feels familiar. The same way other things do, like a memory I lost somewhere.

A footstep behind me makes me turn.

A young scribe stands frozen halfway up the stairs, a stack of books clutched to her chest. She can't be older than twenty; I suppose she can because she's fae, but she looks so young, all elbows and nerves with ink freckles on her hands. Her mouth parts, closes again, and then she bows too deeply, too quickly. The fear in her eyes isn't for me, it's for being caught near me.

"I—" she stammers, backing away. "They said the heir wouldn't be allowed near the gatework."

Then she's gone. Her footfalls vanish like mist into the stairwell.

The word lands like a dropped stone in my gut. *Gatework.* I step beneath the arch, one hand on the wall to steady myself. The stone is cold and smooth, like many hands have touched it. The corridor drops away in a slow slope. By the time I reach the end, my pulse is racing with an energy I don't think is coming from me. The door itself isn't grand, tall and narrow, carved deep with lines that twist like roots or ribs. It feels older than anything else down here, old enough to predate 'the shadows.'

I reach for it without thinking. Just to touch. The moment my fingers brush the surface, the script flares to life beneath my skin. A thrum runs through the stone. Magic folds in on itself and draws back. The glow dies quickly, done with me as if it decided I'm not worth the effort.

I stagger back a step, my necklace flaring to life for the first time in a while. The heat runs up my throat. My heart stutters. I don't know if I've been seen or denied.

"You shouldn't be here."

I whip around, heart jerking hard, half ready to throw a punch before I realize who it is. Emrys stands at the top of the hall, arms folded in that deceptively relaxed way of his, a small book tucked under one elbow like he's passing through. His eyes—gray as riverstone, steady as steel—fix on the door behind me, then return to my face.

"I got lost," I say. It's a lie, but it isn't at the same time. It's not like I was actively looking for this place. I was wandering around only semi-aimlessly.

He nods once. "Of course."

He doesn't believe me, but he doesn't call for guards, either.

Instead, he walks to my side. Looks down at the stone. Tilts his head like he's listening to something I can't hear.

"They bound it," he murmurs. "Not too long ago. Not against enemies, but rather against questions."

I look up. "Who bound it?"

He hesitates. Then, with the faintest edge of sorrow, "Someone who thinks they know what's best for you."

Great. Another male telling me what's best for me. The universe has a type.

"Come," he says after a beat. "You've been missed."

He offers an arm and holds it there until I turn to walk beside him.

There's no conversation, polite or otherwise, as we retrace my steps through the upper halls, back into corridors lit with softer magic, back to the silence of the court that feels more like a cell each day.

At my door, he pauses. "I disagree with the decision," he says, voice low. "For what it's worth."

When he turns to leave, he stops midway. "Aurora, when it all begins to fall apart," he says without looking at me, "look to the isle that forgets time. What was lost waits for you there."

Then he leaves, just like that.

I stare at the closed door long after he's gone. *"Aurora,"* he said. Not Rory. No pet names or pretty titles. My name. The one I've barely begun to understand. And an isle that forgets time. If that isn't a myth, then I don't know what it is.

THAT NIGHT, I lie beside Raef in our borrowed bed, the fire low and restless in the grate. Shadows flicker across the ceiling like they're trying to spell something in a language I can almost remember. Like they're trying to tell me something.

His arm drapes across my waist, warm and heavy. The weight feels protective, but it's also a reminder of how easily I can disappear beneath it.

I should sleep; my body wants it, but my mind is still back in the archives, fingers pressed to carved stone, my chest snagging on whatever history lives in these walls.

I stare at the ceiling. At nothing. My necklace pulses faintly against my breast, as if it too remembers the door. As if it's still listening.

I whisper, barely audible. "You'd tell me if you could...wouldn't you?"

He stirs against me, the mattress dipping under his weight, a low sound escaping as he half-wakes. His breath ghosts over the back of my neck, warm and uneven, his arm tightening around my waist in instinct.

"I would," he says, voice rough with sleep, low, so sweet and real. "I would tell you everything."

I roll toward him, the sheets whispering against my skin. His eyes are already open—gold in the half-light, ringed in shadow, watching me like he knows I've been awake this whole time.

"What's wrong?" he asks, brushing my hair back from my face. His fingertips are gentle, almost reverent enough to bring tears to my eyes. "You're breathing like your heart's broken."

I press my forehead to his chest and inhale a deep lungful of his scent. Smoke and resin and some lingering trace of the mountain he'll never escape.

"I found a door," I say quietly. "In the lower halls. Sealed. It...reacted to me."

He stiffens enough that I feel it in my ribs.

"I don't think it was locked," I continue. "I think it was warded. Against me."

He says nothing, and that silence is my answer.

I pull back far enough to see his face. He's not hiding anything. But he's holding something—some truth he doesn't even know he's missing. It's not his betrayal. It never was.

"I know it's not you," I whisper. "I know."

His hand cups my cheek. "But it still hurts."

I nod, and for a moment, we look at each other.

He leans in—slow, hesitant—and kisses me like he's afraid I'll pull away. I don't. I press into him, into warmth and worry and everything we haven't said since the night he made those vows.

His kiss deepens, hand sliding around the back of my neck, anchoring me to him. And I realize this, too, is a vow. The kind of vow you absorb into your soul, even when the world tries to take it from you.

When we part, his forehead rests against mine.

"You're not alone," he says. But the way his voice breaks, I think he knows it won't always be true.

I kiss him again, harder, hungrier, with no hesitation left. I press my mouth to his like I need it to find air. Like I want to rewrite everything that's broken in us with the shape of him.

Raef responds instantly, a dam breaking apart between us. One hand slides into my hair, the other pressing low on my back, pulling me flush against him, and I know exactly how much he wants me. His skin is too warm, his chest bare, muscles taut beneath me like he's been holding tension for days, weeks, maybe forever.

He kisses like he's starving. Like he doesn't know when I'll be his again.

I shift to straddle him, knees bracketing his hips, my nightshirt tangling around my thighs. His breath catches as I lower myself, and his hands find my waist—gripping, grounding, like he's afraid I'll burst into mist.

I brace my hands on his chest. I can feel his heartbeat. It's not steady.

"Tell me to stop," he whispers. His voice is wrecked. "If this is too much—gods, tell me now."

I shake my head. "I don't want to stop." But something trembles beneath the want. Not fear. Not pain. Just *fragility*.

His hands still. His brow presses to my sternum, above my necklace, my mother's ring, that's still warm. He kisses it, slow and worshipful, and I feel everything tighten in my chest.

He lifts his head, eyes meeting mine.

"I want you," he says. "You know I do."

"I do," I whisper, slipping my fingers into his silky hair.

"But not like this." He brushes a thumb across my cheek, along the curve of my mouth. "Not when you're bleeding on the inside and trying to pretend you're not."

I huff out a laugh, holding his face and pressing my forehead to his. "You're always so noble when I least want you to be."

That earns a low laugh from him, rough and fond. He pulls me back down, wraps his arms around my spine, and holds me like the only way to keep the world out is to close every inch of space between us.

We lie like that, skin to skin, tangled and trembling with everything we almost became. Almost.

I fall asleep against his chest, with his heartbeat in my ear and his whispered promise in the dark. "Next time, we don't stop."

I laugh, but I believe him. But I also know better than to believe in next times. Not here. Not yet.

68

HOW TO NEGOTIATE WITH GHOSTS AND LIARS

THE SHADOW COURT'S COASTAL OUTPOST doesn't have a name, it's a cliff and a watchtower with a promise that no one intends to keep. The stone is bleached pale by years of neglect, ink-black banners are long gone to tatters, but the air is fresh at least.

We ride out under the pretense of peace—Raef in black, me in muted gray, our guards instructed to remain out of sight. The Sea Court's envoy had requested a private meeting, and Shadow Court protocol demands we comply. "An opportunity," Selmire said. "A show of diplomacy and forgiveness."

Forgive? Never. Besides, it feels more like bait on a hook. Forgiveness is for people who believe the wound can still heal. I don't. Not after what they did to Mattie. This isn't peace; I'm performing. A stage dressed in diplomacy, meant to see who bites first. I'm tired of being cast as the fool who still believes in good faith.

459

"This is a mistake," I say as the ocean wind catches my cloak.

Raef doesn't argue with me. He hasn't said much at all since we left the keep, which isn't helping my frantic nerves at all. He only glances over once, eyes searching mine like he wants to say something softer than war but can't find the words.

The sky is bruising purple by the time we crest the ridge. Below us, the outpost clings to the rocks like an old wound—stone buildings weathered by salt, the main hall facing the tide. For a meeting of diplomacy, it's got all the charm of a graveyard.

Raef reins in. "They were supposed to arrive before us."

I nod, the back of my neck prickling. "So, where are they?"

"This place was neutral ground," he mutters. "Shadow-owned but rarely used. A show of trust."

"Trust," I echo. "That's rich."

We dismount, boots crunching across broken shells and seabird bones. A rusted wind chime spins in the breeze above the gate. It's not singing.

I shake off the feeling crawling down my spine, but it stays with me as we cross the threshold. This isn't just uneasy. It feels downright evil in the air.

The doors groan as Raef pushes them open. Inside, the main hall is dim, lit only by the dying red smear of sunset slanting through the open arches. The smell hits first—thick and wet, clinging to the back of my throat before my brain can identify why it's inherently sinful. It's not just blood. It's rot and copper tangled with bile. The stench of fear turned sour. Urine, feces, and that faint, almost-sweet note that means death's had time to settle in. It's been described to me a number of times, but actually smelling it in person... I gag before I can stop myself, eyes watering, hand flying to my mouth. This is a smell that crawls into your hair and stays there no matter how hard you scrub.

Raef steps in ahead of me, hand on the hilt of his blade.

The table is still set. A plate of half-eaten meat glazed in its own grease, fruit already turning brown in the salt air. Two goblets catch what little light remains, one upright, one tipped and bleeding wine into the cracks of the wood. The smell of rot and iron clings to everything, a feast gone rancid before the prayers were finished.

The envoy slumps at the far end—what's left of him. They'd propped him upright, posed him like a marionette whose strings had been cut. His arms hang open in a grotesque welcome, palms slick and glistening. The throat wound cut so deep his head lolls almost backward, the last vertebrae fighting to keep the head from falling clean off.

The smell hits harder now, copper and rot thick enough to taste, bile crawling up my throat, and bitterness coating my tongue. Flies buzz in lazy circles above the table, wings brushing against glass and skin with a sound that makes my skin crawl.

His tongue, pale and leathery, had been cut out and nailed flat to the wood of the table with an Atlantean steel pin. The metal flashes in the dying light, cold and perfect against everything that's ruined. The table creaks when the breeze shifts, and for one wild second it sounds like he's trying to speak.

I choke on air.

"Gods," Raef mutters.

I was already staring past the body when something moves near the side exit—a flicker in the dark, the scrape of hard soles on stone. My head snaps to it. Two cloaked figures fleeing. One, a half-step behind, their movement too quiet.

That second one turns. Just for a heartbeat. Dark blond waves catch in the low light. A flash of pale skin. The shape of a mouth I used to know.

My stomach drops back down, and my ears ring. The room starts to tilt. For one second, everything else—the smell, the sound, even the ruin behind me—vanishes. *No. That's not possible.*

While I hesitate, panic taking over my brain, Raef takes action. He moves the instant I do, no word, no plan, the two of us chasing ghosts.

I race along, legs screaming, lungs raw with salt and panic. We burst out of the stone hall into the open cliffside—in time to see the two figures vanishing into the tree line beyond the broken fence.

"Mattie!" I shout before I can stop myself.

Raef shoots me a look, startled, but doesn't ask. Just runs faster.

The wind picks up with a biting edge. It whistles between the trees like it's trying to speak.

We push through the scrub, past wind-worn statues and gull-slicked stones. The trees thicken. Shadows pull tighter. They are fast, too fast, but the terrain isn't in their favor.

We see one of them crest a ridge and vanish behind a stand of black pine.

Raef draws up short as we reach the clearing. "They're gone," he growls. "There's no way they moved that fast, even fae."

He turns in a slow circle. I scan the ground, heaving. Leaves rustle where no breeze touched them. That's when I feel it, a presence lingering beyond the edge of sight.

"Rory," Raef says, stepping closer. "Don't—"

I turn, and I know he's there.

Remington stands half shadowed by the trees. Not cloaked now. Leaning against a rock as if we were out for a morning stroll. He keeps to the shadows and tips his head when I meet his gaze, slow and lazy, like a man acknowledging an inside joke. Then he vanishes into nothing... again.

The pressure in my chest cracks like ice. My brain still screams Mattie, but my body knows who I actually saw. Remington. The tilt of his head. The smug cruelty. Like it's a game. Like I'm the piece he left waiting too long and now wants to reclaim.

Raef catches my arm. "We need to go. Now."

We stumble back toward the outpost, only to find it crumbling.

Magic had detonated along the foundation. A delayed spell. Trap on trap. *We were supposed to still be inside.* Coral and sea-glass shrapnel litter the floor. The envoy's body has been half consumed in the blast, with nothing left but a curl of silver scale armor and that hideous steel pin.

Raef pulls me to the horses.

"This wasn't a message," I say, heart pounding. "It was a provocation."

He nods grimly. "They want a war."

"But who wants a war?" I ask, my brain whirring through the possibilities. "Would the Sea Court actually sacrifice their own to start it? Or is someone else trying to pit us against each other?"

"You mean Remington," Raef says, not a question I notice.

"You can't deny it's possible," I answer.

We mount fast, Raef scanning the trees, jaw tight, fingers twitching at the reins. But I'm not looking at the forest.

My gaze catches on one of the fallen Sea Court soldiers now appearing near the wreckage from where they were hidden. Half buried under splintered stone and driftwood shards. His cloak had slipped back in death, baring his throat and his collarbone.

The mark. Etched into his skin in raised, blackened lines—twisting like a net closing in on itself. The same symbol I'd seen on the heel of Remington's boots. I stare until Raef tugs my reins.

"We need to move."

I point. He pulls alongside me, cupping my cheek in his hand. "Aurora," he says so gently. "That's ancient magic. A binding brand. Old and illegal throughout the realm. But I need you to focus. That pin," he says, "the one in the envoy's tongue."

I nod, stomach twisting.

"It wasn't Sea Court."

"I know."

"It was Atlantean." His voice is cold now, flat with realization. "They're framing you."

The words hang between us, heavier than anything we left behind and far more dangerous than a corpse.

My breath shudders out. "They used something from my home," I say, eyes burning. "They reached into the grave of a place no one remembers and twisted it into a political weapon."

I look at him, throat tight. "They're not just trying to kill me. They want the world to believe I deserve it."

Raef dismounts, comes to my side, and reaches for my hand. I don't take his.

"I'm fine," I say.

His hand doesn't fall. "You don't have to be."

I stare out toward the sea. Somewhere out there, the waves touch Atlantis.

"They're using the dead," I whisper. "And I don't even know how many of them are mine."

The grief comes quickly. Like seawater through a cracked hull—inevitably cold. Impossible to stop.

That's when I reach for his hand. Let him steady me. If only for a moment. Because I'm not steady. I'm splitting down the middle. Between what I was and what they're trying to make me. Between the girl who ran toward the past and the weapon they're shaping in her place.

We ride forward again, because I can't fall apart here. Not yet. This all became so very real. But something inside me has already started breaking open. And I don't think it can be sewn shut again.

69

ON THE ACT OF DROWNING GRACEFULLY IN YOUR PARENTS' MISTAKES

THE FIRST DREAM COMES LIKE water rising. It presses in around me, slow and heavy, the sea rising with the tide. When it loosens, I'm standing in a sunken hall.

It gleams with broken opal and drifted ash. Moonlight pours through cracks in the ceiling, filtered through waves above. Everything moves with the hush of deep water—but I can breathe.

Shapes emerge.

A figure in white, her hair gleaming like pearl. Her hands are light— literally. They glow at the edges. Healing magic drips from her fingertips, pooling at their feet like silver flame.

My mother. I know it with all my being.

She stands out of step with sorrow and fire in her eyes.

Behind her, a man waits—red-gold armor dulled with salt. A crown of rusted metal. His eyes are bright, hungry, and alive. The same color as mine, even though mine have her shape.

The Sanguine King.

My father.

They don't speak with words. The dream doesn't work like that. Instead, it bleeds memory. Emotion. I feel what they felt.

Their love was a wildfire caught in a glass jar—bright and doomed. Their union was forbidden. One bound to death, the other to healing. But they did it anyway. Against the courts. Against the stars. Or so the others believed.

You were born of rebellion, the voices whisper.

You are balance made flesh.

You are the gate.

The water begins to churn. The walls crack. Something claws at the edges of the dream—a pressure, sharp and cold.

I see faces now. Not just my parents.

The Atma.

Souls of Atlantis. Ancestors. Ghosts. Not peaceful. Not all kind. A legion of watchers who never left, who wait beneath the veil.

They speak together, voices braided.

You are hunted not for power, but for birthright. For blood. For memory carried in your bones.

You are what they could not kill.

You are what they fear most.

The water rises fast now. A shadow passes overhead. I see a ring of teeth. Something vast and ancient.

I wake choking.

Raef sits nearby, elbows on his knee, gaze fixed on the dying fire. He looks up sharply when I stir. We're still in the small cave he found once he believed us to be safe.

"Another one?" he asks softly, worry in his eyes.

I nod. My hands tremble in my lap. I can still hear them.

He comes to my side, touches my arm, but carefully, like my skin might still be scorched with meaning. He doesn't press. Doesn't ask what I saw. He stays. That's the thing about Raef. He doesn't demand your pain. He makes room for it.

I want to speak. To explain. But the words catch somewhere between my ribs and my throat.

"I think I'm changing," I manage. "Not just waking something up—I think it's...writing me. I don't know how to explain what I'm feeling."

His expression folds under the pressure, like something inside him cracked. His mouth twitches, but not toward a smile; it's the ache of someone who knows he can't fix it.

"Magic shifts when it grows," he says. "Especially if it was bound once. Especially if it was meant to be broken or to break."

I look up at him, searching his face for the first flinch, the first sign he's pulling away. "You're afraid of me."

"No," he says. "I'm afraid for you."

He brushes my hair back, and I let him. Let him see what's left of me. But neither of us says what we're thinking. That power like mine doesn't go unnoticed. That people like me don't stay unbroken.

"I miss them," I say, a tear escaping down my cheek.

"I know," he says, catching it with his thumb.

70

HOW TO SURVIVE LOSING THE ONE THING YOU THOUGHT WAS YOURS

W E RETURN TO THE SHADOW Court before dawn. Word travels faster than we do. By the time we pass beneath the obsidian arch, courtiers are already watching from balconies, some cloaked, some open-faced. All silent. How could they possibly know already, know enough to be leery of me?

There's no fanfare this time with trumpets and banners. The great gate of the Shadow Court yawns open like a wound, black stone slick with early frost. The path inside is lit with gentle lanterns and nothing else.

No one welcomes us. No one explains the absence of the guards at the gate. We aren't escorted to the strategy rooms or the council wing. Instead we're directed—gently, politely—back to our respective quarters.

Javi is still gone. Tris, too. Their absence lands like a blow I didn't brace for. I was secretly hoping I'd at least have them back, after everything.

I still have the folded note from Tris with three words scratched across the page:

Stay standing, little star.

It doesn't help. I can feel the shape of their absence like a void around me. My rooms are still and cold, the edges too neat, and the chair beside my bed empty. Javi's folded blanket is gone. Tris's book, left open by the hearth, has been removed. No one asked to take it away, and no one warned my rooms were to be scrubbed of everyone and everything.

I fold the page again with numb fingers and tuck it away. I can't look at it any longer, it hurts too much. I think it even smells like him, steel and woods.

Raef doesn't mention them. He doesn't mention much of anything. He returns to his quarters, not mine, and hasn't left them since.

That continues. When I pass him in the corridors, he offers only nods, eyes distant. He stops meeting me for meals. He stops sleeping beside me. The warmth that had once lived in his voice cools to ash.

When I knock, sometimes he doesn't answer, even though I know he's behind the door. I can smell him and sometimes even hear him moving.

When I ask what's wrong, he says, "I am simply busy."

There's something in him that I don't recognize. Like he's a man walking through a dream that doesn't belong to him anymore. Tired men don't forget how to touch you. Tired men don't flinch and pull away when your fingers graze theirs.

I find myself draining my phone battery over and over to find any solace. Looking at my pictures, my old life I have no hope of returning to, listening to music that used to soothe my soul. It's the only thing I have now that brings me any sense of peace, even if it results in draining all the tears I have left.

The Court watches. Always. Their silence is heavier than their praise, their politeness edged with teeth. Gifts still arrive—fruit trays, rare silks, and scrolls of poetry penned in languages I don't speak, much less read. None of it is for comfort. It's all the usual performance.

The formal letter comes, that proverbial shoe dropping.

Black wax. No signature needed. Everyone knows the king's mark.

The parchment is thick and scented faintly of ash bark and spice. I read the opening line three times, trying to make sense of the words.

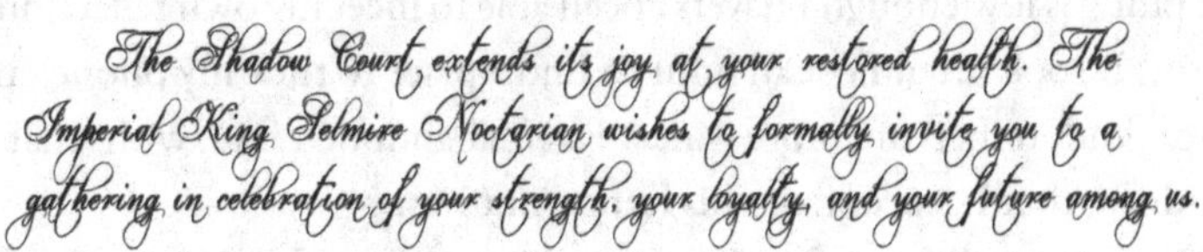

Future. Among them.

I place the letter beside my tea and stare at it until the light dims.

When I return to my room, a dress has been laid out on the bed. Midnight velvet, heavy and beyond soft. Fitted sleeves taper to points at the wrists, and the neckline plunges indecently low. Silver threads stitch through the bodice, catching light and throwing it like a spider's web the morning after a rain.

The air smells faintly of lavender, someone's attempt at comfort that only makes my already tight stomach turn. I can't recall the last time I ate because I'm all twisted in knots. A faint trace of cold clings to the fabric, like it's been waiting in a chest beneath the palace for the right moment.

I don't have to spend much brainpower at all to figure out who chose this monstrosity. The amount of skin it will reveal speaks volumes.

Raef was gone again by nightfall. I wait. Curled in the corner of the bed in a robe too thin for the cold, pretending to read by firelight while the shadows press closer.

He doesn't come. He doesn't knock. The walls feel too quiet. And still—I don't cry. I don't think I know how anymore. Something in me bends, though, the way trees do when they're desperate for water as the wind blows too hard.

The dress still waits on the bed, catching the firelight in its silver threads. A spider's web, not for beauty, for catching prey, for catching me.

THE KNOCK COMES before dusk. Not soft. Not tentative. One sharp rap on the door, like punctuation at the end of a sentence that had been written without me.

I stand from the edge of my empty bed, hands smoothing down the front of my gown. That midnight blue velvet, backless too, with a neckline that plunges low enough I haven't been able to meet my own reflection in the mirror. It took me almost an hour to find a place to tuck my phone, my only armor and tether anymore since Raef abandoned me with that chilly emptiness that I expect from his father, not him.

I open the door to find Raef standing there in full ceremonial attire—midnight jacket trimmed in slate silver, Shadow Court crest at his throat, not a single strand of black hair out of place, intricately braided against his scalp with shadow thread.

He doesn't even bother to look at me. This isn't the man I married. Not the man... the male who once teased me about stealing his cloak or kissed me breathless in the shadow of a war-torn tree.

But it's his body, his mouth, his silence. That makes it so much worse. He doesn't care. Doesn't make one comment about the absurdity of the dress. Can't even meet my eyes or won't. Just turns on his heel and says, "We're late."

I follow him through the halls in silence, the hem of my gown whispering behind me as it drags over obsidian and stone. He doesn't speak once. Doesn't offer his arm, or even glance back to make sure I'm still following.

When we enter the ballroom, the cacophony of sound swallows me whole.

Laughter, lyres, glasses clinking. Dozens of faces turn toward us, each one practiced in polite interest. The ceiling sparkles with floating chandeliers, and the scent of roasted fruit and saffron hangs heavy in the air.

A celebration in my honor. For surviving. For existing to please them.

Raef guides me to the high table with the precision of a soldier delivering a weapon to the front lines. He doesn't sit beside me, though his name is etched in silver beside mine. He stands instead, conversing quietly with a steward, nodding once before finally deigning to take his seat.

He doesn't speak to me. Not when the first course arrives. Not when I reach for the wine. Not when I try—quietly, so no one would hear—to ask, "Are you going to look at me at all tonight?"

He doesn't. His gaze stays fixed on something far across the room. Or maybe it wasn't fixed at all. Maybe there was nothing left behind his eyes to anchor it.

The dancing begins after the third course. Violin-like strings trill from the balcony, and couples begin to glide across the polished obsidian floor.

I make no move to stand.

Raef, however, does. He walks to my side and holds out his hand. Formal and distant.

"I'm not dancing," I say.

His fingers don't waver. "Yes, you are."

Eyes are already on us. Watching. Measuring.

I stand and take his hand. "I expect this type of behavior from your father, not you."

He says nothing. Does nothing other than lead me down the steps to the floor, one hand settling against the bare skin at the base of my spine moving up, the other capturing my hand in his. His touch is careful at first. Controlled. Then the pressure begins.

Each step comes tighter. His grip around my fingers, the press of the palm between my shoulder blades—it all tightens. I can't pull back without making a scene, can't wince without confirming to everyone watching that the fairytale had rotted through.

"You're hurting me," I whisper through my teeth.

His eyes flick down to mine, and for a heartbeat, something cracks. Not the monster I've come to know, the one his father made, but Raef, horrified and lost. Then it vanishes. Snapped shut like shutters slamming in a storm.

I don't understand. I thought I was playing the game. I thought I was winning. But this—this isn't a loss. It's a massacre. The board is gone, as Selmire promised, and I have no idea what to expect next.

I tear free of his arms the moment the song ends. Applause rings out behind me, but I don't hear it. I don't stop. I flee the ballroom and the laughter and the wine, breath caught somewhere between my ribs.

The corridor spills out onto a veranda. I don't think; just walk straight out into the night air.

It's cold enough to sting, but I don't mind. A wind has picked up, carrying the smell of frost and distant woodsmoke. I grip the railing with trembling hands and try to steady the shake in my chest by leaning against the statue. I don't want to cry. I won't. Not here. Not over him.

The door opens behind me in a whisper so soft for stone. No words are said; the only sound is the drag of shiny boots that sound too calm for what I know is coming. I don't bother to turn and meet him. I don't have to. The air already tastes like him, all smoke and steel.

"You shouldn't have walked away," Raef says.

His voice is too quiet and even. The calm that comes out of the mouth of someone who feels nothing.

I have no energy left to play these games, verbal or otherwise.

"You embarrassed me."

I turn slowly. His silhouette cuts sharp against the pale lantern light behind him, face half-shadowed, tunic perfect, and stone-faced. Except for the eyes.

They're not his. Not anymore. His eyes are so...so dark and empty of everything.

"What happened to you?" I whisper. "What is this?"

He stares me down, the anger penetrating deep into my soul.

"You've been cold for days, but now you want to act like—what? My husband? My escort? My warden? My prize stud?"

Still, nothing; he even looks away.

"Look at me!" I snap.

My anger always did get his attention. His gaze lifts to mine—flat, glinting like obsidian under moonlight. And yet...not fully his.

"What did your father do to you?"

"Nothing he wouldn't do to anyone who forgets their place."

I should argue, shout, something—but the way he says it steals the air right out of me. It takes a second for the meaning to sink in, another for the anger to follow.

I take a step back, the cold stone biting through my shoes. He mirrors me instantly, closing the space like it's his right to own it.

"Raef—"

"You made vows," he says. "You swore to stand beside me. To serve the court."

"That's not what I said—"

"You swore your body," he cuts in, voice lowering. "You swore your blood."

My back hits the stone of the balustrade, the chill sinking right into my skin until it hits bone. There's nowhere left to go.

"I swore to the man I *loved*. Not this." My throat tightens. "Not *you*."

He steps into me, close enough that the air between us collapses. His hands plant on either side of me, the stone railing still freezing against my spine. The cold in his expression cracks—something cruel and hungry flickering beneath.

"Arrogant little queen," he murmurs, voice twisting into something familiar and not my bonded. "You thought you were so clever."

"What?"

His smile stretches his lips, but his eyes remain empty. "You gave me everything I needed. Every look. Every flirtation. Every bare inch of skin. You never told him what you were doing—but you showed me. You gave me everything I needed." A flicker of satisfaction crosses his face. "I showed him too."

My blood chills with the sudden realization of what I've done. "What?"

"I showed him the way you looked at me. The way you laughed. How you kissed me. How you begged."

"No," I say, breathless. "That never happened—"

"It didn't need to," he says. "The mind filled in the rest. And he believed it. Believed it when I showed him his king inside your warm, wet—"

My palm cracks across his face before I can even reconsider the action. Pure reflex to make him shut the fuck up. The sound cuts through his words like snapping glass. My hand stings, but I don't regret it because realization slams into me like a dropped blade. He saw. Raef saw all of it. But not through my eyes. Through Selmire's. Twisted and reassembled into something completely fictional.

I never told him. Never warned him what I was trying to do. Because I thought I was playing a king, but I was the bait after all.

Raef is the only one he wanted to break, and I helped him do it.

"I didn't know," I whisper. "Raef, I didn't know—"

"You made it easy," he growls. "You warmed my throne. Shared my wine. Wore silk to bait me."

"I was never yours," I say. "I was trying to—"

He grabs me hard, his hand a manacle on my wrist. "Trying to what? Provoke him? Tempt him? Pretend you weren't already mine while crawling into his bed?"

"I did it to protect you, Raef!"

His grip tightens. "Then why didn't you tell me?" Maybe I'm imagining it, but it sounds like him this time. Raef.

Because I thought I could handle it. Because I thought he'd be fine. Because I never saw how deep the trap was set. I see it now. All of it. The seduction wasn't to ensnare Selmire. It was to make Raef *watch*.

"You broke him," I say, the words barely leaving my mouth. "You broke him and made him think it was me."

He doesn't speak because this isn't Raef. Not all the way. But he's still in there.

"I want to speak to him," I say. "To Raef."

His fingers twitch, one heartbeat of hesitation. But instead of releasing Raef, his mouth crashes to mine. Not with passion, with control. Teeth sink into my lip, and I taste blood.

I spit it in his face. It hits his cheek, bright against his pale skin. His eyes flash while his hand arcs. The slap lands hard, skin on skin, sharp enough to split the moment in two. Light bursts behind my eyes, a white flare.

I stagger back, catching myself on the railing. My jaw throbs, my pulse stutters—but the pain is a gift; it wakes me up.

He lunges, fingers snaring my arms before I can step away.

"You told me," he says, leaning close enough that I can feel the shape of his lips, "you told me that next time we wouldn't stop."

"I didn't mean—" I twist, but his arm shoots out. Grips my wrist, firm and bruising.

"You wanted this," he murmurs against my cheek. "You want me now. Why would you wear this invitation in velvet otherwise?"

"I don't." My voice shakes. "This isn't you."

He laughs, the sound so off it scrapes against my bare skin. If I didn't know better, I'd think he was proud of it.

"It's enough of me."

His free hand drags down my side, calloused fingers scraping over silk and skin until the fabric catches. The seam gives with a rip that echoes too loud in the abandoned courtyard.

The skirt tears easily, cool air slicing up the backs of my legs, in between as his knee pushes mine apart, raising gooseflesh where his warmth had been.

I gasp, half shock, half fury. "Don't, Raef. Stop."

But he doesn't.

"You were bred for this," he says, voice like silk over broken glass, not his voice. "Your job is to breed."

"No," I say. "No. No—"

He presses harder. His hand between my legs groping, fingers probing where they don't belong. I squirm, shoving against his chest with everything I have.

"You're hurting me!"

"I told you to listen."

He releases my wrist and catches my jaw, pinching it between stiff fingers. Slamming his mouth to mine. His kiss isn't hungry—it's punishing. His teeth sink into my lip hard enough this time to tear.

I yelp. The taste of blood fills my mouth. I spit it back in his face again.

Something contorts in his expression. His fist cracks across my jaw before I even see it coming. Stars explode behind my eyes.

I teeter. The world tilts in so many directions. When I catch my balance, his chest is rising and falling at a rapid rate. Unsteady.

My heart is racing. I reach blindly for anything—something heavy, something sharp. He grabs me again, yanking me close.

That's when his tunic tears open at the collar.

Cut into his skin. A mark like the dead soldier. Burned beneath the surface. Shifting with strange light, dark and unnatural.

I stop on a sharp inhale. The world tilts and swirls through the tears gathering in my eyes, sound draining out until it's just him—his hand gone slack, his pulse flickering at his throat like he's the one afraid now.

For a moment, one infinitesimal moment, something human returns to his face. His pupils dilate. His hand loosens more, and his mouth opens—silent.

"Raef?" I whisper, I beg. "Please."

He blinks once. His gaze drops to where he holds me—skirts bunched in one hand again, my lip torn from his kiss, my chest heaving, the bruises sprouting on my wrists, the fear in my eyes.

He looks...horrified. He sees what he's done, and it ruins him.

He reels back as if I'd stabbed him in the chest. "I didn't—" he chokes.

His eyes flick to my bodice.

"What are you—"

He reaches, tearing the silk inlay at my front, exposing my chest bare. "You've been hiding things."

He reaches down. I try to stop him—but he's already found it.

My phone. Tucked between layers of silk and skin.

I gasp, the tears starting to overflow at what I know comes next. "Raef, wait—"

He raises it overhead and slams it against the stone railing. The screen explodes in a spray of glass and sparks. My last tether to hope and joy shattering into nothing but broken pieces.

"No more distractions," he says. His voice isn't even cruel anymore. It's flat. Empty. Like someone standing at the edge of a grave. "No more lies."

He kisses me again, that hard, bruising cruelty. But I know he's still in there. I know he's fighting. I heard his voice and saw his eyes, if only for a moment.

I scream into his mouth.

He pulls back, teeth bared—and for a heartbeat, he hesitates again.

"Raef," His name rips out of me, torn and trembling. My fingers slip against his chest, smearing blood and tears together into a painting of trauma and heartbreak. "Please. I love you. Please... I need you to see me."

His hands tremble. His pupils dilate. The control cracks. He staggers back—staring at his own hands like they don't belong to him. He takes one step, then another, shaking his head like something inside is screaming. And looks up.

But I don't see the look in his eyes. I don't wait. I run.

The ring on my finger burns so hot I think it might brand me.

And then—

Cold.

I don't stop to look back. Not even once. Not even when his anguished scream rends the night.

71

STOP RUNNING WHEN THERES NOTHING LEFT TO FLEE

BRANCHES WHIP AT MY ARMS, snagging my dress, clawing at the wounds already burning beneath my skin. I don't stop. I don't cry. I run. Through the gardens. Through the outer path. Through the forest.

My legs give out halfway down a ravine slope, sliding on wet leaves and loose stone. I hit the ground hard. Roll. Something cracks, my shoulder, maybe. Or a rib. I don't know. I don't care.

The pain barely registers anymore. Everything already hurts.

I crawl. On hands and knees, dress torn and heavy with blood and rain. I make it to the base of an old tree and collapse against it, chest heaving, hands shaking so badly I can't even push my hair out of my face.

I taste copper and earth. Blood runs down my chin from the corner of my mouth. I spit again. There's nothing left to spit but silence.

The ground rises up to meet me. I'm cold and too hot all at once. My limbs are trembling. My skin sticky with sweat and bruises and his fingerprints.

He hit me. Raef hit me. He hurt me. With his hands. With his mouth. He—

I press my palm to my cheek and curl in on myself, dress hiked up around my waist, knees scraped raw. The trees blur. I blink once, twice. Can't get the forest to stop spinning. Can't get me to steady.

The ring on my finger is ice. Sitting on top of the skin, all broken promises. I go to pull it off. Claw at it with shaking fingers, but I can't do it. My hands fail me. My courage fails me.

Tears slip free—not the first, not the last, but the kind that don't come with sobs. A steady, slow collapse, a sad ice sculpture at a summer wedding.

I curl in on myself, knees drawn tight, the cold gnawing through torn velvet and skin. My spine trembles against bark slick with old rain, shame pooling heavy in my gut.

"I don't want to do this anymore. I want to go home."

The trees don't answer. The moon peering through them doesn't care. The stars blink above me like they're pretending they can't see me.

But something moves in the dark—far off, maybe real, maybe not. A rustle of leaves. A footstep too heavy for the wind. I can't even flinch.

Let it come. Whatever it is, let it take me. At least it won't lie. At least it won't look like someone I love.

A LOW GROWL stirs in the silence, deep and reverberating—not a threat.

I blink toward the sound, eyes heavy, vision doubling.

He steps from the trees right out of the shadows.

I know the tall, massive shape of him, all silvered fur catching stray beams of moonlight. Eyes the color of deep forest moss locked onto mine— watchful, unblinking, and full of knowing pity.

I don't want pity.

He moves with purpose, closing the distance in silence. I don't even move. It's easier to let the stillness hold me than to remember how to fight. What would be the point of moving?

He shifts mid-step. One heartbeat, a beast. The next—a male with those damned pointed ears.

Broad shoulders, more so than the others, a sculpted, bare chest dusted with soot-dark hair, and trousers loose around powerful legs. His skin gleams with sweat or dew or magic. A faint line of old scars trails down his ribs. His face is half-shadowed by a fall of shaggy black hair, with a square jaw and a firm mouth. Not handsome in the usual way. More that rough-hewn honesty that is sometimes more attractive.

But it's his eyes. Not a lowly green—alive. Lit from within by something ancient and solemn. They study me without judgment, without demand. Just a quiet, fierce presence.

I struggle to sit up, my arms giving out. A whimper escapes before I can stop it.

He crosses to me in two strides and kneels, massive arms slipping beneath my body with care I haven't felt in days. I gasp as the motion shifts my once again bruised ribs, and my head lolls against his shoulder.

"Easy," he says, voice low and velvet-rough. "You're safe now."

I don't believe him. But gods—I want to.

The warmth of him is immediate. He carries the scent of pine needles and cold river stone, wild and clean. It wraps around me like a cloak. I go limp in his arms, chest hitching with breath that doesn't quite become a sob.

For a while, we don't speak. He walks with me cradled close, moving through the forest with impossible silence. The air turns cooler. The trees shift, older now, moss-covered and twisted. I watch the moon flash between the leaves as we pass.

Eventually, I stir. "I can walk."

He doesn't slow.

"I'm serious. I'm fine."

Still, he says nothing. But after another dozen paces, he stops and lowers me gently to my feet.

I wobble and nearly fall. He steadies me with one hand, calloused fingers wrapping lightly around my arm.

"See?" I manage a pitiful mockery of pride.

He doesn't smile. But his head dips once.

We continue side by side, his presence a silent tether. He never asks questions. Never looks at the torn neckline of my dress or the split in my lip. He lets me be broken without making me feel weak.

At some point, when I think my thoughts might swallow me whole—Raef's eyes, his hands, the ring, the words—I whisper into the space between us, "He would never."

The wolf-man glances down, once. And quietly, in a voice like gravel and river water, he says, "The king is cruel. Raef would never do this to you. His mother raised him better, and she suffered for it."

That was all. But it strikes deeper than any comfort could have. And I wonder if he knew Raef's mother. If he's the one.

I keep walking because I have to. Because someone still believes the man...male I love is worth saving.

The journey takes time. I don't know how long. I don't pay attention. We move through mist and fern-choked paths, across shallow brooks and narrow stone ridges. The sun comes and goes at least twice. I keep walking because he does. Because it feels like giving up if I stop.

At the edge of a thicket, he parts a wall of horned vines with a sweep of his arm. On the other side, a grotto carved into the hillside, lit by lanterns made of bone and blue flame. Vines hang heavy from a thatched roof. Water trickles down into a shallow pool ringed in moss.

She steps out from the mouth of the grotto, her long, silver hair still woven with herbs and bone pins. Her scent of yarrow and smoke already reaching me. Her eyes, sharp and weathered, land on me and soften.

"My gods," she says.

That's all it takes.

I break. I shatter into a million tiny pieces.

All of it, held in my throat, in my ribs, in my marrow, comes pouring out. I stagger the last few steps forward and fall to my knees at her feet. The sobs hit me like a wave, deep and ragged. They don't stop. They tear out of me, guttural and helpless, as she kneels beside me and draws me into her arms.

"You're safe now," she murmurs, voice thick with fury and something gentler. "You're safe, my girl. You've done enough."

And for the first time since I fell into this godforsaken place, I let someone hold the real me while I cry. I let someone see me, the real me, not the character I tried to play. I let someone catch the pieces before they hit the ground.

And I cry.

THE SOBS TAKE time to slow. By the time I can force air into my lungs again, my hands are curled into the folds of the hedge witch's robes, and my knees have gone numb on the stone. She strokes my hair with rough fingers that smell like sage and salt. Nothing about her touch is inherently gentle, but it's something tangible.

"I've got you," she mutters, tucking the edge of her robe around my bare shoulders like I'm something worth keeping warm. "You're safe, girl. You're safe."

I don't believe her. But I want to. I do, much like I wanted to believe wolf-man... wolf-male. Oh, who cares anymore?

Said wolf watches from the mouth of the grotto, back in his fur, massive, silent, and solemn. His green eyes never leave me. When I shiver, his ears tip forward. When I cough, he shifts like he might rise. He doesn't speak again. But his presence stays rooted like a tree behind me.

Eventually, the hedge witch, Wen, guides me to the door of her cottage, one arm around my shoulders, the other steadying the latch as she pushes it open.

The scent hits me first, smoke and dried sage, damp earth, and lavender long since hung from the rafters. A hearth burns low against the far wall, its flame banked with ash and ringed in smooth river stones. The thatch above us creaks with the wind but holds firm, thick with moss and knotted branches. Just as I remember it.

Inside, it's blissfully warm. A warmth that sinks into your bones and tells them they can rest.

The floor is packed earth, layered with braided rugs worn to softness, a respite for my sore feet. Bundles of herbs hang from every beam, yarrow, mint, and dried bloodwort. Her shelves line the walls with cluttered jars of roots and dried petals, bottles of green-tinted oil, and small bones tied with red or blue thread. A new wooden table dominates the center now, scattered with parchment, melted wax, and bowls carved from horn.

In the corner, her narrow bed sits beneath a quilt patched from faded court banners. She guides me there, helps me sit, and wraps me in a woolen shawl that smells like pine needles and thyme. I don't remember undressing. Only the weight of the ruined gown is gone. That the scrape of linen against my skin hurts less than the press of Raef's fingers had.

A kettle hisses on the hearth.

Wen moves and does without needing to ask. She pulls a salve from a carved box and dabs it gently on the split at my lip. Packs something sharp-smelling against the bruise on my cheek.

When she removes the ring from my finger, she doesn't ask. She simply holds it in her palm, whispers a word I don't know, and drops it into a small stone bowl filled with black salt and crushed ash berries.

"It won't wake again tonight," she mutters. "Let it sleep."

I nod. I think.

Sleep. Yes.

Maybe, if I'm lucky, I'll remember how.

MY DREAMS CAME in flashes. Fire. Frost. Blood on my hands and a throne made of bone and salt. A woman with white hair and sea-glass eyes screams my name as the tide swallows her. Remington, laughing in the dark. The king's voice whispering from the hollow of Raef's throat.

When I wake, it's still night.

Wen sits cross-legged near the fire, grinding something into powder with a stone bowl.

I blink into the quiet. "How long have I been asleep?"

She doesn't look up. "Not long enough."

My body aches, but it's dull now. Manageable. The pain you can live with when you have no other choice. When you've already lived through worse.

The fire crackles low in the hearth behind me. Outside, the wind shifts—gentle, but colder now. Somewhere in the trees, an owl calls once and falls silent.

"He's gone," I say quietly, more to myself than to her. "The wolf."

Wen doesn't lift her head from her mortar, but her hands still.

"He'll be around," she says. "He always is when it matters."

I draw my knees to my chest, the blanket slipping off one shoulder. "He didn't say much at all the whole way here."

"He doesn't speak anymore unless it's needed. Not much for small talk. Doesn't stay unless you need him to."

Her voice holds no judgment, just fact.

"He brought your things," she adds after a moment, jerking her chin towards a pack leaning against the wall. I hadn't even noticed. "Your blade. Satchel. What little your horse carried before you fell. He pulled it from the ravine."

I looked down, chest tight. The satchel is torn and streaked with dried blood. But tucked within it, wrapped in pale linen, is my curved Atlantean blade. The one Raef gave me.

"He said it belonged with you," Wen says, returning to her grindstone. "I didn't argue."

I trace the edge of the cloth with a trembling finger. "Who is he?"

She doesn't answer immediately. Instead, she reaches for another jar. Her movements are steady. She works the way people do when they are about to say what can't be unsaid.

"He's your uncle," she says at last. "Half-brother to your father, the ancient Sanguine King. His mother was lower caste, barely marked, but the blood took."

To say I was shocked might be the understatement of the hour. "But then..."

"He's not part of the Court, if that's what you're asking. Never was. Didn't take to the Sanguine ways. Left young. Took the old paths. Saved him from the curse after his brother fell.

The pieces begin to shift into place at an uneasy pace.

"Who caused the curse?" I ask, almost afraid of the answer now.

She looked me dead in the eyes. "Your mother, which could be why he was spared in the end. After they rose against their king and killed her mate."

"My father."

She nods. "Dirty business, that."

She leans forward; her gaze holds more of an edge now. "But what matters to you is this—he was the lover of Queen Mirelle."

I still, brows furrowing as I think on the name but can't place it.

"Raef's mother, the dead queen, as they call her."

My uncle loved Raef's mother. I don't even know what to feel about that, not anymore.

"He loved her," Wen says simply. "Still does, I think. Promised her, long before she died, that he'd protect her son. Help him if the king ever turned full shadow. That day came sooner than any of us wanted."

I close my eyes.

The wolf, my uncle, has been there, watching, helping, from a distance. Not for me. Not at first. But for Raef. And now, maybe, for both of us.

Wens stands, moving to the shelves behind her, and starts to pull jars, bundles, and salves. Her hands work without hesitation. She doesn't speak again, but she doesn't have to.

72

Learning to Let the Past Have a Voice

THE FIRST FEW DAYS PASS in silence. No pursuit comes. No hoofbeats thundering through the woods, no shadow-glamoured scouts peering through Wen's garden herbs. No message from the court. No demand for my return. No mention of the ring. Nothing.

I keep waiting for it. Waking at dawn with my heart in my throat, certain someone will be standing at the edge of the tree line. That Raef would appear, cloaked in remorse or rage or something worse. That the king would send his hounds. That Tris or Javi would be dragged in chains behind them, or their bloodied bodies strung up for all to see.

But the woods stay empty.

Wen finds me pacing at the edge of the chicken pen on the third morning, boots soaked in dew, cloak unfastened. "You keep circling like a hound that's lost the scent," she says, dropping a bundle of kindling into the bin beside the door.

I stare into the trees. "They should've come."

Wen straightens her spine, her hands bracing her aching back. "They didn't."

"He's not even trying."

She doesn't ask who I mean. Instead, she leans against the fencepost and plucks a burr from her sleeve. "The Shadow Court doesn't chase things it thinks it owns. Not until they make a mess too big to ignore."

The urge to make a mess is... getting harder to swallow back down.

Words rise and stall, stuck somewhere between my chest and my mouth.

"And besides," she adds, "they don't know where to look."

I shake my head. "No. They do. Raef would know. He knows I wouldn't run blind. That I'd find someone familiar. That I'd find you or head for Iron Mountain."

Her expression doesn't change. But her hands are still, which in itself is highly unusual.

"Maybe he does," she says at last. "Maybe he's the one keeping them from following."

I don't answer. I don't believe it. Not after his hands...

Not after the ring...

Not after the way he looked right through me.

BY THE END of the week, we'd slipped into a rhythm. I help Wen strip nettles. She shows me how to layer mugwort into oil. We don't talk much about the court, or the mark, or the ring in the bowl on the windowsill.

But news has a way of crawling through cracks, even when all you want is silence.

The first comes on the back of a crow, glossy and black-eyed, talons wrapped around a scroll sealed in wax the color of sea glass. Wen takes it without hesitating and breaks the seal. Reads the letter in full and says only, "Hm."

"What does it say?" I ask.

"Nothing you need to lose sleep over."

Which means everything I need to be worrying over.

Hours later, she returns from the edge of her warded glade with a second message, folded between river stones, lined in silver ink.

She doesn't read that one aloud either.

Just drops it onto the table and mutters, "They're listening."

I pick it up. The paper smells faintly of wax and smoke, cool against my fingers, edges crisp like it wasn't folded by hand. The handwriting is tidy and formal in a way that screams authority without needing a seal. There's no name or sigil to take accountability.

The heir of Atlantis walks free again.

A chill creeps under my skin.

Wen brings tea to the table and drops into the chair across from me.

"The courts are stirring," she says. "Not just the Shade King. All of them. You've been mostly invisible, untouchable, for a long time. But that's over now."

I don't say anything. What is there to say?

I keep reading that same sentence, over and over.

The heir of Atlantis walks free again.

The words feel too large for the page. Too much for the ink.

"I'm not protected by the ring anymore. They won't stay away," I say eventually.

"No," Wen agrees. "And neither should you."

I CHOP KINDLING in the mornings. The axe is too heavy for my left hand, so I use only my right, bad arm bound tight, ribs aching under Wen's wrappings and spellwork. The crack of wood splitting rings out across the clearing, loud as anything I'd screamed on that terrace.

Wen doesn't stop me. She watched once, from the porch, a steaming mug clutched in both hands and her silver braid falling long over one shoulder. She doesn't offer help. Doesn't say a word.

The next morning, the axe is left out by the stump.

And the day after that, the 'should be kindling' pile is bigger. Waiting for me to start.

I grind herbs with the same slow rhythm, angelica root, crushed bay leaf, and poppy seeds stored in little jars tied with red thread. Wen's kitchen always smells like earth and thyme, like something ancient lives beneath the floorboards. I like that. It makes the pain feel older. Makes me feel less alone.

I like pressing the pestle down into powder. I like the ache it leaves in my shoulder, the burn behind my ribs. It's something that feels real while still being contained and controlled.

I feed the chickens, too. They're hateful, pecking little beasts who resent my presence unless I bring beetles in a clay bowl. I do anyway. It feels like penance. Sometimes they let me scratch behind their wings. Sometimes they don't.

I carry water from the stream in pails hanging from a yoke that digs into my collarbone. The cold soaking my sleeves and turned my knuckles raw. I don't care. I don't cry. I don't do much of anything except keep moving.

And it helps.

To hurt where no one can see. To bleed just under the surface. To let my body speak when my mouth can't find the words.

Wen never asks questions. She lets the silence grow around me, like a moss she knows will soften things eventually. When I need space, she vanishes into the woods or takes a nap with her feet up on the hearth. When I don't, she sits beside the fire with a second mug already poured and says nothing as I reach for it. Sometimes, she mutters about the world falling to rot. About the courts and their greed. About how the Sanguine crown had turned inward and began feeding on itself.

"They used to be different, you know," she said once, as we shelled dried beans in a wide wooden bowl. "When the first bloodlines came from the deep places. Before the Shade King decided he could mold power like clay."

She bares her teeth in something that isn't quite a smile. "Now they carve out what doesn't fit and call it tradition."

I don't answer or contribute. Because Wen doesn't treat me like something carved out. She treats me like something buried. Still growing. Still sharp, under the soil. Somehow, that helps. It doesn't fix the nights, or the dreams, or the way I flinch when a log cracks too loud in the fire.

But it helps.

I'm still broken. But I'm beginning—barely—to stop splintering.

73

RECLAIM WHATS YOURS AND REGRET NOTHING

THE RING SITS IN THAT bowl of black salt on the windowsill.

Raef's ring. The one that had once hummed under my skin like a second pulse—warm, insistent, intimate. The one that burned the moment his fingers left bruises on my inner thighs. The one that turned to ice as I ran bleeding into the trees.

Now it's as dull as pewter. Just metal. A band, quiet and cold in the weak morning light, as if it had never belonged to anyone at all.

I haven't touched it since the night I escaped. Since the night he broke something I hadn't even realized I was protecting.

I remember the weight of his mouth against mine and the way his voice twisted into something unrecognizable, cruel, and possessive. I remember the moment his hand closed around my jaw and I saw something else behind his eyes. I remember, too clearly, how the ring pulsed with heat, then

495

withered to cold as I left him behind. I even remember how it didn't release until he betrayed me; that one look at my finger and he would have known what his father showed him were lies, but he didn't. He didn't look to my hand for his answer. He didn't trust me.

Wen never touched it. But she never ignored it either.

She'd glance at it when passing the sill, lips pressed thin, like the presence of it in her home made her jaw ache. She never commented. Never rushed me. Until one night, when the fire had burned down low and the wind whispered through the roof thatch like it's telling secrets.

She poured a second cup of whatever bitter root she always drank before bed and slid it across the table without looking up. "Before you decide what to do with that," she says, her voice gruff with smoke and age, "you should read what he left you."

I look up.

I knew exactly what she was referring to. I follow her gaze to the satchel tucked beside the hearth. The same one the wolf had brought with the blade and what was left of my gear. I hadn't opened it since. Hadn't had the strength.

Now I pull it toward me, fingers slow and cautious. It smells faintly of pine and salt and the copper tang of dried blood. I open the flap and reach past the folded linens, the hilt of my blade. At the very bottom, nestled against the worn leather base, sits the book.

Emrys's book. Bound in cracked dark leather, the spine smooth with use, the edges worn soft by time and weather and—maybe—love.

I pull it out with both hands and set it gently on the table.

Wen doesn't say any more. She reaches for the poker and stokes the coals.

I open the cover for the first time. The first page bears no title. Just a single line, written in a spidery hand, every letter pressed hard enough to dent the thick paper.

For the girl born between tides.

The space between breaths feels too narrow to hold what's rising in me.

The next pages move like lost memories.

Ink so fine it might have been sketched from dreams, capturing my mother as if the artist had known her skin and her silences. Her white hair is braided with pearls, and her eyes are the color of seashells, calm and endless. She sits tall on her throne, carved from sea glass and stone, her feet bare, her hands glowing with power.

A queen.

Not a bride. Not a consort. Not someone's precious bargaining piece.

A sovereign in her own right.

At her feet stands a circle of consorts—men and women both, some with markings of court allegiance, others who bear none at all. Every one of them shows admirable inner strength, chosen by her, and it's an incredible thought.

My eyes sting, but I turn the page.

There, the Sanguine King. Younger than I expected, regal and severe but not unkind. Beside her, never above or below. They hold hands in one panel, bound at the wrist by woven bloodroot and gold.

Their love had been legend. Their defiance of the ways of their world infamous.

But still, they had made me.

I flipped on, hands trembling, stuttering on each word. The birth of a child in secret. The hiding. The long silence. The betrayals. The fall of Atlantis. Their lives boiled down to a few simple pages.

One page held nothing but a smear of dark ink across pale parchment, like someone had begun to draw a gate, then stopped.

The last page bears a single line, written in that same spidery hand, below a watercolor sketch of my mother standing in the surf, her hair caught in the wind, her crown half-lost to the tide.

She called the tide to drown the gate, hiding her child from all who would hunt her—but lived long enough to watch her court fall.

Beneath it, another line had been added, messier, rushed—as if someone had returned later and couldn't bear to leave it unsaid.

Her consorts died before her. One by one.

Loyal to their horrid end. The Sanguine turned

on their own king. And still, she stood.

I stare at the words until they blur. The thought of losing all of them, Javi and Tris, even Raef to a certain extent, is terrifying, and that's what she lived through.

I can see it. Her, alone on that shattered throne, sea salt drying on her lips, watching as her council—those she loved, those she chose—were dragged from the chamber and cut down. Betrayed not by strangers, but by the courts she once held in balance.

By the Sanguine Court.

By blood.

I turn another page, but there are no more images. Just one final line, scrawled at the very bottom corner like a footnote no one dared to center.

No pyre. No cairn. No song. Only silence.

And the deep.

My hand closes around the edge of the page, fingers curling tight.

She didn't die.

She'd been erased, unmade.

Buried without rite or honor, forgotten by the very people she bled to protect.

Finally, my grief crystallizes into something colder, in perfect clarity.

Not rage—not yet.

But close.

THE FIRE BURNS low in Wen's hearth, no more than glowing coals and the soft crackle of half-spent pine. Outside, dusk spreads like ink across the clearing, painting everything in shades of quiet.

I sit alone at the table, Emyrs's book still open beside my elbow, its pages heavy with ghosts. My hand hovers over the last line again—*no pyre, no cairn, no song*—and the ache behind my ribs deepens into something that feels more like truth than pain.

She died forgotten. Stripped of every rite and every name. The woman who raised a throne from the sea, who called the tide to close a gate no one else could breach, who chose love over politics and still stood tall when her court fell—had been left with nothing but silence and the dark.

Not even a stone to mark where she lay.

And her daughter had been hidden for millennia. Buried in another life. Taught to be small, quiet, and unremarkable.

Until now.

I let the book fall closed. The weight of it feels different in my hands now. Not like a burden. It's like a beginning. My story is finally starting; this was only my prologue.

My gaze drifts to the small bowl, the ring still nestled in the black salt, washed in that last stretch of dusk light, the metal dulled to shadow.

I lift it from the bowl with two hesitant fingers. It's cold—just metal now. No pulse of magic and promises, no whisper of light. But it's honest, and I'll take honest.

I turn it over in my fingers, feel the cool of it settle into my skin like a memory half-buried. I remember how it burned when he touched me like a stranger. How it chilled. How it stayed, even when I tried to forget. But I remember other things too.

The way he looked at me in the woods the first time I bled and couldn't stop. The way he said *you are not your pain.* The way he pressed his forehead to mine and whispered a vow like a prayer, not a chain.

He's not gone. He can't be. Not yet.

The king's shadow lives inside him. But Raef—the boy who never asked to be born with that blood, who stood in fire for me and still tried to hold a line—was in there too. He's buried and bruised and needs help, not more hatred. He's still living in there somewhere, feeling alone and abandoned, and I can't leave him that way.

I'm not sliding this ring back onto my finger because I forgive him. I'm also not doing it because I believe in fate. I'm doing it because this is mine. My choice. Not the Court. Not the bond. Not the vow.

Mine.

What we were. What we still *could* be. What I would one day burn the world down to find again—if he was still in there, if he ever reached back.

I slide the ring onto my finger. It sits cold. Quiet. But it doesn't fight me.

74

REMEMBERING WHAT WAS BURIED

T HE CLIFF SMELLS LIKE SALT and lightning. Wind tangles through my hair as I step closer to the edge, boots crunching over old black sand and crumbled rock. Far below, the ocean roars—wild and alive and uncaring. A storm churns on the horizon, distant but coming. Clouds like bruises spread their shadow over the sea.

I'm not scared or worried at all. My calm is inspiring even to myself.

The wind tears at my cloak. The waves hurl themselves against the stone. But I stand, unmoved. Let them rage.

This place is older than any court, older even than the names carved into its worn altar stone—names that were never meant to be forgotten.

I step into the center of the circle. And they come. Not with thunder. Not with screams. The Atma move like smoke caught in moonlight, formless at first, then distinct. One by one, they emerge from the wind, clothed in seafoam and memory. They don't speak or whisper prophecy or demand blood.

They bow.

Each of them. Tall and slight. Crowned and plain. Consorts, queens, warriors, lovers. Mothers who gave too much. Sons who died too young. Witches who drowned the sun. All the lives that had come before me. All the voices I have heard in sleep. They had faces now. Names. I can feel them pressing beneath my skin, lineage made real.

They bow to me. And then they vanish, like mist burned away by the sun. No fanfare. No chant. Just acknowledgement.

I stand alone again. But not empty.

I WAKE WITH a gasp and sit upright in Wen's cot, drenched in sweat, lungs clawing for air that doesn't smell like sea salt and ruin. Only herbs— that's what I smell, herbs and ash. The low embers crackle in the fire.

Outside, the first hints of dawn paint pale streaks through the fogged window. My hands tremble as I reach for the chain that hangs heavy at my throat. The dream clings to my skin like tidewater coming in.

I pull the ring free. My mother's ring on the chain around my neck. The one I've worn forever, beneath every layer of magic, every borrowed name, every tether and illusion. It's always been here, warm and waiting for me to wake up.

I slide it onto my right ring finger. And everything stops. A holding of breath—the kind that lives in the marrow, ancient and instinctive. The kind that wakes predators. The kind that stirs the deep places no one speaks of.

The ring pulses once—then again, harder. The air cracks like the snap of a frozen branch.

A wave of magic bursts from my chest, not in sound or light, but in pressure, a pulse that slams through the ley lines of the world down through rock and up through salt and sky. It howls into the bones of every fae still awake, jolts seers from sleep, splits scrying mirrors, and shatters spells mid-whisper. I can see it all.

A wave slams through my chest, old and ancient, dusty and grasping for water and light.

The pulse starts in my chest, a bloom of pressure that bloats and cracks outward. This magic needs no runes or sigils, no ancient words or spells. It's innate and thoughtless.

Every thread my mother had ever woven, every spell pressed gently into the hollows of my bones to keep me unseen, unremarkable, and safe—burns to dust and ash.

One by one, they peel away. Soft at first, like silk unwrapping. Then sharp, sudden. Gone. And as they fall, the visions come.

A roaring tide. The Sea Court's deepest trench yawning open as if gasping. Pearls spilling from shelves. Glass globes of prophecy shattering as the water surges too fast, too hard. Someone screaming in a language I don't know but know at the same time.

A grove of ancient Greenwood trees groaning, their roots rippling with a sound like mourning. Bark peeling back to reveal sigils older than kings. Leaves turning to silver as they bow toward the coast.

Shadow Court halls plunged into sudden dark—candles snuffed, mirrors cracking. Glamours failing. Magic fraying like threads in a torn tapestry. Somewhere deep in the marble halls, he rises.

Raef's father. The Shadow King. He stands in his long hall of ash and silence, draped in void-colored robes, his fingers curling on the arm of his throne. He lifts his head slowly. His mouth twitching into something that's not a smile.

"She's awake," he says.

Stone splits in the Iron Mountains. They don't shatter; they open to new life. A heartbeat echoing through the oldest tunnels as old wards crumble. A wolf lifting its head.

In the Sanguine Court, firelight flickers. Wine sours in its cups. And far below the vaulted palace, Tris staggers where he stands. A silver basin of vision water cracks at his feet, and his reflection ripples with my face.

"Rory."

The vision snaps like a chain pulled taut and broken. My chains.

My knees strike the ground hard, hands braced in dirt that steams beneath my palms. The wind howls. My skin blazes with it. But I don't burn.

I blaze back.

I kneel at the center of it all. Power humming under my skin, no longer sealed. My pulse thunders in my ears, too loud and fast, like it doesn't belong in this body anymore. My skin crackles with heat that doesn't fade. I can feel it now, running under every bone, through every nerve. Magic, yes, but not only that. It's memories flooding my blood. A truth that was always mine and never given.

I scrape in a little air. My throat is raw, lungs dragging in air like I've clawed my way out of the sea.

"You are the gate," they said.

I understand that now. I don't carry the blood of Atlantis. I am what they tried to lock away. The seal and the key to it all. The storm waiting behind every silence. I understand why they are so afraid.

A distant tremor rolls beneath my knees, like the land itself has remembered my name. Behind my eyes, the visions don't stop. They flicker like torchlight on water, broken and shimmering.

Raef staggers in a shadowed hall, dropping to one knee, not in obedience, but in pain. In agony. His mouth moves, but no sound escapes.

Javi stands with his hand on a door that should never open, light bleeding beneath it in threads of gold. His knuckles are white. He doesn't move.

Tris screams in a chamber of cracked mirrors, each one reflecting a different version of me. His voice lost in the din of splintering glass and water boiling in silver bowls.

A stranger with startling light green eyes grins in the darkness.

The world has turned its head.

And it's looking straight at me.

75

LETTING THE DEAD TELL YOU WHAT TO DO

THE DAYS SLIP INTO ONE another like dusk into fog. I mark time by the smoke of Wen's fire, the sound of the kettle, and the ache behind my ribs that never quite fades. There are no messengers. No birds. No sign of Tris or Javi...or Raef. Not even the glimmer of a ward-flare in the distance.

I stay anyway.

Because what else is there?

Wen still doesn't ask questions. She leaves things unsaid the way some people leave offerings at shrines—carefully, respectfully, always enough. She hands me a mug each morning with a nod and nothing more.

I still haven't touched the blade leaning near the door. I'm not ready to hold it again.

Not yet.

Some mornings I see shapes in the mist. A flicker of brown hair. A dark silhouette on horseback. A flash of silver through the trees. But when I blink, they're always gone.

Just fog. Just wind. Just hope pretending.

Each day passes heavier than the last.

It comes to a head when I spill a basket of dried sage, and instead of sweeping it up, I stare at it for nearly half an hour—watching the tiny leaves scatter like something broken. When Wen steps in from outside and finds me on the floor, hands limp in my lap, she only says, "It's not the waiting that kills. It's the thinking someone else will come."

I look up.

For the first time since I arrived, I say aloud what has been circling my chest like a storm-hawk, "They're not coming."

Wen kneels down, picks up a single sprig of sage, and says, "Then it's time we decide what to do next."

THE MIST HASN'T burned off yet. It presses low against the cottage hands on clay, curling around the porch beams and swallowing the trees whole. I step outside with bare feet and a shawl thrown over my shoulders. The dirt and moss are cold beneath my toes. The morning smells like dew and rosemary.

My blade is somehow leaning against a post outside now, its hilt catching the pale light. Simple. The leather wrapping dark with old sweat.

I don't remember putting it there.

But there it is—like it's waiting.

My bad arm reaches for it, but I don't stop. My fingers close around the hilt. The balance is still right. Still familiar even though I only held it once. But the weight no longer feels foreign.

It's not Raef's. Not anymore. Never was, really. It's *mine*.

I stand slowly, testing the pull of it at my side. The ache along my ribs flares, then steadies. The steel feels cold against my leg. Comforting in a strange way.

Behind me, Wen leans against the doorway with a steaming mug in hand.

"About time," she says.

I feel my lips stretch into a smile as I slide the blade into a loop at my hip, straightening my spine, and turn to face the mist.

I'm done waiting.

THE SUN IS low by the time I make the climb. Wen doesn't follow me this time.

The hill rises behind the glade—steep and brambly, ringed in bent pine and thin white birch. From the top, I can see the forest stretch in every direction, dark and rippling like a sea of its own. The wind tugging at my cloak, dry leaves whispering against stone.

The ring on my finger, my mother's ring, pulses hello.

The blade hangs at my hip. My mother's ring is warm on one hand and Raef's cold on the other. I hold a scrap of dry wood, carrying it all this way without knowing why. I don't even understand the rune I carve into it.

I crouch by the small stone firepit that Wen and I used to burn herbs for protective charms and feed the wood to the coals. It flares blue, then gold. I stare into the heart of it.

"I will return to Atlantis," I whisper. "I will reclaim what was mine. I will burn every throne that tries to take it again."

A wind rises behind me. As if the forest itself has heard my vow. Somewhere beyond the trees, thunder rolls. I turn away from the flames and don't look back.

76

EVERY FIRE NEEDS A NAME

I T'S LATE AFTERNOON WHEN THEY finally come.

The sky above the glade is streaked with soft clouds, and the scent of crushed rosemary clings to my hands. I've come back from the stream with a bundle of sweetflag and moss for poultices. Wen is at the edge of the garden, muttering at a sprig of dying feverfew, her apron dusted with powdered root.

I hear it first—a shift in the rhythm of the forest. The rustle of a bird taking off too fast. The crack of a branch under boots that don't belong here. A whisper too close and shallow, on a path no one should know.

I straighten slowly. Wen's hands pause over the herbs. That's when the figures step out into the light.

They slip from between the trees like smoke made flesh—hooded, masked, cloaks dark as crow feathers, their boots leaving no sound in the moss. Shadow Court scouts, each bearing a weapon, blades shaped for speed, throwing knives at their belts, and coils of black cord on their hips that shimmer with binding spells.

Wen stands up from her herbs, slow, eyes narrowing.

"Back inside," she says quietly.

"No," I say. They're already too close.

One steps forward, breaking formation with a confidence that says they know they won't need to work very hard. Their boots barely disturb the moss—a whisper of crushed green and damp earth. The charmed masks hide everything: their breath, expressions, and humanity—not that I was expecting any. Only the shimmer of runes across the surface betrays the magic humming inside.

Their hand drifts down to the blade sheathed tight against their thigh. The sound is soft, leather against metal, but it thrums through the clearing like someone breaking a piano string. A signal. The other shift in unison, shoulders turning, balance shifting heel to toe in a ripple of motion so smooth you know it's been rehearsed sunup to sundown for years. The smell of iron and pine thickens until I can taste it. Every instinct screams that these aren't soldiers; they're executioners waiting for a cue. They aren't here to talk.

"You have no right—" I start, my hand finding the hilt of my blade, fingers curling tight around the worn grip. It pulses against my palm, ready. I don't hesitate. Raef had drilled that out of me.

Wen raises a hand without turning. "Leave now."

Her voice is steady and firm. There's no harsh edge to it or volume, but it somehow cuts through everything.

I wait, hoping they listen on one hand, and ready for a fight on the other.

The scouts don't respond. The move, instead, is small, silent adjustments that speak louder than words.

The tallest of them, wide in the shoulders with a charcoal cloak and twin knives at his hips, shifts a half-step left, weight settling over the balls of his feet. The motion ripples outward like he gave a command. Beside him, another—lithe, fast—glides forward, mask glinting as their hand ghosts toward the dagger at their wrist. The third tilts their head, studying us through runes that flare dull amber, the faintest hum leaking into the air in warning.

The rest fan out, fluid and well-trained, flanking us with predatory grace. Not hesitation, but intentional choreography. They flow around us like water around a stone, soundless, inevitable. The scent of ozone prickles against my tongue.

Wen moves first. No warning or hesitation, like any trained warrior. A guttural word, snarls from deep in her chest, and a snap with her fingers. Her hand lights with ancient flames. A spell knotted like roots and grief, unraveling down her fingers in threads of bitter gold. The air snaps. The ground buckles beneath two of the scouts as vines surge upward, lashing tight around their ankles.

The tall one staggers back as it hits, stopped, like they'd walked into a wall carved out of the earth itself. The scent of stone and pine and something burning fills the glade.

I move. My blade comes up in a sharp arc, catching the nearest scout mid-step. He ducks, faster than I expect, but not fast enough. The edge catches his arm. A shallow cut, but it hisses and sizzles. The flesh turning bright white around it.

He reels back; no healing magic comes.

I lunge before he can recover, the blade sliding between his ribs with a sound that's more wet than loud. His body jerks once, the air leaving him in a single, startled exhale. No scream—the thud of armor and bone as he collapsed into the trampled moss. The smell of copper floods the air, hot and metallic, mixing with the scent of pine and burnt ward light.

I pivot hard, boots skidding in the dirt. Another scout surges toward me from the right in a flash of steel, a hiss of breath behind a mask. I bring my blade up in time to meet his, the clash ringing through my bones. Sparks leap where the edges kiss. He presses hard, faster than I expect, forcing me back a step. His blade grazes my shoulder, shallow but burning cold where it touches skin. Wen's wards catch the rest of the blow, a faint shimmer across my sleeve and the smell of singed air.

My heartbeat pounds against the grip of the sword, raw and racing. I drive forward again, teeth clenched, the world narrowed to motion and thoughts on the next strike.

To her left, Wen lets loose a word that cracks like thunder. A wall of dirt and roots slams upward, shifting my flank. The scouts regroup, but not fast enough.

Wen strikes again, one hand flinging powdered salt and ember ash into a scout's face. The magic catches, turning his own breath against him. He claws at his throat, stumbling into the garden wall.

A third scout vaults over the low hedge and lands on me with the force of a falling tree. We hit the earth rolling—mud and crushed rosemary spraying my face—blade against blade, metal singing in my ears. His gauntlet slams into my ribs; the shock blossoms white-hot and stupid, but I don't let go. Fists find leather and throat; my hand tastes of dirt and blood.

I twist and drive my heel into his knee, and he stumbles off like a puppet with no strings. I gulp air that tastes like smoke and iron. My ribs scream, a bright flare with every inhale; stars prick at the edges of my vision, blurry and loud. Still, my grip is steady.

I drop low and lash out, the edge whispering hot across the back of his calf. He goes down with a thud that rattles my teeth. There's no time to watch him die—no time to watch anything—so I shove the blade home, the strike clean and merciless, and wrench it free from his chest before the world can catch up.

Two down. The others are closing fast.

Wen stands behind me now, both hands weaving sigils in the air. They float over her head, symbols older than the courts, older maybe than any of them remembered. Her lips move faster with incredible intensity.

But she's too exposed.

Another scout breaks through the smoke, sprinting straight for me, dagger flashing sickly green in the dim light. Poisoned—my mind registers that a split second before instinct takes over. I pivot hard, the world narrowing to motion and my blade meeting hers with a metallic shriek that vibrates through my arms. Sparks spit between us, brief and bright as lightning bugs. Her hood slips, revealing a strand of red hair stuck to sweat-slick skin, eyes blank behind the glamour of the mask.

She feints left, low and fast. I follow—too focused, too certain. The hiss of steel on air is the only warning I get before I feel it: another presence, close, the whisper of movement behind me. I start to turn—and Wen slams into my side, shoving me hard enough that my feet skid across the dirt.

The air splits with a sound like tearing cloth. I hit the ground, shoulder first, the impact punching the breath from my lungs. My blade clatters beside me. When I look up, she's still standing where I was—the hilt of a black dagger juts from beneath her ribs, deep.

"No," I say. My voice cracks. "No—no—"

The scout tries to pull back—retreat.

Wen isn't done. She grabs his wrist. Whispers something low. And both of them burst into light, him frozen in place.

Wen drops to her knees.

I scramble along the scorched grass, catching her before she hits the ground. Blood soaks her apron, her blouse, my lap. Too much. Too fast.

Her eyes flutter. Her mouth moves. "Not your fault," she whispers. "He...he was raised better. Her love protected. Love protects. Remember that."

"Don't—don't say that, just—stay—" I beg, hands pressing to the wound, but I can't remember how to call the green light. "Wen, *please*. I can fix this—"

"No fixing this," Wen sighs. "But you—can still burn."

She's gone.

Gone in a single fleeting moment.

I can't find the light; I can't feel what I felt last time with Javi.

I fall forward, over Wen's body, sobs wracking my chest in broken gasps. My breath is coming too fast. I press my forehead to Wen's shoulder, as if that will bring her back. As if warmth can be begged back into a cooling body.

"I tried—" I whisper. "I tried, I—" But my voice breaks.

This wasn't supposed to happen. Not her. Not the only one left who had nothing to gain from my survival. Not the one who never asked for anything. Who brewed tea when I cried and tied my ribs with spells that didn't leave bruises. Who had known our mother's names.

Something lodges in my throat and stays there as the world tightens around it. The scouts don't advance; they hover at the edges of the ruined glade, masks turned toward me, heads angled like carrion birds waiting for the twitch that means it's over. They're studying me. Measuring the space between mercy and death. Watching me fall apart.

I raise my head.

Something breaks. A shatter that happens inside bone and behind my teeth, beneath my skin. It's grief first—hot, raw, uncontainable—but grief curdles quick when it has nowhere to go. It becomes pressure. Then light.

The blade in my hand lights like a forge woken suddenly from sleep, white runes lashing up the steel in wild arcs that sear the air. My chest pulses with light. Something jagged and starless, sharp with sorrow, hammering its way out through ribs that can't contain it.

The scouts shift, boots whispering against the scorched moss. Even through their masks, I can feel it—the hesitation. The flicker of fear. They don't know what's standing in front of them anymore.

Heat blooms outward in ripples, shimmering like the air above a forge. My pulse roars in my ears, too loud and fast, until it drowns out everything else. The ring on my finger brands itself against my skin, a final, desperate warning I don't—or can't—heed.

The world breaks.

The glade erupts. A crack tears through the air, not sound, but force, a pressure that shreds leaves to dust. Trees convulse—bark blistering, trunks splitting open with screams of splintering wood. Roots wrench free, thrashing like dying serpents. The earth itself heaves, soil glowing in veins of molten white.

The closest scout doesn't even make a sound; one heartbeat he's there, the next he's ash collapsing into his own shadow. The second staggers back mid-step and simply ceases to be. The light eats him whole. The last one, she manages half a breath, fingers clawing for a charm at her throat before her hand crystallizes—skin turning gray and grainy. She exhales, and her fingers crumble to salt that the wind snatches away.

And it's done—

I drop to my knees in the smoking ruin. The ground is hot beneath me, vibrating like it's trying to remember what living felt like. Ash drifts through the air in slow spirals, soft as snowfall, clinging to my skin, my lashes, and the back of my tongue. Everything smells of ash and rain that will never come.

Roots still twitch like burned nerves beneath my feet. The trees at the glade's edge have blackened to husks. Wen's body lay near me, untouched by the blast, wrapped in stillness.

I lower my blade. The heat still clings to the steel, faintly glowing in the seams of its runes before dimming to dull metal. My fingers ache from how hard I've been gripping it. I don't realize I'm shaking until I hear the sound—a crack. A single branch giving way under weight.

Footsteps follow, solid ones. I turn, every muscle quivering, the air thick with scorched sap.

He steps from the tree line.

Mattie.

For a second, my mind refuses it. His curls are longer now, damp with sweat and dirt, tangled around his temples. His clothes are torn, his hands raw, but his face—his face—is exactly as I remember. That small crooked scar near his jaw. Those eyes—too kind, too human for the blade trembling in his grip.

He looks at me like I'm the ghost here.

"You're alive," I whisper, too stunned to cry, too empty to get up.

He flinches but doesn't lower the dagger. His voice is quiet and ragged, a thread barely holding on. "They said I have to. If I ever saw you again. If you lost control."

I say nothing. Can't. My heart has already broken open once; there's nothing left to break again. They sound rehearsed and foreign in his mouth, those words.

Behind him, the forest shifts—branches sighing, shadows bending, something moving that doesn't belong.

Vaeryn steps out of the smoke like he's been carved from it, a living shadow. His bow is already drawn, the string pulled taut, the arrow aimed square at my heart. His eyes, which used to be all sly humor and lazy defiance, are rimmed in red, wet at the edges, and gone to something harder. Something that looks like grief wearing a mask of duty.

My lips part, but nothing is said.

He looses the arrow. It hisses past my cheek, so close I feel the wind of it slice the air. It buries itself in the blackened trunk behind me with a sound like a heartbeat stopping.

I don't move an inch.

Vaeryn lowers the bow with slow precision, his shoulders tight, his jaw locked. His mouth, stretched with some emotion I can't name, barely moves as he speaks.

"My queen."

There's a tug in my stomach, behind my belly button, like a hook catching something invisible inside me, and it all disappears.

EPILOGUE

THE THING NO ONE TELLS you about ruined thrones? They smell like rot and salt. Like memory gone sour.

I lean against a cracked pillar and watch the morning sunlight die against sea-damp stone. It slants through broken glass, painting my boots in the colors of a crown long buried. The sea-glass throne is still here—crooked now, leaning like it's tired of waiting. Moody little thing.

I toss a pebble at it. It clinks off the base with the saddest little sound. "Rude."

No echo. Of course not. Even sound knows better than to linger in this place. But apparently I didn't get that memo.

I wander a bit. Running my fingers over the murals—faded paint, chipped detail, history bleeding into myth. There's the queen, crown of starlight. There's her pretty corpse-king. And there, barely visible in the center, the shadow of a child they hid like a sin.

I smile. "Found you."

It's been a long wait. A bloody one. But I'm nothing if not patient. Well. Except when I'm not.

517

I sit on the steps. Cross my legs. Tap a beat on my knee. One and two and—nothing.

Again. Still nothing.

Ah, there it is, or rather, there she is.

The air splits in half. Magic punches through the weave, tearing a hole clean into the heart of Atlantis. Smoke pours out. Salt and heat. Mmm, and her.

She falls into the room like a secret ripped from someone's ribcage.

She doesn't crash, exactly. She...lands. Hard. Knees hit stone. Hands catch her. Head lifts. Dark hair tangled. Eyes like something starved and furious all at once.

Oh, she is beautiful.

Not pretty, nor delicate. Beautiful in the way fire is, right before it eats the roof off your house.

Hmm. That makes this harder. I don't know if I can kill her after all.

I stand at attention. "Well, finally," I say, brushing off my coat. "I was starting to think I hallucinated the whole thing. Again. Gods know it wouldn't be the first time."

She spins, blade half up, teeth bared.

I raise my hands. "Careful, darling. This is a brand-new jacket, and I quite like my spleen where it is."

She doesn't speak. That's fine. First impressions aren't for everyone.

I step closer. She doesn't back up. Brave. Or stupid. Or both. My favorite kind.

"You're shorter than I imagined," I say, peering at her like I might bite. Which I will. "Not in a disappointing way. Just observational. Also," I grin, "you've got blood on your lip. Yours? Someone else's?"

Still no answer, but her magic is twitching beneath her skin. Glorious and raw, waiting to be formed into something new.

"Right, stunned silence. That tracks. Betrayal, screaming, shadow kings, dead witches, boom-boom magic. Very rough day." I tilt my head. "Also, fun fact—you're standing exactly where your mother died."

Her fingers tighten on the hilt.

I drop my voice lower, softer. Let it slip under the door.

"They'll come for you, you know. All of them. Every throne. Every crown. Every monster who wants your blood bottled and branded. They'll come."

I step into her space. I never have been a fan of personal bubbles, they get in the way.

"I'll help you, of course," I whisper. "Because I now find you are far too interesting to kill."

Her breath hitches.

"But first," I say, smiling like a blade unsheathing itself, "you're going to do something terrible. Something unforgivable. And you'll be brilliant at it."

She stares with those deliciously dark eyes, blinking at me like a lost little doe.

I can already see it—her hands dripping with light and ash, the sea splitting open behind her, the world on fire.

Oh, this is going to be fun.

* * *

Acknowledgments

This book did not happen in a vacuum. It was written in the chaos between school runs, medical appointments, bad coffee, and the occasional existential crisis. If you're holding it now, it's because a lot of people caught me when I wanted to drop it.

First, to my daughter: you are the reason I walked away from a safe career and into the wild, terrifying world of story. You taught me that soft doesn't mean small, that fierce can look like getting out of bed on the hard days, and that some risks are absolutely worth taking. Every page I write is, in some way, for you.

To my family—by blood, former marriage, and choice—who listened to me rant about fictional people like they were real, who reminded me to eat when I forgot meals, and who didn't flinch when I said "I just need to fix one more chapter" for the fiftieth time. Thank you for loving me through deadlines, doubts, and drafts that deserved to be burned in a blazing inferno.

To the teachers, librarians, and booksellers who put stories into my hands long before I started writing my own—thank you. You taught me that books can be both escape and anchor, and that there is always room on the shelf for another strange little tale.

And finally, to you, reader: you chose to spend your time in this world with these characters, and that is no small thing. Stories don't feel complete until someone else steps into them. Thank you for turning the pages, for feeling with them, and for letting this book live in your hands for a while.

If this story made you laugh, cry, stay up too late, or whisper "just one more chapter" when you knew it was a lie—then it did exactly what I hoped it would.

Thank you,

Arin

ABOUT THE AUTHOR

I was the second child of four; ideally, I would have been a boy. They said I was a boy, and that would have been it for my parents, but alas, another girl. Actually, I was born with my cord loosely curled around my neck, and I was blue, not from being strangled by the ever-important highway of oxygen and nutrition from my mother's womb, but because of those bright, blinding white monstrosities attacking my poor eyes from above. I simply had the breath scared out of me. My father loves to tell the tale of the doctor who needed to return to medical school, as when he was asked whether I was a boy or girl, he responded, "I don't know." Stunned, I tell you. In truth, he simply had not had the time to look yet as well... I was blue. My silence only lasted for so long, as when they suctioned out my airways, my father was sure they could hear me throughout the whole hospital in rural South Dakota.

We did not stay in South Dakota for long. By the age of two, we came to New York, Buffalo area to be precise, and I have lived here for the entirety of my life so far. I have traveled much, but Buffalo is still home. My father is a minister and historian, and my mother studied biology and medical technology but works for a bank now. Hospital mergers would have prevented her from seeing her children growing up due to insane schedules. The three from South Dakota became four in New York as my youngest brother (of two) surprised my parents two   years   in.

Family trips always had some element of history mixed in, a fort along our route or living history museums. History and its importance were always a large part of our lives. As young adults, my youngest brother and I, and eventually our parents, got involved in living history education at a local fort and engrossed ourselves in the 18th century. We now spend most of our summer weekends traveling back in time, educating the local populations on life during the French and Indian War (Seven Years's War) and the American Revolution. For me, this wasn't enough. I needed more history. I pursued a degree in archaeology in college and eventually earned my doctorate. While I love the 18th century, and it is a passion of mine, the medieval period is my heart and soul. It is a fascinating and complicated moment in history, especially so in Ireland and Scotland, the place of my roots. This is what inspired my first b   o   o   k   ...

During graduate school I fell in love, got married, had a beautiful baby girl, discovered I married a lie, a fictitious character created and played to woo me into a false sense of security, survived an abusive relationship, freed myself and my daughter from that physical, mental, and emotional prison, and earned my doctorate as a single mother living with my parents as an adult. But here is where it gets interesting.

Remember there at the top of the page... I was supposed to be a boy. My siblings, of course, having not suffered in a poor relationship as I, have moved out and have lives of their own. I am home helping my older parents with their house (the first they've ever owned and a fixer-upper) and am quite handy with power tools, projects, designs, gardening, and herbal healing. I, the second daughter, have achieved the ever elusive 'favorite son' status; guess they were right after all ;).

Echoes of a Queen
Atlantis Rising Book Two
Coming June 2026

Five years ago...

They say he drowned.

No body. No note. Just a jacket washed up on the shore and some shaky eyewitness claiming they saw a man walk into the water and never come out.

That's it.

I sit on the edge of the bathtub, fully clothed, the water still running like background noise for someone else's grief. My fingers dig into he edge of the porcelain. I can't stop shaking. My brain keeps skipping like a scratched record—Remy is gone, Remy is gone, Remy is gone. The words won't land. They feel like someone else's headline.

He wouldn't just disappear. He's not the disappearing kind.

He leaves his mugs half full on the counter. He folds his socks into weird little squares. He kisses my shoulder in the morning before I'm even awake enough to appreciate it.

People like that don't just vanish.

But grief doesn't follow rules. It opens doors. It rewinds tape.

And suddenly I'm not in the bathroom anymore. *I'm in his arms. The rain tapping glass.*

"Do you think power changes people?" He asks.

We're curled together on the couch, a blanket around us and the sound of rain ticking against the windows. My feet are cold. His hands are warm. He smells like bergamot and something else, like a cedar chest left open.

I look up at him, half-smiling. "That's a weird segue. You bored with my movie pick already?"

He doesn't laugh. Just tilts his head slightly. "I'm serious."

I shrug, shifting against him. "I think it can change the way people act, sure. But the core stuff? No. That stays the same."

He's quiet for a beat, his eyes locked on mine. "I think power unmasks us," he says, finally. "Strips everything back. Shows you what was already there."

"Sometimes you sound like you've lived a thousand lives."

He smiles. Not the crooked one, I love, or the playful one. The weird one that never reaches his eyes.

"Would that be so bad?"

I don't answer. I don't know what to say to that. So I lean in and kiss him slow, like maybe I can figure out what he's thinking between his lips.

His hand finds my wrist. He presses a kiss there, right where my pulse beats fastest. "You don't have to understand," he whispers.

"What?"

But he doesn't repeat it. He just holds me a little tighter.

I blink. The water in the tub has overflowed, dripping onto the tile. I still haven't moved.

They say he's presumed dead.

Presumed—like guessing the weather. Like maybe he's not.

But I know something's wrong. I know it in my bones. I know it in the space he used to fill.

He's not just gone.

He's *missing*, like a chapter torn out of my story. Like a door slammed shut before I can ask why.

His coat still hangs by the door.

His voice still echoes in my head.

Aurora.

No one else says it like that.

CHAPTER ONE

That echo doesn't go away.

His voice is still hanging in the air like a bad aftertaste.

You're going to do something terrible. Something unforgivable. And you'll be brilliant at it.

God, I hate that I remember the exact tone he used. Like he was handing me a gift. Or a bomb.

I don't answer. Can't.

My legs are still shaky from the fall, or the magic. I'm standing, at least...barely. Sword half-out, lip bleeding. Chest tight. Every nerve in my body screaming *do something* and not agreeing on what.

Who the hell is this man?

He's not armed. He hasn't moved. But he's standing like someone who could gut me without blinking and look good doing it. Tall, lean, sharp at the edges. Not the kind of pretty that fades under bad lighting, the kind that's either ageless or expensive. Skin like sunlight never quite touches it. Hair dark and awfully neat for someone skulking in a palace no one's stepped foot in for ten thousand years. His coat is immaculate, boots polished like they've never seen dirt, which is funny considering the moss cracking through the palace floor.

Eyes like they've seen the world break a few times and just got bored of watching. Pale. Blue? Silver? I can't tell in this light. But he doesn't blink enough.

He's got that kind of face. Knife-sharp. Too much charm, but eerily still. Too clean for a place that's supposed to be dead.

He could pass for human. Probably has. But something in my gut curls tight, warning me that he's playing the part. Like someone dressed him up in civility and dared him not to break it.

And he's smiling now, pleasant and polite. It's the kind of smile that makes me want to count my organs. Just in case.

And the worst part?

He's the only one here who doesn't feel like a lie.

I take a slow breath. The air tastes like salt and metal, like a thunderstorm again. The stone under my feet should be cold, but it's not. There's heat. Unsettling heat.

Behind him, the throne waits. Still as glass, but the air around us feels alert. Like stepping into a room mid-conversation and realizing you were the topic.

I try to focus. My vision's still doing that fun thing where the edges blur if I move too fast. Great. Another reminder that m body's not caught up to whatever just happened. What I'm trying very hard not to think about.

"Do you ever shut up?" I ask, finally.

He grins like I handed him a cookie. "Eventually. You're fun, though. I might make an exception."

I tighten my grip on the blade. "Tell me who you are."

"I'm Jules. Obviously."

"Obviously?"

He gestures to himself like that explains anything. "I did just welcome you dramatically into your birthright, didn't I?"

I narrow my eyes. "Try again. Slower. With fewer riddles."

He sighs, dramatic and full of mock sorrow. "Atlantis is very bad at instructions, you know. I'm just the knife it left out on the table."

That is *not* helpful.

I take a step sideways, adjusting my stance. The weight in the air shifts. Glass overhead clicks softly. Light angles differently, like the room is adjusting its gaze.

The light brushes my shoulder like a hand that didn't ask permission. I flinch before I can help it, eyes scanning the corners of the room for movement. Nothing. Just those murals and that throne.

I don't like this. I don't like any of this.

Jules just watches, or studies. Or whatever flavor of creepy he prefers. He hasn't stopped smiling.

"Is this how you greet all your royal guests?" I ask, testing my balance. "Weird riddles and third-degree murder vibes?"

"Oh, I won't kill you." His smile sharpens. "On purpose anyway."

"Wow. Comforting."

I edge toward the nearest archway. The light shifts again. Subtle, but I clock it. My legs aren't cooperating. Too slow, too heavy. Something's off and I don't know what it is yet. But I keep moving. Because standing still feels worse.

Jules falls into step behind me without asking. Of course he does.

The next corridor opens on its own. No hinges groan. No grand fanfare, just ghosts.

I pause.

"You're bleeding," he says casually, like he's commenting on the weather.

I wipe my lip and check my fingers. Still red.

"I noticed."

"I could help, you know."

I snort. "I'm good."

"You're really not."

He's not wrong. But I'm not saying that out loud.

The hallway ahead stretches long and pale, veined with what looks like silver. The floor reflects just enough to give me a warped shadow. I watch it. Half to stay grounded, half to make sure it doesn't start moving on its own.

I take three more steps.

Then the floor lurches.

Not visibly. Just in me. A sharp pull behind my ribs. My knees buckle.

I catch the wall before I drop, sword clattering from my hand to the smooth tile.

Jules doesn't touch me.

Thank god for small mercies.

"You always this dramatic?" He says, voice almost kind.

I breathe through the wave. One, two, three seconds of everything going white-hot behind my eyes, and then it passes.

Mostly.

"I'm fine," I manage.

He hums. "Sure."

I retrieve my sword, slow and careful, like my body's made of glass. My lip's bleeding again.

"If you collapse now, I'll be so disappointed. I haven't even gotten to the good part."

"Bite me," I manage, dragging in a breath. Everything's too hot. My skin, my spine, my teeth.

He tilts his head. "Tempting. But I usually wait until someone begs."

My hand shakes around my sword more than I'd like. He watches, says nothing.

I straighten slowly, eyes lock on him. "Enjoying the show?"

He shrugs. "You fall well. Bit dramatic. But I suppose you've earned it."

"Is this fun for you?"

"Oh yes," he says."Watching you stumble around like a newborn fawn with a sword? Utterly captivating."

The corridor yawns open ahead of us. The air's cooler now. Or maybe I'm imagining that part. Hard to tell, with everything spinning at the edges.

I push forward anyway.

Behind me, his boots click softly on the stone. He's not rushing, only following at my pace. Like a cat waiting for something to twitch.

I pass a column carved with overlapping scales. A mural flickers at the corner of my vision, figures half-hidden in shadow. I don't stop to look closer. I don't trust what I'll see.

"You're taking this well," he says after a while.

I grunt. "Define 'well.'"

"No screaming. No tears. I've seen heirs do worse with less."

I pause. "I'm not an heir."

He chuckles. "Aren't you?"

I don't answer. Because I don't know. Because my parents are dead, Wen is ash, Mattie looked at me like I was a stranger, and I'm here. Bleeding in a palace that shouldn't exist.

I press forward, needing space. From the throne, from the blood still drying on my lip, from the man who keeps smiling like he knows the ending and wants to ruin the surprise.

The corridor bends slightly, the edges of the walls catching light that isn't coming from any obvious source. It's colder here. Not freezing, but sharper. The kind of cold that sinks past skin and starts threading itself into your muscle.

Behind me, Jules doesn't speak. I can still feel him back there. Watching me.

The next step is harder than the last.

I try to ignore it, blame it on the adrenaline crash. But there's a pressure building deep in my chest. A warning my body is too slow to explain.

Then everything tilts.

There's no stumble to catch. My knees give with no resistance. I don't even register the fall until Jules' arm catches across my ribs and hauls me upright.

"You aren't supposed to die yet," he mutters near my ear. "It'd be rude."

I twist out of his grip, throat burning. My shoulder slams into the wall to stay upright.

"What did you do to me?"

He doesn't answer. He just watches me like I'm part of the palace now, some artifact he's cataloguing.

The silence that follows is too quiet. There's pressure in it.

A crack slices through the air above us. Clean and high. I glance up to see a hairline fracture spider across the nearest skylight. The glass doesn't break, but the tension in the corridor sharpens like it wants to.

Jules raises one hand, not to me, but enough to hush the air around us. His eyes flick toward the noise, lips pressed together now.

Something's coming.

I force my body upright again, fingers clumsy around the hilt of my blade.

Footsteps break through the silence. Heavy. Running.

I turn toward the sound heart lodged somewhere below my ribs.

And Mattie is there. Breathless, wide-eyed and alive.

Bound in Ash & Gold

Fyrala Chronicles Book Two

Coming February 2026

Chapter One

Elora

I'm downright giddy, and it's the strangest feeling in the world. I walk so light on my feet I'm practically bouncing along a few paces ahead of Jadis in these now familiar hallways. I clasp my own arms behind my back because I simply don't know what to do with them and the energy buzzing through me.

"Did you know the library has an entire section of fae written fiction novels?" I ask Jadis, spinning on my toes to face him. We keep moving, so I not so gracefully start walking backwards, still holding my arms behind me.

"Considering the Day Court has the best library in the kingdom, I'd imagine it has the largest collection of fiction. But I don't spend much time in the library." His eyes sparkle with the same intensity I feel running through my veins, the corner of his mouth curling into an amused smirk.

I slow my pace, letting him get a little closer. "There are at least three shelves of spicy novels, too. I knew that was popular in the mortal realm, but I was pleasantly surprised to find that subgenre here too."

"Spicy?" He's not playing. He raises that single eyebrow in question, and the same expression reaches his bright green eyes.

"You know, makes you sweat like when you eat spicy food." I don't know why I'm a little embarrassed considering what we've done together, but I can't just spit it out. I swing around to settle in next to him again, my legs tiring of walking backwards.

"Why would reading a book make you sweat? You're not making sense."

"You're really going to make me say it, aren't you?" I pause, but he doesn't do anything other than slow our pace a little. "You know, hot and bothered? No fade to black, no closed doors, open doors for everyone to enjoy..."

"So, porn in a book?" He stops and turns to me ever so slightly with his question, and my cheeks flame.

"No," I say, shushing him. "Well, maybe...essentially, but more tasteful than that."

"And mortals are into that?"

"Many of them are. It's a huge market. Mortals love stories of the fae, and romances between mortals and immortals are a big thing these days."

"Why are mortals so enamored with beings who would readily kill them as easily as swatting away a fly?"

"I don't know, I think it's the magic, the idea of fated mates—" Jadis stumbles slightly, but when I move to steady him, he just waves a hand in my direction to continue. "I think some people have a wing fetish or something; there are a lot of winged MMCs."

"A wing fetish? They like the looks of them? Why would wings be so appealing?"

"I don't know. I never understood that one, other than they're different, not everyday. Plus, there are sex scenes while flying that got a lot of attention—" I add, voice lowering slightly.

He looks at me completely aghast.

"I know, I could never figure out how that worked either. Never could wrap my head around it. I mean, epic crash and burn both literally and figuratively, right? But I suppose that's what fantasy is, suspending reality and simply living."

He rights himself, the quizzical look on his face telling me he's also trying to figure out how they managed the whole flying sex thing, and that has me smiling. He stumbles again, this time on a step he misjudged, and catches himself with a muttered curse. I laugh quietly.

"Anyway, I find it really interesting that the similar genre in this realm centers on fae finding mortal lovers. I never would have thought they'd seek out or fantasize about something like that."

"No, I wouldn't think so either; that's very strange. And you're reading this, these spicy books."

"All the time." I smirk.

He nods, his eyes trailing off to the distance. "I get the impression that they like mortals because they live in the moment and are more passionate. Because life is always limited to them, they don't hold back like the fae. The fae have all the time in the world and hold back."

"I don't think that's entirely true. What do you think about fae passion, hmm?" He spins me around to face him, pinning my arms that I'd still been holding behind my back, pressing me up against him.

"I don't know; my personal experience is limited," I start, and he squeezes me tighter. "I may have to experience more to be sure and be completely scientific before I claim either way." He chases my lips with his own, but I dodge as much as I can with him pinning me against his chest.

When he settles for trailing kisses along my neck, I finally have room to continue. "I think it's less about passion and abilities, magical or otherwise, and more about finding the right person. I think it's about feeling lonely and not finding love for so long that you assume it only exists in the most fantastical of places, in the obscure and otherworldly. People find love and belonging finally because they worked for it under the most difficult circumstances and came out, against the odds, on the other side. It's a metaphor against instant love, easy love."

"Mmm," he says, finally devouring my lips with his.

"Oh, please, enough already, the both of you." Brandis walks up behind me, and I laugh against Jadis' face, his forehead pressing into my hair. "The council is here, and I don't need them all seeing this *relationship* and tarnishing your image, Elora."

"I don't care, Brandis. You really need to get over this nonsense. Plus, it's too late, as you know." I turn in Jadis' arms to face my brother, my increasingly irritating brother with his antiquated ideas, and gesture to my stomach.

"Yes, it's bad enough that he's beneath your station, but you couldn't possibly have been more careful? I know for a fact that your maid prepared you for all possibilities before you left."

Jadis wraps his arms around me from behind, cradling said stomach in his hands in a move he never would have attempted in front of Brandis before. Brandis glares.

"He's not beneath my station, not that it matters, but he's a prince in his own right."

"You can't be a prince of a political entity that no longer exists."

"His lands diminishing doesn't change his blood, Brandis. Isn't that what royal matches are about anyway? Matching bloodlines for strong lineages and alliances? Why does this bother you so much anyway? Oh, wait, you're jealous, aren't you?"

Jadis lets out a low snicker in my ear, resting his chin in the crook of my neck as Brandis' face explodes into something bordering incredulous.

"That's it, isn't it? Your marriage was already arranged by our parents."

"Yes, well before they died. The princess of the Summer Court."

"Day and Summer, that makes sense, but our parents have been with the stars for over a century now. Are you leaving your poor bride hanging for that long? Waiting...pining over you? They say absence makes the heart grow fonder, but I think even a century is a bit much."

Jadis' laughter musses my hair, and his hot breath mists into my shoulder as Brandis clenches his fists.

"She disappeared shortly after you left for the mortal world, if you must know. No one has been able to find her, not that we have the time or resources to invest in that kind of search anyway."

I press my lips together, trying not to laugh. I'm trying so hard to hold back, but I fail miserably. "The thought of marrying you was so disturbing that she up and disappeared? Left her family and everything? You poor male..."

"I much preferred you before all this," he says, pressing his lips firmly and waving his hand at the two of us. His shoulders rise like he's about to argue, but then slump with resignation.

"That ship has sailed, dear brother; you're stuck with me now, as is."

He smiles, a smile that lights up his entire face, and extends a hand. "Come on, we're late already; they're all waiting."

I take his hand, and he pulls me forward, out of Jadis' now limp arms. I swing my other hand back, grabbing a handful of his shirt to drag him along.

"I don't expect you to hide this relationship from the council. You wouldn't even if I asked you to, and as you say, he is technically royalty, so we can explain it away, but Elora, let's keep the child quiet for now. A little information at a time, yes?"

"Ok, Brandis. I can agree with that. I don't want my child to become a target anyway." The words feel heavier than they should, but I mean them. My joy is real, but so is the danger.

Brandis' entire being changed the instant we walked through the doors to the council chamber, putting on the airs of a High Lord of Fryala. The marble underfoot cools beneath each step. The air thickens with silence and the weight of watching eyes.

Jadis whispers in my ear, pulling me gently closer to him as I release Brandis' hand. "I do believe I need to read some of these books of yours, my moonflower. I can't possibly be shown up by some fictional characters."

I grin, drawing him close, and bring our lips together in a gentle kiss that holds promises of more. And just before the doors open, I murmur, low so only he can hear, "Whatever happens in there...this is ours."